Love on Board

Aries Skye

BLACK ODYSSEY MEDIA

WWW.BLACKODYSSEY.NET

Published by
BLACK ODYSSEY MEDIA

www.blackodyssey.net
Email: info@blackodyssey.net

LOVE ON BOARD. Copyright © 2026 by ARIES SKYE

Library of Congress Control Number: 2025916801

First Trade Paperback Printing: February 2026
ISBN: 978-1-957950-73-0
ISBN: 978-1-957950-74-7 (e-book)

Cover Design by Ashlee Nassar of Designs With Sass

10 9 8 7 6 5 4 3 2 1

Manufactured in the United States of America

Distributed by Kensington Publishing Corp.

The authorized representative in the EU for product safety and compliance is
eucomply OU, Parnu mnt 139b-14, Apt 123
Tallinn, Berline 11317, hello@eucomplianceprtner.com

Dear Reader,

I want to thank you immensely for supporting Black Odyssey Media and our ongoing efforts to spotlight the diverse narratives of blossoming and seasoned storytellers. With every manuscript we acquire, we believe that it took talent, discipline, and remarkable courage to construct that story, flesh out those characters, and prepare it for the world. Debut or seasoned, our authors are the real heroes and heroines in *OUR* story. For them, we are eternally grateful.

Whether you are new to Aries Skye or Black Odyssey Media, we hope that you are here to stay. Our goal is to make a lasting impact in the publishing landscape, one step at a time and one book at a time. As always, we welcome your feedback and kindly ask that you leave a review. For upcoming releases, announcements, submission guidelines, etc., please be sure to visit our website at www.blackodyssey.net or scan the QR code below. And remember, no matter where you are in your journey, the best of both worlds begins now!

Joyfully,

Shawanda Williams

Shawanda "N'Tyse" Williams
Founder & CEO, Black Odyssey Media

NAME GLOSSARY:

This is how I pronounce the characters' names. It's meant to be lighthearted, fun, and entertaining, but feel free to skip past them and dive straight into the story.

AQUILA: *It's Ah-KEY-lah, like Akeelah and the Bee. Not Ah-QUILL-lah.*

JOEL: *It's JOEL. One word, one syllable.*

ROMAN: *It's Roman, like the empire.*

ROMERO: *It's roh-mEH-roh. The name is Italian, but he isn't.*

NIA: *It's KNEE-ah, like Long.*

TAMIA: *It's tah-ME-ah, like the singer.*

ANGELA: *Like Davis. Like Bassett. Like Simmons.*

KINSTON: *It's KEN-ston. Not Kingston. The "G" is not silent. It is nonexistent.*

NISSI: *It's KNEE-see, like Jehovah Nissi. If church isn't your thing, like Niecy.*

KANNON: *It's KAY-none, not CANNON. This pronunciation and spelling are also my prerogative.*

NISANTE: *It's KNEE-sun-tay, and probably the one that you needed most, LOL.*

SANTE: *It's SUN-TAY (just remove the knee).*

KAIN: *It's CANE, like Cain and Abel.*

NISAN: *It's KNEE-sun, like the car.*

JANSEN: *It's JAN-sin.*

JANA: *It's JAN-na.*

ABIGAIL: *It's Abigail.*

CIARA: *Like Russell Wilson's wife and Future's ex.*

ZACH: *It's short for Zachary.*

FAWN: *It's just how it's spelled, like Von with an F.*

JOVAN: *It's JOE-vaughn, like Von. Not Van.*

THURGOOD: *It's THUR-good, like Marshall.*

IVY: *It's I.V., like Poison Ivy, like Blue Ivy.*

MACIE: *It's MAY-see, like the department store.*

WREN: *It's REN, like Ren & Stimpy.*

JORGE: *It's HOR-hey.*

DR. SOTO: *It's SO-toe.*

GRACYN: *It's GRAY-sin.*

CYN: *It's SIN. Like Gra-CYN.*

ROBERT: *It's Robert.*

GENESIS: *It's GEN-nes-sis, like the first book in the Bible.*

TRIGGER WARNING—FROM US, WITH LOVE

Aquila here. Aries made me write this after I had to convince her that my story even *deserved* to be told. If "earning your spot" was a person—it's me.

Roman here. I had to jump in before this whole thing got shelved. I ain't gon' hold you. This story is straight *fiyah*, and unless you're under the age of eighteen, there's no reason not to read it. The way I put it down? Yeah…this one *ain't* for the kids.

Aquila again, back before Roman takes it too far. If you're into open-door spice and laughter, this romantic comedy might be just the stress reliever you need. Who doesn't love the idea of a romantic getaway? But when the cruise ends, real life…well, *lifes*. We get into some deep stuff: divorce, co-parenting, sexuality, and finding your sense of self. If any of that feels too heavy right now, it's okay to set this book aside and come back when you're ready. Our hope is that this story helps you heal, not adds to any hurt.

Roman tapping in again… and I co-sign all of that. Please, take care of yourself while reading, sweethearts. Self-care first, always.

But if you're ready for us?

We're more than ready for you.

Welcome to the final installment of the Richards sisters: *Love on Board*.

Forever Yours,
Aquila and Roman

Prologue

AQUILA

PULL YOURSELF TOGETHER, internally, I coached myself.

Parking my G-Wagon in the empty church parking lot, I flipped down my visor and peered into the mirror. I breathed deeply in and out as I closed my eyes and tried to center myself. I couldn't fathom how I practiced thirty minutes of yoga every day and went to the gym four days a week to be still this stressed out.

When I left the house twenty minutes ago, I was determined to do as planned and have a girls' night out with my sisters—a night that I'd advised my husband of for the past month. He knew that our sisters' quality time had been limited since Nissi married Kannon and Angela had solidified her relationship with Kinston. Having been in their position, I understood. All they wanted to do was have "couple time" with their significant others, and I couldn't blame them. Once upon a time, I'd been in their shoes with Joel back when it was Joel and Aquila Oliver forever. Those days now seemed to be a far-distant memory. It made me feel reduced to a group member in the Oliver clan instead of his wife and life partner, as if he were David Ruffin, and I was the Temptations. But he forgot the main rule: No one was bigger than the group. Everything—and I do mean *everything*—was centered, focused, surrounded, and concentrated on Joel and his needs and desires over anything and everyone else.

Just like tonight. He waited until he came home to announce that he was invited to some function supporting one of his mentors, and I needed to be available to attend. I was taken aback for a few reasons: his lack of asking but rather demanding, his lack of concern for who would babysit our children, and his lack of thoughtfulness over my previously discussed plans. Thank goodness our kids were already at my parents' house. After reminding him that I had planned an evening with my sisters, I slipped on my celadon sleeveless, ankle-length bodycon dress, which paired perfectly with my gold YSLs. Rather than concede and attend the function unaccompanied or stay at home for all I cared, he began ranting about my attitude and absences of late, as if he had any room on his moral barometer to chastise me on one's attitude and absences. The same man whom none of my family members or friends wanted to endure. The same man who made me feel as though I were a single parent in my marriage. The same man who made me feel as though I were a single woman masquerading as a married one. I'd become accustomed to biting my tongue over the years, so much so that I had lost who I was aside from being Joel Oliver's wife-turned-handmaid.

Lately, though, I'd been finding my voice more and more, and tonight had been no exception. A full-out argument ensued, with me leaving the house and heading for Angela's place—Joel and his demands be damned.

However, halfway there, I reverted to the doting wife, and guilt began to gnaw at me, not necessarily for Joel but for the guest of honor. Jansen Carlyle had helped us bail out financially when Joel's restaurant had taken an unexpected hit. Being among the elite with friends in high and well-off places fared well in dire circumstances. Jansen had been our ram in the bush, and I'd always be eternally grateful for that. Had my husband taken the liberty to notify me ahead of time, I would've gladly been present. And that's what chipped away at me now. As much as I loved my sisters, it would have felt disrespectful not to attend Jansen's soiree, given the measures he'd taken to support my family. It was for that reason that I sat in this empty lot, coaxing myself into a façade so that I could support Jansen as the dutiful wife of Joel Oliver.

"You've got this, Lah. Just head home, apologize, slip into a little black dress, and do what needs to be done."

Smoothing the edges of my hair, perfectly pulled into a slick ponytail meeting at the nape of my neck, I cast away the negative vibes of earlier and pulled out of the lot, heading back to my house. Thankfully, my phone call to Angela went unanswered, allowing me to disappoint her and Nissi via voicemail. As I drove, my eyes kept bouncing to the three-carat princess-cut diamond on my hand. *Be his wife.* If Joel did nothing else, he afforded our babies and me a lifestyle that most longed for, so I couldn't be upset that he wanted to honor the man who helped continue making that American Dream a reality for us. With that, I resolved to make this right with my husband.

As I eased into the house, I expected Joel to be in our bedroom getting dressed for the event. When I didn't find him in our bedroom or bathroom, I went on a search for him throughout the rest of the house.

"Joel?" I called out, checking in our family room. *"Humph."*

Then it dawned on me—his man cave.

Schlepping toward his private mantuary, I opened the door when I heard a sound resonating from the television. "Joel, baby, I'm sor—"

The words were lodged in my throat as the entire scene unfolded in my view as if it were in slow motion. There sat my husband on the couch, jerking off to the sight of two men on the screen, straight barebacking. Tears filled my eyes as my hand flew over my mouth, trapping the wail that could barely squeak past my closing esophagus.

"Shit, Aquila!" Joel scrambled, trying to cover himself and turn off the television simultaneously. "I thought you were with your sisters."

Hot droplets fell from my rapidly blinking eyes as I tried my best to gather my bearings before I fainted. Joel had somehow managed to turn off the porn and reclothed by the time I found my voice.

"Aquila…"

"So, this is what you do while I'm not at home? Get your rocks off on gay porn?" Joel moved to touch my arms, and I swatted him away. "Don't you dare."

His face fell, and worry lines spread all over it. "Baby—"

"Baby? Baby?" The audacity of his words was displayed in mine. "You're standing here with precum leaking through your slacks from watching men…*men*…have sex, and now, you want to call *me* baby?"

"Just let me explain, please. It's not like I was cheating on you."

The rage of every disrespected married woman in the history of marriage set my soul ablaze, and I reached back to the depths of before Christ and smacked the hell and probably the rest of the ejaculation out of him. His head snapped so far to the right, it appeared as if I'd sprained his neck. I could only hope.

"You sorry sack of shit. When I accepted your hand in marriage, you promised this would never be an issue. You told me—*swore* to me—that you loved me and only me and that I'd never have to worry about your infatuation with men."

There it was. Our closeted bones laid bare.

Joel and I had met through mutual friends when we were in college. We'd become fast friends and eventually decided to explore being lovers. I'd broken it off with him because while I loved and cared for him, something didn't seem quite right between us. Joel had pleaded with me to give him another chance, but I didn't. We agreed to remain friends, and we did. We became the best of friends, in fact. We were so close that one night, in a drunken binge in my apartment, he confessed his greatest secret: He was bisexual. Before we could delve into his admittance, we passed out in my living room, senselessly inebriated, and the next day, the encumbrance of his confession came down like the weight of the world. He tried to backpedal, but after reassuring him that our friendship was a safe space, he admitted that his confession was the truth. Though he stated he'd never cheated on me when we were together, and I'd believed him, he said that he still had urges from time to time. According to him, it wasn't every man he was attracted to, just whoever caught his eye.

As far as women, he was attracted to them, and he was still head over heels for me. He'd even confessed to having slept with two men in his past. One guy was in his senior year of high school, during a band competition. The other guy came during the summer of his freshman year in college, during a summer internship. He claimed that neither was a relationship, just mutual sexual attraction and intimacy.

While I had been devastated because he didn't disclose this information before we dated and slept together, I put our friendship above my angst and disappointment. Besides, we'd both been tested and yielded negative results, so I could at least be thankful for that. But in that moment, it became painfully obvious why he insisted that we test before we had sex. He claimed that I'd been the only woman—hell, the only person he'd ever been in love with—and he wanted to ensure our safety. He'd only been the second man that I'd slept with besides my high school boyfriend after our senior prom, but I went along with it because I'd never tested after intercourse with my old boyfriend. Therefore, I saw the benefit. It only took one time to contract a disease, just as easily as it was to get pregnant after one time. Now, here we were, back here again.

"And I've kept that promise to you, Aquila." Frustration oozed from him as he scrubbed his bald head. "I've never cheated on you with a woman or a man."

"No. You jack off to men when I'm not around!" The patter of my footsteps created a cadence as I paced. "So now I know why our sex life has been nonexistent."

His hand flailed up as he held up his index finger to cut me off. "Don't. Don't do that. You know I've been stressed. The financial struggles we are powering through with the restaurant have left me drained and depressed. You know that. My focus has been on securing a future for my family, and I'm sorry if intercourse and intimacy are not on my menu."

"But clearly, men and pornos *are* on your plate right now." I squinted as I stalked up to him and poked him in the chest. "We haven't had any type of relations in a year, but instead of arranging quality time with me and instead of showboating this farce of a marriage in front of your power-elite friends, you'd rather bust quickies from gay porn."

"Like your rose doesn't get overtime," he said, seething. "I've come home plenty of nights to hear that *thump-thump-buzz* setting getting more action than me."

The incredulous scoff that I released echoed throughout his den of lies. "Excuse me for creating time to nurture *my* needs that you haven't bothered to take care of. At least my rose time was spent thinking of you, Joel, instead of thinking of John and James, like *you*."

The reality of what was transpiring suddenly tumbled on me, and I couldn't stop the sting of fresh, hot tears from clouding my eyes. I swallowed and blinked to no avail. A guttural wail emanated through my body as I began to shake uncontrollably. My marriage and my life had fallen apart. Only it'd been falling for a few years now. The friendship we'd built had long since withered away, and the vows we'd recited were nothing more than devalued words on paper devoid of any truth they once held. We had officially become two people joined by babies and businesses. This was not what he promised me; he owed me so much more—a lifetime of forevers.

His eyes and demeanor softened when I glanced at him as I leaned on the bar to support myself. He looked genuinely concerned about me, an emotion I hadn't witnessed or felt from him in so long that it appeared foreign on his features. It dawned on me how asinine it was that my husband's concern felt unnatural. He was the one person whom I should be able to lean on for love, care, concern, and comfort, yet he wasn't. My parents, my sisters, my babies, and my friends had filled that void for so long that I hadn't realized that he'd vacated the spot that only he was supposed to fill. They were supposed to be the supporters. He was supposed to be my one. My person. My husband. I'd been his wife a million times over without reciprocation. And that thought shifted my heartbreak into rage.

Swiping my hand down my face to wipe away my tears, I turned unemotional and hardened eyes to him. "I stood by your side as your friend even after you weren't forthcoming about your attraction and intercourse with men before we dated and slept together. I stood by your side as your woman, even after that, when you begged me to give you another chance because you stated that I was the only one for you. I swallowed all of your deceit and secrets because I loved you when any other woman would have left, leaving you to pray she kept your hidden desires to herself. But I stayed. I forgave. I supported. I trusted you. I loved...you a hell of a lot more than you were ever capable of loving me."

Droplets fell from his eyes as he sniffed and cupped his hand over his face, sliding them away. "But I do love you so much. Baby, I realize how this may seem, but you must believe it's still you for me. I still—"

I rolled my eyes, and a knowing smirk crept onto my face. I peered into his deep-set, russet eyes, which once held the charm to convince me of anything short of disavowing my faith and separating from my family...only to feel emptiness coursing through my veins. Nothing about him could sway me—not his dazzling Colgate smile; his creamy beige bald head, which I used to caress; or his plush beard that used to tickle places on my body that once made me submit to his every will. Nothing.

"Not this time, Joel. What is it that you need from me now? To ensure you're included in more of your family's business ventures, or are you just holding on so you won't get cut from your father's will?" I exhaled. "What type of sacrificial savior must I be for your gain this time?"

He was stuck on stunned because he knew I was correct. When Joel first asked me to marry him, I knew we weren't ready, despite how much we loved each other. Initially, I'd asked to wait, but he kept pressing, so I figured that perhaps my insecurities about his past were holding me back. I loved him, and he loved me, so marriage seemed to be the next progressive move. It wasn't until the night of our wedding rehearsal dinner that another hurtful truth was revealed.

Our wedding rehearsal dinner had been one for the history books. It was filled with delicious food, beautiful family, and entertaining music. The DJ had the atmosphere poppin', and I found myself dancing with my future husband, my sisters, and my entire wedding party. I was sweaty and exhausted when we finished every Black person's slide dance imaginable. Earlier, my future father-in-law had wrangled my future husband off the floor from me to talk, so I decided to grab some fresh air and locate my man.

When I languidly waltzed out on the patio and into the plush green gardens outside the restaurant, I heard Joel and his father before I saw them. I almost called out to them when I heard Mr. Oliver express his pride in Joel. I didn't want to interrupt such a precious moment, so I waited in the background for him to finish.

"Son, you don't know how proud it makes me that you've chosen Aquila to be your wife. She is a marvelous young woman and will be a wonderful and doting wife."

"Thank you, Father."

"And I'm so glad you let that other lifestyle go. I knew it was only a fad. I couldn't have my only son out here ruining the Oliver legacy. We're thoroughbreds. Now, with Aquila by your side, you'll bless your mother and me with the grandchildren we deserve."

"Can you not bring that up? I love Aquila, but it's not like you gave me much choice but to rush into marriage."

"You love her. She loves you. Where's the rush? Marriage is the natural progression of love for two young people in a relationship." He cleared his throat. "And we both know there was no way I'd pass the restaurant on to you if you continued sowing the wrong oats. There's no place for that sassy shit in our family or our family business. Besides, your mother wanted me to retire early so we can travel the world." He patted him on the shoulder. "I only guided you to do the naturally right thing."

At those words, I bolted from around the corner as if someone had lit a torch on me. "Joel!" I cried out. "Is that the only reason you wanted to marry me—to obtain your father's restaurant?"

Mr. Oliver and Joel spun around at my words. Joel looked mortified, but not more so than me. Running over to me, Joel grabbed my hands and pleaded. "No, baby. Not at all. It's just that my father, he—"

"He wouldn't turn over his business to you until he felt secure that you'd be with a woman and not a man." The words came out softly as realization poured over me.

Mr. Oliver walked over to me, gently turning me to face him. Cupping my face, he peered into my teary eyes. "Aquila, my son loves you. So, for that, I owe you a debt of gratitude. You're the only woman he's ever loved, and quite frankly, you saved him. You shouldn't look at this as him settling, but rather as him setting you up in life. As his wife, you'll have total access to all things Oliver."

"I don't care about all things Oliver. I care about Joel. I love him, and up until this moment, I thought he loved me. How can I go through with a wedding with a man who's unsure of this union because of his sexuality?" I tossed a glance at Joel, who appeared outright terrified.

"Oh no, darling," Mr. Oliver coaxed me. "He's not confused at all." He turned a stern glare at his son. "Don't you see your future wife needs you? Get over here and settle her."

Joel walked over to me, taking my hand and guiding me away from his dad. "I love you, Aquila, and yes, Father wants me to take over his restaurant, but that doesn't negate how I feel about you. I love you. I'm sure we both would've been right where we're at sooner or later, but my father wants to retire."

"And he's going to need a wife to assist," Mr. Oliver cut in.

"Father," Joel said, exasperation lacing his tone, "can you let me talk to my fiancée?"

"Sure, son." He came to me, attempting to comfort me by touching my arm. "Don't walk away from this opportunity. My son can and will provide a wonderful life for you." With that, he made his way back into the restaurant.

I slapped Joel before the door could close. "You used me."

"No, I did not. I love you, Aquila, but is it so bad if that comes with perks?"

"If it comes at the price of not living your truth—yes."

"My truth?" he whispered, caressing my face and leveling me with his mesmerizing aura. "My truth is that I'm completely in love with you. I have been since the moment I laid eyes on you. Have I dabbled in the past? Yes. But I only have eyes for you. I only love and am in love with you. If you take my hand in marriage, I promise you'll never have to worry about me with any other person, woman or man. I'm committed to you and the life that we're building. I'm dedicating my life to us, Qui. Please. Just trust me."

I loved that man so much that he could've told me he walked on water, and I would've believed him.

"I trust you."

Joel and I stood there in a test of wills. However, I refused to be the one to give in this time. Not this time. This time, I was putting Aquila first.

"Baby, I don't know what to say. I—I love you," he stammered.

I closed my eyes as a solitary tear streaked down my face. "Say your truth. Not for me. For you. You love me, but you're no longer in love with me, Joel, and you haven't been for a long time. Free us both."

When I opened my eyes, he stared at me with a gamut of disappointment, confusion, and regret stirring in his orbs. "I…uh…I think. I want to explore…men."

He'd said it. Spoken his truth. Now, it was time for me to speak mine.

"And I want a divorce. Get out of my house."

Chapter One

AQUILA

TWO YEARS LATER

"JUNIOR, RUN UPSTAIRS and grab your backpack. I'm not bringing it to you this time if you leave it."

An irritated huff escaped as Junior rolled his eyes and haphazardly got up from the breakfast nook with his empty plate, heading toward the sink.

"Hey, hey. Don't get that attitude with me, young man. If you'd remember to bring it with you when you first come down, then I won't have to remind you every morning."

"I'm going, Mom. *Geez.*"

That was my oldest son, Joel Oliver, Jr., whom we affectionately called Junior.

Have kids, they said. It would be fun, they said. The thought ran through my mind as I tried to rub the impending headache from my frontal lobe. It only threatened to magnify as I heard my insouciant nine-year-old schlepping up the stairs to his bedroom. Shaking it off, I turned to see my six-year-old, Sante, shooting fadeaways into the syrup with bits of his French toast sticks, and I gently thumped him on the shoulder.

"*Ouch,*" he hollered in an overly dramatic fashion.

"Quit playing with your food and eat. We'll be leaving in a few."

His obedience to my instruction was to shove an entire stick into his mouth at once. With a mouth full, he garbled, "Look, Mom." When I focused my attention on him, he continued, "I'm eating seafood. See? Food." His mouth flew open to reveal a mushy mess of cinnamon sticks and gooey syrup swirling around. It was a sight that I could've lived the rest of my days without witnessing.

"Stop being disgusting."

He giggled as if I'd told the most hilarious joke in the world and scarfed down the rest of his food. Boys. God would bless me with boys. After making sure they had all their belongings, securing the alarm system, and shuffling us all into my Lexus RX 350, a stylish and comfortable downgrade from that monstrosity Joel had insisted I get, I pulled out of the driveway, ecstatic to get them off to summer camp for the day. I loved my sons, but on days like today, when they tested every one of my nerves, I welcomed the break because being a single parent wasn't easy.

Their father, Joel Oliver, Sr., and I had been divorced for nearly two years. Taking care of my sons sans my ex wasn't new. I had always been their primary caregiver, even during our marriage, but the few things he managed to do—like washing and drying a load of laundry now and then or taking out the trash and handling other household tasks—are what I miss. Now, it was solely my responsibility, along with my two unreliable, broke best friends. I share some of the blame because I pampered them during the divorce and for a time afterward, due to the guilt I felt for initiating the loss of their two-parent dynamic. Furthermore, the emotional toll affected not just Joel and me; it also impacted them. In my haste to care for their mental and emotional well-being, I neglected to enforce some household rules.

Now, I was dealing with the scars from the bruises those bumps caused as I tried to help them learn to be responsible little humans, teaching them that I am Aquila, their mom, not Aquila the maid.

"Hey, sissies." I smiled into the FaceCall.

"Hey, sis," Nissi and Angela said in unison.

"Have you dropped the boys off yet?" Nissi asked.

"No, I'm—"

"Hey, Auntie Nissi and Auntie Angela," the boys boomed boisterously at once, cutting off my response while my sisters cheerfully waved and gushed over them.

"We're in the drop-off line," Sante yelled, flashing his snaggle-tooth grin over my shoulder at the phone's camera.

Out of left field, Junior hit Sante on the arm. "Sit back, stupid."

Retaliating, Sante swung back at him but missed as Junior dodged with his quick reflexes. "Shut up, stupid." Not wanting to be outdone, Sante resorted to his "I'm the baby" go-to move of dramatic tattle-telling. Gripping his forearm, he whined, "Mom, Junior hit me."

As if I didn't see the shit unfold in 4K.

"Aye, y'all stop aggravating your mama," Angela chided as I pinched the bridge of my nose.

"And apologize to her," Nissi added, her typically soft and bubbly demeanor transformed into a deep scowl.

The boys' faces immediately fell, revealing their heartbreak because heaven forbid their favorite aunties be upset with them. I carried those little terrors for nine months. I fed, bathed, clothed, and drove them around all their lives, but to hell with my feelings. As long as their aunties were happy, that was all that mattered in life. The joy of being a mother was priceless.

A unified "Sorry, aunties. Sorry, Mom" flowed from their mouths.

Of course, my wussy sisters folded like wet papier-mâché to a chorus of "It's okay, just don't do it again." Meanwhile, I knew they would do it again.

"I've told you boys to stop fighting a billion times." My eyes darted to the rearview mirror to meet my eldest son's gaze. "And Junior, you know better. You're the oldest. Knock it off." Before he could respond, my eyes darted to Sante. "And Nisante Thurgood Oliver, you better not stick out your tongue."

Upset that his plan was thwarted, he slammed back into his seat as I inched my car forward, grateful to be at the front of the drop-off line.

"That kinda morning, huh, sis?" Nissi asked sympathetically.

"Anyway. Where's my nephew?" I asked Nissi in return.

Her smile brightened whenever anyone mentioned her eighteen-month-old baby boy, Kain Nisan Jordan, named after both of his grandfathers. That's because he was still in the adorable stage. I'd see how she felt about it once the terrible twos began.

"My little KJ is with his daddy. Kannon took him to daycare for me this morning on his way to the station." Nissi sat up from her vanity as if she had just remembered something. "And it's nice of you to ask since you reneged on keeping him for me on Sunday."

"How many times do I have to apologize? I swear it had to be one of those twenty-four-hour bugs I caught from these boys from one of their little playmates at camp."

Nissi looked unconvinced as she continued to apply her makeup, but it was the truth. Rather than continue to press that issue, I focused on Angela, who was getting a kick out of the back-and-forth between Nissi and me.

"Okay, Ms. Sniggles and Giggles, where is my favorite niece?"

"At 5:10 in the morning on the West Coast for a teenager on summer break? I'm pretty sure she's still in bed, fast asleep. I bet Fawn would be doing the same if she were here on the East

Coast. She left this past weekend to visit her best friend back in California. She'll be back in a week to spend her last two weeks with us before returning to her mom's."

Before I could respond, my car door swung open, revealing a beaming camp worker. "Good morning, Ms. Richards. Hey, Joel and Nisante, are you guys ready for today?"

The boys roared their excited answer to the young lady as they began to exit the car.

"Hey, y'all, I need to go. I'll see you both tonight, right?" I asked my sisters.

"Wouldn't miss it," they said in unison. "Love you."

"Love y'all roundtrip," I bellowed before disconnecting my phone to send my children off. I rolled down my passenger-side window. "All right, see you this afternoon, boys," I shouted as they barreled out of the car. "Be good, and stay safe—"

Both of them turned to me, leaning into the open window. "We will."

"Love you, Mom." Junior flashed a gleaming smile my way.

"Love you, Mommy," Sante shouted, adding a blown kiss.

I caught it and hugged it to my heart. "Love you boys more. Have a good day."

"You, too!" they screamed as they rushed to the sign-in table with the other kids.

My heart was full as I doted on my two heartbeats before pulling out of the line to head back home and start my day. Despite the stress of our morning routine, those boys were my entire world, and I loved them immensely. The joy of being a mother was truly priceless.

The bustle of noise caught my attention as I sat waiting for my children's talent show to begin. When I turned to see what all the commotion was about, I facepalmed as I realized my sisters were making their way down the aisle to sit beside me, followed by a chorus of "Excuse me. Pardon me."

When they reached me, I removed their programs from their seats and rushed them to sit down. "You know, when you arrive ahead of time, you don't have to worry about being disruptive."

"First of all, I got off work late, and then I had to drop your nephew off to Papa Kain so I could make this talent show." You know he stays across town," Nissi said, huffing as she planted in her seat.

Angela's rebuttal came on the heels of Nissi's comment. "Who's worried about being disruptive when the show hasn't even started yet? We're here, right?"

My lips curled up as I gave her the side-eye. "Yeah, but Nissi has a valid excuse. She had to drop off her baby with his grandfather. What's yours?"

Leaning over Nissi, she smirked. "Well, I was riding my husband's—"

My hand shot up. "Angela! Couth, please. *Geez.*"

Shrugging, she sat up. "It was none of your business, but since you wanted to know, I was going to answer. Now *that* was disruptive."

Nissi cackled. "Y'all are certifiable, I swear. Anyway, where's Joel?"

Angela high-fived Nissi. "I know that's right. You're up in arms about us. Where is their father for his sons' summer talent show?"

It was my turn to shrug as I lifted my phone to see that my text message inquiring about his whereabouts still had gone unanswered. That man seemed to irk my nerves even more now than when we were married. Our marital woes focused on the diminishing relationship between him and me, but now that we were divorced, it became clear that his fathering skills were lacking. Now that I was no longer part of the equation, I could clearly see that none of us in the Oliver clan were his priority, not even his kids. Ignoring me was a type of foolishness I could overlook because I didn't care, but when it came to ignoring our sons, I was ready to unleash on him because his absenteeism hurt them.

"I can't worry about Joel. Otherwise, I'd ruin the night for Junior and Sante." I let out a breath to release my thoughts about his selfishness. "If he comes, he comes."

We settled in as the talent show began, quickly becoming immersed in the teary-eyed laughter of kids sharing terrible jokes, performing non-magical magic tricks, and belting out horrendous singing. However, we applauded each participant with love and encouragement. Junior and Sante showcased a dance routine, which I suspected was inspired by their TikTok-famous Auntie Nissi. They missed a few steps, but it was incredibly cute, and their aunties stood up to dance along while everyone clapped. My sisters and I gave my little ones a standing ovation at the end. When it was time to announce the winners, every participant received a participation award, and my boys secured second place. A little boy named Jonah came in third for crafting a semi-decent balloon animal. A girl named Misty earned the coveted first-place trophy for her lip-sync performance of a Taylor Swift song. Afterward, we all gathered for refreshments.

Nissi and Angela doted over my sons for their dance routine and play-danced around them for a minute before we hugged and congratulated them on their win.

"Mom, can Sante and I eat our cupcake with our friends?" Junior asked, pointing at a table with other little boys who appeared to be around their age.

"Yes. Go ahead. We'll be leaving in about five to ten minutes."

They barreled off to their friends as we smiled at them.

"I still say they should've won first place," Angela fussed, after swallowing the last bite of her cupcake. "Now, that was delicious."

Playfully, I tapped her arm. "Stop that." I giggled.

Nissi shrugged. "I mean, she's right. Anybody can lip-sync. It takes skills to break out dance moves."

My face flushed red. "OMGeee! Do y'all not see that little girl and her parents standing right over there?" I whispered, leaning in close to our huddled circle.

Angela peered past me and huffed. "Don't threaten me with a good time."

"Lord, have mercy. They're children."

"Fine." Angela rolled her eyes. "Let's switch subjects to why their sorry-ass father didn't show up tonight."

Honestly, I had temporarily forgotten about Joel. I had been so caught up in enjoying the children's performances and celebrating my sons' second-place victory that his absence hadn't even crossed my mind. This prompted me to pull my silenced cell phone out of my purse. Halfway through the performance, he had responded to my text:

> **The Boys' Father:** Oh shit! The talent show was tonight? I thought it was tomorrow.
>
> **The Boys' Father:** I guess you're ignoring me now. I got my days mixed up, Qui, damn. You know I would've been there for the boys.
>
> **The Boys' Father:** All right. I'm going to assume that you're busy watching the show. Since it's my weekend, I'll pick them up early tomorrow and get them a gift. So let me know if 7:30 am is cool. Tell them I'm sorry for me, please.

I don't know what irritated me more: his nonchalance in prioritizing our sons, his delayed response, his attitude toward me for not hurriedly replying to his late message, or his audacity in assuming it was my responsibility to apologize to our sons for his irresponsibility.

Nissi noticed my expression. "He must've replied. You look like you're about to blow a head gasket."

I handed my phone to her, and she and Angela read the messages.

"That sorry SOB. I wouldn't tell the boys a damn thing. If they ask me, I'm gonna say their daddy is a deadbeat, and that's why he's not here," Angela spouted as Nissi handed me my phone.

"Ang, don't." Exasperation oozed from my tone.

"I'm not going to say that for real. As much as I loathe him, that's still their sorry father."

"And they love him," Nissi added, "for whatever godforsaken reason."

I raised my hand. "Thank me for that. I try my best to shield them from their father's lack of accountability when it comes to them. I know he loves them, he's just—"

"Selfish," my sisters said in tandem.

It wasn't as if they were wrong, so I pointed and nodded. "That's the exact word for it."

Nissi laid a soothing hand on my back. "At least he's coming to get them early in the morning so you can get a break."

"If he doesn't get the days mixed up," Angela chided with an attitude.

Nissi and I snickered. If there was one person who did not miss an opportunity to take a dig at Joel Oliver, it was Angela. If she could swap DNA samples with another man, she probably would, to remove the Oliver genes from her nephews so we could be done with him forever.

"I love my boys, but I'm glad to get a break. I haven't truly had one since Thanksgiving. He picks them up for a day here and there, but this is the first weekend visit since November, and I'm tired."

"I'm sure you are." Nissi rubbed her hand down my back.

"I *know* you are. Sis, I know you'll probably spend the weekend sleeping, cooking, and working out, but you need to take some real time for yourself," Angela said.

"Yes. Go to the spa," Nissi added.

"Go get some dick."

I choked on the last remnants of my lemonade at Angela's words as they both patted my back through my coughing fit. "You're going to kill me."

Angela waved away my comment. "Stress will do that before I will. I'm just advising you on how to relieve it before it does. It's been two years, Lah. I'm not saying run and start dating or hop into another marriage, but a little something something will do more wonders than that damn yoga mat."

Nissi dropped her head, trying hard to contain her laughter as I stood there, biting my lip, caught between wanting to say something snarky and laughing myself. Angela really needed to take her comedy show on the road.

"I have my means to take care of that, thank you very much."

"And I'm sure you've outworn the warranty on those means, too," Angela clapped back.

Nissi placed her hand on Angela's shoulder. "Girl, stop." She laughed before turning to me. "Even if you don't take our advice about the companion, at least jot down your ideas for your business. You've been planning to dive into the chef arena, so it's time to pursue your dreams. However, Angela makes a valid point about the other subject. You're going to turn into a robot if you don't get something real in your life. Just because you're a mother doesn't mean your life has to end."

"No. It just means my life becomes all about my children."

Angela shook her head vigorously and pointed at me. "No. Those boys are *part* of your life. When they grow up, they will live their lives to the fullest, not revolving around you or Joel. Live *now*." Angela's phone chimed, and she glanced at the message before continuing. "Listen, sis, take both of our advice. Tomorrow offers no guarantees, and you don't want to look back and find you have nothing for yourself and no one for yourself." She embraced me. "I've got to go. Kinston wants me to pick up food from this new Thai restaurant, and I need to get there before it closes."

"And I need to pick up KJ from his grandpop before that boy makes him throw out his back again." Nissi leaned in and hugged me.

We made our way over to the boys, and they gave their goodbyes to them before I corralled my troops and headed to my car.

"Hey, Mom," Junior called out after buckling in, "what happened to Dad?"

I pressed the start button on my SUV. With my eyes straight ahead, my heart turned cold considering Joel's antics. "I don't know, Junior. But you and Sante can ask him yourselves in the morning."

I caught his face in the rearview—hurt written all over it—but he didn't push. As much as it gutted me to see that look, I wasn't cleaning up Joel's mess. Not again. Not ever. The days of shielding him were over. My cape? Burned. Let the villain explain himself because this superhero was done. Seven-thirty couldn't get here fast enough.

Chapter Two

AQUILA

I SAT IN the summer camp parking lot for a few extra minutes, enjoying my alone time before I had to go inside and sign out my boys for the day.

The weekend had been a blur. Joel kept his promise to pick up the boys that Saturday at his proposed time. No sooner had he walked inside than Junior and Sante flooded him with questions about missing their talent show. The shocked expression on his face showed that he was surprised I didn't come to his usual rescue. His subsequent stuttering indicated that he also expected me to defend him. My days of running interference to spare him were officially over. As his wife, I felt it was my duty to have his back, even when he was wrong. As his ex-wife, I had enough burdens to manage on my own. He'd better learn to step up or be prepared for the fallout.

In typical Joel-avoidance fashion, rather than giving them a straight answer, he sidestepped their questions by heaping praise on them for winning second place. While they were basking in the moment of praise, he quickly switched the subject to going toy shopping, and just like that, his no-show act was long forgotten. He avoided eye contact with me throughout the entire farce because he knew I wasn't pleased. I wasn't his wife anymore, so his whereabouts were no longer my concern. Therefore, I didn't ask. However, as the boys dashed to his Audi A8, I made it a point to tell him that I didn't appreciate him missing the boys' moments and then buying their affections instead of owning up to his actions. To avoid making a scene, he gave me a half-hearted promise to do better and left me standing at the threshold of the house, waving goodbye to them.

When they left, I followed my sisters' advice and began compiling my ideas for a business plan. I got started, but then I remembered that I needed to load the dishwasher from breakfast earlier. The rest of my weekend was consumed with cleaning, meal prepping for the week, working out at the gym, and doing yoga. By the time I finally settled down to return to the business plan, Joel rang my doorbell to drop the boys off early Sunday evening. My night was filled with making sure the boys were ready for the next day and for bed. As soon as their heads caressed their pillows, I was good for nothing except a nice hot shower and my bed.

Not even my adult toys saw action the past weekend.

As I entered the building, I saw a man of tall stature waving me down from my peripheral vision. I stopped and turned to see Daniel Goldman, the camp's director, headed toward me in his usual attire: a lime green polo shirt and khakis. His identification lanyard was swinging from his neck.

"Ms. Richards," he called out as he got closer. "May I speak to you for a moment in my office?"

My Spidey senses immediately made me tense, and I thought something had happened to one of my children. "What's wrong? Is everything all right with Joel and Nisante?"

He raised his hands to stop me, his demeanor conveying a sense of calm. "Oh no, nothing like that. I'm sorry to alarm you. I just wanted to talk with you."

Releasing a sigh of relief, I followed him to his office, away from the ruckus of rambunctious children and camp workers.

His office was adorned with the camp's lime green, white, yellow, and purple logo. A cloth rolling chair sat behind a small standard desk. A few papers were scattered about, alongside a laptop computer. The small bookshelf nearby displayed his degree in public administration, a picture of his daughter, who was one of the middle-school campers here, and his fraternity paddle, along with other black-and-gold fraternity memorabilia.

"Ms. Richards," he said, gesturing for me to take a seat.

I stayed stoic, my arms crossed over my chest, as I sensed that something troubling might be amiss. "I'd prefer to stand, thanks."

He let out a small chortle. "Aquila," he called out my first name, dropping the pretenses. "I assure you that everything is all right with your sons."

On that note, I felt thoroughly convinced that I could relax, which only left me more perplexed. I knew I didn't owe anything financially. I had paid for the boys' camp costs in full upfront before the program started.

As I settled into the chair in front of his desk, my brows furrowed. "Daniel, I'm sorry. What's this meeting about?"

He took his seat, smiling brightly at me. "This is actually about the cupcakes you brought for the reception after the talent show."

A gasp escaped as I pressed the panic button. "Oh, goodness. Did someone get sick? Was someone allergic? I tried not to use commonly known ingredients that cause allergic reactions."

Now, his brows furrowed. "So, *you* made those cupcakes?"

Swallowing a lump, I nodded the truth. "Yes, I did."

He shook his head. "*Wow,*" he said, looking amazed. "I know Joel is a chef, so I figured either he'd made them or you bought them."

I had to force my face from converting into a frown. Everyone believed that because Joel was a world-renowned chef, he always prepared the meals. I wished they knew he reserved his precious five-star hands for his upper-echelon clients only. It was Mama Bear who cooked for the commoners, also known as my boys and me, as well as for all of their functions.

"No. I made them from scratch. My ex-husband is a chef; however, we are both skilled in culinary arts."

My tone must've been a bit more abrasive than I'd intended because he apologized profusely. "My apologies, Aquila. I didn't mean to offend you. Quite the contrary, actually. I wanted to commend you. Those cupcakes have been the talk of the day camp. Everyone wanted to know who made them. If I'm honest, they are the best cupcakes I've ever had, and many have echoed that sentiment."

Talk about being floored. I knew I could bake and cook, but I wasn't expecting this kind of feedback. To be fair, my family was usually the only ones eating my food.

"Are you serious?"

"I am." He smiled. "I wanted to compliment the baker, and since I now know that's you, my next question goes to you."

Curiosity had me quickly inquiring. "What's that?"

"Would you be willing to bake more cupcakes for the season-ending program reception? Of course, we'll pay you."

Falling back into the seat, I blinked rapidly as I processed his request. "*Um.* Well, I…*Wow.*"

"Before you decline, please say you'll at least consider it."

"No, it isn't that. I wasn't expecting this."

He swayed his head from side to side. "So, you will do it?"

"Yes. I mean, what are the details and the budget?"

"You tell me. Just provide me with an invoice that has a due date, and we'll handle the rest." He opened the top drawer of his desk and pulled out a business card, offering it to me. "My business number and cell number are on here, and you'll find my email address as well, so feel free to reach out to me anytime."

Taking the card from him, I clutched it like a lifeline. "Oh, my goodness. I'm still in shock. Thank you so much, Daniel."

He flashed an award-winning smile at me. "Perfect."

Up until that point, the conversation felt professionally poised. With a hint of admiration in his eyes, I sensed a shift in the atmosphere. It was subtle, but it existed. I hoped this man wasn't lying about this opportunity purely to get my number. My children had been attending this camp every summer since Junior was five. I didn't want a failed advance to jeopardize their ongoing attendance.

As I stood, Daniel stood with me. "You know, after you assured me that my children were safe and I hadn't caused anyone harm with my goodies, I almost thought you might be trying to shoot your shot." I levied the comment jokingly to ensure I hadn't misread the situation.

He released a nervous titter and eased his hands into his pants pockets. "Would that be such a bad thing?"

Is he serious? My head cocked to the side in disbelief. "You're my children's summer camp director."

Daniel's shoulders relaxed as he leaned back, his brows knitted in confusion. "Yes, and being the summer camp director doesn't make me blind. It makes me a single man who's interested and happens to work at the facility your sons attend."

"Mr. Goldman—"

"Daniel," he stressed, interrupting me.

I took a beat before posing the real questions that had run through my mind in the few short moments since he'd confirmed his interest. "Daniel. Is this newfound attraction why I suddenly have a catering offer, or have you been watching me since I was a married woman?"

It may have been crude, but I was fed up with men and their manipulations. I considered myself well-versed since I'd been married to a master. From what I could determine of the current dating pool, they'd only multiplied like Gremlins. I'd thought better of Daniel, so I certainly hoped he wasn't revealing the unmasked version of himself.

He quickly dispelled the notion of hiring me to bake the cupcakes as a diversion. Emphatically, he waved his hands. "No. Absolutely not. My approach to you for catering services for the end-of-the-summer program is strictly professional and has no bearing on our private conversation." With a sigh, he levied a scornful stare at me. "Aquila, you've known me since your sons were babies, even before the program. I believe you know I'd never do anything like that." After a moment, he stepped into my personal space, his stare shifting to a longing gaze. "And regarding my interest, I won't pretend that it hasn't been piqued since you were Joel's wife. I have enough respect for myself and the sanctity of marriage not to disrupt a relationship. But as a single man, I have no hesitation about shooting my shot at a gorgeous and single woman."

Help me, O Lord. Daniel's towering frame could easily bring down the walls of Jericho. I couldn't deny that he was an exceptional man. He had always been that way. While he was slightly taller than Joel's five-foot-nine frame, Daniel's caramel-colored skin stretched over a solid, muscular build, in contrast to Joel's slender physique. He was handsome, from the wavy coils atop his head to his dimpled smile, extending to his strong, athletic thighs. Even the square black-framed glasses he wore added to his attractiveness.

I'd had the pleasure of meeting him at one of his fraternity banquets. Joel's restaurant was hired to cater the plated affair, and Daniel, then the president of his fraternity chapter, invited Joel to the black-tie event as an official guest due to the generous discount Joel had offered for the promise of future business. I went as Joel's plus one, of course, and we had established a fast and friendly relationship with Daniel.

Unlike me, Daniel had never been married but had a daughter with his college sweetheart who'd since moved on, gotten married, and started a family. He'd never been inappropriate with me before, so I trusted that what he'd said was the truth. My truth was that, as handsome and downright sexy as that man was, I didn't think it was appropriate to date someone who was friends with Joel or someone who was as close to my children as Daniel was. At least, that was a significant part of it.

"Daniel." My tone softened, and my eyes fluttered up to him as I touched his forearm. "You're right, and I'm sorry, but honestly, I don't think it would be in our best interests to date each other. I met you through Joel, whom you still communicate with, and I don't want the boys to be confused about the nature of our relationship."

Daniel paused before speaking, gently patting the back of my hand. "Aquila, be straight with me. Joel and I are hardly associates, and the boys see me infrequently during the summer, if at all. I'm not responsible for their direct care and learning; I supervise their teachers. They only catch glimpses of me during passing moments or at special events, like the talent show last week. It's perfectly fine to tell me you're not interested."

Given my failed marriage and poor decisions surrounding Joel, I struggled with a sense of gullibility. My lapses in judgment aside, I had to admit that Daniel gave me grown-man vibes. Even though I didn't need his permission to say no, it was reassuring to know that rejection felt safe, considering the current climate of overly aggressive and mentally unstable men—an episode of *The First 48* I would not become. While everything I'd explained to him was the gospel truth, the *unspoken* truth was that despite his undeniably good looks and reassurances, I had trust issues—with my own decisions.

Shrugging, I reluctantly admitted, "You've got a point. While I still have reservations because of my kids, I guess the real reason is that I don't think I'm ready to try again. I hope you understand."

He took my hand in his and squeezed it. "Totally."

It felt like a weight had been lifted off my shoulders, and air rushed out of me like a confession. Gripping his hand, I acknowledged my silent thanks for his kindness and patience.

"And for the record, if I were ready, I'd be crazy and blind not to be interested."

A blush tinged his face as he chuckled. "I'll make sure to remind you when you're ready to test the waters." He stepped aside and gestured for me to walk ahead of him out of his office. "In the meantime, you have my number and email for the catering. We can't wait to taste your cupcakes again."

Our conversation detour almost made me forget about the new incredible opportunity. The reminder made me bounce giddily. "Right. Thank you so much. I'll be in touch about the details and invoice. I know the program is in August. I just need the exact date."

"Sure thing. I have you covered."

Giddiness washed over me. I was ready to do backflips and somersaults all the way to the car. This unexpected hiring reignited the fire within me to settle down and take my plans to pursue a professional career in culinary arts seriously. I decided then and there that this would be my test run. If all went well with this booking, I would actively pursue my entrepreneurial career. I could already feel it in my bones: It was my time.

Turning to leave, I exited Daniel's office with an extra pep in my step. Even though I wasn't ready to date, I was curious to know if I still had it, so I took advantage and went full Loretta Devine in *Waiting to Exhale* and added a little jiggle as I walked. Curiously, I glanced over my shoulder, and sure enough, Daniel's eyes were on my slim, thick waist. I couldn't help but grin. *Yep. I've still got it.*

Chapter Three

ROMAN

SITTING IN MY office, I could already feel the electric energy in the air as clients and their family members streamed into our open gym area. I only had one Saturday a month to be the lead training coach, and my favorite day was Family Fit Day. For one, it meant we could try to retain spouses or significant others and their older teens (if they had children) as permanent clients. What excited me even more was seeing families committed to physical fitness. Usually, having family with them—even if it's just one person—helps keep them motivated to continue their fitness journey. It also added a bit of competition because who wants their fifteen-year-old or spouse to outshine them on the turf? Whatever the reason, it kept people healthy and kept my best friend and business partner, Kinston Jordan, and me in business. Together, that was a win-win.

After verifying that the inventory order was correct, I closed my laptop and reached behind me to grab my black-and-gold KinRo Fitness short-sleeved compression t-shirt from my leather chair. I slipped it on and checked my reflection in the mirror. Today was a scorcher, with an estimated hundred people filling the facility, so staying as cool as possible was essential. Therefore, I opted for all-black athletic compression gear and mesh shorts instead of my usual pants. I connected my headset and microphone before stepping out the door and into the hallway. While stopping at the employee lounge to pick up my jug of water, I noticed my favorite family, the Jordan-Richards clan, huddled together, getting ready to head onto the turf floor.

"What's up, fam?"

"Roman," they all shouted.

I slapped fives with Kinston before we pulled each other into a one-armed hug and repeated the action with his brother, Kannon.

"What's up, Kann? When are you going to get your wife in here with you?" I teased him as I pulled his son, little KJ, from his arms and flipped him up on my shoulders as he beat pretend drums on top of my head.

"When someone agrees to watch that little rascal afterward, so she can rest. She said this is her 'me' time." He shrugged.

"And I know you weren't going to argue with that. What do they say? Happy wife, happy life."

Kannon pointed at me. "And you better know it." He reached and grabbed KJ from my shoulders, much to the little man's dismay.

"*Aww*. Sorry, li'l buddy. You have to go to the KinRo Kid Zone, but one day, you can hang with the big dogs." I rubbed his back as he settled down and laid his head on Kannon's shoulder.

"Let me take him right now before he gets fussy again," Kannon said. "See you on the turf, bro."

With that, I turned to see Angela and Fawn stepping out of the restroom. Fawn ran up and hugged me tightly.

"Uncle Roman," she greeted.

"'Sup, li'l Kinston?"

She pushed out of my embrace and folded her arms across her chest. "Why do you always say that?"

Angela nudged her. "Because you look just like your daddy, child. You know that." She shook her head and side-hugged me. "What's up, Roman?"

"Just getting ready to kick y'all's asses on this turf."

"And don't we know it," Aquila's voice rang behind me.

As soon as we turned around, Aquila's sons, Junior and Sante, ran up to me, and I gave each of them our special handshake. For Junior, we slapped hands three times and then chest-bumped. For Sante, we slapped hands once, dabbed, and did the Griddy dance. It always pumped them up, and me, too, if I'm being honest. Those boys were the ideal kids for any parent wanting to bring their children. They worked hard, never complained, and had fun while doing it. I hoped they could come more often, but they weren't quite of age yet. Junior kid's membership started at thirteen. However, kids aged five to twelve could work out with their parents on Family Fit Days only, and Aquila and her boys never missed a Saturday Family Fit Day session.

"Mr. Roman, aren't my muscles getting bigger?" Sante asked, flexing his arm with the brightest beam on his face.

I stepped back, as if genuinely eyeing and considering his form, then walked up to him and lightly squeezed his bicep. "Boy, look at those guns. Gonna put all those first graders to shame."

He balled a fist and pulled down his arm, shouting, "Yeah!" Then we high-fived each other. "I'm gonna be just like you!"

"In no time." I curled my bicep, and his eyes lit up. "Gimme some." We slapped hands three times.

Junior walked up to me and whispered, "That's cap."

I burst into laughter and playfully mushed his head. "Stop hatin'. And what do you know 'bout some cap?"

Sante scowled at his brother. "He just wants to be like us, Mr. Roman."

I stifled my laugh because I knew those boys, and the last thing I wanted was for them to get into a tiff. So instead, I said, "Hey, no competition here—"

"Only results," they both shouted.

"That's right. Leave it all on the turf."

Aquila grinned, watching us. "Y'all are a mess. What's up, Roman?"

The sound of Aquila's voice caught me off guard. I was so engrossed in the banter with her sons that I didn't notice her watching us. When I looked at her, she felt like a breath of fresh air, and I had to suppress a smile. Instead, my thoughts turned to my admiration for her. She'd been through a lot in recent years with her divorce, though I didn't know the details. What I understood was that divorce had to be tough. It's already challenging when you tether your life to someone else, but bringing shared lives into the world and raising them while navigating a divorce must be an even greater feat. I couldn't imagine investing my faith in forever with someone only to watch it all burn to the ground. I was in awe of her strength in standing tall amid all the adversity, especially with a man like Joel. I'd had the displeasure of witnessing their interactions as a married couple, and from my brief encounters with him, I'd never understood how he ended up with Aquila. A guy like him didn't deserve a woman like her.

We side-hugged each other. "Not much. Like I told your sister, just getting ready to put this workout on y'all."

Aquila clapped. "Let's go then! I'm ready."

This time, I did smile. Her excitement always amped me up. We slapped hands three times in quick succession. "That's what I'm talking about right there. You stay ready."

Those were all facts. Aquila wasn't new to this. She was true to this lifestyle. She had been with KinRo since nearly its inception as one of Kinston's first clients. We often used her as a poster client because she was faithful and consistent. She was friends with every trainer at both locations and was just as much a part of KinRo as we were. We even tried, albeit unsuccessfully, to bring her on as a trainer. While she loved to exercise, she didn't want to train others in that capacity. She feared making it a job would dull her vigor. I understood that wholeheartedly. Some things were meant to be our pastimes, not our passions.

"On that note, we better stretch because your uber-competitive auntie is not about to have me tweaking my back," Angela said to Fawn as they all began to file out and head to the turf.

Before they left, I shared another round of our special handshakes with Junior and Sante, and Aquila high-fived me before speaking. "Thank you for making them feel special. They adore Mr. Roman. To be honest, they've been the ones dragging me to these Saturday sessions lately."

"No need to thank me. Those guys are my dudes. Besides, it seems like I should be the one thanking them for keeping our top client on track."

We shared a laugh about that, and it seemed like she was going to say something else, but my other trainer, Cami, came through the door to tell me the time. Instead, Aquila left, heading to the turf.

"Ro, you have two minutes until the start," Cami said, waving hello to Kinston, my business partner and best friend, who was approaching me.

He waved back at her before he turned to me. "Yo, man. You're awesome with kids. I see how you are with Fawn, the boys, and KJ. It's a damn shame you never wanted to settle down and have a family of your own. You'd be an amazing dad."

"Ninja, please." I *tsk*ed. "You get married and wanna marry off every man. We can't all have an Angela."

"Hell nah 'cause she's mine. But you could have a close second if you tried," Kinston joked.

"I'ma leave that for you and Kannon." We touched knuckles. "I'll see you out there in a second."

Kinston patted Cami on her shoulder as he walked out to join his family for the workout. Cami was co-coaching with me today due to the large crowd. She walked over to me with a sympathetic expression plastered on her face.

"Don't give me that look, Cami."

She raised her hands. "I'm not here to pick a fight or get you all in your feels. But you know it's never too late to find love and start a family, especially—"

Not this again. My ears instantly tuned out the rest of her words. I wasn't up for this conversation today. All I wanted to do was get in this workout and see us transform our clients' lives. Besides, that ship had sailed and sunk a long time ago. KinRo Fitness was my wife, and as long as it was good, so was I.

"I have found love…in this." I pointed to the KinRo Fitness logo on the wall. "And all these folks are all the family I need." I finished my statement, pointing out to the massive crowd.

Cami eyed me skeptically. "Roman," she said, stretching my name with a sigh.

Ignoring her, I pressed play on my music playlist and turned on my microphone as I opened the door, waltzed across the hall to the glass doors, and pushed them open. The beat of the Terror Squad's "Lean Back" dropped over the loudspeakers, and I sprinted through the room, high-fiving everyone, thrilled beyond belief.

"What's up, KinRo Krew! I am your trainer for today, Coach Roman, and joining me is Coach Cami. Today is Core and Cardio. We have eight blocks today and one hour of time. Give your neighbors a high-five, and let's get started with some warm-up jumping jacks when I say KinRo on three, KinRo on me."

Chapter Four

ROMAN

I WAS FINALLY getting out of this house tonight, and it felt remarkable. These days, it seemed the only reasons I left were for work and grocery shopping, as if I were an old maid with six cats and a garden in the backyard. For the first time in…well…*ever*, there wasn't a woman around to occupy my time. My love life felt like a drought; the Sahara had more action than I had in these past few months. Usually, initiating a hook-up for a night out and a nightcap wasn't a challenge. Being a business owner and well-known in the city had its perks in that department. It wasn't that the number of prospects was dwindling; it was more that my interest in the selections was. Only one woman had truly piqued my interest, but the chances of that ever happening were so slim, they were practically non-existent.

Sure, I had a list of numbers for women I could connect with, but I wouldn't be dying of thirst if those women had held my interest. At thirty-six years old, I was finally growing weary of superficial satisfaction. While I couldn't foresee family life being in the cards for me, I'd also outgrown one-night stands. Even though I still held out hope that a good woman would come along someday, no woman had measured up recently. But tonight held promise.

Last week, I went out to the club with some other trainers. They were all younger than me by at least five years and up to ten years at the most. And it showed. Those men were wild and down for whatever, whereas I was on my chill vibe. I knew I was with the wrong crowd when they jokingly called me *OG* Roman. I wasn't even given the benefit of the coveted "Unc" title, just mad disrespectful, but who else did I have to hang with? Kinston and Kannon were married men with families, and though I was cool with Travis and Jovan, they were associates to me who I only knew because Travis was Cami's husband and Jovan was Kannon's best friend. With no other meaningful friendships, I figured hanging out with the younger trainers wouldn't be so bad, and it wasn't. It was horrible. That night assured me that those guys were not my speed, aside from working together at the gym and work-related outings.

Despite my failed guys' outing, one positive came from that night. I'd met a little hottie at the club. Madison caught my eye because while her friend group was wilding out with alcohol and twerk moves, she sat regally in the booth, sipping on her cocktail. When we locked eyes, I was prepared to walk over and spit my game to get her number, but she beat me to the punch. Without hesitation, she eased from her seat, walked those sexy stilettos over to our section, and sat beside me. The other guys I was with ogled her, but she gave me all her attention. Although she was a tad bit more slender than I preferred, she had a little body on her with a tiny yet supple round ass. Not to mention, her face card wasn't ever declining. Baby girl was gorgeous. I found out she was twenty-nine and a nurse. Beauty and brains. That was the perfect combination for me to ensure that we exchanged numbers that night, and we did.

Tonight, we are going out for dinner. Throughout the week, I tried to call her to get to know her better, but her work schedule was packed, which I understood due to her profession. Since I didn't know her preferences or dislikes, I decided that a simple date at LongHorn would be decent. I wanted a juicy steak, and they offered other options like chicken, seafood, or vegetarian meals if she wasn't a fan of red meat. If I had known her a bit longer or could have talked with her to plan in more detail, we might have gone to a place like Prime 112. But I wasn't a fan of wasting money. I'd prefer that she disliked LongHorn on a budget than dislike Prime 112 on a dime. If all went well tonight, we could work our way up to that.

We decided on casual dress attire for the date, so I kept it simple—a silk button-down shirt paired with chino pants and all-white sneakers. My short waves were brushed to perfection, and my beard and goatee were neatly trimmed low. One thing I didn't skimp on was my grooming habits. I visited my barber, and although he charged a pretty penny, the service was top-notch. The haircut included a complete grooming session and a facial. We may have kept it simple tonight, but I made sure my appearance was top tier.

At 7 p.m., I pulled up to her townhome in my black-on-black Dodge Challenger. She'd asked me to call her when I arrived, and she'd come to my car. I didn't particularly care for that because I considered myself a chivalrous gentleman. My parents taught me the importance of walking to the door and greeting a woman properly. However, we lived in different times, so I yielded to her independent and safety-conscious views that were now the norm in the dating scene. It was bothersome, but I understood. The delusional men out there were why women would risk their lives facing a bear rather than running to safety with a man.

"Hey, Madison," I greeted her when she answered on the third ring. "I'm outside your house."

"Hey, Roman. I'll be out soon."

We hung up, and I checked my work emails while waiting. After answering my fifth email, I looked up to check the time on my radio, which read seven-thirty. I knew that couldn't be right, so I checked my cell phone, and sure enough, thirty minutes had passed since I'd called her. Now, I was panicking. Maybe I was at the wrong address, and she thought I was playing games by not being at the correct location. I redialed her number.

"Hey, Roman," she said, not offering anything more.

"*Umm,* are you all right? Am I at the right house?" I was about to rattle her address when the front door opened, and she waltzed out.

"Yeah. I wasn't finished getting dressed," she said before ending our call.

My eyes lingered on the ended phone call. "What the hell?"

Aside from being slightly perturbed because she kept me waiting for thirty minutes without a heads-up, I was also somewhat confused when I saw her. We had agreed to dress casually, yet she appeared in a dress that was much skimpier than the one she wore at the club, paired with sky-high heels— definitely true Miami nightlife attire. We were heading out for dinner, not to South Beach. Still, I got out of my car to open her door, flowers in hand.

As I went to hand her the bouquet, she shooed them away. "*Eww.* I don't like flowers. That's such a waste."

Well, damn. Here I was, attempting to be a gentleman. I could understand her shunning them if she was allergic, but not being rude just because she didn't like flowers. *What's the harm in accepting them and appreciating the gesture?*

Shaking my head, I let the notion go and opened the car door for her to enter. Once she was secured, I opened my back door, placed the bouquet on the back seat, and then eased back into the driver's seat, heading to our destination.

"I apologize about the flowers, and you look very nice."

I wasn't sure if she had heard me as her head darted around the vehicle. After a few moments, she finally acknowledged me.

"Thanks," she said and shook her head. "I'm sorry, but didn't I see you driving a Maserati at the club last week?"

I looked over and flashed her my pearly whites, although I was unsure whether to be impressed or cautious that she remembered. We talked at the club until our sets of friends were ready to leave. When we left, my car had been valeted, so I passed by her and her friends in my sports car as they walked to the parking deck where their vehicle was parked.

"Yeah, you did. That's my other car. Since we kept it light, I figured we'd go out in my everyday car."

"Your everyday car," she repeated, a hint of irritation pinging in her tone.

"Yes. My Dodge Challenger is the vehicle I typically drive. Is there something wrong with that?"

She scoffed. "I mean, if you're trying to be a young dope boy, I guess. I figured your *everyday* car would be a luxury car."

Time out. Red flag on the play. Just when I thought I'd met someone I could vibe with, she was proving to be the type of Miami chick I had grown tired of. Gripping the steering wheel, I decided to test my theory.

"Nah. One luxury vehicle is enough. Do you drive a luxury car?"

Though I focused on the road ahead, I heard her slight sneer and caught her side-eye from my peripheral.

"No, but why did you say it like that? Like you're trying to check me."

My temple started to throb immediately. Nope. This felt like familiar territory, so I offered the information that would decide if we made it to dinner.

In my gentlest voice, I offered comforting words. "Hey, let's just relax and have a good time. We'll be at LongHorn in a few minutes."

"*LongHorns?* Oh, hell no. You have a freaking Maserati, and you wanna take me to some ol' regular-ass chain restaurant? Unbelievable." Without giving me a chance to respond, even if I had planned to, she retrieved her cell phone from her purse and dialed a number. "Girl, you won't believe this. Remember the guy from the club? The one you said owned those gyms? This dude had the nerve to pick me up in this ol' mid-ass car, girl. Then he wondered why I kept him waiting for thirty minutes. 'Cause I'm like, who's at my house? *Righttt.* Period."

Now, I had been through—and probably put some females through—a lot of bullshit in my life, but this was a first. She had the unmitigated gall to talk about audacity. Not only was she sitting in my vehicle disrespecting me, but she also had the gall to double down by discussing me with her friend right in front of my face. She was on some new kind of bold.

"Then he brings me some flowers. I'm twenty-nine, not forty-five. The hell?" She laughed and continued, "Then he says we're going to LongHorns. Yes, girl. Long-freakin'-Horns. Like whettt? Be so for real."

While she talked, she didn't even realize I had turned around and headed back to her house. I didn't bother interrupting her tirade as she continued with her little co-signing friend. This was why I was in a drought right now, and if this was all the dating pool had to offer, I'd shrivel up.

She was so absorbed in her rant that she hadn't even noticed she was back at her house. I spotted a basic ass mid-size SUV with no perks or features parked near her townhome with a license plate that read MADDY 1. I chuckled. Unbelievable. She was pressed about riding in my Challenger instead of my Maserati, even though she couldn't afford either vehicle. That's not a knock against her or her ride if she couldn't, but how does someone set a standard for someone else that they can't even meet themselves? Typical bird behavior.

Parking, I exited my car, walked around, and opened her car door. She was so busy cackling with her friend that she stepped out before glancing around.

"Wait a minute, girl. I know he didn't. Let me call you back."

As the realization began to sink in, she hung up her phone frantically, as I rounded my car and settled back inside.

"Hey!" She hit my window as I locked my doors. "I know you didn't bring me back home."

As my car idled, I rolled down the window. "Oh, now, you're off your phone so that we can talk? Yes, I did."

"Why? I'm hungry."

It wasn't even shocking that she had the nerve to ask me why, so I didn't address it. "I'm sure you have groceries in your house. Cook something."

Her eyes shifted as worry lines creased her forehead. "I… don't. My check hasn't hit yet. I'm a CNA, and I don't make that much." Her words were soft and shaky, a stark contrast to the vibrato she had with her friend just moments ago.

That's when what she said struck a chord with me. *Wow.* Now, she was not only disrespectful but also a liar. Nurse my ass. She wasn't a RN. Hell, she wasn't even an LPN.

"Sounds like a 'you' problem, sweetheart."

She smoothed down her dress and approached the door, still trying to persuade me to let her back into my car for a dinner date. "Come on. I know I was put off by the restaurant at first, but that's only because I know you can do better. I'm totally worth it." I shook my head, and she continued, "We can go to LongHorns. I don't have a problem with that."

"Oh yeah?" I sounded like I was asking a question, so she nodded happily, thinking I had changed my mind. "Well, I do.

Next time, maybe be appreciative when a real man wants to treat you. *Another* man. Not me, though, because I'm out."

She struck my car door with her purse. "So. Don't nobody care about you anyway. I can find another baller just like that," she declared with a snap of her fingers.

Lifting my brow, I flicked the tip of my nose with a sniff. "Yeah, a'ight. Back up," I ordered as I put my car in drive. "Oh, and one more thing, sweetheart." She gave me her full attention, probably hoping a second chance still lingered in the atmosphere. "The restaurant is LongHorn, not *Horns*."

Her mouth fell as I peeled out to her screaming expletives at me. I looked at the time, which read 8:25 p.m. I still had time to make it to the restaurant to get my steak.

Chapter Five

AQUILA

TO SAY I was excited about baking 250 cupcakes for the summer camp end-of-season program is an understatement. The day was filled with running errands, comparing prices, and preparing invoices. I felt exhausted when I shuffled into the house to start dinner prep before picking up the boys from camp. However, I couldn't complain. The sheer joy that enveloped me at realizing I was about to live out my dream was enough to make me forget any momentary hassles.

Kicking the garage door closed with the toe of my ballet flat, I toggled the mega-size box of chips and mail in one hand and the grocery bags in the other as I headed into the kitchen to put away the items. Tonight's dinner was going to be super easy—vegan spaghetti with cheesy garlic bread and a meatless pasta salad.

Placing the bags on the counter, I retrieved all the ingredients needed to prepare the meal and put the other items away. I was just about to unload the dishwasher, but a letter sitting on top of the stack of mail I'd just placed on the counter caught my attention. It was from an attorney. Joel's attorney. That made me come to a full stop. I picked up the envelope and retrieved the letter opener from my junk drawer. My brief perusal of the letter ignited an inferno inside me, so I took a deep breath and reread it slowly, knowing I must've misinterpreted it. When I reviewed the details again, I concluded that I hadn't lost my mind because I knew Joel had lost his. I directed my cell phone to call his cell phone before I even knew what I was going to say to his conniving ass.

"What the hell is this, Joel? Alimony reduction?" The words were out of my mouth before he could answer.

He blew out a harsh breath. "Hello, Qui—"

"Don't you 'Qui' me. Answer the question, Joel."

"Well, you read the paperwork, dear. It is what it says it is. I'm petitioning the court for a reduction."

If the kitchen were carpeted, I was sure I would've worn a hole clean through it with how much I paced around. I had to keep moving because if I stopped, I might've physically tried to put my hands through the phone to lay hands on him, and I didn't mean praying ones either. Joel was a perfectionist at creating problems where there were none. I didn't ask him for more alimony. I didn't ask him for more child support. I was satisfied with what we had. It was enough to sustain us, pay the house bills, take care of the boys' necessities, cover school tuition, and breathe easily. Could I take lavish vacations or go on monthly shopping sprees? No. I wasn't looking for any of that. I just wanted to provide for us without living paycheck to paycheck. The only parts of my alimony that were strictly for me were my biweekly hair appointments and gym membership. Those were included in the payment because they were part of my care during our marriage. Every dime outside of that went into this household and for our children.

"Thank you, Captain Obvious. I gathered that. What I need to know from you is *why*, hence the phone call. We agreed on this through our divorce settlement."

"Honestly, *Aquila*," he said, grating my nerves by stretching my name the way he used to when we were in a heated argument.

"We've been divorced for almost two years now. It seems you should've found something to provide supplemental income."

I dropped my phone on the counter like it was a hot potato. "Excuse me? I am the sole caretaker of our two children, or did you forget that?"

"Plenty of single mothers hold jobs. It's a ubiquitous phenomenon these days."

Oh, he had all the audacity today. Well, so did I. "I missed the part where you mentioned that when we married, you asked me to be a stay-at-home mother to support you and the restaurant and our future babies."

"Yes, when we were *married. You're* the one who wanted this divorce, or did I miss the part where you mentioned that?" Joel barked back.

"No, you didn't. I think it was lost in translation, along with the portion about you being more interested in dicking down men than dicking down your wife, which led to said divorce." My response to his bark spewed as harshly as a pit bull's bite. "So, if you want to go there, then let's go all the way there. Otherwise, cut the shit and tell me what this is about because I haven't contested a thing from our divorce for you to initiate this ridiculous and unfounded claim."

There was a pregnant pause between us. I'm sure Joel was flustered, trying to figure out how to bounce back from my verbal assault. He wanted to take it low, but I'd dragged him to purgatory and I wouldn't apologize for it. Since the day I'd agreed to continue our nuptials, I'd swallowed my pride, feelings, desires, and needs to protect Joel. It hadn't served me when we were betrothed, and I'd be damned if I continued as his ex-wife. No longer would I make myself digestible for his benefit. He'd choke first—if he didn't make me do the honors.

"The second investment Jansen promised hasn't come through, and the restaurant is still recovering financially. I'm focused on the advancement of the Oliver Brand future, which includes my sons."

"Your sons also need to be financially secure in the Oliver present. Instead of using me as your punching bag for your financial woes, why not reach out to Jansen to see what's going on? He's our friend and has already approved the initial investment to help save the restaurant. I'm sure he has no intention of reneging on his word."

"Jansen has done enough. I'm a grown man. I can't keep asking another man to bail me out. My father is also disappointed. He doesn't understand the hits we took after COVID. It's why I began private catering again," Joel seethed in frustration.

With more clarity, I sat on the barstool at the island counter and rubbed my throbbing forehead. "I remember, Joel. I was there. I lived it with you. I understand you're still climbing out of that hole, and your father is unhappy. However, taking food from your children's mouths is not the solution. So, call Jansen or come up with another plan because I will fight you on this in court. Guaranteed."

"You'd contest this knowing what I'm experiencing with the restaurant?" Joel asked, incredulity lacing his words.

"For my kids? Every time."

Chapter Six

ROMAN

"WAIT. WHAT DID she say you were again because of the car you drove?" Kinston howled.

"Bruh, you know what she called me. I've told you this story twice already."

"And it gets more hilarious every time." He howled. "Yo, she really didn't know you turned around to take her back to her house?" Kinston asked again, leaning against the receptionist's desk for support.

"Nah." I shook my head. "She was too busy thinking she was clowning me on the phone with her friend, so I dropped her back off to go lead the circus."

Kinston collapsed against the receptionist's desk, doubled over as tears streamed down his face while he fruitlessly wiped them away. He was enjoying this date-night-from-hell story a bit too much. Although I couldn't help but join him in laughing about the comical night, I was admittedly disheartened by the whole incident. Not only had that chick wasted my time, but she'd also low-key gotten my hopes up. Okay, well, high key. That's the part I couldn't admit because he'd make a bigger deal out of it than necessary.

We'd finally calmed down to help our coach-in-training, Jeremy, prepare for today's opening when Cami and Brooke, two additional trainers, strolled through the door, greeting us with cheerful "good mornings." No sooner had they clocked in than Cami doubled back to me and asked how my date went. As soon as the question left her lips, Kinston nearly lost a lung again as he eagerly recounted the whole story to the ladies and Jeremy. Needless to say, I was the only one getting our gym ready for opening while the rest of the team, including my so-called best friend, enjoyed themselves at my expense after the failed date.

"Wait. You went to the club with Jeremy and the trainers from the second location?" Brooke asked after they began to settle down. When I nodded, she balled her fist to her mouth and let out a small chortle. "That was your first mistake. I know these young cats didn't take you anywhere to meet someone who actually had potential."

Jeremy laughed until he snorted. "First, I don't know why OG Roman was trying to meet someone his age in a club. *That* was his first mistake. All her homegirls were assed out on the club floor, but he thought she was different. Those birds chirp the same language."

Kinston pointed to Jeremy. "Facts." Then he tapped me on the chest with the back of his hand. "You're old enough to know how birds of a feather get down."

Eyeing Kinston, I stretched my arms wide. "You and Kannon hang out with Jovan, and we all know how *he* gets down."

"*Ooh,* factsss," Brooke and Cami yelped, twiddling their fingers together.

Kinston smirked, his head bouncing up and down. "True, true." He slapped fives with me. "Okay, so let's chalk it up to a bad judgment call. But real talk, you're not trying to settle down anyway, so why don't you go through your cell phone and spin the block?"

"Probably because most of those chicks are similar to that same one he met in the club," Brooke commented before I could answer. "He may be tired of entertaining these little gold diggers and clout chasers, but he doesn't have anybody of substance to call because we also know everybody on that contact list is not a real type, but a right-now type."

Everyone looked around at one another. The expressions on their faces clearly showed their agreement with Brooke, yet no one spoke up. Instead, the words hung in the air. I certainly wasn't going to comment because, for the most part, she was right. I'm sure there were some potential matches among them, but they weren't meant for me beyond the good times we'd already had together. They needed to find the right man for them, rather than waste time with me.

On that note, I put my hands up. "A'ight. A'ight. Enough about me and what y'all think y'all know about my life. Let's get this place together. As for me and my love life, we're straight."

I left Kinston and the crew as I entered my office in the back of the gym. I needed a break from the conversation, knowing it would keep going if I stayed. Brooke had pulled my card, which I wasn't comfortable discussing with anyone, not even my business partner and best friend.

After a few minutes, Cami tapped on the door and entered before I could give her permission to do so.

"Are you all right?" she asked, easing inside and shutting the door.

"Man, I don't want to talk about that. We have a full day ahead of us."

She pumped her hands at me. "Hold on. I'm not trying to discuss the date or what Brooke said. I only wanted to make sure that you were okay."

Rearing back in my seat, I bobbed my head, running my hand over my close-cut waves. "I'm straight, Cami."

She raised her hands. "If you say so, but let me say this: you might be searching for something that's right at your fingertips if you stop being afraid to open your mouth and say something."

"See, that's where you have your facts wrong. I am not *searching* for anything."

She stood there for a moment as if she were contemplating whether to believe me. I realized she didn't when she crossed her arms over her chest. "You know, you can put on a fake front for everyone else, but you don't have to do that with me. I still don't understand why you won't just talk to her."

My eyes fell as I tapped the desk, wanting desperately to drop the subject. "I'm aware, and *again*, I'm straight." This time, my tone was curt, signaling my desire for finality.

"Fine." Cami shrugged. "I'll leave that alone. I had an idea and thought I'd share it with you." When I gestured for her to continue, she did. "There's a singles cruise coming up, and I think you should go. Take a vacation."

A hearty laugh spilled from my gut because she couldn't be serious. *Is she serious?* One glance in her direction told me that she was. That killed my chuckles quickly.

"A singles cruise?" I repeated. "What the heck is a singles cruise, Cami?"

She sat down in the chair opposite my desk as if that were an invitation for her to pitch this to me like some pushy timeshare agent, but I'd enjoy being entertained.

"It's just like a regular cruise, but for single people—both men and women. They enjoy outings with friends and possibly link with other single and available people. They have onboard activities so singles can mix and mingle there or on the island excursions."

"You seem to know a lot about a singles cruise, Mrs. Married Woman."

She squinted at me, her mouth forming a tight line. "Don't do that. Travis and I are solid." She pursed her lips at me before continuing. "My friend met her husband on a singles cruise."

"Yeah, well, how long have they been married?" The skepticism dripped from my inquiry.

"Only one year, but they've been together for five years."

Of course, she'd have the one friend who'd met and married the love of her life from a singles cruise. Only Cami. She was a zealot for love. If left to her, everyone would be married and living in a utopian galaxy. The next thing I knew, she'd whipped out her cell phone. It appeared she was sending a text.

"I sent you the details about the one that sets sail in a few weeks. It departs right here from Miami and only lasts seven days. You should check it out. If for no other reason, take time for yourself. Since the inception of these gyms, I've only seen you miss work a day or two here or there, but never take a full vacation. Perhaps that's exactly what you need."

With that, she rose from her seat and headed toward the door. As she opened it, she returned her gaze to me and said, "Just think about it." Then she exited, closing the door behind her.

Curiosity got the better of me, so I picked up my cell phone and clicked the link. It was a seven-day, six-night trip from Miami to Turks and Caicos to Bimini, Bahamas, and back to Miami. As Cami mentioned, there were plenty of onboard activities and both daytime and overnight excursions. Though I had my doubts, it seemed like the perfect getaway. While I didn't expect to find my forever person on this trip, I could find an island baddie to lift me out of my funk and rejuvenate my spirit. What initially seemed like an asinine idea was now taking shape, and by the time I headed to the gym for my first private training session, I'd decided that a week-long cruise between exotic thighs might not be a bad idea. If all else failed, Cami could always be a timeshare agent after all.

Chapter Seven

AQUILA

THE SCHOOL YEAR couldn't return to session fast enough. Between preparing for this end-of-season program and the boys' activities and outings, we were always on the go, which is precisely why I reconsidered household responsibilities. Now that I had my blinders off about having the boys assist around the house, I implemented a chore list for them to manage so that I wouldn't wear myself out.

Pushing my laundry cart down the hall, I glanced into the boys' bathroom. Junior had cleared all the toiletries from the sink and used a scrubbing pad to clean it. I looked over at the tub and saw it was sparkling clean. The old shower curtain, mat, and slip pad were piled to the side, ready to be discarded and replaced with fresh ones.

"Did you clean the toilet?" I asked, slightly startling him from his routine.

He flinched and turned to me, ripping his earbud out of one ear. "*Geez,* Mom. Yes. I've cleaned the toilet."

I gave him a thumbs-up. "Good job. Don't forget to clean the mirror—"

"With glass cleaner, refill the soap dispenser, and sweep and mop the floor," he finished, waving his hand in the calm-down motion. "Relax, Mom. I've got this."

I tossed my head back as I placed my hand on my hip. "You got it, sir."

Did this child hit me with a head nod? He did, then turned back and informed me, "And I pulled my linen off the bed. It's by the door."

My soul sang at his thoroughness. I knew this was my child. I left him to his devices as I boot-scootin' boogied my tail to his bedroom, grabbed his bed linen, and tossed it in my laundry cart. Moving to Sante's bedroom, I saw him neatly sorting and folding his clothing. His superhero-themed bed was all made up, and the matching rug had the invigorating smell of carpet freshener, indicating that he'd vacuumed. One more scan showed me that his desk was neat, and all his toys were placed inside the open toy chest.

"See, Mom," Sante called out to me, displaying his stack of neatly folded underwear. "Did I do it right?"

"You sure did." I waltzed into his room, draped my arm around his shoulder, and placed a kiss on the top of his messy mop of curls. "Now, we just need to tame this hair." I tousled his locks, much to his dismay.

Dodging my hands, he stepped to the side. "Please, Mom, don't. You're messing it up. I like my hair."

"We need to tame it, though."

"It's perfect like this. Can the barber just give me a tape, but not cut my hair this time?"

"You're not old enough to maintain that."

That answer sent him into an entire whine session. "*Aww,* Mom. Please. Pretty please. Please. Please. Please," he begged, gripping my arm for dear life.

This was not a battle I wanted to face, so I tossed my hand up. "I'll think about it. I'll tell you by Tuesday when I take you boys to get your hair cut."

Sante jumped up and down. "Yeahhh."

"I didn't say yes." I pointed a stern finger at him. "We'll see."

He hit me with that side smirk he stole directly from his father. Joel used to give me that exact expression when he knew he'd gotten me to do what he wanted without my even realizing it. I used to love it when Joel did that. Apparently, it still had the same effect. While Joel no longer affected me, Sante surely did. He was just so adorable, and it irked me that I'd been freed from one Oliver man only to be charmed by his carbon copy.

"Okay. Thank you, Mom." He climbed onto his bed and planted the sweetest kiss on my cheek.

"Finish folding and putting away your clothes," I ordered and walked out, rolling my eyes at the pull on my heartstrings. He had me pegged, and he knew it.

In my laundry room, I sorted my colors from my whites and darks, then tossed my first load of clothing into the washer with my scented beads while rocking out to the music blaring from my earphones. Just as I was about to break into a soulful rendition of Reyna Roberts' "Raised Right," my music was interrupted by a notification. My level of irritation reached a fever pitch when I listened to the alert. I whipped my cell phone out of my pocket and paused the music. Scrolling to my banking app, I logged in. When I confirmed that the notice was true, I saw red. My anger could be summed up in one name: Joel.

Gripping my phone in my hand, I almost dialed his number but decided this matter deserved an in-person visit to resolve. Instead, I dialed my mother's number.

"Hey, sweetheart. How are you?" she answered with her usual greeting.

"Mad as hell. Can I drop the boys off with you for a little bit? I need to meet with their father."

"Oh, dear God. What has that man done now?"

"Mama, I don't mean any disrespect, but I don't want to talk about it right now. I'm too fired up, and I need to save all this venom for Joel. Can I drop the boys off and discuss it later?"

"Sure. Of course. Be careful. I don't want you to get into any trouble."

"Trust me. The only thing saving me from trouble is the two lives I ushered into this world, which he obviously doesn't give two damns about." Fumes bounced off each syllable. "I'll be there in twenty minutes."

As soon as I hung up the call, I rushed through the house at warp speed. I'm sure the boys thought I'd lost my mind the way I had demanded they hurry up so we could leave. I was so livid that I didn't even answer any of their concerned questions, and once they realized I wasn't in the mood, they fell silent like church mice. I didn't even get out of my car when I arrived at my parents' house. I just dialed my mother's number and told her the kids were coming in. She came running out to bring the boys inside. I knew she probably wanted to calm me down, but there was no stopping my runaway train. Before she could turn back to my car, I sped away from her house so fast that I probably left tire tracks on the street.

Twenty minutes later, I parked my car in front of Joel's house and stalked up the driveway. As I approached the front porch, the door swung open, stopping me in my tracks. The shrubbery partially obscured me from their view, but I had a clear angle to see everything happening on the porch. Jansen stepped out, holding Joel's hand. They exchanged words that I couldn't distinguish, but they appeared to be a bit heated. Then, Joel leaned into Jansen, cutting off whatever he was saying with a kiss. When Joel pulled away, Jansen bit his lip, and they moved closer for a deeper, more intense merging of their lips. Not a mere air kiss. Not a quick peck. Not just a smooch. It was a full-on, tongue-thrashing exploration. Joel wrapped his arms around Jansen's neck and pulled him in tighter, while Jansen melted against him, savoring the passionate exchange.

Bile threatened to spew from my esophagus as I clinched my stomach at the sight before me. Everything made sense now. My brain began piecing together the last few years of my life at such a rapid pace that I silently wished it wouldn't to spare me the realization of the whole scope of the situation. Joel and Jansen. These two sneaky bastards.

"What the hell?" I screeched, emerging from the shadows to make my presence known.

The two culprits speedily jumped apart as they scrambled to figure out what to say or do next. They didn't have to. Whatever astonishment I'd held immediately refueled my initial emotion—rage.

"Oh, so this is why you wanna screw men? *Jansen.* You've been sleeping with Jansen this entire time."

Jansen faced me with worried eyes. "Aquila, darling, it's not what you think."

"Oh, you're right about that, Jansen. It's not what I think. It's what I *know* and saw with my two very capable eyes." I turned my attention to Joel. "So, this is why we're divorced? You claimed you never cheated. It was just the 'urge.' I should've known that *urge* wasn't the only reason you'd give up on us. And Jansen, you were *our* friend. *My* friend."

Panicked, Joel trotted down the steps toward me. "Aquila, it's not like that. We never slept together while we were married. I swear it."

My face contorted as I cast a doubtful look between Jansen and him. "The lies you tell. You expect me to believe you'd allow your family to be dismantled over a possibility. You expect me to believe that you didn't cheat on me while Jansen has a whole wife at home whom he's cheating on. Speaking of…" I said, peeking over his shoulder to Jansen, "how's Jana?" I stepped back from Joel as he reached for me. "You better find someone safe to play with because I will air all this shit out."

At that proclamation, Jansen was off the steps and by Joel's side in a nanosecond. "Aquila, please. You can't tell anyone, especially not Jana. Please."

My eyes widened. Just when I thought I'd heard and seen it all, the earth tilted its axis again to show me that I hadn't seen anything yet. This man, who was the culprit behind my ex-husband's wandering genitals, had the nerve to ask me to be an accomplice to his secret love life.

"You have got to be kidding me?" I glanced around, looking for the hidden screens and people. "Where are the cameras? I must be on a reality television show. That has to be it because this cannot be real."

Joel moved closer, his hands in a pleading position. "Aquila, please listen to me. You can't say anything. If you do, Jansen won't be able to come up with the money—"

Jansen interrupted him. "Jana found gay porn, and it took all I had to convince her to stay. If she found this out, she'd bury me. It's why I've been cautious with my money," he explained, trying to get me to understand the severity of his marital status.

"I know you're here because the alimony payment was short," Joel added. "I needed to buy some time—"

"Wait a minute. *Wait.*" I flailed my arms, halting their explanations. "You shorted me without a discussion, have an open petition for alimony reduction still in place, and are sleeping with the source of your money and our divorce, and you both expect sympathy and leniency from me? *Wow.* Both of you must have plenty of fun sucking on each other's gigantic-sized balls because this is next-level fuckery."

"I'll pay you," Jansen blurted, his fingers interlaced atop his head in frustration. "I'll pay you right now, whatever he shorted you."

"Don't you dare patronize me. I do not want your money. It's Joel's debt to pay."

"Right now, he needs money from me, so my money *is* his money. Take it, and don't tell Jana," Jansen said.

My body involuntarily jerked backward—nearly leveled by the arrogance in his tone. *I know he didn't make a demand of me, and with his whole chest.* Clearly, he must've been funding delusion, too, because he'd bought it in bulk tonight.

"*Knee-grow,* I'd starve first."

Jansen threw a warning glare at Joel before Joel pulled me to the side. "Listen, Aquila. Do you want the truth? Fine. Truth is, Jansen and I grew attracted to each other when you and I were together, and we engaged in a few moments that shouldn't have happened while we were married—intimacy, but not sex. You can blame, curse, yell, scream, and fight me all you want. I deserve that. But think about our boys. If you do something erratic because you're unhinged right now, you'll affect my ability to care for you all. I know this situation isn't ideal, but I need you to be levelheaded and consider the bigger picture here."

This man was so lowdown. The mere fact that none of these repercussions would exist if it were not for his unfaithful actions escaped him, yet my reaction would be the culprit for any mishaps. Never mind that his actions were the catalyst. At this point, I wasn't even shocked that he used our sons as gambling cards to force me to agree with keeping their treacherous secrets. The difference is that he knew I cared about our children's welfare, so if anything would make me yield from a fight, it was the promise that they would be taken care of. An image of Junior and Sante floated through my mind, and I cast my eyes down, considering them. Every fiber of my soul hated Joel and Jansen, and I wanted nothing more than to toss them and their secrets over the Brickell Avenue Bridge. However, thoughts of my sons took me off the ledge that I wanted to push their father off.

I stepped into his space, staring at him directly so he'd know the seriousness of my following words. "Send me my three thousand dollars right now, Joel, and then you work it out with Jansen. I'm not taking any hush money from him. Secondly, I expect my five-thousand-dollar alimony and child support payments to stay the same. If you take me to court, there will be no limit to the lengths I will go to ruin you. And neither Junior nor Sante will stop me from coming for your jugular. If you put me through the dirt, I will drag your ass through the mud. Try me."

Joel dipped his head. "Send it right now?"

"If you think I believe you're that hard up for money, you must've forgotten I was married to you for ten years. I know exactly how you, Olivers, operate." My next words were meant to call his bluff. "Run me my coins, or I'm running to Jana and everyone else who'll listen."

My stoic stance gave the impression that I meant every word I'd said. After a few seconds, Joel sucked his teeth and slipped his cell phone out of his pocket. Within minutes, my phone dinged, and I checked the notification. My shorted three grand had been deposited into my account.

"Received," I said snootily before walking to where Jansen stood in desperate anticipation. "He sent my money. You do what you need to do regarding the investment, and don't worry about me blabbing anything to Jana. And don't think it's because I wouldn't tell her for one second. It's simply not my business to do so. But as her husband, it's yours. I'll let you take that up with your God and your conscience, if you have either one of those in your heart."

Turning on my heels, I began to trek back to my car.

"Aquila, thank you," Jansen called out to me.

Standing at the driver's side, I said, "Don't thank me. Both of your mothers should have done to you what you two seem to do so well...swallowed."

With that, I settled into my car and drove back to my mother's house to explain the foolishness of the day before my sons and I headed home.

Chapter Eight

AQUILA

O NLY ANGELA WOULD'VE *thought of something like this.* I pulled into the parking lot, not feeling up to going out. I was still drained from the catastrophe last weekend and was still attempting to recover from that incident.

When I arrived at my parents' house last weekend, all I wanted to do was grab my babies and head home. My mother accepted that with the promise that we would discuss it later. I quickly made that promise so I could get home to my bed. The incident at Joel's house had taken such a toll on me that I ordered pizza that night for the boys and allowed them to stay up late playing video games. I'd only eaten one slice of veggie pizza and chased it down with a bottle of ginger ale. Afterward, I immersed myself in a lavender and chamomile bath, hoping it would deliver on its promised relaxation sensation. By the time I'd exited the tub two hours later, I swore I'd cried enough tears to refill the tub to capacity. When my boys came into my room that night to cuddle with me and then opted to spend the night in my bed, I knew I was a train wreck of emotions.

Once Joel and I divorced, I promised myself I had dropped my last waterworks show for him. Learning about his deceit with Jansen, who was our mutual friend, brought up feelings I thought had long since died. The revelation made me mourn my marriage all over again, and I loathed it because I didn't want to admit that it hurt, but it did.

To add icing on that tiered cake was Jansen's betrayal. I had never considered any of Joel's business associates or friends as my friend, except for Jansen. He and his wife were like family to me. We regarded them as the unofficial uncle and aunt to our children. He was like the big brother I had never had, only to discover he was the brother-husband who stole my spouse. I was betrayed by not one but two men in my life. What's sad is that I never suspected anything between them. Sure, Jansen had a little sass, but I saw him as a metrosexual man, not a bisexual one. Besides, that wasn't the measure for determining sexuality. There were plenty of men who appeared in ways that would deem them gay by society's standards. And why should I have to run around scrutinizing behaviors and mannerisms when both of them were married and should have been faithful to their wives? I never judged Joel about his sexuality, but I expected loyalty and faithfulness as his wife, the same as Jana expected from Jansen. The same as I expected from Jansen, as my friend. Still, it troubled me that I couldn't see the connection.

The reality was I had loved Joel with my whole heart. At the rehearsal dinner, I put aside my reservations because I trusted him to have my back forever. I skirted away his transgressions by blaming everything on his father instead of placing the responsibility where it belonged. After discovering Jansen and him, I now understood that Joel was the replica of his father... conniving. Perhaps he'd always been that way, and I didn't recognize it. Perhaps somewhere along the way, he'd gradually changed. Either way, when we divorced, I realized that the Joel Oliver that existed today was not the one I thought I'd married. With this new revelation, he proved to me that this current man was precisely the type of man I had married. His admission peeled away the film covering my view. Now that it was plain, I had to reckon with the reality that Joel Oliver never truly loved and cared for me the way he claimed. If he had, none of this would've happened...quite possibly not even my marriage, had he been honest with himself.

At any rate, after my mother didn't hear from me for a couple of days, she scheduled a mother-daughter intervention. She and my dad drove to my house, and my dad took the boys out while my mother and sisters, whom my mother had also ordered to come over, sat with me while I recanted the horrid details at Joel's house that evening. They were as alarmed and incensed as I had been, not only by Joel's lies but by his and Jansen's treachery. All we could do was accept Joel's word that he'd never cheated on me, but that didn't stop me from doing my due diligence regarding my health. I'd had an STI screening completed after my divorce, which had been negative the two times I had taken it. Once I had advised my mother and sisters of that, they seemed to breathe easier regarding my health, but Joel was a different subject. Whatever ill feelings they had harbored for him previously tripled after hearing the story. They soothed me as best they could, and I was grateful to have them in my corner. My spirits were lifted when they left, but my heart still ached from the betrayal.

When Kinston reported to Angela that I hadn't been to the gym, she knew I was still in the dumps over the situation and planned this outing for us. When I walked into the building and saw that both she and Nissi were there before me, even I had to admit I needed to find a way out of the black hole because never in the history of outings had I been the last sister to arrive.

"Both of you beat me here? This building might burn down," I teased as we hugged.

"Whatever." Angela smiled. "We're waiting on Ciara and Nia."

"Good. So I'm not too late. When they arrive, can we not bring up the whole Joel situation?"

"We wouldn't mention it unless you brought it up," Nissi reassured, placing a comforting hand on my shoulder.

"Right, sis. We respect your privacy and, honestly, Joel's. Until or unless he wants to come out, we're not sharing that information with anyone. That's your and his business," Angela added.

The sentiment brought tears to my eyes, and I fanned them away hurriedly. That was why I loved and respected my sisters. Even in their hurt and anger, they were considerate. We agreed as a family that we wouldn't reveal why Joel and I divorced. No one outside of us, our spouses, and my parents knew about Joel's sexual preference. To our friends, I explained that we were no longer in love and wanted a divorce. They had seen enough of our heated interactions to buy into that theory, so it worked. My sisters loved me and their nephews more than they wanted to lash out at Joel. Anybody else might have screamed about the ordeal to the mountaintop for revenge, but they understood the fragility of the situation. I appreciated them for that. While we didn't owe Joel our kindness, his bad behavior didn't justify discarding our morals.

Angela and Nissi rubbed my back until the wave of sadness had passed. When it did, I cleared my throat. "So, a smash room, huh?"

Nissi pointed at Angela. "Her idea."

"And was." Angela curtsied. "I figured since you couldn't put your paws on Joel, you could take it out on smashable objects. Us, too."

Now, I was intrigued. "Does it help alleviate anger?"

"It does." A woman approached us. "My apologies. I heard you ask the question. I'm going to be your safety instructor. My name is Wren. And yes, it helps alleviate anger, reduces stress, and gives you a bit of a workout. So, whatever brought you in here today, take it out in the room."

Just then, Ciara and Nia walked in and hugged us. We all signed our releases and followed Wren to get suited for our smash-room experience. I thought it was comical that we appeared as if we were a hazmat team with white suits and plexiglass head coverings until we entered the room and saw it filled with every smashable item imaginable. There was a battered wooden table that housed an entire bar of glass liquor bottles in all different sizes and shapes. Scattered around on the floor and on other smaller tables were plastic items like calculators, POS machines, DVD and VCR machines, and even laptops and PCs. Along the wall were various weapons: bats, mallet hammers, crowbars, golf clubs, wide wrenches, and frying pans.

After explaining the safety rules inside the room, Wren said, "All I need to know is what type of music you ladies would like to play, and you have the room for an hour."

"I think we all pretty much have the same taste," Ciara said as we looked at one another.

"Wait. Nope. All of us, except Aquila." Nissi giggled.

Angela pretended to faint dramatically. "Oh, no. We'll be in here crying over spilled milk instead of busting windows out the cars," she joked, and snickers spread throughout the room. "We'll go with gangsta rap, but the ones that are bops."

Wren nodded. "I got you." She grinned, then walked over to the speaker and pressed a few buttons.

The next thing I knew, my sisters, Ciara and Nia, bounced around shouting about not being able to get on their level. I stood in the background because I had no clue who even rapped the song. I prayed my soul wouldn't be more irritated when I left than when I came. Let's just say my musical tastes were a far cry different from those of my sisters' and our friends' circle. They carried on, smashing items as I tried to stay clear of flying particles and glass.

After fifteen minutes had passed, Nissi realized I hadn't participated and stopped everyone. "You need to release some stress, sis. Smash something."

Nia and Angela began chanting, "Smash it. Smash it." Soon, Nissi and Ciara joined in.

The playlist changed, and a universal song started playing that I knew by heart, even if I didn't know any others. That amped me up, and I gripped the golf club off the wall and took aim at a glass liquor bottle as the words of a song called, *"Knuck If You Buck"* pumped through the speakers. As soon as it did, I crushed the bottle in the middle and sent the remaining shards flying into the smash wall, which completely shattered. I shrugged and popped my neck with satisfaction. That felt good.

"Remind me not to play golf with you," Nia joked as I turned to face them.

"Right. Your fist may be lightweight, but your swing don't miss, sis," Angela said, impressed by the handiwork.

Gleefully, I smiled at them and admitted, "When you used to entertain potential clients and business owners on the green, you develop one hell of a drive."

"Instead of commas, you were on the course effing up some balls," Ciara joked.

"What?" I asked, amused yet confused.

They all looked at each other and howled. "Never mind."

"Let's continue letting you have a shot. I know that felt good, didn't it?" Angela asked, passing me a crowbar.

"It did." I accepted the new weapon of choice.

Angela leaned into my ear. "Pretend these are Jansen and Joel, and go to work, sis."

Gripping the crowbar, I signaled for them to crank the music volume up, and I went to town on a PC to some song by a rapper identified as Bone Crusher. After another ten minutes of using the crowbar, frying pan, and golf club again on more bottles and the laptop, I was sweaty and bopping my head to the constant blare of rap music. I was slightly fatigued, but I felt invigorated. Yoga and exercise centered me, but I understood Angela's logic. Sometimes you needed to fuck some shit up.

Once our hour was over, we opted to grab a quick bite to eat at the Smash Room restaurant. Although their vegan options were limited, their veggie burger hit the spot, paired perfectly with my bottled water.

As I finished my meal, I leaned over and side-hugged Angela. "I have to admit, Ang. This was fun—a lot more than I thought it would be. The problem is I can't smash things every day."

"That's because you need a vacation, Lah," Nissi countered.

"She's right." Angela pointed at me. "I don't remember the last time you took a trip to relax and rejuvenate."

She couldn't remember, but I did. It was before Sante was born. In fact, it was the trip when Sante was conceived. It was the last good year of my marriage. When Sante turned one year old, my marriage was in disarray and on its way to being irreconcilable. Until this moment, I hadn't realized how long it had been.

"I don't have time for that."

"No. Vacations are things you make time for. It's a part of self-care," Ciara said. "I must have Zen in every facet of my life. I try to keep my work office as peaceful as possible, but still, I have to have a work-life balance. We all do. At the center of that is time with oneself."

Nia snapped her fingers. "My co-worker and I were going to go on this singles cruise, but I can't go. It departs when I start on a travel nurse assignment for sixteen weeks. If there are any rooms available, you should go."

"I couldn't do that. Who would watch my boys?"

"*Hello,*" Nissi stressed, her eyes as wide as saucers. "You act like Angela and I aren't capable aunties who love our nephews."

"Exactly. We'd take turns watching them for you."

"I also have the cupcakes to make for their summer camp."

"When is the program?" Nissi asked.

"In August."

Nia whipped her phone out. "Oh, that's perfect. The trip is in July, and it's only for one week. Mid-July."

"That's basically in two weeks," I said, trying to avoid going on the trip. "And I don't have any good girlfriends, I mean, besides you all, but you know what I mean."

Angela downed the remainder of her wine and placed the glass on the table. "Sis, it's a singles cruise. You don't need a bosom buddy when you're there to find a fuck buddy."

While the rest of them found Angela's declaration hilarious, my mind automatically drifted into mommy mode. "I definitely can't think about that. I have kids."

"And that's how you conceived them," Angela countered. "Besides, that has nothing to do with the price of tequila in Mexico."

I pursed my lips, turning my eyes upward. "It's tea in China."

"Well, I don't like tea, and I've never been to China, so I said what I said. You stop avoiding the topic at hand."

At that, they all completely keeled over, causing a few patrons to stare in our direction. Of course, they couldn't care less, but I sat there with a blush of embarrassment etched on my face.

When they settled, Nissi motioned her finger at Nia. "Text her the link."

With a press of a few buttons, Nia answered, "Done."

My cell phone dinged with a message that I knew was from Nia. In the nick of time, the waiter came over with the bill, but Angela retrieved her card to pay the tab for the table. Once the waiter returned the card to her, we gave him some cash for the tip. Thankfully, Nia and Ciara had errands to run, so we said our goodbyes and dispersed to our cars. Of course, my sisters followed me to mine.

"Seriously, Aquila, take some time for yourself. You deserve it," Nissi said.

"And you can't be any good to your boys if you're running on empty. What does Mama always say? You can't pour from an empty cup," Angela coaxed.

"Now you want to use the correct saying."

She shrugged, clearly ignoring my slight, and pulled me into an embrace. "Nissi and I have the boys. Do something for yourself for once."

Later that night, as I sat in my bed watching television, the conversation from that day inundated my mind. Reluctantly, I picked up my phone, scrolled to Nia's unread message, and clicked the link. The trip was a seven-day, six-night cruise for singles leaving from Miami to destinations at Turks and Caicos and Bimini, Bahamas, then back to Miami. No travel was necessary since it departed from my city. The cruise was with Island Skye Voyages aboard the *Sensation of the Skye* liner. Admittedly, the activities looked exciting, the amenities were to die for, and the excursions appeared full of wonder and adventure. A few rooms were left in the MegaSweetie suites, which were geared toward the wealthy at ten grand for the trip. However, FriendlySkye Suites had two ocean-view rooms available for two grand. That was more my speed and my budget. I threw caution to the wind.

"Here goes nothing." I grabbed my purse from the nightstand to retrieve my credit card. "Vacation, here I come."

Chapter Nine

AQUILA

TWO WEEKS LATER

*D*AY 1 OF 7. *I'm on vacation. Now what?* I wrote in my daily journal app as I sat on the terrace of my ocean-view suite aboard the *Sensation of the Skye.*

True to their word, Nissi was watching my boys for half of the week, and Angela would have them for the second half. Earlier this afternoon, Nissi dropped me off so I wouldn't have to leave my vehicle at the port. Now that I'd made it through security and check-in, I'd performed my usual room cleaning and safety rituals and was relaxing in my suite before the onboard safety meeting. From what I'd seen of the ship, it was exquisite. I planned on checking out the restaurants, the casino, and the nighttime comedy show. I'd even promised Angela I'd attend the welcome party tonight. I wasn't as excited about that because I wanted to rest, but I came here to enjoy everything the trip offered, so I'd entertain the welcome party for a little while before calling it a night.

In my journal, I jotted down my descriptions of the ship and my room and logged what activities I planned to partake in. My week-long living quarters weren't exactly spectacular, as most cruise ship rooms aren't, but I loved the cute touches that enhanced the quaint space. The room was decorated in pearl white linens and ocean sea blues. The best part about its presentation was the bucket of champagne on ice placed on the round table and the towels neatly folded into octopuses on the bed surrounding a charcuterie board of cheeses and meats.

My cell phone rang out of the blue. Junior's name and face lit up my screen, so I hurriedly answered.

"Hey, Pooh," I sing-songed as soon as our FaceCall video connected.

"Mom, please stop calling me Pooh. I'm almost ten years old," Junior whined.

"You're nine, and I don't care how old you get, you'll always be my Pooh."

Before he could respond, I heard a slight commotion, and the next voice I heard was Nissi in the background.

"Leave my nephew alone," Nissi ordered. "I wanted him and Sante to call before you set sail. The next time we want to hear from you is on day seven when you're back in Miami. Don't bother us while you're on vacation, and we won't bother you."

I kissed my teeth. "Whatever. He's *my* Pooh. And since you're restricting me from communication with my kids, let me talk to my baby at least."

"Hey, Mommy." Sante's voice crashed through the receiver as his face came into view. I loved it when he called me *Mommy* instead of imitating his brother with the *Mom* moniker. I knew he missed me when he called me *Mommy*, which warmed my heart.

"Hey, sweetie. I love you."

"I love you, too. I miss you, Mommy."

Be still my heart. I wanted to find the nearest exit and flee this ship. Being a single mother may have had its difficulties, but I loved my little tribe fiercely. The greatest joy of my life was being the mommy to those two boys.

"I miss you guys, too."

"Have the best grown-up fun," Junior added.

"I will. I promise." I exhaled deeply. "I miss you and love you, Junior."

"I miss and love you, too, Mom. Auntie Nissi wants to talk to you."

Before I could respond, Nissi appeared on the video. "That's enough. I hear you getting sappy with them."

"*Ugh.* I miss my babies, Nissi. Maybe I should leave before we set sail and—"

"These children will be here—well, at Angela's when you return. Besides, you have $2,123 worth of reasons to stay put."

She had a point there. As much as I missed my kids, I was not a fan of wasting money. I refused to throw any of it away, especially not after I had almost gone ballistic on Joel about my shorted alimony.

"When you put it that way, I guess I better have $2,123 worth of fun, rest, and relaxation."

"That part!" Nissi pointed at me. "Anywho, I need to get off the phone and get the tribe in order. I'll see you in T-minus seven days."

"Love you roundtrip," Nissi and I said in loving unison before we ended the video chat.

Smiling, I reopened my journal app and tapped the page for a new entry.

Day 1 of 7. Fuck them kids.

What have I let my sisters talk me into? Checking my appearance in the mirror, I immediately felt uncomfortable and out of place. The welcome party was set to start in fifteen minutes, and I was holed up in my room contemplating changing outfits or changing into my pajamas. Why? The outfit that my sisters chose for me. Tonight's party was a luau-themed event, and instead of the shorts and silk camisole I had planned to buy for the evening, my sisters insisted on buying my outfits after giving me a twisted look at my choice. I was in such a rush that I only glanced over what they'd chosen because, at first sight, the choices seemed nice enough. It was a tad sexier than I would have gone, but I had vowed to let my hair down. This outfit and, quite possibly, the others they'd chosen gave the impression that I wanted to let my panties down instead.

The Hawaiian floral wrap skirt stopped just above my knees, but the split stopped mid-thigh, and the matching top was a short-sleeved off-the-shoulder crop top with a cleavage cut so low I might as well serve my tatas on a platter beside the pineapples and coconuts. I couldn't deny that I looked sizzling hot, but I hadn't dressed this provocatively since college, and a young tweeny bopper I was not. Just as I was about to abandon the idea and head for bed, I turned to see my journal app open to my last entry. A deep, roaring laugh belted out of me, and I had a thought. I was still acting as if I were Aquila Oliver. I wasn't married. My kids would not be in attendance. What did I have to lose? I knew how to turn down offers, and I had my pointed fingernail file for anyone who wanted to get too friendly without consent. Tonight, I could relish being Aquila Richards and enjoy exploring who I was in this new phase of life. Besides, it'd been a couple of forevers since I'd seen the vixen standing before me.

"Screw it."

I pulled my fresh knotless boho braids into a high ponytail, applied a fresh coat of nude lip gloss, and placed the gloss, cell phone, Skye key card, and nail file in my clutch before slipping on my cute pink open-toed flats. Then, I headed to the upper deck to see what this party had to offer.

It was barely standing or sitting room only on the deck. I located a seat at a table near the back and settled in as we listened to the activity coordinator introduce the executive-level staff to our applause. Once the captain gave his speech, they kicked the festivities into high gear. Plenty of water, wine, and other distilled spirits floated around, with several bars filled with fruits, veggies, seafood, and other finger foods. I filled a small platter with fruits and veggies and grabbed a glass of wine before returning to my seat, which luckily was still available. The music blared smooth island-vibe tunes that had almost everyone swaying in their seats to the beat. I'd even introduced myself to two ladies who were friends who sat at the same table as me. We had fun gabbing it up as we ate our food and bobbed our heads to the sounds. Off in the distance, a shuffleboard game had begun, and other people were playing with the life-sized chess pieces. Some people had opted to take advantage of the water activities. It was a chill vibe. Once my two new ship besties finished eating, they decided to head to the jacuzzi. They invited me, but I chose to stay put, content with checking out the scene.

As soon as I started to get comfortable, one of the activity assistant coordinators queued the "Macarena" song and began a Macarena dance line. It tickled me watching the offbeat people try to keep up. That was until the coordinator started pulling people into the line involuntarily. *Oh, hell no.* That was my cue to exit stage left, except I couldn't. From where I sat, I'd have to walk through the line to leave, so I tried to sit back and be as inconspicuous as possible. Leave it to him to find me out of all the sea of people.

"Come, *señorita*," Jorge, the assistant activity coordinator, tried to coax me.

"No, I'm good." I held my hand up in defiance.

The look in Jorge's eyes made me want to take the chance and sprint to my room or toss myself overboard. Since I didn't feel like busting my tail on this deck or dying, I kept motioning no, hoping he'd keep going. Of course, he wouldn't. Joined by the other coordinator, they both made their way toward me and lifted me by my arms to a standing position. Reluctantly, I grabbed my clutch, tucked it into the front of my top, and joined the line to the cheers of those around me as we danced around the deck. Once I saw a clearing where I could duck out, I knew that when I made it there, I'd strike out and head back to my room. I pretended to be having a blast, and as soon as I bopped around to the clearing, I dashed for it. My one mishap was that I didn't calculate that someone would step right into my pathway, and I clumsily collided with a hard thud. Just before I embarrassingly plummeted to the floor, two strong arms captured and steadied me. With my footing in place, I stood as he held me to ensure my legs were stable. My eyes fluttered up to a wall of caramel-coated chest muscles and abs carved to perfection as his opened Hawaiian shirt left nothing to hide. I'm ashamed to admit that my gaze drifted downward, focusing on the thin patch of hair between the bottom of his washboard abs and the V-cut at his waistline. The swim trunks he wore seemed to hug his thick, godlike thighs, and the bulging print in front—my God today—was evidence that he was all man. My pulse raced as other parts of my body that had been dormant for years came alive.

"Are you okay?"

My brows furrowed, and my face turned upward in a flash when I recognized the voice. "Roman?"

His eyes gradually ballooned, and a barely audible gasp was breathed from his lips as his face contorted. "Aquila?"

A stunned silence fell over both of us. For me, it was due to two reasons. First, I was shocked to see anyone I knew on the cruise.

Second, the man who sparked this instant drool session was none other than Roman Patterson. I tried to regain my faculties as he stood before me, looking like every bit of an African god. As many times as I'd seen this man, not once did he make my breath hitch. Granted, that was before pre-exposed abs and swim trunks, but tonight, the sight of him nearly collapsed my lungs. Had he been dipped in chocolate gold? Inhaling, I shook my shoulders and head to clear the inappropriate thoughts running through my mind.

"What are you doing here?" we asked simultaneously.

A slight snicker passed between us as we fell into a comfortable silence. I realized that he was still cocooning me in his arms. Nervousness and slight embarrassment overcame me, and I cleared my throat before taking a cautious step backward. Roman realized that he was still holding on to me and stepped away as well.

"My bad. I'm sorry. Are you okay, though?" he asked again, easing his hands into his shorts' pockets.

"Yeah. You just usurped my getaway."

Confusion etched his features until his eyes landed on the never-ending Macarena line dance, which had grown in number since my departure. A grin curled the corner of his lips as he nodded. "I got it now. Not a fan of the Macarena?"

"Not a fan of dancing in front of strangers."

He folded his pythonic arms and lifted a finger to his lips, assessing my reasoning. "Why? They're not afraid of dancing in front of you."

I bit my lip to quell the desire brewing as I continued to lust after him, despite my best efforts to stop. For goodness' sake, it was Roman. *Get it together, Lah.*

"I'd prefer not to be the butt of jokes because there are a couple of people who surely are the butt of mine," I teased as we both looked to see one man whose hands were on his head when everyone else's were on their hips. I pointed in his direction. "Case in point."

"True, true." He hid his chuckle behind his cupped hand. "But it's all in good fun. That man is living his best life. We should do the same."

"So, that's why you're here?"

He shuffled in place with nervous energy seeming to ping off him suddenly as he squeaked out, "That's one of the reasons."

That's when a realization struck me, prompting uneasiness to creep in, and my eyes darted around. "Oh, goodness. Did you come alone, or did you meet someone here?"

My energy shift must've caused him to calm down because he brought his hands to rest on my shoulders, leveling me with his pearly whites. "Relax, Qui. I'm here alone."

Due to the overload, my brain struggled to function. Joel used to call me Qui. It was his nickname for me, which is why I loathed it when he attempted to call me by the sobriquet these days. Hearing the name fall from Roman's lips surprised me because he'd never called me anything except my full name. Still, coming from him, it sounded calming, sweet even. It immediately settled me in a way that I was unfamiliar with yet appreciated.

That only turned my focus to his touch. The heat from his large hands on my shoulders pebbled my skin, sending misfires to my cranium. No man's hands had been anywhere near my body since Joel, and the sensation felt as tender as it felt strange. I didn't know how to react. Why were my senses out of sorts? It was only Roman. I'd been around this man a thousand times in a thousand different settings. Now, all of a sudden, my brain wanted to register everything, like his perfectly white and aligned teeth. Had his smile always been this gleaming? Damn. *Okay, Aaron Pierre, that's Mufasa.*

"*Aquila.*" He stretched my name out slowly, breaking me out of my discombobulated musings.

"I…*uh*…I'm sorry. You…you called me Qui." My eyes found his. "Why?"

He shrugged. It was his turn to look awkwardly uncomfortable. "I'm not sure. It just came out. It felt friendly, I guess. If I offended you—"

"You didn't," I interjected quickly. "It didn't offend me. It just caught me off guard. That's all." My answer visibly eased his trepidation as his shoulders relaxed.

"Good." That cute side smirk was back. "Let's say we walk around and explore this ship. Honestly, I don't feel much like this party myself, and I'm happy that there's someone here that I know."

"Oh god, same," I admitted, tilting my weight into him. "That was on my checklist, so I'm down." I stepped back, pulled my small clutch from my breast area, and adjusted my top. "I'm ready."

Roman stood there for a minute before he proffered his bent arm to me. I looped my arm into his, and we headed away from the crowd on our mission. We walked in contented silence, admiring the euphoric atmosphere and the warm breeze kissing our skin from the ocean air. A calmness fell fresh over me, and my mind and body easily drifted into a state of relaxation. It was the most peaceful I'd been since I'd boarded the ship. Honestly, it was the most peaceful I'd been in years.

Suddenly, it dawned on me that neither of us had answered the other's question. Tilting my head to glance at Roman, I broke our solitude to revisit the conversation.

"You know, you never told me what brought you here." When he looked down at me, I held up my pinky finger. "I'll tell you my story if you tell me yours."

His eyes twinkled in consideration before he locked pinkies with me. "Deal." A deep breath was released from his body. "Cami suggested it to me. I thought it was insane, but after the last date I was on and the pool of prospects I've bumped into lately, I figured, why not?"

Shock filled me at the revelation. "What was wrong with your last date and current prospects? It's not as if you're the settle-down type."

The rumble from his belly vibrated between us as he released a boisterous bellow. "What's that supposed to mean?"

"I don't mean any disrespect, Roman, so please don't take it the wrong way." I winced at the words on the edge of my tongue. "Based on some of your prior choices, shallow and frivolous seem to be your speed."

He clutched his chest with his hand and pretended to stagger. "Stab a brother straight through the heart, the jugular, and the balls." He lifted a brow at me. "Let's say I'm not the settle-down type; why must I want a woman of little to no substance?"

I lifted my hands in mock surrender. "My bad. I'm only basing it on your past flings, and they were sketch at best."

He stood aghast. "*Wow!* Got any more bullets you'd like to unload into my corpse over here? Damn, Aquila."

Snickering, I slid my hand up and down his back. "I'm sorry. I don't mean to come off judgmental. You just seem to have a type."

He stopped walking and faced me. "Well, maybe I'm trying to have another type."

The intensity in his tone and the gravity of his demeanor knocked me off-kilter. Was it me, or had the temperature increased a few notches? The way he stood there, unwaveringly staring at me with those deep, coffee eyes, increased my anxiety. Was he...was he flirting, or was I reading too much into it? Steeling myself, I let that notion go and probed further.

"So that means you didn't come here for a quick hook-up?"

"*Ahh,*" he said as he guided us to continue walking.

"*Mm-hmm.* That's what I thought."

He drew in a breath, swiping the waves at the top of his head. "I mean, honestly, I hoped to find someone I meshed with, but I was doubtful, so I kinda sorta decided to find a little island baddie for a quick hookup," he reluctantly admitted as we shared titters.

"I knew it." I pointed my finger into the air.

"So, why are you here then?" He sucked his teeth. "I mean, because you *are* on the same singles cruise with me."

"What are you trying to say?" I playfully punched him on the shoulder.

This negro playfully pushed me right back. "That you are on your hot girl hookup shit, too. Don't try to play me."

Although I knew he was joshing with me, discomfiture crept into my bones and crowded my face. *"Mm,"* I groaned and bit my lip timidly.

Sensing the shift, Roman stopped and faced me, lightly caressing my hands in his. His thumbs brushed softly over my knuckles, sending ripples up my spine. Care and concern swooshed over me. It reminded me he wasn't some man I'd just met on this boat but one I had a friendly history with. He'd been a part of our circle of friends for a while, and from that alone, I knew I could trust him. The moment was enough to bring down my walls of awkwardness.

"Okay." I palmed the side of my face with one of my hands. "My sisters forced me to come. They said I needed a vacation," I admitted. "And some dick."

That last confession was mumbled, but he still heard it, evidenced by his horrible attempt to withhold his doubled-over hysterics.

"See," I said, huffing, "this is why I didn't want to say anything." I stomped off.

"Aquila," he called out to my retreating back. "Hold up." He easily caught up to me with his long strides. "Listen, I'm sorry. It caught me off guard, and I didn't think you'd say that."

I shrugged. "Well, it's the truth." The chip on my shoulder was still showing.

He gave me the side-eye. "It's true that your sisters forced you or that you need some vitamin D?"

He burst into laughter again, and this time, I joined him. I'd walked my snooty attitude right into that dig.

"You know what? Let's drop the subject and say we're both here to have a good time. How about that?"

His chuckles diminished into the softest beam. "Agreed." With outstretched arms, he prompted, "Come here."

He embraced me with a gentle cuddle, and I melted into his chest. It was intended to be a friendly ceasefire, but being held like that by him suddenly sent mixed signals again. My core stirred again, and confusion engulfed my mind as I tried to understand why my emotions and body reacted this way.

Never mind the fact that this man smelled like lust and sin—the kind of delectable temptation that made you scream yes without concern for consequences and repercussions because you'd accept every one of them to have that moment. His body felt like seduction, and his hands…my god…his hands gave me that after-sex feeling that you knew would have your skin glowing and your cheeks burning from endless cheesing. Schoolgirl-crush type vibes. Breakfast-in-bed type vibes…lunch and dinner, too, because you couldn't bear separating from his caress.

"Excuse us." A voice came from behind. A group of friends was attempting to move around us to go up the stairs.

Roman released me from the embrace, and the vacancy was felt immediately.

"Sorry," we said, sliding out of their way.

"Let's finish taking our tour," Roman said.

With a nod, I gripped his bicep with my hand, not bothering to wait until he extended it. I did this partially because I wanted to continue our exploration, but mostly because I needed to hold on to him to fill the void left when I was no longer in his arms.

We headed to the next deck, lost in the grandeur. Our surroundings were steeped in vacation oasis opulence. Each deck offered a different perspective. If I never stepped off the vessel, Island Skye Voyages ensured a tropical experience onboard. On the other side, there was a galore of water slides—several colored tubular ones for those who enjoyed the ride, minus the thrill. The riptide and boat slides were the more thrill-seeking slides, which had clear tubing and used either mats or tube floats to careen down the slide with a magnificent and bold ocean view. Either one flowed into two massive pools.

"Oh, yeah. I'm trying both of those," Roman said with the giddiness of a little boy.

"I might try the regular tube slides." My comment, though audible, wasn't necessarily for him, but rather, they were my inward thoughts being verbalized.

Excitedly, he turned to me. "Oh no! You have to try it with me." The skeptical gaze I cast at him was shot down before my mouth could protest. "Come on. Live a little."

"I live every day. It's death that I'm trying to steer clear of."

"I'll make sure you don't die." He pouted playfully. "Don't you trust me?"

A girlish blush reddened my cheeks. "Just a little." I indicated by pressing my fingers together.

Leaning over, he muttered, "*Humph*. I'll have to prove it to you." His breath tickled the top of my earlobe.

Shivers. Tingles. Chills. All of them traveled through my body, rendering me speechless. And that was for the best. *Heaven help me.*

The next level mimicked an entire waterpark, with two Olympic-sized pools and three smaller ones, two of which were wave pools. A surf wave pool completed the outdoor experience, which looked exhilarating and terrifying. Wrapping up this level was a breathtaking indoor aqua dome theater. The amphitheater boasted a water stage with three wide screens. I could only imagine how enchanting it must be when the stage was lit and the performers gave their show. I couldn't wait to be engrossed in the whimsical experience.

When we finally made our way to the promenade, I was impressed a million times. The main deck was reminiscent of the boardwalk in California. With shops, arcades, and bars throughout, guests didn't want for anything. In the center was a gigantic carousel, and a walkthrough art museum on the other side.

"What doesn't this place have?" Roman asked in wonder. "Now I see why people want to retire and live on a cruise ship for a year. Everything you need, want, and can conjure is all in one place."

A yawn slipped out, which I hurriedly tried to cover.

"You're tired," Roman said sympathetically.

I wanted to fib, but I was sure my face told the story of my fatigue. "Yes. I need to call it a night."

Roman gazed down at me. "I can walk you to your room to take a nap. Later tonight, one of those water-acrobatic shows will be in the aqua theater. We should go."

"I should probably stay in. Besides, I don't want to ruin any plans you have. You came here to have fun, not babysit me."

He lifted a hand to his chest. "The only plans I have are to enjoy myself on this trip. And for the record, you're not a babysitting job for me now or ever. We're both here solo. We're both here to relax and have fun. We're both friends. Why can't we spend this trip together?"

For a few moments, I contemplated what he'd suggested. Neither of us had a guest, and two was always better than one. I also felt safe knowing a man I trusted was around.

Releasing a deep breath, I agreed. "Sure."

This time, he held his pinky finger out to me. "Let's make a pact: These seven days, we'll make sure that we take advantage of the time we have before we get back to the real world—vacation accountability partners. Swear."

His silliness tickled me. *Vacation accountability partners*, I repeated internally. But I'd bite. I locked my pinky finger with his. "Swear."

He walked me to my room, and just before I entered, he reminded me, "I'll stop by and pick you up at 9:45. The show starts at 10:00." Before I could respond, he turned and walked back down the hallway, solidifying that I'd better be up and ready at 9:45.

Chapter Ten

ROMAN

WHEN I RETURNED to my suite to prepare for tonight, there was only one thing on my mind: Aquila Richards. I couldn't believe it. Talk about a plot twist. One chance encounter with her changed the trajectory of my trip. It called into question everything I used to believe in, which wasn't kismet. Then, Aquila Richards landed smack against my chest on a cruise neither of us knew the other was taking.

My mind ran rampant about what this meant. Cami would call it fated destiny. Why? Let's just say she was the only one who knew I had been crushing on Aquila for quite some time, and I blame Kannon. Leave it to Kannon to fall in love with her baby sister, which led Kinston to meet and fall in love with her other sister. Suddenly, Aquila was no longer just a member of the gym. She and I were now part of our family and friends' circle. As Kinston's client, our interactions were limited, so I didn't really know her, and why would I? She wore that enormous wedding ring just as well as her workout clothes. Had I been attracted to her? Abso-fucking-lutely. Her being married didn't make me Ray Charles. But I didn't go for married women. That automatically killed my attraction to Aquila. Until it didn't.

Being around her in our friend circle introduced me to a different side of her. Sure, she was reserved, but there were glimpses of the true woman inside that emerged when we were together, which she seemed to hide from everyone, especially when her husband—or rather, now ex-husband—was present. Her ex drained the energy from those around him, so I could only imagine what Aquila experienced. However, when he wasn't around, she was much more open. I kept my little crush on her at bay because she was married, but I distinctly remember the day I knew I had to stay away from her as I felt that crush evolve into a deeper attraction: the all-white yacht party for the grand opening of our second gym location. To this day, I recall that moment as if it were yesterday.

Aquila and her sisters had arrived at the same time. Nissi had come into view first, and when Kannon spotted his wife, his eyes shone with love and lust. His motioning for her to come over brought our eyes in their direction. When Aquila came into view, it was as if time had slowed down. I was perched on the arm of a sofa chair, taking a sip of cognac, when I spotted her walking toward the group. She was runway model fine. The all-white pantsuit she wore was every bit of the astute Aquila we knew, but the way it contoured to her tight, petite frame with her cleavage on display almost had me frothing from the mouth. The way she glided in those nude red bottoms could put Naomi Campbell to shame, and with her hair sleeked back and flowing down her back, she was serving nothing but sex appeal. When they finally reached us, I could barely keep my eyes off her.

When Kannon complimented his wife, I felt compelled to acknowledge how beautiful all the ladies were. However, when I made that statement, I was definitely referring to Aquila. Hell, I was definitely *looking* at Aquila. However, I couldn't give such bold praise to a married woman directly. At the time, Kinston and Angela were stuck in the impasse of their situationship, and Kannon and Nissi were focused on their lives as newlyweds, so my comment and lingering gaze went unnoticed—at least by them. The only one who caught on was my nosy friend and employee, Cami. As soon as she had the chance to tease me about low-key flirting with Aquila, she took it. That's when I admitted that I had a slight crush on Aquila but would never pursue it for many reasons—the most important was that the now Ms. Aquila Richards was Mrs. Aquila Richards Oliver at the time. I'd never confess to Cami or anyone else that just that one moment ignited my crush into a raging inferno of attraction.

But that was then. Since Aquila's divorce, I'd clung to all the other reasons not to pursue her. I've used every excuse—from her being a client to my belief that she wasn't interested in me. Cami has consistently pressured me to approach her, which is why she eventually gave up and suggested this singles cruise. Now, the thought of Cami setting me up crossed my mind, and the only reason I felt our meeting was a coincidence was that Cami would've given herself away if that had been her plan. If she didn't, Aquila's sisters surely would have. Nope. This is what Cami would've called fated destiny.

The only issue that plagued me was how to approach this. Of course, I was going to find any excuse to spend time with Aquila. This was the closest opportunity I'd ever had to see if there was a connection beyond my attraction. Still, I had to be sensitive to the situation. She was not only still a client of KinRo, but she was also my best friend's sister-in-law. I needed to let this unfold naturally. I would be on whatever time she was on. If she never gave me any indication that she was attracted or interested, I'd scale back and keep it strictly platonic. But if she showed any hint of interest, I would begin my mission to claim her as mine. I may not be the kind of man who envisioned marriage in my future, but I could imagine Aquila as more than just a friend or a friend with benefits. One thing about me: Anything I set my sights on, I always achieved. My sights were locked on Aquila Richards. It would start with our date night at the water acrobatics show, and hopefully, it wouldn't end there.

Chapter Eleven

AQUILA

DAY 2 OF 7. I'm already exhausted.

Last night was an absolute blast. After a refreshing shower and nap, I was ready by 9:40 p.m. on the dot. True to his word, Roman was right on time. Since it was cooler, I slipped on a pair of leggings and a short-sleeved white, collared top tied at the waistline. My sisters ensured that this top showed plenty of cleavage as well, but at least I felt more modest. Roman must've had the same idea because he donned a beige linen pants outfit with cognac casual mules. We had great seats at the water-acrobatic show, where we sat mesmerized by the talent, athleticism, and the laser and water lights. Afterward, we grabbed a quick bite at one of the bars on the promenade before heading back to our respective rooms at one in the morning. That's why waking up at seven was already kicking my tail, and it had only been an hour.

The promise of Turks and Caicos was enough fuel to revitalize me. Roman and I decided to spend the morning exploring the island before it got too hot and then go on a couple of excursions. I had to give it to my sisters—more than likely Nissi—for today's outfit. The tangerine-and-yellow floral bathing suit was a two-piece, but the top was a halter, and the bottoms were high-waisted shorts, reminding me of a retro seventies style. It also included an uber-cute matching sarong, which I paired with my yellow slides. When I heard the knock on my door, I tossed on my shades and sun hat and answered.

All the air in my lungs escaped when I saw Roman standing at the threshold, full of early-morning smiles and a rippling bare chest. He'd donned another island-inspired button-down, but just like last night, it wasn't buttoned up. Every pec and ab muscle was visible like a thirst trap, and apparently, I was parched. I dared not venture my eyes to his lower section for fear I'd combust. I needed to get myself together. Roman was my friend and the co-owner of my gym. We'd never shown an inkling of interest in each other nor been inappropriate. These lustful thoughts had to be the culmination of this vacation and years of a lack of intimacy, or my sisters infiltrating my thoughts.

"Is something wrong?" Roman's concerned voice filtered through my roaming, salacious thoughts.

Shaking my head, I assured him, "No. Not at all. I was going over my checklist in my mind."

Yes, I lied and gladly did so to keep him from becoming privy to my true internal musings.

"Good." He shared that dazzling smile with me. "Are you ready?"

"Yes. Let me grab my tote."

My tote indicated that I was a mother because I was always prepared, most of the time overprepared. He came down with his wallet and cell phone, and I had everything except the bedroom furniture.

"Would you like me to carry that?" Roman asked.

"Would you, please?" My face lit up while handing it to him.

He nearly dropped the darn thing. "Damn, girl. What you got in here? A body?" He hoisted it on his shoulder.

"It's not that heavy." Playfully, I bumped his hip with mine.

"Tell that to my rotator cuff," he smarted and sprinted a few steps to stop me from popping him again. He turned and walked backward, and I speed-walked to catch up to him. "Can I store my items with yours since everything else is in there?"

"You're toting it, so why not?"

"Just so long as you take care of my massage, it's all good." He stretched his neck and rotated his arms for emphasis.

Was he referring to me or spa services? He had to be referring to spa services, right? Of course. I had to let go of the notion that Roman might be flirting. To be honest, I was so out of the loop that I couldn't tell when or even if he was being serious. This new era of my life was so difficult to navigate. My intuition and common sense seemed to have taken an early retirement, and on top of that, this getaway had me out of character around a man who had zero interest in me. I wasn't even sure if I had an interest in him beyond the fact that he exuded sex appeal. Based on that alone, I decided I needed to get a grip on reality, enjoy my trip, and not mess up my friendship with Roman.

"I'll be sure to purchase you a spa service."

Once we exited the ship, we headed to town to soak up some of the culture and shops. We went from place to place, exploring the island and enjoying the sights. I found quite a few keepsakes and gifts to give to my boys, my sisters, and their kids. Roman also purchased a couple of items. The entire time, our conversation was light and refreshing. Initially, I didn't believe that he and I could have fun together aside from working out in the gym, but Roman was truly a breath of fresh air, and he matched my brand of comedic relief.

As we walked past this one storefront, it smelled heavenly, reminding me that we opted not to eat breakfast. However, my stomach growled, alerting me that I was on my way to being hangry. Yes, hangry—one mile past hungry and three steps before starvation.

"Let's stop here." I grabbed Roman's hand and pulled him into the restaurant as if he were a rag doll.

"So, I assume you're hungry," Roman joked as I stopped and smelled the flavorful aromas surrounding us.

"Famished. Aren't you?"

He patted his bare belly. "I could eat."

"Hello," the hostess greeted us. "Welcome. I hope you brought your appetite."

"Yes, we did. Everything smells delicious," I gushed.

"Well, you've come to the right place." She eyed Roman standing beside me. "Table for two?"

Roman nodded. "Yes, please."

She escorted us to our table and placed the menus before us. There were so many things I wanted to try, but I decided on the Johnny cakes with fish stew, and Roman decided on the snapper and veggies.

"I can't wait to try the food. The flavors are so bold, and all the platters look so vibrant. I've been dying to make island cuisines."

Roman drank a sip of his water and sat back. "You love to cook?"

"Absolutely. These days, I only get to cook for my boys, but their summer camp hired me to bake cupcakes for the end-of-season program."

"Interesting." He sat forward. "I didn't know that. I thought you were only into the culinary arts because of your ex-husband. I didn't realize you have a passion for it as well."

I covered his hand with mine. "No worries. Everyone thinks the same. Joel comes from a lineage of restaurateurs, so it makes logical sense. But I love to razzle-dazzle."

"Are you a baker or a cook?"

"Cook by nature. Baker by necessity. So, both." I took a sip of my water before continuing. "I began learning to bake because I refused to buy birthday cakes for my sons' birthdays. Besides, vegan options were even rarer a few years ago."

He snapped his fingers. "That's right. You are a vegan."

"One hundred percent—loud and proud, baby." I pumped my hands in the air. "When I can help it, anyway. When I cook, you can guarantee it's all vegan, but out and about, such as on vacation, I try. I stick with seafood and vegetarian options as my backup plan."

"Do you or the boys have food allergies? I'm just wondering about your decision to eat completely plant-based."

"No. Those boys eat any and everything. I jokingly call them part-time vegans because my sisters and Mama aren't all the way in for my journey, so when they're with them, they eat what they prepare. As long as they steer clear of red meat, I'm not arguing. As for my decision, it was because I saw the struggles my father had when he was first diagnosed with diabetes and soon after with high cholesterol. I didn't want those problems for myself or my offspring, so I knew I had to make a change. I started in college and haven't looked back since."

He leaned forward, gliding his thumb across his bottom lip. His eyes shone in admiration as he digested what I'd explained. "That is remarkable, Aquila. I'm impressed." He shrugged. "But then again, your fortitude has always been commendable."

Curiosity got the better of me. He'd only just now heard of my ability to cook and my choice to be vegan. "How so?"

"You're our most loyal client. You stay committed to your workout regimen and your yoga exercises. You've never let being a mother, married, or single deter you from your health goals and fitness mindset. I know you enjoy it, but it still takes a level of commitment that few can maintain. It doesn't surprise me in the slightest when you state that you converted in college. In the grand scheme of things, it tracks."

I'd never considered that. When he pointed it out, it made me want to pat myself on the back. But the credit went to my mother and father. They were alike in that way. When they committed to something, they were locked in. I'm pretty sure that's the reason they were knocking on forty years of marriage...happily.

When our food was returned, Roman reached for my hands to bless the meal. I dove into my stew immediately afterward. As soon as the food touched my palate, I knew I was in heaven. A moan escaped, and my eyes rolled backward as I savored the flavors.

"That good, huh?" Roman smirked at me.

Slightly embarrassed, I nodded, lifting my hand in praise. "Hallelujah. Thank you, Jesus, for the meal. This must be the manna from heaven. How's your food?"

"It's good, but I'm slightly jealous because I don't think mine is as good as yours, delivered straight from Jesus' dinner table."

"Stop." I giggled. "It's probably just as good."

"Would you like to try some?" Roman offered.

Of course, I accepted that offer because I was a foodie. When I went to grab my fork, Roman had already gathered a portion on his other fork and extended it out to feed me. When I opened my mouth, he slid the food gently inside—next-level deliciousness. Again, I reacted in like fashion to his meal as I had with mine. Our eyes met as a sinfully sweet grin spread across his lips. Quickly, I darted my eyes away.

"It's good, too. I think you should try a bite with the veggies and see if it enhances the taste."

"Good point." He pointed at me with his fork and gathered the fish with veggies as I'd suggested. As soon as his lips closed on the fork, he melted back into his seat. "Damn. That's good."

"See."

"Look at you over there knowing your shit." He gathered another bite for me, but I declined. "Come on, Qui. You gotta try it with the veggies to do it justice."

There was that nickname again—Qui. It stirred something in me every time he uttered it. I quelled whatever that feeling was and allowed him to feed me again. This time, I closed my eyes to avoid contact. Thank goodness I had. That bite tasted so delicious that my skin pebbled with goosebumps.

"Now I'm jealous that I didn't order what you have."

"Well, I still need to be the judge of that," Roman declared with a wink.

Licking my lips, I reached and grabbed his spoon, then dipped it into my fish stew. When I went to hand him the spoon, he gave me a curious stare.

"Feed it to me," he said, and a lump lodged itself into my throat before he said, "You allowed me to feed you, so I'll allow you to do the honors."

Calm down, Aquila. Don't make a mountain out of a molehill. I lifted the spoon to his lips, and he lightly blew on the stew. I kept my focus on the utensil, but I could feel his gaze like a hot laser on me. When he slid the stew into his mouth and hummed his appreciation, I nearly lost all of my composure.

"Excuse me. I need to use the restroom." I skedaddled away from that table so quickly that I'm sure I left a trail of smoke.

Inside the restroom, I washed my hands and took a few deep breaths to settle my nerves. Once I was confident that my heart palpitations had diminished, I waltzed back to the table with Roman none the wiser and with a bubbly demeanor intact.

"Sorry about that." I slid into my seat and began eating again.

He held a hand up. "No problem. Handle your business."

We fell into a comfortable conversation about the island cuisine with the waitress who came to refill our drinks and left our tab for whenever we were ready to check out. I was grateful for the reprieve because it restored balance to this lunch date. Once she left, it dawned on me that I'd spoken so much about food that I hadn't bothered to learn more about Roman.

"So, do you cook?"

He laughed as he finished the last remnants of his food. "You razzle-dazzle, and I dabble. I know how to grill, and I'm a wiz with an air fryer and a griddle. But no one is going to ask me to cook Thanksgiving dinner."

I held my hand over my mouth to prevent my food from spewing. "You almost made me choke. But you're a single guy, so you do what works for you, ya know?"

"Precisely. I'm not vegan, but I do watch my red-meat intake."

"Moderation is better than gluttony."

"Oh, for sure." He wiped his hands. "I think it came with sports. Protein intake is a big part of an athletic diet."

"I forgot you used to play football with Kinston in college. What made you stop?"

"A knee injury took me out. I was never one for major contention like Kinston. Without injury, if I had entered the draft, I might've gone in the fourth or fifth round. Football, for me, was more of a committed pastime. I've always wanted to do exactly what I'm doing in some capacity. My bachelor's is in sports medicine, and I have a doctorate in physical therapy."

This time, I choked on my Johnny cake. "Wait a minute. You're a *doctor?* Dr. Roman Patterson?"

He shrugged it off as if it were a minor feat. "Yes, but I prefer Roman. The only time the doctor portion matters to me is when it's time for certifications and securing clients. Aside from that, I don't even harp on it."

"And he's humble," I chided. "You're an anomaly."

He released a throaty rumble as amusement danced on his lips. "I guess you can say that. My parents raised me to be a man in all things. I do the work and earn my achievements, but those things don't make me who I am. They are a part of my life."

There was more to Roman than met the eye, and I sat in admiration of him. Though we'd known and been friendly with each other for years, I hadn't known him more than surface level. To me, he was a cool guy but a bit of a conceited playboy. I hadn't known the intricate details of his makeup, and admittedly, I was beginning to believe that I had him pegged all wrong.

Standing, he retrieved his wallet from my tote and picked up the tab. "Excuse me. I'm going to use the restroom and pay our bill so we can get going."

"Oh, let me give you my portion—"

"Aquila," he said in a manner that halted my speaking, "I can handle paying for our meals. It's no big deal, seriously."

My lips parted to protest, but his buttoned lips and raised brow paused me again. Instead, I lifted my hands in surrender and mouthed, "Thank you." His serious expression turned into a pleased one as he winked at me and walked away.

I was still lost in thought when Roman re-emerged. "Ready?" he asked. When I nodded, he pulled my chair out so I could stand, grabbed the tote, and offered his arm to me, which I accepted. "It's time to meet at our excursion point."

"This is absolutely gorgeous." I snapped pictures of the turquoise ocean water and scenic views as we rode the catamaran to our diving location to snorkel.

Roman and I exchanged phones as we captured shots of each other against the picturesque backdrop. My mood was tranquil because there were only four other people on our excursion tour, thank goodness. With the popularity of the island, I appreciated every opportunity for peace and privacy that we could get.

During the ride, we learned some brief history about the islands as we soaked up the sun, sipped cocktails, and basked in the cool breeze. We all swayed to the beat when the captain began playing Bob Marley tunes. The other guests stood and began dancing around as the music changed from a relaxed vibe to a more upbeat and vibrant note. Roman glanced in my direction and jogged his eyebrows. Hesitancy shrouded my face as he stood and gently captured my hand.

"Vacation accountability partner, checking in for duty," he said under his breath, biting his lip as he salsa-danced from side to side.

I picked up my cup to gulp down a little more liquid courage and gave in to his request. Standing, I matched his movements, sashaying left to right. At first, I was timid in my moves, but soon, I loosened up, and we sang to the music. When Roman twirled me around so that my back was against his chest, we snuggled together, slowing our motions into a sensual sway.

Roman's arm wrapped around my waist as my head fell against his shoulder, continuing our rhythmic pace.

"It's wonderful to see you carefree and enjoying the moment," he murmured in my ear. "This is the Aquila I've been longing to see."

Curious, I inquired, "Oh yeah? Why is that?"

He twirled me to face him and gently pulled me close to him as we continued swaying. "Because you're always in a mode. All business. No nonsense. Even when you're having fun, there's always an air of tension. There's a time and a place for that, but there's also a time and a place to have fun and live life. If only you realized how well carefree looks on you."

The cocktails had me slightly inebriated, so his words landed as intended without my ability to overthink them. "*Mmm.* Carefree feels good *to* me, too."

Our gazes meshed together as his lowered lids blinked slowly. "To me, too."

My breath quickened under the watch of his sultry eyes roaming over my face. It was as if he were searching…hoping… maybe longing even. My pulse raced when I felt his fingertips gently caress my back, urging me closer to our already diminished space. Roman's tongue slowly glided over his bottom lip, making me gently nip on mine. His eyes narrowed as if he were homing in on me, and my skin pebbled with ignited anticipation. Our heads angled when we heard the blare of the intercom.

"We've reached our destination point, everyone. Who's ready to snorkel?" The instructor's voice interrupted our brevity of serenity.

Slowly, we pulled apart, neither of us daring to speak. Instead, we gathered our gear and instructions. I had been excited to go on this excursion until we prepared to jump into the ocean. I'd swum, but I'd never snorkeled before. I was more of an above-the-water adventurer, so I had no clue why I thought I could tackle snorkeling.

"Wait. I don't think I can do this." My voice trilled while talking to the instructor. "I think I need to turn around."

"Of course, it's no pressure," he stated, stepping to the side so I could turn around.

Roman walked up to us. "What's wrong?"

"She has changed her mind," the instructor answered before I could explain.

Roman turned to me, and I shook my head. "I can't do it. My nerves have gotten the better of me."

"What if I go with you?" Roman asked, then aimed his next question at the instructor. "Can we jump together?"

He shrugged. "Of course. If it makes her comfortable."

Without waiting for my answer, Roman stepped beside me and took my hand. "I've got you."

Biting my lip, I eyed him doubtfully. When my legs began to shake, my head bounced side-to-side, indicating that I was bowing out. I felt Roman clench my hand and interlace our fingers. That snapped my attention to him, and his orbs seared into mine.

"We'll do it together." His stern yet reassuring voice soothed me instantly. "I promise I won't let you go. Trust me, Qui."

Just the utterance of *Qui* from his lips quelled my anxiety, and his reassurance gave me the courage I needed to give him the green light. On Roman's count of three, we gripped hands and jumped off the boat into the water. Just as he promised, he never let my hand loose. When we plunged into the water and resurfaced, he pulled me into him.

"I'm here. Are you good?"

I let out a yelp from the pit of my belly. "*That was so exhilarating!*" Roman burst into laughter, and I threw my arms around his neck in a tight squeeze. "Thank you."

For a moment, we floated there enveloped together. He waded through the water to balance our buoyancy.

"I told you, you can trust me."

"I'm starting to see that more and more."

A blush graced his cheeks before I unraveled from around him. Pulling down our snorkeling masks and breathing tubes, we held hands and swam, our flippers creating ripples around us as we explored the fish and other animals in our midst. We had fun discovering all the ocean had to offer while never letting go of each other. By the time we emerged from the water back to the boat, my heart had begun to thump, but this time, it was due to more than just Roman's water-glistened, rippling chest. I had become smitten with Dr. Roman Patterson, but since we were friends, I refused to admit that aloud.

After we reached our starting point, Roman said, "I want to go back to the shops."

"Oh. I thought we had another excursion."

"It was canceled. I'm sorry I forgot to tell you."

"It's no problem," I told him, although, low-key, I was disappointed.

Roman and I had both planned an excursion for today. Mine was to go snorkeling, and his was to go ATV riding. I was looking forward to his, as I'd never ridden an ATV. The only vehicle that came close was a golf cart, which I was more hyped about because I felt safer on land. But if it were canceled, there was nothing that he could do about that.

When we arrived at the area with the restaurants, Roman walked me to the back, where a group of people was. The host from the restaurant we'd eaten at earlier appeared. She walked over to us and winked.

Now, I was totally confused. *What is this?* Before I could levy Roman with my looming questions, another woman announced herself.

"Hello, everyone. Welcome to Island Cuisine. My name is Chef Yuri, and today, I will be your instructor." She pointed to the lady who was our hostess and stated, "And this is Zora. She will be my assistant and your guide."

Zora stepped forward. "That's right. I hope you came a little hungry and prepared to use your hands as you get ready to learn how to make authentic food from the island of Turks and Caicos."

My eyes ballooned as I spun around and faced Roman. "What? What is this?"

Roman gave me one of those panty-dropping commercial smiles and licked his lips. "After you fawned over the food, I figured the ATVs could wait. Forgive me for fibbing, but I went to ask the waitress if any places taught us how to cook island food, and she told me about this tour and when it would start. After I had paid for our meal, I paid for this tour and canceled the ATV excursion. That's why we had to hurry back. I wanted to surprise you. Seeing how you gushed over our meals and the passion in your eyes about learning to cook authentic food, I had to make this happen for you if I could. I hope you're not upset."

I was floored, but the shock of the surprise was short-lived as I bounced on my toes and clapped like a spry schoolgirl. "Upset? Absolutely not. This is one of the sweetest things anyone has ever done for me. OMG! Thank you so much." I hopped into his arms, and without thinking, I kissed his cheek. "I'm sorry. I didn't mean—"

"No offense taken, I promise."

I slid down from his arms and gave my undivided attention to the instructor as she handed us a bowl and an apron and assigned us to our stations. Roman sat beside me, content to watch me master this skill, and my beam couldn't stop at the fact that one of my culinary dreams was coming true, and Roman was the reason.

Roman and I couldn't stop discussing our fun-filled day as we returned to the ship. After I learned to make conch ceviche, we indulged in the meal for dinner. The chef awarded prizes for the best cuisine, and I won the best overall. Afterward, I had a pleasant and promising conversation with the instructor, during which I explained my love for cooking. She invited me to come back any time. Honestly, I would try to take her up on her offer.

Roman agreed he'd go with me if I did. He had to because he was the one who made it possible. As we entered the hall where my room was located, I slowed my pace because I didn't want the day to end. The idea of having to wait another day to continue this journey of carefree enjoyment chipped away at me.

"So, this is me," I said slowly as we reached my door.

Roman turned to face me and sighed. "Yeah. This is you."

"I had a great time—" We uttered the sentiment together and chuckled.

His fingertips grazed mine before he asked, "So, what's on the agenda for tomorrow?"

I wagged my finger at him, then dug in my tote until I found my cell phone. Pulling up the Island Skye Hub app, I scheduled a spa session for him. "Tomorrow, you have a two-hour massage. Be there at 10 a.m. As for me, I will rest and then hang out on the promenade."

"What? You didn't have to schedule that for me for real, Aquila. I was only joking."

Turning my phone in my hand, I playfully teased, "So, you don't want a massage. Is that what you're telling me?"

"Hell no. I'm not crazy now. I'm definitely taking that massage. Just know you didn't have to do that."

As our fingertips lazily toyed together, I locked pinkies with him. "You didn't have to plan the island cuisine tour, nor jump off the boat with me during our snorkeling excursion. You did it because you wanted to. I wanted to do this. Let me."

"Duly noted." He bowed his head with grace. "But it also sounds like you don't want to hang with me tomorrow."

"Oh, you can't get rid of me that easily. Tomorrow night is on you. You plan it, and I'm there. Vacation accountability partners, remember?"

"I got you," he bellowed.

A brief silence passed between us before I retrieved my keycard. "Seriously, thank you for today. You made my day."

He brought my hands to his lips, delivering a soft kiss to my knuckles, and murmured, "Mission accomplished."

Removing one hand from his, I reached up and palmed his cheek before tiptoeing and planting a supple kiss on it. "Good night, Dr. Patterson."

We stood there staring at each other in silence while still communicating so many unspoken words—words that neither of us dared utter aloud. When I thought one of us would take steps that we couldn't recover from, Roman parted his lips, and truthfully, I hung on every breath, waiting for him to speak.

"Good night, Ms. Richards."

I quelled the disappointment that bubbled inside. Before dwelling on the regret, I surmised I had set my expectations too high. It was clear that he preferred to maintain our platonic relationship, and perhaps that was for the best. We couldn't allow our vacation brains to outweigh our reality.

As I turned to go inside, Roman left for his room, which officially ended our day. Inside, I hurriedly kicked off my shoes and disrobed, running straight to the shower. I aimed to rush and wash the day away, but as the water cascaded down my body, soothing my tired muscles while making a trail along my plump breasts, my second heartbeat began to thump with visions of one Roman Patterson dancing through my psyche. My eyes fluttered closed as I reminisced over...*him*. His boyish grin that made me redden all over, the way he licked those kissable...*suck-able* lips, the sinful winks that sent my heart racing, those python arms that engulfed me into his warm and soft embrace, the way his whispers tickled my earlobes, and his glistening and chiseled chest with those powerful thighs, topped with his tender kindness and gentle care—my god. I hadn't realized the path my hand had traveled until an old familiar friend rumbled in my belly, flooding my core. And I took flight.

"*Ahhh!*" I hollered so loudly my ears rang as my sticky fluids leaked on three of my probing fingers, panting until I gradually came down from my Roman-induced orgasm.

My back fell against the shower wall as euphoria overcame me. Biting my lip, I smiled, considering the naughtiness I'd just experienced. Since I couldn't partake of the real deal, my private explorations would do. Immediately, I knew I had to write one more entry in my journal app to top off the ending.

Day 2 of 7 was purr-fect.

Chapter Twelve

ROMAN

MY CELL PHONE, blaring its irritating alarm music, annoyed me as I sat up and silenced it. "Damn it." I swiped a hand down my face.

It wasn't that I wasn't used to my alarm, but when it interrupted the best erotic dream of my grown life, I had a justified reason to be slightly perturbed. To add to my frustration, I was almost at completion. The woman who was the central focus of my dream was none other than Aquila-fucking-Richards. She had my head, my heart, and my hard-on all disconcerted. As I lifted the covers to stare at my morning wood, exacerbated by my erotic fantasies, I wanted to do nothing but fall back into my bed and release the pressure off my valve to thoughts of her.

When I booked this vacation, I decided to hook up with either a baddie on the boat or one on the island. My bet was on both to have a little of this and a little of that, which was why I booked the MegaSweeties suite, although the island felt more probable to meet someone because I'd never have to see the chick again. This vacation was supposed to be strictly to clear my mind, have fun, and have hot sex. Then, Aquila collided with me, literally.

The moment I laid eyes on her in that skirt with the split and the top showing her midriff, impure thoughts invaded my mind. Aquila had always been attractive, but she'd been married the entire time I'd known her, and I'd never seen her in any outfit that wasn't workout gear or professional gear, aside from the all-white party and Kannon and Kinston's weddings. Nothing like the outfit she wore the first night on the boat or the swimsuit she donned yesterday. She exuded the aura of a goddess. Sheer perfection. However, she only saw me as a friend, so I tried to keep my reactions to her at bay. But it was getting hard—damn hard. The way she smelled, her banging body, and the softness of her skin threatened to bring out the wolf in me, but what quelled those instincts were the other facets I was learning about her. At home, she could come off as arrogant to those who didn't know her, but I'd been around the jokester, the loving sister, the loving mom—hell, even the loving wife—so I knew that wasn't true. Here I was reaping the benefits of her softer side as she settled into a carefree spirit—her timidness, gentleness, and zest for food and culture. And I looked forward to learning more above being sexually turned on.

That was rare. It was unusual for me to be interested in the makeup of a woman. Of course, I'd gathered some information about the women I previously dated or only had flings with because it was the nature of the beast. I'd grown too old to have one-night stands with women I knew zero about. But I hadn't actively *wanted* to know more than what was necessary, solely in case I had to get the law involved. I'd been down that road with an ex-stalker chick, and it wasn't pretty. But Aquila, I *desired* to learn.

That still didn't negate that she had a brother over here with the blue balls, trying to respect her space and our friendship. When she kissed my cheek that second time and called me Dr. Patterson, oh my god, I came dangerously close to breaking every rule I'd set for myself when it came to her and claiming her body. What was wild to me was that for a split second, I could've sworn that we were feeling each other in the same way, but then I remembered she'd had a few drinks. I was not about to take it there only to have her regret it today and avoid me for the remainder of the trip. Then, there was no way I could face my best friend to explain that his sister-in-law and client felt I'd taken advantage of her. Hell nah. So, I tucked away the instinct I had to sex her down until the sun told us good morning. But apparently, my dreams had not.

There was no time to handle that, as I had a massage appointment to keep. The fact that Aquila took what I'd said seriously and booked the session for me almost broke me down. Aside from family and select friends, I'd never had anyone give such consideration to my needs. Her attentiveness was top-tier without even trying. It was just who she was. Although I wished we were getting this massage together, I planned to enjoy my gift.

After I hopped out of the shower, I wrapped a towel around my waist, plopped on the bed, and picked up my cell phone from the nightstand. As I scrolled, I opened the app for the restaurants. Since it'd be late, I figured we could stay on the ship and enjoy the amenities on board. I made reservations for two at one of their premier restaurants called The Skyeline. Afterward, we could possibly chill at one of the clubs or the casino. I'd flow with whatever the vibe called for.

"Good morning," Aquila answered groggily.

"Good morning to you." I tried to hide my excitement at hearing her voice. "Look at you getting all that beauty rest. I didn't mean to wake you. I thought you might be up already."

She sounded as if she were stretching and sitting up in bed before she responded. "Normally, I'm up at five without fail, but this vacation has made me so lazy I haven't even followed my workout regimen, or perhaps it's my late nights with a certain individual."

"First of all, you're not the only one skipping workouts. I figured I'd just pay for it when I got back home. Secondly, as long as you're having a good time, I'll gladly take the wrap for that."

My declaration was met with a giggle and a long yawn. "Good, because I totally plan on blaming you for the fact that it's going to take a month to get back into my routine when I return home."

"That's why I have wide shoulders to *shoulder* the blame."

"Oh, god." She snickered with a playful scoff. "Whatever. Don't start getting cocky now."

"No promises," I joked before peeping at the time. "Listen, I have to get ready to go to my massage appointment that some sweet lady scheduled for me."

"A sweet lady, huh? In that case, I take it back. You can be a little cocky," she teased.

"Whatever." I laughed. "Be ready tonight at seven o'clock. We have a dinner date at The Skyeline."

"So that means I get to sleep a little longer?"

"Woman, that's all you got out of that?"

"Nope. I heard I'll be eating very well tonight, and I have plenty of time to rest up for it."

This version of Aquila was hilarious. I could banter with her all day. Unfortunately, I couldn't at the moment because I had to go.

"As long as you're ready at seven. But right now, I have to get going."

"Enjoy your time," Aquila cooed ever so sweetly.

"Enjoy your rest."

We disconnected the line, and I slid on some lounge pants and a t-shirt before heading to Skye's Mystical Massage.

After the day I had, I owed Aquila majorly. My time at the spa had been, as the name suggested, mystical. I'd had sports and deep-tissue massages before, but there was a magical power in those ladies' hands and products. The facial with the herbal poultice massage had me feeling like a bathed and burped baby. I even purchased the essential oils they used to take home with me. When I returned stateside, I planned to have a serious discussion with Kinston about adding some spa services as add-ons or as a whole new start-up. I could see it now: KinRo Relaxation and Spa services.

Staring at my reflection in the mirror, I admired my black-and-gold silk button-down, fitted black jeans, and casual black pull-on boots. My gold Cuban link necklace and bracelet completed the look. With a few sprays of my cologne, I headed to pick up Aquila for our dinner reservation. Since I'd allowed her to rest the entire afternoon, my anxiousness to be in her presence was heightened. I couldn't believe it, but I missed her while we were apart. In just a couple of days, she'd embedded in me, and I was surprised by her emotional pull on me. Strangely, I wasn't mad at it at all. I believe it made me that much more eager for us to spend time together. I hoped that we could talk and get to know each other better. I took pride in being the person who helped her unwind and fully embrace this time to herself. Once she returned to reality, she had time to worry about other factors in her life, as did I. Right now, our primary concern was to make the most of the opportunity to center our minds, bodies, and spirits.

Per usual, Aquila was dressed to impress, making me wonder why her ex-husband was foolish enough to let her walk away. I didn't know her intimately, but what I did know of her, in addition to her beauty, was that she was the perfect culmination of the type of woman any man would be honored to have in his corner and on his arm. Then again, I remembered she was married to Joel. That man was so self-absorbed, I'm shocked he even knew how to land *any* woman, especially Aquila.

"This restaurant is stunning. The décor and accents are picturesque. I'm sure the food will live up to the aesthetic," Aquila cooed over its elegance.

When her eyes found mine, she smiled demurely to see that while she was checking out the surroundings, I was checking her out.

"Why are you staring at me?" she asked softly.

My elbows were propped on the table, and I fanned my hands out, stating the obvious. "I was admiring the beauty *inside* the restaurant."

Her cheeks reddened at my compliment before she picked up her water glass and drank a sip. "You should stop trying to butter me up. I already agreed to go clubbing with you afterward."

Soft chuckles erupted between us. During our earlier discussion, I begged her to go to the club with me. She deemed herself too old to bop around clubs, even if it were on a cruise ship. I had to remind her that we were vacation accountability partners, to which she reluctantly agreed, only because of my generous gift to her with the cooking class. Yet, I also knew the joke was her obvious attempt to skirt past my compliment.

"Don't pretend you're not down to have a good time."

She pointed to herself with fake surprise. "Who, me?" She shook her head. "No, sir. I am quite boring."

"No, it's not you who is boring. It's the company you keep. I've been with you for three days, and you've had the time of your life. I want to think that I had a little something to contribute to that."

Flicking her fingers at me, she rolled her eyes and tossed out, "Whatever. You're all right."

I faked heartache when I leaned back in my seat and clutched my chest. "I'm just a'ight? Bet. You'll see."

Just then, the server came over and placed our appetizers down, along with the bottle of wine I'd ordered. She attempted to pour it, but I held up my hand, indicating that I would do the honors. As I poured, Aquila took a bite of her food, and the savory sound that emitted from her was orgasmic. The sounds and faces she made when partaking in her meal made me shudder with thoughts of how she'd feel in my arms, making those noises. Then, I scolded myself for the thought. She was my friend, and I needed to accept and respect our time for what it was.

"Help me see more."

I lightly beat my chest to clear the cough from nearly choking on my wine. Either I was putting too much on what she'd said, or I didn't hear her correctly. Either way, her request sounded both intriguing and flirtatious.

"Excuse me?"

She sipped her wine and leaned closer. "Tell me more about what makes up Mr.—Wait. No, *Dr.*—Patterson."

If she had twenty-one questions for me, I would have an answer for every one of them. I'd never had a woman take that type of interest. Gradually, they would get to know some things about me if we were involved, but not an outright interest above what they saw on the outside and my material possessions.

Matching her energy, I mimicked her movements. "I'll tell you whatever it is you'd like to know as long as you promise to do the same."

She held up her pinky finger, and I held out mine as we locked them together.

"You first," she said, finishing off her wine, and quickly dived in, leaving me no chance to object. "Tell me more about college life with Kinston."

"We met from being teammates during college. I was a walk-on for the team, and we wound up being roommates, and then we became the best of friends."

"So, you also knew Jah." She huffed, her eyes rolling at the memory.

Jah Michaels was the black sheep and a taboo topic among the Jordan family. He had been Kinston's best friend since they were teens. He was also our third roommate, a teammate, and a man I never trusted. I'd always had a keen ability to discern people, and when it came to Jah Michaels, he reeked of bad energy. I couldn't tell Kinston that. Jah had been his friend far longer than I had been. Besides, I had no proof other than my gut, so I kept my thoughts private. To keep the peace, I always kept it cordial on an associate basis with Jah, but Kinston and I were joined as if we were blood brothers. When the news broke that Jah was sneaking around with Kinston's longtime girlfriend back in the day, I wasn't the least surprised. I wished I could've spared my boy the consequences of the aftermath then and later.

"Yeah, he wasn't my favorite person," I admitted to Aquila. "I never trusted that dude, but he was Kinston's friend, so I backed off."

"It's such a shame what Jah did, marrying Kinston's ex-girlfriend and claiming to have gotten her pregnant with Fawn, only to find out all these years later that Fawn is Kinston's child. I'm just happy that all of it panned out for my sister and Kinston. Angela would've lost her mind without him."

"Trust me. Kinston would've, too." I chuckled. "One thing I know for sure is that regardless of his relationship with Lilah back in the day, he's never loved her like he loves Angela. I knew that even with finding out all these years later that he had a child with Lilah, he wouldn't allow that to destroy his relationship with Angela."

"Good to know." Aquila nodded.

Realization struck me, and I shook my head. "Wait. Did you play me for information?"

"What kind of sister would I be if I didn't?" She grinned. "But back to you. Speaking of family, does yours live in Miami?"

That one caught me by surprise. "Oh, so we're getting deep, deep."

She relaxed into her seat, shrugging her shoulders. "Between me and my sisters, you've been around and privy to my crazy family drama. I think it's only fair that I know a smidge about your family dynamic—I mean, unless there are some underlying circumstances like they're contract killers for a secret government agency or the black mafia drug cartel."

When I didn't answer and took a sip of water, her eyes widened to the point of near explosion, and I couldn't help the bellow that ripped through me. "I'm kidding. No. Nothing like that."

She placed her hands against her chest, taking deep breaths. "I nearly fainted. I was about to run out of here and move my gym membership. I am not about either of those lives."

"Good to know you're not a ride or die, geesh." I pretended to be butthurt.

"Hell no. I'm a ride and live. I'm not about to put my life on the line to prove my love."

Jogging my eyebrows, I quipped, "Oh, so you love me?"

Waving her hand back and forth, she let me know quickly she wasn't going there with me. "I'm starting to think there's some truth in my assumption because of the way you're trying to swerve this conversation. You're not slick. Stay on topic, sir."

"Allow me to put your conspiracy theories at ease. My people are normal American citizens. Rest assured, we're not affiliated with any B6-13 programs or involved with any Frank Lucas organizations. Nor are they members of an elite squad known as the Special Victims Unit."

In unison, we simulated in the deep tenor voice of the *Law & Order: SVU* opener, "These are their stories," even adding the sound effect at the end.

She tossed a linen napkin at me. "*Hahaha.* You think you're so funny." Then we looked at each other and keeled over. "That was hilarious, though."

"Anyway, before you claim that I'm changing subjects again, my family is from California. I'm a West Coast baby, born and raised. My parents did all right for themselves—my dad is a techie, and my mom works in the medical field. I grew up in a two-parent household, by the way. My mom and dad have been married for forty years as of this past June, and I have a younger sister." Her eyes grew wide, causing me to furrow my brow. "What's that look for?"

"If I can be frank—"

"As you always are." I held my hand up when I saw the defensiveness in her orbs. "And I'm a fan of that, as I am the same way."

When she reeled her horns back in, she gazed remorsefully in my direction. "I'm ashamed to admit that I am shocked by your revelation. Most people would assume that you grew up in a single-parent household under meager means and used football and academia to aid your plans to improve your life. Before you answered, I must admit that I was one of the 'most people', which was wrong and inconsiderate. As a mother of two little brown boys, I'd hate for them to be stereotyped. I apologize."

"And that's why I love frankness and frank people. You own up to your words and actions as swiftly as you stand on them. The apology isn't necessary, but it is appreciated. Besides, there's some truth to your assumptions. I did use football and academia to aid in my success."

She reached across the table and gripped my hand in thanks, and it was all I could do to stop myself from caressing it. I'd never been so carefree discussing my life, especially my family, but Aquila had me all out of sorts in more ways than one.

"With such entrenched family values, now, I'm wondering why you're not the settle-down type. You were born and bred to be a man with a wife and 2.5 children." She propped her hand under her chin, examining me. "Are you a heartbreaker, Dr. Patterson? What type of hearts were you breaking back then—or now?"

"None. I'm pretty straightforward about what I want and don't want. My career path shows that I march to my own beat."

"Career and core family values are light-years in difference. You've had to have broken some hearts."

"I didn't say hearts weren't broken. However, it wasn't my fault. People want honesty, but can't handle the truth. That's not my cross to bear."

"Like the woman you all had banned from the gym."

I fanned my hands. "Please don't summon that bad juju on this trip. But yeah, exactly like that."

When Kinston and I first went into business together, we didn't have a no-fraternization rule. While we didn't flirt in the gym, we weren't above dating a client as long as it remained outside the facilities. Leave it to me to link up with the one crazy woman who couldn't accept when our time had ended. It led to us banning her from the gym, and I even had to take out a restraining order and threaten her job. After that, the strict policy was enacted, and I kept my head on a swivel for nearly a year.

We joked about that moment for a few minutes as we continued dining and drinking.

Our meal was on par with the rest of the amazing food we'd eaten on the trip, simply delicious. As we began to wind down our dinner, the effects of the wine were coming in. I'd always been a brown-liquor connoisseur, but this wine packed a powerful little punch, evidenced by Aquila's next question.

"So, what is it that you want?" Her question was laced with a touch of seduction behind glossy eyes as she slowly licked her lips of the last remnants of the red wine.

Lifting my glass to my lips, I leaned back, took a sip, and stared into her eyes. "As of right now, I'm exactly where I want to be with who I want to be with."

A seductive grin spread across her lips as she rubbed the edge of her wineglass with her fingertip. "*Hmph.* So am I."

By now, the wine was speaking languages that we were nearly close to verbalizing for ourselves. Inwardly, I calmed the piece of me that was full-on kung fu fighting me to chance it with Aquila to see where this brewing intimacy could lead us. I could no longer sit still because this confined area between us felt like a raging inferno. I needed air and space to contain my rampant emotions.

Standing, I offered my hand to Aquila. "Let's get out of here."

Chapter Thirteen

ROMAN

THIS WAS PRECISELY what I needed. We were in the ship's hip-hop club, and the DJ knew exactly what he was doing. Dr. Dre's "California Love" was blaring when we walked in, and Tupac's vocals automatically had me ready to C-walk through the crowd. I loved Miami. I'd made it my home because it was the only city that compared to the streets of California, in my opinion. I'd wanted a home-away-from-home experience when I went to college, and Miami gave me that, and I had no plans to leave. But home was still home. Whenever I got the opportunity to rep my West Coast roots, I did so full throttle. Dre and Pac's music was nostalgic and a surefire way to amp me up. Mostly, it tamped down those earlier feelings at dinner because I was two seconds away from getting kicked off that boat for lewd acts.

When the track changed from Dre to E-40, I was up on my feet, dancing in front of the booth I had rented for Aquila and me to chill. She was still sitting in the booth, drinking her SkyeRita, a margarita with an island blend of flavors and tequila, while I sipped on Dussé. By now, I was feeling right and wanted to move on the dance floor. As soon as Kendrick Lamar blessed the airwaves, I couldn't be held back. I reached back for Aquila's hand but didn't feel her grasp. When I turned, she sat almost statuesquely in her seat as she mouthed for me to go ahead without her. She was finishing her second SkyeRita, so I sat beside her to check on her. I figured perhaps she was tipsy, and that's why she didn't want to dance with me.

"Are you feeling okay?" I asked as I leaned my mouth to her ear so she could hear me.

Leaning into me, she answered, "I'm fine. It's just not my vibe. But you go and have fun."

I shot her a side glance. She already knew I wasn't going to do that. We were in this together. I'd already spent the first part of my day without her, and tonight belonged to us.

"Nah. If you're not going, we'll stay here."

"No. Don't let me stop your fun."

She placed her hand on my chest to urge me to go. In a sneaky move, I gripped her hand and stood, urging her to stand with me. The DJ fused Kendrick's latest banger into the mix, and the crowd went up, including me. I wanted her to be with me… in the moment.

Slowly, she stood and rocked with me. While the rest of the club patrons and I shouted the lyrics to the rooftop as we danced, I noticed Aquila hadn't said a word. While she was present with me, her energy was off. It wasn't as if she didn't want to be there, just that she seemed uncomfortable.

Drawing her close to me, I inquired, "Talk to me. What's wrong?" I could see the denial forming and raised my brow to prevent her from being anything less than the frank person she was.

Sighing, she leaned into me. "This isn't my scene."

"The club?" I mouthed.

"The music." She winced.

Record scratch. The music? What Black person didn't love hip-hop? It was an ancestral rite of passage. I knew we were all individuals with unique tastes, but we shared a commonality as a people—music, typically, being one of them. Then I deduced maybe it was West Coast music. Several people had a preference, whether regional or local, when it came to the various styles.

"You don't like West Coast rap?"

Sheepishly, she shrugged. "I don't listen to hip-hop at all."

That news was more like a record breaking. I get that hip-hop might not have been her favorite genre, and call me crazy, but to say she didn't listen to it at all stumped me because my fitness sets—and I'm sure Kinston's—were both loaded with hip-hop music. There's no way she wasn't at least a casual listener. How Sway?

By this time, the song had ended, so we sat down and both took shots of the Dussé. The look of shame plastered on her face was enough for me to make our exit. Of course, she protested. She wanted me to enjoy myself, but how could I if she wasn't? Finally, she agreed to leave with me. Still, I was intrigued by this, so as soon as we were out of the club, I opened my mouth to ask a question, but she was already prepared.

"Before you ask again, I don't listen to hip-hop music. It's not that I haven't. I've heard some catchy ones that stick with me. I wish I had some scholarly reason as to why, but the truth is, for the most part, I don't like it."

"Hip-hop is mostly seventy percent of our playlist at the gym."

"I'm aware." She rolled her eyes. "I've learned to tune it out. But I love your intro song and both you and Kinston's outro song," she said, referring to "Lean Back," "Dedication" by Nipsey Hussle, and "Put On" by Jeezy.

"At least one West Coast rapper," I celebrated, shaking my fist.

"Which one is that?"

And just like that, I was back to square one, surprised and partly slighted by her non-existent knowledge of hip-hop.

"My outro song," I said sadly. "Listen, this is a hard pill for me to swallow. That's my favorite music, so forgive me for having difficulty understanding how anyone could not listen to it."

Her lips pursed as she eyed me with a smirk. "You mean any *Black* person," she joked.

Guilty as charged, and the chuckle I released sold me out. "In the words of KevOnStage, it's for Black people anyway."

"OMG," she said, howling. "I can't with you." She paused walking and placed her hand on my arm. "I never said it was intolerable, so I'll go with you if you want to return to the club. I felt awkward because I didn't know the songs, but anywhere is a good time with you."

Instant gratification overcame me. She could never listen to another rap song in her life, but to hear her willingness to bend on my behalf simply because she enjoyed my company had me overjoyed like a little boy getting a kiss on the cheek from his crush. Then, it dawned on me: her admission.

"So, you admit having a good time *is* about the company you keep."

"You just want to hear me say you make everything better." Before I could respond, she stepped closer into my space. "Well, you do. Or maybe *I* make you better." With that, she sashayed off.

"You couldn't let me have that one, huh?"

She twirled around. "Of course not," she teased.

But honestly, I felt that she was right. Something about Aquila Richards made me want to be better.

Catching up to Aquila, I fell in stride beside her. "Well, I appreciate you thuggin' it out with me in the club." Gently clasping her fingers, I halted her steps, and she faced me. "But tell me what a night of fun looks like for Aquila."

She tolerated the hip-hop club for me, so I wanted to give her an experience she could enjoy.

"Oh, I club every night with MC Blanket and DJ Pillow on the ones and twos."

"Woman." I grinned. "Besides hanging with your homegirl, Beauty Rest, what else do you do?"

She was about to say something when she whipped around at a sound. Grabbing my hand, she pulled me into another club we were about to pass. Her eyes went wild with excitement as she ushered me through the crowd. It was smaller than the hip-hop club but still had quite a few patrons. When my ears tuned in as I took in the atmosphere, I reared back in utter disbelief.

My eyes landed on the club's name, Neon Skye, before I said, "Country?" as Aquila began to belt the chorus of the current song from the depths of her country-girl soul. All I heard was something about "raised right" as Aquila began bouncing to the beat like everyone else.

"Reyna Roberts!" Aquila belted out to inform me.

"Wait. You like country music?" I asked for clarity.

"I love it." She beamed. "This is one of my favorite songs."

I tuned into the lyrics, and I could see why. In my opinion, this song perfectly summed up Aquila. To my surprise, the song slapped. Country wasn't my preference, and I wasn't a fan, but I had to admit this track had my head bopping.

Once the song finished, Aquila turned to me. "You know what else is for Black people, anyway? Country music."

This woman. She kept me entertained with her antics. "Well, I don't know about now, but I know it came from Black people."

"It did. And I, for one, love our roots. Contrary to your belief, it is making a comeback in the community." She gave me a sympathetic gaze. "But we don't have to stay—"

"We're here. I want to hear more music and learn what you love so much about it."

With the way her face lit up, it may as well have been Christmas in July. We walked to the bar and had a few drinks as she gave me a very Aquila-esque lesson in Black country music.

Although I could tell the effects of the liquor were getting to both of us, I was intrigued by her vast knowledge and off-key karaoke.

Amid her schooling me on all things country music, we'd made our way to the dance floor as she taught me to line dance and two-step to several songs. When they slowed it down a bit, I pulled my little cowgirl close in my arms and slow dragged with her as if we were the only two in the room. As we swayed to the rhythm, Aquila lifted her arms around my shoulders, caressing my neck. Her lids slowly lifted, showing me her lazy, liquor-induced eyes. Still, the sultriness in their depths sucked me into her suffocating aura. Aquila held me entranced, and I caressed her waist as she stood flush to my chest. Our exhalations pinged off each other in an erotic cadence.

"Thank you," she said, barely above a whisper.

"No, thank you." I dipped my head so that she could see my sincerity. "You introduced me to a world that I never would've explored without you. Qui, you are rare air."

Her eyes twinkled with the sexiest glint. "As are you, Dr. Patterson. As are you."

We couldn't control the magnetism if we tried, nor did I want to. Our heads tilted until our lips collided into a tangled mesh as our tongues danced in tandem to our gentle sway. I could taste the notes of tropical fruits and the hints of tequila on her plump lips. All my senses exploded, each coming alive. Her skin pebbled yet warmed to my tender embrace. She smelled of fresh citrus—a light bergamot that wafted in the air every time she moved. The sound of her subtle moans moved melodically through my ears, piercing my heart. This kiss was drowning me on the shores of Aquila's riverbanks, and damn if I would ask for a life preserver.

When we pulled out of the sweetest kiss I'd ever had, I was about to lead the charge to my suite when over the loudspeaker, we heard Beyoncé's voice croon out the hook to her song, "Sweet,

Honey, Buckin','" and the DJ announced that the bull-riding competition was about to begin. He asked for female volunteers to line up.

"I wanna ride the mechanical bull," Aquila slurred, and before I knew it, she was up off the dance floor and headed that way, pulling me along with her.

She was the second volunteer out of five women. Each one had to stay on the bull for ten seconds. Whoever lasted the longest received one hundred dollars. If that person lasted ten seconds, they won two hundred dollars. In the event of a tie, the one who lasted the longest won the grand prize.

The first woman lasted all of two seconds. When Aquila went to go up, they handed her a cowgirl hat and went to help her on the platform, but of course, I intervened. Another man wasn't about to put his hands on her. We both might have been a little lushed, but I was her only vacation accountability partner, and after that kiss we shared, I felt even more territorial about her than before.

"Are you sure about this?" I asked worriedly as she climbed the bull, barely making it on.

"I've got this," she declared, gripping the makeshift handles.

Taking her in, I sucked in my bottom lip. She looked sexy, straddling that bull to the point I felt a bit jealous that she hadn't mounted me that way. Those thoughts aside, I encouraged her with a wink. "Get 'em, cowgirl."

Stumbling off the platform, I gave the thumbs-up when my slightly intoxicated self was out of the way. Once the bull started, Willie Jones' song "Down by the Riverside" began to belt out over the airwaves, slowly building up steam as the bull began to gyrate and buck back and forth in a paced motion. Aquila held on to the horns, getting hyped over the song and singing it lyric for lyric as she held on to the strap with one hand like a pro. After she passed the two-second mark, the crowd joined in singing with her, and by the time she made it to the five-second mark, we all began a deafening cheer to see if she could hold on for another five seconds. By then, the bull was bucking so fast and hard that she was being tossed back and forth and side-to-side with force.

"Hold on for a little while more, Qui!" I was excited that she might make the entire ten-second round.

Yet, the liquor proved to be the winner as she suddenly gripped her stomach. The move jerked her to the far left, and she tumbled off the bull onto the air mat at the eight-second mark. I rushed up the platform to help her, and we rolled and tumbled over, laughing at ourselves. Yep, we were two sheets to the wind. Finally, the bouncer and one of the club employees helped us get to our feet and off the platform. As soon as Aquila stepped off, she raised the cowboy hat in the air, and the crowd went up in an uproar for her. Even drunk, the other three competitors were no match for Aquila, each coming in at six, three, and four seconds, respectively.

"The winner and undisputed champion is competitor number two. She wins one hundred bucks. And because she did it a little bit faded, our manager threw in twenty-five extra bucks. Come and claim your prize."

"I won," Aquila screamed at the top of her lungs and jumped into my arms, wrapping her legs around me.

I held her tightly, just as enthusiastic as she was. "Hell yeah, baby."

I walked her to the podium, still wrapped in my arms. When we reached the DJ booth, they counted out the money to her and slapped it in her hands. She tucked it inside her bra and raised both arms in the air like she was Rocky Balboa. And to be honest, she was. Qui rode that bull like she was the eye of the tiger. The DJ flipped the tunes and played the winner's song for Aquila, and she stood on the platform screaming the lyrics to Tanner Adell's

"Buckle Bunny" with the rest of the women as she gyrated and threw her ass in a circle, aiming all of her words at me. As for me, I just stood there, immersed in the show she gave.

When she finished, she reached for me, and I outstretched my arms, allowing her to jump into them. We hugged as she bounced up and down on her tiptoes.

"I won," she yelled, before screaming more lyrics of the song.

"You absolutely left no crumbs, Qui. Not even a morsel," I added, grinning at her.

"Roman," she called out in a dreamy-eyed fashion.

"Yes," I answered, hissing out the word.

"This is the best night *ever*."

Chapter Fourteen

AQUILA

*D*AY 3 OF 7 *had to be the worst night ever.*

The thumping in my frontal lobe woke me from a sleepy haze as I struggled to part my heavy lids. That proved an even worse idea because the intense pain only increased with the motion. The filtering sunlight, which normally energized me, only aggravated my current situation. Lifting on my elbows, I touched my head and realized my bonnet had slipped off, so I felt around for it. When I didn't feel it, I peered through slit eyes to see if I could quickly spot it. A quick scan of the room revealed that this was not my room. That thought sent me into a panic, and despite the pain, I quickly opened my eyes to see exactly where I was.

It was clear that I was in a bed, but it was also clearly not my bed in my room. *What the hell?* I tried to recall the last events. Flashes of dinner with Roman and the club came to mind, but nothing else. Hurriedly, I lifted the comforter and saw that I still wore the dress from yesterday. On the nightstand was my phone, and on the floor was…a cowboy hat? I needed to locate Roman, find out what was happening, and get away from wherever I was. I pray I didn't leave with anyone or get taken. With that thought, panic set in, and I scurried out of bed and slipped on my sandals, almost slipping on coins. I had no clue why money was on the floor, but that made me check myself. My panties were still on.

That was a good sign that I hadn't done anything strange for some change. However, when I checked my bra, a slew of twenty-dollar bills fell out, which concerned me.

Aquila, what did you do?

When I ran to the bedroom door and opened it slightly, there was another room—a living room with a bar and sliding glass windows that opened up to a private deck with an immaculate view of the ocean. Good. I was still on the boat. I quickly closed the door, locked it, and ran back to my cell phone, which I spotted on the nightstand, and dialed Roman. I heard the faint buzz of a cell phone in the living room and hung up.

Is this his room?

"Oh, Aquila, what did you do?"

Suddenly, a queasy feeling overcame me, and I rushed into the bathroom and faceplanted into the porcelain god. After my body was done rejecting and ejecting everything I'd placed in it from last night, I stood and washed my hands in the sink. That's when I noticed a corded bead bracelet on my wrist. *Where the heck did this come from?*

After I rinsed my mouth and then washed and dried my face with paper towels, I peered into the mirror and nearly died a slow death at my appearance. It seemed like I'd been in a fight with Laila Ali and her daddy. Now that my faculties were returning and I realized this had to be Roman's suite, I knew that I'd partied entirely too hard with Roman last night. I couldn't believe that I'd gotten college white girl wasted in a foreign country with him, as if I weren't a fully grown woman with two kids at home. He probably thought I was as wild and loose as the women he dated or used to date or whatever. Just an embarrassment. The only thing I knew for certain was that we didn't have sex. My walls still felt locked up tighter than Fort Knox and drier than the Sahara. Though I desired Roman, at least I wasn't wild, loose, and a whole heaux. I could at least recover from the drunken night with some semblance of dignity. I finished in the bathroom, grabbed my phone, and prepared to apologize and do the proverbial walk of shame back to my own room.

When I opened the door, I found Roman sitting up on the sofa, shirtless, in a pair of joggers. His elbows were propped on his knees with his cell phone in his hand. When he turned his head to face me coming out of the bedroom, I halted my steps. Our appearances matched. He looked as if his night was just as rough as mine. We stared at each other for a few seconds until suddenly, he began a slow laugh that spread to me, and before long, we were doubled over. I ran to the sofa and hit him with a throw pillow.

"Don't laugh. It isn't funny," I whined, plopping down beside him.

He rested his hand on my knee. "We both look and feel like crap. That's a sign of an epic time that was had."

Leaning forward, I massaged my temples. "Don't remind me. I'm already embarrassed enough."

"Why are you embarrassed? We are grown and had a good time. Truth be told, it was good to see you in your most uninhibited element. You were fun and carefree."

"You mean wild and loose."

Roman took my hands into his and turned me to face him. *"Fun and carefree."* He swept my braids from my face and brushed my cheek with his thumb. "That is the Aquila I've been trying to tap into since we made the pact. We all know that you are responsible, dependable, consistent…all the qualities that make you a mature human. But it's okay to put that hat down and be free when you can. You have the rest of your life to be on your grown woman shit. But for your 'me' time, do you. That's equally as important to reset and balance the scales."

There's no way he could realize how impactful those words were to me. I'd spent most of my adult life being Joel's wife and Junior and Sante's mom, and all of my life being the eldest sister and the oldest child, that I'd forgotten how to simply be Aquila—to have fun and enjoy being who I am. Roman's reminder soothed my spirit, and unexpectedly, my carefree night of fun didn't feel so damning.

Squeezing his hand, I nodded. "Thank you. I needed that."

We lingered at that moment for a second before he bent his lips to my forehead and gently kissed it. "You're welcome."

"So, since you enjoyed this version of Aquila, can you fill me in on that version from last night?"

"Wait. You don't remember anything?"

"*Umm,* I remember dinner and the hip-hop club, but everything after that is a blur or non-existent."

"Honestly, some parts of last night are a blur to me, too." He stood and stretched. "Let me make us some coffee and try to catch up on last night's festivities."

I lay across the sofa, propped up on a pillow, and placed another in my lap as he headed toward his bar station to make the cups of Joe. "*Ooh,* I like my coffee—"

"Black with two packs of sugar," he finished, tossing a glance with a curt smile over his shoulder at me. "I remember how you make your coffee when you come to the gym."

"*Wow.* You remember my coffee preference?"

I could see his body visibly steel before he cleared his throat. "Yeah. I mean, when you're a regular gym member who makes coffee before every workout, it tends to stick."

"Good point," I agreed as I took in my surroundings.

This two-room suite made my quarters look like a shack. The modernistic furniture was highlighted with sea-inspired accents. This room carried a sports theme and showcased portraits of Black swimmers, divers, surfers, and the first all-black rowing team. The kitchen island top was a surfboard, the couch throw pillows were images of the different cruise liners of Skye Voyages, and the base of the coffee table was made of seashells. A fisherman's net with decorative sea crustaceans in it hung above the mounted television. The outside deck was an all-white wraparound sofa with a hot tub in the center. This suite was an immaculate array of the sea meets Black water sports culture. "This is the MegaSweeties suite, right?"

"*Uh*, yeah," he answered, bringing over our freshly brewed mugs of coffee and some ibuprofen and returning to his seat beside me.

"Sir, you must've really planned to party with a few chicks on this boat. I saw the cost of these rooms and immediately went to the lower tiers."

"*Nah*. I'm a big guy. I like to be comfortable wherever I lay my head." While that tidbit of information may have been true, I still gave him the side-eye because I knew him well enough to know a larger bedroom could've sufficed, not an entire suite. "And I initially planned on having fun with a few chicks," he admitted jokingly.

"*Mm-hmm.*" I joined him. Placing my mug down after taking a sip, I put my hand up. "Now, don't let me stop you."

Although I was joking, he didn't find the humor in my off-color comment. He stared at me with the most serious expression I'd ever seen on his face. "My plans changed, and you are the only person I want to spend my time with on this trip."

A tickle formed in my throat that I couldn't clear, and I picked up my mug to sip on more coffee because this man had me all in my imaginary feels. Over the past few days, we'd made a few flirtatious remarks, but it always seemed all in fun from his end. This morning, it felt genuine and heartfelt. That led me to realize I needed to find out what happened last night.

When I finally regained my composure, I ventured into the dire portion of the conversation, although I was fearful of what I might learn. "So, about last night—"

He set his coffee mug on the table and rubbed his hands down his head. "Certain parts are still fuzzy to me, but I do remember some. I know for a fact you were way more wasted than me by the time we hit the second club."

I sat straight up. "Second club?"

Roman's eyes grew in astonishment. "Wait. So, you don't remember dragging me into the country club, Neon Skye?" Shame cast over me as I shook my head. "Okay, so our night started with dinner, then we left because I reserved a booth in the Lit Skye hip-hop club. You had some SkyeRitas. I thought it was two, but hell, it may have been more. I was getting toasted on Dussé. But I saw that you seemed uncomfortable, so I convinced you to leave. When we left, we talked for a bit about our music tastes before we ran into the Neon Skye club. You dragged me in there. That's where the lines start blurring for me. My memories are coming in waves. I remember more drinks and a mechanical bull. I think you won some money. I'm not sure."

He paused, trying to make heads or tails of his thoughts, but that's when a flash of the money I'd taken out of my bra came back to me. *Oh, dear god. Please tell me I didn't do anything too out of character to get that money.*

"After that, I'm not sure. I remember cool air and palm trees, then carrying you to the bed in my room and crashing on the sofa. That's it."

I was about to speak when I noticed the same corded bead bracelet on his wrist as mine. I outstretched my arm so that our wrists fell beside each other. "Any idea where we got these from?"

Roman scratched his temple in deep contemplation. "I think a street vendor."

"That would explain the cool air and palm trees." I pressed my hands against my face. "I apologize for getting drunk and forcing you to take care of me."

"Woman, that's the best time we've had. You never have to apologize to me for that. Besides, I like taking care of you. Nothing was forced on me or you, just so we're clear."

Inadvertently, I placed my hand in his. "The last thing I'd worry about is you doing something ill-intended to me. I trust you."

Instead of moving his hand, he interlaced his fingers with mine, and my breathing hitched. For moments, I couldn't remove my fixed gaze from our interlocked hands. My heart pounded uncontrollably, causing me to take deliberately slow breaths, and the light churning in my belly let me know that these feelings I'd developed for Roman came from a real place and not just lust, but also that they were being reciprocated by him for me. I'd been able to ignore it before, shooting the idea down as overactive hormones, but the poignant emotions radiating between us felt blissful and wondrous. Worthy of exploration. It felt like that moment when you knew that person was *your* person—like fated destiny. My mind tried to convince me to question why Roman, but my heart begged to differ. Why *not* Roman?

My lowered lids lifted to find his stare intently fixed on me as if he were waiting for me to catch up with him. Swallowing softly, he used his other hand to turn my chin so we could face each other. He dipped his head, bringing his lips near mine, and we hovered there.

"I want to kiss you so bad," he purred, his ticklish breath wisping against my mouth.

I offered him the same serious expression, and my next words were barely audible. "What are you waiting for?"

His lips descended onto mine, landing softly as if to test the reality of what was transpiring. The first was a simple peck, but when I leaned into him, he ignited and savored on my lips. Energy I'd never felt before coursed through my body like electric currents charging places that hadn't been awakened in years. Our mouths meshed, and our tongues tangled together in a coordinated tempo that spoke more volumes than we could ever verbally express. An image flickered in my mind. At first, I thought I was daydreaming, but I quickly recalled that it was a memory. We'd kissed before…last night. When Roman finally lifted to give us the air we so desperately needed, he offered three soft, supple pecks to my bruised lips and doubled back for one more before he eased back. I'm not ashamed to admit that I tucked my bottom lip inside my mouth to catch the lingering remnants of his taste.

Turning sideways on the sofa and propping up against my elbow, he did the same as we sat with our fingers toying together and never breaking contact. We were mentally communicating and exchanging nonverbal thoughts.

Surprising myself, I conceded. "Can I say I've wanted to do that for a few days?"

His mouth curled into a beaming smile. "As long as I can confess, I've wanted to do the same. But I also must confess that this is our second kiss."

"You remembered the first one, too?"

"As we were kissing." The admission flowed out together.

Giddiness spread through my being. Just sitting there with him brought me such joy and serenity. We could do everything under the sun or nothing at all, and I would be content to be in his space. I'd heard others speak of this feeling, but I'd never experienced it for myself—until now with Roman. What spoke to my heart was that he seemed to appreciate this time just the same.

After a while, I leaned my head on the sofa and asked, "So what do we do now?"

He scanned my face and brought his hand to my cheek, caressing my face with his thumb, a move I was quickly coming to love. Fully embracing it, my cheeks warmed to his touch, causing his orbs to shine brightly.

"Continue having fun and enjoying our vacation. While doing so, let's explore this—at our pace." He leaned forward, hovering in front of my face. "Apparently, we're now in Bimini, Bahamas. What would you like to do today?"

Following his lead, I leaned closer to his face so that our breaths brushed against each other. "A lazy day at the beach."

He stood and held out his hand for me. I accepted it and stood. "Whatever the lady wants, the lady gets."

"I'll go to my room, shower, and change. Meet me in a couple of hours?" He nodded and walked toward the door. "But first, let me grab my winnings. I don't know what I did to earn it, but I will put that windfall to use."

I was ready to see what Day 4 of 7 had to offer.

Chapter Fifteen

ROMAN

$\mathcal{E}$VERYTHING ABOUT TODAY felt perfect. The weather was perfect. The water was perfect. My company was perfect. Since I'd picked up Aquila a couple of hours ago, we'd been stretched out on our rented loungers in a partially secluded area on the beach, basking in the fresh ocean air and sipping drinks. I'd wanted a beer, but leave it to Aquila to have me drinking a fruity drink out of a pineapple with an umbrella. Like I'd said earlier, anything the lady wanted, the lady got, even if that meant me indulging in a very feminine beverage.

She'd gone to buy some sunscreen while I continued to relax. When I looked toward the gift shop, I saw her strolling out, walking toward me, appearing as if she was working the runway instead of vacationing. As much as I loved the bathing suit she'd worn when we went snorkeling, the bikini she donned today was my favorite. She'd be sexy in a paper sack, but the way the fuchsia color blended with her sun-kissed complexion and the two-piece melded on her bodacious body oozed sensuality. Her stride caused her hips to sway with a level of confidence that I hadn't seen from her in a while. Her modelesque features were highlighted behind her oversized shades, floppy sunhat, and braids. My bohemian goddess. Still, the brightest and sexiest part she wore was her smile. It radiated with the beam of a thousand rays, and it was aimed directly at me, piercing me right in the chest. Rather than question how something so fresh could feel so right this quickly, I chose a different route. I chose to embrace the feeling. I'd been running around claiming I wanted something of substance, and I had substance, sex appeal, and smarts wrapped up in one woman who was headed in my direction.

"Hey, you," Aquila cooed, handing me the bottle of sunscreen and causing me to cheese widely like a tickled toddler.

Yes. Aquila has entered the chat.

Retrieving the sunscreen from her hand, I opened my legs, motioning for her to sit between them. She slipped off her sarong and sat down. When she swiped her braids to the side, I squeezed a generous amount of lotion into my hands and began kneading it into her back, starting from the nape of her neck down her shoulders and arms to the remainder of her back. My hands over her smooth skin were nearly too much to handle. All of the sensations were sending sparks to the epicenter of my thighs, so much so that it ached.

"Thank you," she uttered once I'd finished. "Do you need me to do you?"

In more ways than one. The thought crossed my mind. "Sure."

Her hands on my back felt divine. My head fell back as she applied sunscreen and massaged my muscles. Forget the spa with her blessed hands. My body was totally confused about what it should be feeling. Either way, it felt remarkable. When she finished, she had to pat me to let me know she was done. My mind was so far out of the zone that I was nearly lulled to sleep.

Standing with a stretch, I couldn't help but heap praise on her. "I think you missed your calling."

A smile danced on her lips as she held up her hands and wiggled her fingers. "Just good with my hands."

My eyelids closed as a groan escaped that I couldn't cease before it left. I reached out my hand to hers. "On that note, let's dip in the water."

She took my hand to stand, but to my surprise and appreciation, she never let go of it as we casually walked to the shoreline and entered the ocean. The crystal-blue water was warm yet refreshing. Once it covered us about the waist, we stopped, and I wasted no time pulling her into my arms. She pressed against my chest and rested her arms around my neck.

"I can't let the day continue without thanking you."

I reared back, grateful but genuinely surprised by her gratitude. "For what?"

"For not judging me as the Aquila you already knew and the drunk Aquila from last night." We tittered before she continued. "Seriously, for showing me the importance and joy in being me. I've never felt so carefree in my life, and without you, I know I wouldn't have done that. Your efforts forced me to tap into a different side of me, one that I've denied for far too long. I appreciate you for seeing me."

Her sentiments had me ready to plant another one of those earth-shattering kisses on her when she asked me a question that threw me completely off-kilter.

"What happened between you and Nia?"

Of all the times to bring up Nia, this *would* be the time. I could expect nothing less from Aquila and all her frankness. Although I knew we'd have to cross that highway at some point, I hadn't expected it to be right now. I'm sure it plagued her, and perhaps before she could fully come to terms with what was transpiring between us, she needed that bit of peace of mind, and I'd grant that wish for her if that meant we could resume this new path we were on. Hence, this was the ultimate reason I never felt comfortable approaching Aquila after her divorce.

Nia—the woman in question—was her sister, Angela's best friend, whom I'd slept with a few times. I couldn't call it dating because we'd never gone out or truly gotten to know each other beyond what we already knew from hanging out in our friend group. Nia wasn't a bad woman and would probably make some man a great wife when she decided to settle down, but I hadn't been interested in her. All I wanted was sex, so when Nia and I pursued something more than friendship, we both agreed to settle on fuckship. Plain and simple. Since then, I have desired something more with the right woman. While I didn't think marriage was in my cards, slowly, I began to wind down and decided that, at most, a steady companion would suffice. With the recent failed attempts, I was convinced that I would be stuck in sex-only situations.

And then Aquila Richards entered the chat.

"Nia and I were never a real thing. Please don't take this the wrong way because Nia is a good woman, and we're cool, but outside of sex, there was nothing more between us. We just weren't meant for each other, if that makes sense."

Her eyebrow quirked, indicating that she wasn't satisfied with that answer. "So, there was absolutely nothing? That seems a tad far-fetched." She removed her arms and placed her hands on my chest, distancing us. "And I must ask because she's my sister's bestie. I need you to be honest about where you all stand."

Whereas other men may have gotten upset at this, I admired it. Aquila stood on business, which I appreciated, but so did I. Being straightforward was in my DNA, so I had no problem confirming that I wasn't interested in Nia, nor was I out here trying to run through our circle of friends.

"I understand that. When I stopped communicating with Nia, it wasn't because we had a falling out. This will sound downright doggish, but I stopped communicating with her because I was bored. We agreed to have a sexual situation only—hook up whenever we wanted to release tension. I maintained that I'd like to be the initiator, and she agreed. So, once I had my fill, I stopped initiating the hookups."

"You're right. It does sound doggish," she scoffed, adding a mean side-eye.

Grasping her hands, I held her in place. "But have I ever lied about that? I've always been open about my situation and my stance. I didn't lie to myself about what it was between us; more importantly, I never lied to her. She knew and *agreed* to what it was from the beginning." Moving my hands to her waist, I dipped my head so that she could see the sincerity of my next words. "We're not supposed to attach ourselves permanently with everyone that enters our life, and I think the world would be better if people understood that and stopped trying to force what isn't meant to be. Learn to accept the seasonal people for who they are—temporary."

Aquila's breathing seemed to cease as she grew still beneath me and fell into a distant stare. After a few seconds of calling her name, she blinked and returned to me from wherever she'd gone inside her head.

"I'm sorry." She cleared her throat. "I found myself pondering over your assessment. And although your way of dealing with women seems a bit crude, I guess it's better than being a liar and a cheater."

In hindsight, I understood how she perceived it that way, but it wasn't. That much I wanted to clarify. "Honestly, that comes down to the difference between men and women. You all are naturally nurturing, so you feel everything. I think many of your personal relationships are developed from the heart. Men, we are led by our minds. Not saying you all don't think, but I believe our approach begins with that, and eventually, we consider our heart.

These born and bred instincts are fostered as we grow. Even in today's society, most women are raised to consider being a wife and having a family a top priority, regardless of whether they're taught to be independent bosses. Most men are taught to be the boss and then pursue a marriage and family if that's what they want. Those variations give us different mindsets and skew our perceptions."

Aquila didn't readily react, but I loved that about her. She considered a thing before giving her opinion or feedback. In a time when people were quick to hear and speak rather than listen and comprehend, it was invigorating to see her truly contemplate what I'd said. That alone made me feel both seen and heard; she had no clue how much that meant to me.

She inched nearer to me. "You present a compelling argument, and I must concur. I've never had any brothers, but when I think about my dad and how he operates, it closely aligns with what you're saying." Feeling more secure with what I'd divulged, she wrapped her arms around me again. "And thank you for being upfront about your situation with Nia and giving me the scoop on how you men process. Your blunt truthfulness is rare and attractive, Dr. Patterson."

A moan slipped through my lips, and my jaw clenched, trying to bite back the sexual energy she'd just conjured. Instead of allowing the moment to pass, she pressed on, igniting the flames.

Squeezing her arms tighter around me made her body flush with mine. No room was between us, so we could feel the heat penetrating our connected space. And not just the heat from the sun. "Tell me your thoughts, Dr. Patterson." Her breath tickled my face.

Licking my lips, a sly smirk formed. "Can I be frank?"

"As you always are."

My stare penetrated hers. "I want you." My confession caused her eyes to flutter, and her knees slightly buckled. "Can

I taste you?" I asked, descending my lips against hers. The flavor of our earlier Belgian waffles and mixed drinks lingered on our tongues. "Can I have you?"

She gasped and held my shoulders when I slipped my hand inside her bikini bottom, and my middle finger strummed her love button. The ocean water made the destination smoother, but when I eased the same finger inside her silky folds, I realized she didn't require any assistance from Mother Nature.

"Damn. You're already wet for me." I growled my pleasure against her ear.

"Ro...Roman." My name released from her lips with a stutter.

"Nah, Qui, go back to Dr. Patterson. I love that shit."

A moan slipped out, and by now, I was two fingers deep as she nearly climbed me as if she were scaling a mountain. I knew the stimulation was probably too much to bear, but it also felt too good to stop. Her folds heated around my digits, but her insides were tight, gripping my fingers with a sealed suction—a clear indicator that she hadn't been pleased in a long time.

"I...I love it," she panted. "When...oh gawd...when you call me *Qui*." She stretched out her name, barely able to contain herself.

"*Mmm*. Like this, baby?" My scorching gaze invaded the depths of her soul. "*Qui*," I ground out from the pit of my belly.

"Oh gawwwddd," she creaked out, her head falling forward into my chest. Her hips desperately caught a rhythm as she rode my fingers at a frenzied pace. "Yes, yesss."

By now, the waves were rocking us back and forth, and my legs were becoming unstable. I didn't want to risk hurting us, so I knew I had to put a halt to this. Besides, I didn't want her to finish by my hand. That was the pregame setup. We still had a championship to play.

"Can I make you come?"

"*Yesss!*" she hissed, almost screaming the word to the heavens.

Slowly, I removed my fingers from her warmth, but not without protest.

"No, no, nooo," she whined, upset about the loss of my touch.

"I know, baby. I want our first time to be where you can savor every ounce that I'm going to pour into you. Let's head up to the room."

We'd decided that we would finally take advantage of an overnight excursion at the host resort hotel in Bimini, so when we exited the ship this morning, we checked in for one night at Bimini Blue Resort and Hotel. Before we ventured to the beach, we stopped, and I reserved their luxury presidential suite, complete with our private soaking tub, a dual stand-in shower with multiple showerheads, a private hot tub, a full bar, and an extra-large king-sized bedroom.

By the time we got to our room door, we couldn't keep our hands off each other. The teasing kisses and not-so-subtle caresses had hit a fever pitch when I tried to retrieve the key card. We moved down the hall awkwardly as I backed her toward the room, and we continued capturing each other's savory kisses. Air supply be damned.

"Hold on, baby." I struggled to talk between kisses. "I gotta grab the key."

She giggled against my mouth. "So, grab it."

The issue was that our hands and mouths were everywhere. As I went to reach inside my pocket, I felt her suckle on my neck and pulled her close. I didn't even know I had a sensitive spot until she discovered it.

"*Mmm,* Qui," I panted, holding her tight. "Give me a sec."

When I placed her behind me, she eased her soft hands around my midsection and began planting sugary kisses up my back. Another damn spot. This woman was going to mess around and go back to the States with a belly full of my baby because, at this point, I didn't give a damn if I buried myself raw inside of her. Once I fished the key card out, I lifted her with one arm and spun her in front of me, pressing her back flush against the door and clasping both of her arms above her head by her wrists with my free hand.

Our noses circled each other as our breathing grew ragged. "I'm gonna fuck the shit out of you, woman. Do you know that?" I uttered before my lips crashed into hers.

"Do it, *Dr. Patterson,*" she panted, her chest heaving once I released her mouth.

That'll do it. I scanned the card, and it beeped but didn't open. Aquila didn't make it easier as she began kissing down my chest, her hands massaging my abs. I scanned it again, and nothing happened. If this door didn't open, I'd satisfy our urges in this hallway. Snatching the card out of my hand, she spun around and scanned it, then punched the code that I'd forgotten, accompanied by the entry. When we heard the door unlock and saw the green button flash, I pushed the door open, and before she could react, I picked her up and tossed her over my shoulder, heading straight to the bathroom so we could wash the remaining sand away.

"Roman," she squealed in laughter as I carried her effortlessly.

Using one arm to balance her on my shoulder, I used the free hand to open the shower door and turn on the water, activating the multiple shower heads. Then I placed her on her feet. No sooner than she was steady, I wasted no time reaching behind her and unfastening her bikini top. It fell into her hands as she tried to cover up her breasts.

Gently, I pulled her hands down, allowing the top to fall to the floor and expose her perfectly round breasts with chocolate areolas and gumdrop nipples. I could already tell they would be my favorite.

"Nah, baby, don't hide anything from me. I want it all." I bit my lip as I captured her face between my hands. "This is a safe space."

Those words boosted her confidence, and she stood back and peeled down her bikini bottom, allowing it to slide down her thighs and legs before she stepped out and discarded it to the side. *Jesus Christ.* I hadn't ever seen a sexier woman. Aquila was slim-thick, and though I could clearly see the results of her constant exercise regimen, there was evidence that she'd brought life into this world. From the small scar with the slight FUPA to the beautiful array of small stretch marks over her hips, it created a beautiful masterpiece of a grown woman. That in itself made me adore her that much more. I was in awe that she could do something I wasn't physically capable of doing and still look fucking amazing.

Seduction invaded my eyes as I squinted and bit my lip. "Your body should be revered. Damn, Qui. Just sexy."

I could almost see the gratitude swell in her chest as a blush brightened her face and exploded into her beautiful brown orbs.

"May I?" she asked, placing her hands on the waistband of my swim trunks.

"Do with me what you will, baby."

Her eyebrow quirked at that, and a sinful glint lit up her face. She slid her hands inside my waistband and began to slide my trunks down, wrapping her hands around me, and grabbing and rubbing my butt before continuing down my powerful thighs. I loved that on the way down, she stopped and admired my body. Every cut and muscle seemed to turn her on in the best way. When my dick sprang forth, she swallowed long and hard. And this was only at half salute.

Cupping her chin with my hand, I lifted her face. "Don't be scared."

"It's just so thick and pretty."

A smirk crossed my face. I'd never had my man described as pretty, or at least not to my face, and it made me blush to hear it. She stood, and we took a moment to take each other in. I wanted to commit her physique to memory. The sound of the water cascading and pulsing against the shower door broke my concentration. I opened the door and allowed her to step inside, and I followed. As soon as we stepped in, the warm water sent soothing sensations all over our bodies as it washed the sand down the drain. Picking up her mesh loofa, I drizzled some body wash over it and on her back. Swirling the loofa over her back, I washed down her body as her pleasurable moans made music to my ears. When she turned to face me, the sight of the water and suds sliding down her figure almost made me bust one right then, as if I were an unseasoned teenage boy. I drizzled the body wash over her chest and began the washing process again.

As the water rinsed the soap away, I couldn't help but drop the loofa and cup her breasts in my hands, massaging them as I toyed with her plump nipples. *I knew they were the perfect fit.* Aquila's head fell back, resting against the shower wall as she used the soap in her hands to massage my shaft.

"*Ahh*, Qui," I moaned, loving the feel of her hands all over my length and balls as she had her way with me.

She wasn't playing fair as I continued to grow with anticipation. So, I didn't either. I dropped my mouth to her left breast and captured the nipple in my mouth. Her hands immediately released and gripped the back of my head. Just as I'd figured, they were my favorite.

"*Ro…Ro…man.*" The way she uttered my name made my heart and my dick gallop.

I took my time devouring and fondling each one as her moans grew louder and louder. When I finally lifted, she was dazed and heaving as if overloaded with feel-good bliss. Bending to my knees, I hoisted her legs on my shoulders and inhaled her sweet scent.

"Amen." I blessed my meal before I began to partake.

My tongue was long and thick, just like my dick, and I darted it in and out of her succulence. It tasted like a cold, tall glass of lemonade on a sizzling summer day in August. Quenching. Delicious. Revitalizing. I'd never feasted on a woman more appealing to my palate. The more I consumed her pussy, the wetter it became, and the more my tongue watered for her. I licked and sucked and slurped on her endless faucet as she heaved and panted uncontrollably.

"*Aghhh*, right there. Right fucking there. I'm gonna cum."

When I peered up, her entire back was arched off the wall. She used her hands to brace herself against me as she rocked into my mouth, chasing her release. I flicked my tongue fluidly over her bud and then sucked it, and that initiated the countdown. Three…two…one…liftoff.

"*Roman!*" she wailed, with her thighs locking my neck in a vice grip and her toes bending like Beckham.

"Mmm," I growled, enjoying my feast. "Good shit."

When she hit her crescendo, she tried to move away from me, but she forgot that I couldn't have dinner without dessert. I gripped her ass in the palms of my hands and kept her right there.

"*Babyyy*, I can't. I can't take—"

She never finished that statement. Her words became a jumbled and garbled mess of broken cadences. Her sweet nectar had filled my mouth, but I wouldn't be content until I received the downpour. I kept inflicting pleasure while she damn near tried to push my head off my neck. But I was relentless. Soon, her build-up came, and without warning, a sticky shower glazed all over my mouth, chin, and beard, and a roar ripped through Aquila as if she'd just discovered what an orgasm truly was.

"Dr. Motherfucking Pat...ter...son!"

As soon as my name rolled off her tongue, she slumped, and I had to catch her. I lifted her in my arms as if I were rocking a baby, as she begged me to put her down and not to touch her as her body succumbed to mini convulsions.

Stepping out of the shower, I placed her on the bench and retrieved a towel. When I turned to dry her off, she was curled up in the fetal position with her head resting on the wall. It was the cutest scene ever and turned me on even more. Her eyes grew wide as I kneeled to towel dry her skin.

"Don't you look at me like that. I'll probably still be quaking when we arrive back in Florida." She fanned her hands. "I don't think I can handle any more."

I chuckled with a nod. "It's whatever you want to do. I told you anything you want, it's yours. This is all about you."

When I stood to towel myself, my man below clearly wasn't taking the memo that my mind and mouth had just agreed to. He jutted outwardly, primed to chop through logs; I was so stiff and ready. But I'd ride the wave for Aquila. As I toweled dry, I heard soft sounds emitting from Aquila and saw that she'd fallen asleep on the bench. The sight was one to behold. Peacefulness cloaked her angelic frame.

I lifted her into my arms, and she didn't move a muscle. Carrying her into the bedroom, I laid her on the bed and searched through our bag until I found one of my T-shirts. I didn't want to disturb her slumber by trying to fiddle with the lingerie sets she'd brought. They were nice, but I preferred seeing her wrapped in my clothing. To me, that was far sexier. I slipped on the oversized shirt and tucked her under the comforter. Then, I slipped into a pair of sleepwear loungers and crawled into bed beside her. Inadvertently, she snuggled against me, and I wrapped my arm around her, securing her next to me.

Are you sure about this, Patterson? I questioned myself as I lightly brushed her forehead with my lips. But as I tried to talk myself off this ledge, I realized I'd already dived off the deep end. I desired a companion, but with Aquila, I wanted…more. And I wouldn't hide that. I only prayed that she also wanted more with me.

Chapter Sixteen

AQUILA

IF DAY 4 OF 7 was the appetizer, then Day 5 of 7 was the entire seven-course meal, I typed into my journal app as we sat on the rented yacht, cruising and enjoying the scenic sights and the ocean breeze.

We were still in Bimini, Bahamas, but rather than plan an excursion, we opted for a relaxing private sightseeing tour. It was late afternoon, and the weather was perfect for the outing. I finished up my journal entry and then glanced out at the pristine blue water, admiring it as the cool ocean spray misted my skin. This trip had been nothing short of paradise. The atmosphere, culture, foods, and vibrations had been renewing my spirit, but mostly, this feeling was in part due to a certain man who had taken me by complete surprise and was slowly sweeping me off my feet. Hell, let me be honest. I was already swept, even though I wasn't ready to admit that to him or myself. My mind was still blown away that out of all the people in the world, I'd connected with Roman. Although he had changed regarding intimate relationships, I never would have guessed that *we* would be intimately involved after all of these years of knowing each other. We'd never been attracted to each other, so it was nearly unbelievable. *I* wouldn't believe it if it weren't me in the situation. Life was curious in that way. All this time, this man had been my friend and one of my workout coaches, who knew he'd also become the man who helped me rediscover myself after a tumultuous marriage, and the one who was steadily making me want to claim him as my own?

Through my oversized blacked-out shades, I admired Roman as he gabbed it up with the captain. Besides the fact that he looked scrumptious, he seemed in his element, standing with his hands in his shorts pockets, commanding attention like the boss that he was. Here I was surrounded by God's exquisite natural formations, and all I could focus on was His original creation—the Adam who was currently setting my Eve ablaze. My thoughts drifted back to yesterday and this morning. I didn't know how I'd be able to get off this cruise and return to real life. So lost was I in reminiscing that I didn't notice when Roman plopped down beside me.

"What's going on in that pretty head of yours?" Roman asked, catching me off guard when he pulled me into him and kissed my temple.

Shaking away the haze, I beamed, "Nothing. Just admiring the view."

He scanned my body and nodded. "Yeah, me, too."

When I playfully pushed his chest, he grabbed my wrist and yanked me into his lap. "Crazy man." I let out a giggle-yelp, wrapping my arms around him.

"Nah. Just crazy about you."

Both of us paused at his declaration. Sure, we'd shared some kinky banter, but that statement felt like my earlier thought about him sweeping me off my feet. What was really happening between us? This was supposed to be a feel-good, fun time. Undoubtedly, it was starting to feel like more—to both of us.

"I have a day planned for you when we get back." His sudden detour indicated that he couldn't have possibly meant that in the intimate way that it sounded. Rather than press the issue and make him uncomfortable, I ventured into a discussion about this surprise.

"What do you mean you have a day planned for me?"

"I figured after these past couple of days, you needed a bit of pampering as well, so I planned a massage, a facial, and a mani-pedi when we return. Afterward, we'll have dinner on the beach before we board the ship." When I parted my lips, he held a forefinger to them. "And I know I didn't have to do it. I wanted to do this for you, just as you wanted to gift me a massage. Let me do my thing, woman."

I lifted my hands in surrender. "Do your thing. Besides…" I rolled my neck around to stretch it out. "I have a few muscles that do need to be worked out."

"I wonder why," he teased.

My lips pursed at his feigned innocence. "Oh, you know exactly why, sir."

He turned a dreamy-eyed stare off into the distance. "*Ahh. What a time to be alive.*"

"Shut up!"

We both howled, and I smacked his shoulder at his antics.

"But you liked it, though." He nipped at the sensitive spot on my neck, causing me to curl up in his arms. "Hell, we both did."

Flashes of this morning floated through my mind as I rested in his arms. Having two children was evidence that I'd had sex before. What wasn't evident or even truthful was that I'd had mind-blowing, back-breaking sex. That's what happened this morning courtesy of King Roman when Day 5 of 7 terminated my three-year drought.

After our romp in the shower, we slept until dinnertime. Opting for room service instead of going out, we sat up in bed eating, joking, and watching television as if this were our daily routine as a couple. To get rest, we showered separately, and by the time he eased into the bed again, I was lights out. It had been years—if ever—since I'd been thoroughly pleasured, so my body was beyond depleted.

However, in the wee hours of the morning, I woke up feeling revived and aroused. It dawned on me that I had been selfish. Roman had poured all of that superb oral satisfaction on me, and he hadn't received any reciprocation. Sure, he agreed to forego his pleasure to appease me, but that seemed like a cruel punishment in hindsight. He had urges just as I had. He deserved to have them fulfilled, so I was determined to fulfill them.

Peeking over at Roman, he was just as gorgeous sleeping peacefully as when he was wide awake. How could a man be so fine even in his resting state? If he ever bragged that he woke up like this, he would not have told one single lie. Slipping under the comforter, I eased his mushroom head out of his boxer briefs. Even at half-mast, it was thick, juicy, and beautiful. This man had the prettiest penis I'd ever laid eyes on. Slightly darker than his caramel complexion, veins protruded all over it like art sketches into a slightly curved angle, and it was surrounded by one large sack holding two perfectly round balls. Seeing his massive manhood and bulbous beauties caused my mouth to water in anticipation. I lowered my head and slowly worked him awake while cradling his sack in my hand. He twisted and groaned for a few seconds before I felt a tug on my braids.

"Ooh shhiii." *The sound grunted out through clenched teeth.*

He opened his eyes, and all he could see was me lying between his legs, swirling my tongue around his thick tip before making it disappear in my mouth.

"Aquila." My name came out strained as he loosened his grip on my hair, trying not to pump inside my mouth.

Suddenly, I popped it out of my mouth. "Nah. Go back to Qui. I love that shit." I mimicked his earlier thoughts before descending back again.

His fingers found my braids again and clutched them tightly as he fought to restrain the inner beast that he wanted to unleash on me. When I attempted to go lower, I gagged a bit, and he expanded even more. His mass was so lengthy, firm, and expansive that I could barely contain the half of it that I had been able to handle as I came up for air.

"Quiii. You gotta get up." His hoarse voice pleaded with me, but instead, I attempted to swallow it again, and he clasped my chin. "Not like this. Not this time. I need to be buried inside you. Now."

I sat up with disappointment dancing in my eyes, but obeyed his request. He twirled his finger, motioning for me to turn around. He sat up against the headboard as I straddled him in reverse cowgirl. He leaned my back forward, and my head fell between his legs. Looking over my shoulder at him, I could see his heated, lustful stare on my body. His huge hands caressed my cheeks before he delivered a thunderous smack to each of them, causing them to jiggle. I yelped at his touch and held my breath in excited anticipation. He continued his tantalizing love taps, and my pussy heated with each one. When he swiped his finger between my folds and sucked the juice off it, my belly quivered. The flicker inside me went from a match to a five-alarm blaze. We'd both be in trouble today.

"Lie on your back." The simple command came out filled with lustful tension.

He rose from the bed, sliding his boxer briefs down his powerful thighs with his focus still intent on me, and I did as he said, spreading my legs to give him a full view of what was to come. I was trying to put on my big girl pants for this experience, but I could tell he could still see the timidness on my face. He bent down in the overnight bag we'd packed and slipped out a couple of condoms. Tossing one on the nightstand, he sheathed himself with the other before climbing onto the bed.

Our mouths found each other again before he pulled back and asked, "Are you sure?"

Exhaling, I brought a hand to his face. "I love how you always check on me first." My countenance faltered at my following words. "I want this. It's just been three years. Be gentle, please."

At this point, I was basically a born-again virgin. Three years. That tidbit of news seemed to excite him and take him off guard, judging by how his face contorted between shock and amusement. Both expressions were mixed with a touch of concern. For that reason alone, I wanted to ensure he was comfortable with this newfound information.

"Do you still want me?" The words flowed more timorously than intended.

His face softened, and he bent down and pressed his lips ever so sweetly against mine.

"Absolutely. Don't ever doubt that for a second." With an exhale, he began to explain. "Your revelation jarred me for a second. My first thought was that it would make this experience beyond pleasurable for both of us. Then, I thought, you've been celibate for years, which means this moment is intentional. That thought also makes me nervous. After a divorce and years without intimacy, you chose me. Damn."

At his words, any doubts, fears, or hesitation that threatened to withhold me from this moment were released into the atmosphere as my heart melted. "And I'd choose you again and again."

He gently kissed my forehead and purred, "Slow and steady."

I visibly relaxed as he began his entry into heaven. As soon as he penetrated me, I knew there was no one else that I could allow here. As he crept inch by painstaking inch inside my oasis, I knew without him confirming that he felt the same when he had to stop and relish the feel of me surrounding him. Our breathing stilled and released simultaneously, and then he slowly went to work on eradicating my thirty-six-month drought.

Slowly, he curled his body into my tightness. He eased up a few times, but it wasn't necessary. It may have been three years, but my body opened up to him as if it had only been three days. When he started moving freely, he dove even deeper into my depths, and I was lost at sea, never to return. My grunts and wails were evidence of that.

"Qui, baby. I know I said slow and steady—"

Knowing precisely what we both desired, I gripped his shoulders and leveled him with the words he desperately wanted to hear: "Go harder."

Access granted. That was all he needed. He hoisted my legs, and they fell into the crook of his arms as he pistoned in and out of my sweet spot in a combination of fast and slow grinds. This was exactly what I'd been missing in my life. This. Right. Here. My sugary secretions covered him in a messy delight.

"Fuck, Roman. Don't stop. Please don't stop," I cried out, gripping his forearms with a brute strength I didn't realize I had.

Dropping my legs, he leaned forward, angled them to my chest, and dove deeper. I was about to lose my mind because this man didn't understand the commodity that he possessed. Otherwise, he'd be a menace in these streets. This man was guaranteed to drive me certifiably insane.

"Oh, yesss! You're so deep. Don't stop, baby. Please."

"Damn it, Qui. You feel fucking amazing."

My response to his praise was to cry out. He'd slammed so deep inside of me that my stomach muscles clenched, and my neck strained as sweat beads populated on my forehead. I was so close. When he brought his thumb in front to play with my precious pearl, my eyes ballooned, and my lips and legs started quivering simultaneously.

"I'm...oh I'm...com—"

I couldn't even finish what I was about to say before I exploded with such force that I almost knocked him backward. As the feeling spread throughout my entire being, my arms wrapped around him as I forced him to lean in so I could hold him close as aftershock after aftershock consumed my body.

"Mmm. Oh gawd, oh gawd, my gawddd."

A smile formed on his face as he watched my lids close, committing this moment to memory. He kissed my forehead, nose, and lips before *slowly grinding inside of me again. It was as if I couldn't get enough, and he couldn't get deep enough, although I was filled to the hilt.* Ooh, *I was so wet. He was so deep. And this was so damned good. My grunts and encouragement sent him entirely over the edge, and damn if I wasn't going over it with him again myself.*

"Get yours, Dr. Patterson. Get yours," *I uttered between salacious moans.*

That did it.

He swelled to max capacity inside of me. His snakelike movements ground into me as if he were trying to discover new land and hidden treasures—winding deeper and deeper as he uncovered my secret garden. For a moment, I became afraid because my body was uncontrollable as I pelted out a yelp so loud that it could've broken the sound barrier, and then I gushed a downpour on him. Squirting. He made me freaking squirt. Never had I ever.

Tears pooled and streaked down my face as I tightened my hands over his ass and secured him into my crevices. All kinds of expletives were yelled out as he delivered one final thrust.

"Fuckkk, Qui. The best. Shit. The besttt!"

As we lay there regarding each other, we struggled to calm our breathing. Our hearts thumped so loudly, we couldn't distinguish our beats. I wanted to say something, express what was on my mind, discuss how I felt, or hell, crown him king for that performance, but I could do none of that. As I lay encapsulated in his arms, I could only close my tired eyes and fall asleep.

My hands flew to my mouth as I gasped at the beautiful arrangement on the beach. This was going to be the end of an epic day. Once we returned from our yacht outing, the concierge whisked me away for the spa day that Roman had arranged for me. It was exactly what Dr. Patterson had ordered because my aching muscles had been massaged to perfection. My nails were dazzling, and I had a fresh coat of peach color that glowed against my glistening skin. When I returned to our room, I found an all-white flowy sundress waiting for me. It was completely backless and curved just above my waistline to give a hint of seductiveness and still be just enough to keep me completely covered.

When my eyes landed on Roman, he stood in all-white linen pants, an all-white collared shirt, and tan mules holding a rose. His sun-kissed caramel skin appeared golden set against his ensemble. His face beamed the instant he noticed me strolling down the boardwalk. The romantic backdrop was a cabana filled with a wide mat and pillows so that we could lie down and peer out at the swishing waves. Plates of food were placed about, and wine, chilled in an ice bucket, filled the space. Flowers and candles adorned the area, giving it a romantic ambiance. When I reached Roman, we stretched out our arms and fell into each other's warm embrace.

"You look radiant, Qui." Roman's compliment landed against my temple as he held me close.

I peered up at him, blinking flirtatiously. "And you are handsome as always."

We released each other, and he handed me the rose, which I graciously accepted. Roman situated the pillows so we could dine next to each other. Taking my hand, Roman helped me sit, and then he saddled up beside me. We toasted our time in Bimini before sipping on our champagne.

"*Ahh*. It's so serene and breathtaking out here, isn't it?" I asked, lowering my flute.

"Yes, it is," Roman agreed, but when I turned my face, he was staring at me and not the same ocean view to which I was referring.

"That's the second time you've directed that sentiment toward me, sir. I was talking about the ocean and the atmosphere."

"When it comes to you, not even the world's Seven Wonders compare." Of course, I felt he was putting on a little too much, but he doubled down. "What? I see you doubting me. But it's the truth. And also, correction, this is the *third* time I've addressed that sentiment toward you."

I swallowed a cracker with dip before I leaned back on the pillows. "Roman, I'll be honest: When you say things like that and do things like this, I'm not sure how to take you. I mean, you're Roman. You've been out here in these streets for years. I come on this trip, and suddenly, you're this other type of man."

"So, because I've enjoyed my share of women in the past, it means I don't know how to treat you?"

I wagged my finger at him. "That's my point. You've had so many women, I'm not sure if I should feel special or gamed."

He sat up and wrapped his arms around his knees. "Let me ask you this: Do you think I treated Nia the same way I treat you?"

Feigning nonchalance, I shrugged. "I'm not sure."

"Humph." He frowned while bobbing his head. "After all this time we've spent together, you don't know if I treated Nia or my situationships the same as you?"

"I guess it's more that I'm unsure. I mean, aren't we a situationship?"

"What I thought we were was friends who'd found a common connection above that and were exploring our attraction to see where it leads, not just having sex." He took his time sipping on his champagne and contemplating his words before he spoke again. "Since that wasn't clear, allow me to make it plain: Just because I haven't been interested in serious relationships doesn't mean I don't know how to be cordial and treat women respectfully. Just because I don't want marriage doesn't mean I don't want companionship." He placed his flute down, letting out an exasperated sigh. "Aquila, I know we don't have all the answers about what this is between us right now, but let me assure you that what's transpiring between us is new and different for me, too. It's special, and I find myself in uncharted waters. I've given more of myself than I expected, and I'm not mad about it, but I'm also not dishing it out to every pair of stilettos that struts my way. I'm unsure how to explain to you in a way that you'll believe that this isn't just a hookup for me."

Open mouth, insert foot. I could tell he was a bit irritated because I questioned the sincerity of the time we'd spent together. Honestly, I'd never seen how he interacted with women aside from professionally, not even with Nia. However, I also knew his stance on relationships. On this trip, I found that the Roman I thought I had pegged was anything but, which led me to question it. Now, hearing that I was special and he was plagued with the same insecurities gave us common ground. The part that I didn't feel comfortable sharing with him was that trusting people at face value was more difficult for me now than ever, given my marital woes with Joel. However, my vacation was too exceptional to bring up that sore subject.

Reaching over, I grabbed his hand. "Understood. That's the last time I'm going to question your motives. You've been phenomenal to me when you didn't have to entertain me at all. Trust me, I appreciate everything."

He squeezed my hand in return, and the tension diminished between us. Solemnly, he said, "The same way I appreciate you."

The rest of the time was carefree as we drank, ate, and people watched. I'd met my match when it came to the art of people watching. I loved figuring out where people were from, their personalities, and their professions. Ironically, so did Roman. For the most part, we had similar answers with only a few differences, except for this one couple.

"I'm telling you they're from Minnesota. He makes cheese, and she crochets for a living. Their net worth is three million," Roman teased.

"You sound like an episode of *House Hunters*." Erupting in shoulder-shaking snickers, my hand clasped his shoulder to catch my breath, and I matched his energy. "The hair is throwing you off. I'm telling you, he's a second-generation trust-fund kid with an entry-level position in his daddy's firm because he trekked through Europe during all of his college years. She owns a consignment shop. Their net worth is two million."

There was a brief pause before we barreled over in teary hysterics. I'm sure the onlookers thought we were insane, but neither of us cared. We were in our bubble, and no one could penetrate our fortress.

"You know, all of this 'people watching' has me wondering: I know you love being a mom to your awesome sons, but are there any aspirations that you have for *you*?"

"Well, I'm using this opportunity to make cupcakes for my sons' end-of-summer camp program as a test run, so to speak, to dip my toe into the business."

"That's right." He snapped his fingers. "Kinston was upset about those cupcakes at the talent show."

"Right! The ones Angela bragged about but didn't bring him. Kannon complained about that, too."

"Were you ever interested in taking culinary arts?"

"Actually, I went to college for it."

Roman's neck reared back, completely stunned. "Wait. You took up culinary arts in college?"

My mind drifted back to those days and Joel. Sadness overcame me as I nodded to his question. I couldn't offer more than that. Reflecting on my deferred dream, my ex-husband would do nothing but disrupt my peace and make me more upset with myself than I already was. I still couldn't believe I put my life on the back burner for that bum.

"Is that how you met your ex?" he asked before I could answer the first question.

Swallowing the lump in my throat, I answered earnestly, "Yes and yes."

"*Wow.*" Sensing my sensitivity to the issue, he toyed with my fingers. It was such a small gesture, but it gave me a sense of reassurance that he was offering support, not pity. "You wanted to be a chef. That's your dream. Why not just go for it, instead of wading the waters?"

Leaning back on my elbows, I shrugged. "It was, but honestly, I'm unsure where to start. My boys consume so much of my life, and I feel I must concentrate on them instead of chasing my dreams."

Roman lay back, snuggling me against him. "On the contrary, I think that's exactly why you should pursue your dreams. Show your boys that you can still fulfill your goals, no matter what life throws at you. Financially, it provides another source of income in your house, which, with boys, you'll most definitely need. Plus, I'm pretty sure that they would be proud to see their mother kicking ass as a mom and a mompreneur."

"You're right. I know it, but I'd like to be a private chef and have a place where I prepare meals. Maybe open a small delicatessen to maintain a consistent income flow. I want my home to remain my home, not my business. That's why I'm hesitant. It takes money, and I'm uncomfortable investing money I'm saving for their future. If it's meant to be, it'll be. Meanwhile, I don't mind picking up smaller gigs to keep my skills sharpened and still do what I love." Curling up into him, I directed the same question his way. "Enough about me. What about you and your aspirations?"

"I'm pretty settled between the two locations at KinRo. Eventually, we'll add another. Our vision is to spread throughout Florida. We also host student-athlete training sessions for specific strength, agility, and speed drills. After receiving these massages, I'll ask Kinston if he'd like to add spa services to our membership."

"I think that's a great idea. Help to rejuvenate the muscles of your members. Sign me up. I'd take advantage of that."

"As our number one client, you better," he joked, holding up his pinky finger.

I playfully bumped his shoulder, then hooked my pinky with his. "Here's to us fulfilling our goals."

On that note, we continued our night before gathering our things and heading back to the ship. In T-minus one day, we'd be back in Miami and back to reality.

Chapter Seventeen

ROMAN

WE WERE nearing the end of the cruise, and no lie, I was both reluctant and nervous for our time to end. Reluctance set in because while I knew I had to return to normal life, I was having a ball enjoying this vacation with Aquila. Nervousness set in because I didn't know if Aquila wanted to continue seeing me and possibly take things to the next level once we returned home. I hoped to Jesus on the cross and baby Jesus in the manger that our time together wasn't solely on this cruise. I'd accepted that I wanted to pursue an actual relationship with Aquila.

Since being on this vacation, I'd thought of no one else except her. I'd enjoyed our time together and never wanted to leave her side. The time we spent apart ached, and I was worse than an addict with his score when we linked together. Not to mention, she just got me—my silly banter, my jokes, my drive. Even when she didn't understand me, at least she tried. At dinner yesterday, I was going to broach the subject and ask to continue dating her. The spa day was already in the works because I knew she needed the recovery, but that's why I'd had the boutique deliver the dress and created the ambient setting on the beach. I wanted to impress her, show her that I wasn't on some player shit, but when she doubted my intentions, I didn't want to push. She couldn't get over the hump of me not taking my previous dealings seriously, and it seemed like she was content with us being friends with benefits. So, I knew it wasn't the right time. And I won't lie, neither my ego nor my heart could take the rejection. So, yeah. I punked out.

Today was my final chance before we got back to the city, and I didn't want to chance her reverting to the overly cautious woman who could put more protection around her heart than Fort Knox had around the nation's gold. I needed the magic of the land, air, and sea to seal the deal, and I hoped they all aligned in my favor.

"You better not laugh at me." Aquila's voice caught me off guard.

We'd been waiting in line at the FlowRider on the cruise ship when my mind drifted to how I could convince Aquila to take the plunge while we waited to take a water plunge on this ride. We'd opted to enjoy the boat and all the amenities we could squeeze in before our trip ended.

"I promise I won't." The look she tossed me told me she didn't believe that for one second. "Much. I won't laugh too much."

"*Ooh*. That's so wrong." One of the women standing behind us laughed. Aquila had introduced me to them when they got in line behind us. She'd met them on her first night of the cruise before she bumped into me.

"Right," Aquila concurred with her before she tossed her hands on her hips and turned to the attendant. "See how he does me."

The attendant chuckled as Aquila stepped onto the platform. "I'm not getting in the middle of that, but if I were you, I wouldn't laugh at this little lady. She seems like she packs a punch."

Aquila put up her fists and eyed me. "Don't make me two-piece you."

"Woman, you've got me out here holding a purse while stalling. Get on that ride. Besides, you were on the mechanical bull like a professional rider; you can handle this."

She tooted her apple bottom to me, and of course, I smacked it, making it jiggle. She jumped around and blushed. I couldn't resist the seductive wink I gave her.

"It's a beach bag," she yelled back at me.

"Whatever."

"I love to see playful couples together," the attendant said before giving Aquila the boogieboard.

Neither one of us commented on his reference. Instead, Aquila positioned herself on her stomach as the attendant started the waves on low. Watching Aquila reminded me of my old college football days. We were hyped and playful during practice, but at game time, it was go time. She had that look that said she would not be defeated. We'd placed a friendly wager on who would last the longest, so I was low-key a bit intimidated. The current took off, and she made it up to her knees, riding the wave for a bit. When she tried to move to her feet, she toppled over and wiped out, rolling down to the bottom of the ride. The ladies she'd met on the cruise the first day cheered her on as she exited.

"A measly twenty seconds," I joked as she flung sprinkles of water in my face.

"Let's see you go then, Mr. Westside," she teased, throwing up a "W" hand sign. She high-fived the ladies and stood to the side.

Handing her the beach bag, I stepped on the platform next. "Light work."

Aquila and the other two women all sucked their teeth and gave me the universal side smirk. In my head, I considered that all I had to do was beat Aquila's mark, and then it wouldn't matter if I wiped out. Unfortunately for me, I barely gripped the board well when I lay on my stomach, so I swerved side to side before I could gain control and attempt to get on my knees. Then, Aquila proved she couldn't play fair because she sexily tossed her braids over her shoulder and gave me the bedroom gaze. The second it took to trap me in her lair, I wiped out horribly, getting swept away to the top of the rider and spinning over multiple times before the attendant had to help me get up. I was on the board for barely a few seconds, although it took thirty seconds to get out of the water. When I exited, everyone was in tears laughing at me, but they gave me a courtesy cheer for my effort.

No sooner had I set foot before Aquila than I proclaimed, "I win by default. You cheated."

"You wouldn't have lasted twenty seconds anyway." She stretched her arms out to her sides, shaking her head. "Besides, you can't establish rules after the fact."

"And you can't be flashing sexiness after the fact." I pulled her into me and began tickling her. Her pleas for me to stop fell on deaf ears.

The other two women snickered at us and slapped hands with each other. "Well, it was good to see you again, girl. You all continue having your *fun*." They each gave her a knowing glance.

We said our goodbyes and continued walking along the deck, taking in the sights and sounds. A section of the deck near the railing was free, so I interlocked fingers with Aquila and walked over to it, staring out into the water.

"What's wrong?" The concern in Aquila's voice was evident.

"Nothing." I inhaled the smell of the fresh salt water. "Just wanted to take a beat and enjoy the calm as we wind down on the day."

She slipped in front of me and outstretched her arms. "You just want to relive Rose and Jack's famous scene," she teased, referring to the lovers from the movie, *Titanic*.

"Nah. I prefer you not to risk it all on the railing. I'll jump in if you go over, but I'd rather live a little while longer."

"That is not the scene where Jack met his demise." She snickered with a slight scoff.

"All I know is his ass died in that water, so the scene doesn't matter." She lowered her arms and fell backward into me in a fit of giggles at my taunting. After a minute, we settled down, and I used the opportunity to dive into what was on my mind. "Speaking of couples, you didn't correct the attendant when he called us one."

"*Umm,* neither did you."

"I did not." I shifted her so that we were facing each other. "So, about that—"

Before I could finish, Aquila jumped from the vibration of the bag on her shoulder. It startled me, too, because the entire time we'd been on the cruise, neither of us had received phone calls. She fished in her bag and retrieved her cell. One glance at it, and she smacked her teeth, then silenced it, shoving the phone back in her bag. The call clearly irritated her.

"What? Somebody checking on your car's extended warranty?" I tried to make light of the situation to avoid spoiling the mood.

"Joel." She rolled her eyes.

I shared her sentiment, but I didn't want to express it.

"He probably heard I was on this cruise and wants to inquire why his alimony is going to frivolous trips."

Since Joel had interfered with my plans, I opted to shelve the conversation for later and have the one it seemed she needed. "That doesn't surprise me about him."

She huffed in response.

"He's always been a bit of an asshole. I never asked because it wasn't my business, but is that why you two divorced?"

The question sucked the air around us dry. Aquila steeled, her eyes downcast. "No. I mean, yes, but no." She shook her head. "I don't want to discuss that."

"It just seemed like you needed—"

Her hand flew up, stopping my words. "What I *need* is not to have to mansplain why I don't want to discuss my divorce from my ex-husband. This is my vacation, and I do not want to talk about Joel Oliver."

Woo! Talk about a one-eighty. I raised my hands, indicating that I was backing away from the subject. The last thing I wanted to do was upset her any more than Joel already had, nor make her feel as though she had to explain anything regarding her past to me when she wasn't ready.

"I'm sorry. I didn't mean any harm. Consider the topic off the table."

"Thank you." The words floated plainly out of her mouth, and with that, she turned on her heels and continued walking.

I followed closely behind on mute, asking myself what had just happened.

Chapter Eighteen

AQUILA

DAY 7 OF 7, and I feel terrible.

It was the last day, and we were back in the Port of Miami. Yesterday, I acted like a complete donkey to Roman after Joel's surprise call, and my attitude didn't adjust much after. Joel's disruption had placed me in a funk, so while I went through the motions with Roman, I opted to head back to my room to pack my luggage and rest once we ended our time with the light show and dinner.

Roman deserved much better than what I'd given him. He'd done absolutely nothing wrong, but I was still reeling from my last interaction with Joel before the trip, so when he called, it brought me back to that incident. It reminded me of the reality that this Cinderella was about to lose her glass slipper. Admittedly, I didn't want this trip or this time with Roman to end.

Then, there was the elephant stampeding through the room. Roman's request to be a couple. No, he never finished what he was asking, but I knew where the question was headed without him having to. Thinking about my kids and the possible litigation with Joel, I couldn't drag Roman through that. Sure, it was all love on the cruise, but back in Miami, it was all life. He may have wanted me—and hell, I wanted him, too—but neither of us was ready for everything that truly entailed.

All that aside, the way I'd treated Roman was foul, and I needed to make amends for that, at least. I owed him that much. He'd spent his entire vacation with me, ensuring I had the best time, which I did. I didn't want it to end on a sour note. Since I'd finished settling my onboard bill, I would apologize before disembarkation began. I double-checked that I hadn't left anything and was headed to Roman's suite. To my surprise, Roman walked up when I opened my room door, and we bumped into each other. Once we had gathered our bearings, we stood speechless, gazing at each other.

"We have to stop meeting like this." Roman broke the silence, causing us both to titter.

"Where were you—"

"I was headed—"

We started and stopped simultaneously.

He bowed his head. "You first."

"Actually, I was on my way to your room." He lifted a curious brow as if he didn't believe me. I rested my hand on his shoulder. "I was coming to see you to apologize for my behavior yesterday. Would you like to come inside?"

Without a word, he slowly breezed past me, and his scent made me want to climb Mount Roman again for good measure. Clearing my head, I closed the door and faced him. "Roman, this trip has been more than I dreamed it could be. I've had the time of my life and owe much of that to you. The phone call from Joel took me out of my element, and I wrongfully took that out on you. I'm so sorry for ruining your last day. I'm not sure how I can make it up to you, but I hope you can forgive me and we can move past it."

Roman slowly strolled up to me with his hands clasped behind his back. When he stopped, we stood face to face. "Thank you. I appreciate that. Because I was coming to say that I know that your ex pissed you off, but whatever problem you have with him is with him. As your official vacation accountability partner,

I don't mind being a shoulder to lean on while you process your emotions, but what I can't do is be your punching bag for shots intended for him. As long as we're straight on *that*, we're straight."

Did he just politely put me in my place? Did I like it? Yes, and yes. I stepped closer to him, eliminating any space between us. "We're straight, but you still didn't tell me how I could make it up to you."

His hands found my waist, and he held me flush against him. In hushed tones, he said, "Cancel your transportation and ride back with me. I need a little more of your time."

His woodsy scent, mixed with the seduction in his voice, lit an inferno inside of me. Being as suave as he was had to be a cardinal sin. No one could convince me otherwise. Being wrapped in his alluring essence felt hypnotic. He made me feel like the woman from *Coming to America* shouting, "*Whatever it is you like.*" Stepping back, I reached into my purse and retrieved my cell phone.

"Hey, sissie!" Nissi answered groggily, then shrieked. "OMG! Are you here?"

"Stop scrambling, sis. They don't start disembarkation for another hour. Besides, you don't have to pick me up anymore."

"Huh? How? I'm confused," Nissi asked, trying to process what I was saying as she came out of her sleepy haze.

My eyes flicked to Roman, and I bit my lip. I wasn't prepared to disclose what transpired, so I did the next best thing: I lied. "My disembarkation time moved up, so I'm catching an Uber."

"Nonsense. Just tell me what time I need to be there. I can adjust. Kannon will be here with KJ."

"Nissi, I've scheduled the Uber. Get some sleep. I know how few and far between rest comes when you have a small child."

"Well, when you put it that way…" She relinquished, and I could tell she was settling back in bed. "Just so you know, I had no issue with picking you up."

"I know, but I'm good. I promise."

"Okay. Well, call me later so I can hear all about the trip. The boys are at Angela's."

"Will do. Let me grab some breakfast before it closes down."

"All right. Thanks for the pass. I do need the rest."

"You're welcome, sis."

"Love you roundtrip," we said in unison.

When I hung up the phone, Roman winked at me. "I appreciate you giving me your time, but I won't talk about how smooth that fib rolled off your tongue."

Playfully, I scoffed, amusement dancing on my lips. "Do you want this time or not, sir?"

"I'll take the time for two thousand, Alex."

Pulling him close by the hem of his shirt, I confessed, "Well, I didn't lie about one thing." His brows creased, and I continued, "Let's get breakfast. I'm famished."

Breakfast was light and quick. Before we knew it, we were disembarking. Roman managed his luggage and my bigger suitcase while I pushed my smaller suitcase. I expected to walk to Roman's car, but I was taken off guard when an all-black, fully tinted Cadillac Escalade pulled up.

"You ordered an Uber?"

"No. I ordered through RoadRide. So, technically, you didn't lie to your sister at all."

"I've only used Uber once. Is RoadRide good? I've heard of them but never tried the service."

"They're the best. Just watch."

The RoadRide driver exited the vehicle and greeted us, introducing himself by name and his title of private chauffeur. He was professionally dressed and loaded our luggage into the trunk, then he opened the back door for us. Roman helped me inside and then eased in behind me. The inside was extra spacious, as it was built like a limousine. Once we settled in, the driver turned to us.

"Your preferences have been set, Mr. Patterson. Is there anything else you need before we head to your destination?"

"No, Josh. We're good. Thank you."

"My pleasure, sir."

When he turned around, a privacy glass rose, ambient lighting illuminated our interior, and a side cabinet lifted, unveiling a bottle of champagne with two chilled flutes. Soft, sensual R&B music began to play.

"What is all this?" I stared around in awe at the lush details.

Roman slid close to me, his arm draped around my shoulders. "This is the Premium Presidential ride with the romantic package." He handed me a flute of champagne. "It's set for a private and intimate travel experience for guest riders."

His heated gaze fell on me, and his scent again invaded my nostrils. My heartbeat quickened as I was drawn into his hypnotizing aura. My free hand clutched his shirt, and my brow quirked with curiosity. I lowered my flute and barely breathed. "How private?"

Roman licked his lips and shouted, "Josh." No response came, so he pushed a button on the side panel, and the intercom activated. "Josh."

"Yes, Mr. Patterson. How may I help you?"

"Take the longest route."

"Yes, sir."

Roman pressed the button again and shouted Josh's name, but there was no response. "That private."

With that, Roman's lips descended on mine in an excited fury. Our tongues lashed each other, tasting the sweet hint of the champagne. As our passion grew, so did the intensity of the kiss. We warred and caressed, understanding the urgency while at the same time savoring it. Air rushed back into my lungs when Roman lifted.

Huffing deep breaths, Roman commanded, "Slide those panties off."

Doing as he said, I rose from my seated position and slid my ruined panties down and off. The flood between my thighs sopped the leather seat when I dropped back down. Roman motioned with his finger for me to hand my garment to him, and like the entranced goner I was, I pushed them into his hands. He inhaled the scent and groaned. When he stuck them in his mouth and sucked on the seat, I almost came. So nasty. I couldn't believe he did that. I couldn't believe *I* was doing *this*. All of this was so unlike me, but Roman had a way of making me forget any reservations and unleashing an uninhibited side that I never knew existed. Since he'd unlocked it on the ship, the coo-coo was flying free from the clock.

He beckoned me with the crook of his finger, but I denied him and pointed at his pants. "Take yours off."

So, he did. I was on the floor between his legs, thirsting to swallow him. I massaged his thickness as it grew increasingly to life, even though he was impressively hard when I first captured him. When I lowered my mouth onto him, he bit into my panties, gritting his teeth and baring down on the seat cushion.

"Fuck, Qui." He panted, his voice hoarse with raw emotion.

My mouth slid up and down his pole with saliva dripping at the corners and pooling at the hairs of his balls. His fingers dug into my braids and tightened on them as he pumped into my mouth. My gagging reflexes caused him to calm down and lift me. Again, I was disappointed that I hadn't completed it, but I didn't even have time to dwell on that before his mouth was back on mine. His massive hands lifted me by my ass and seated me on his lap. The friction of my clit on his steel caused me to cry out.

"I need you inside of me."

He shifted to grab his pants, fished out his wallet, and located a condom. In no time, he'd snapped it in place, lifted me, and slid me down hard against him.

"*Shhiii,*" we both belted.

Gripping my hips, he rolled me back and forth as he gyrated in and out of me. I found the flow quickly, even though it hurt so deliciously good. He was so deep inside of me that I could feel him in my belly, penetrating my soul. I fell forward, so consumed with lust and pleasure that I could barely stand it.

Roman bit his lip and slapped my cheeks. "Nah, come on, baby. Take that shit."

My juices slicked him as the smacks ignited stamina in me that came from out of nowhere. My hands pressed on his shoulders as I jockeyed him. When I hit my stride, Roman's eyes rolled upward, and his head fell against the seat.

"Just like that." He grunted, his muscles straining against the building release.

He pulled my braids, and my head fell back, exposing my neck. He leaned up and sucked on my tender spots. Between the heat on my neck and the euphoric feeling in my core, I couldn't hold on. I felt a trembling inside my sweet spot that ripped through my belly, and I came hard and fast.

"Romannnn!"

He held me in place and pounded faster and harder inside of me as I wailed out from the insurmountable desire coursing through my body. I wept and whined because it simply felt too damned good. His dick swelled inside of me, pulsing uncontrollably, and I knew he was near.

"Got damn it! This pussy," he yelped as he spurted his release.

He held me in place as we calmed and our breathing returned to normal. Amazingly, he was still hard, and I felt him giving me light thrusts. My head fell into the crook of his neck as I whimpered. I was overloaded but couldn't tell him to stop because it felt too sensational.

"I know you must get back to your boys, but please, stay the night with me. Just one night, and I promise I won't hold you."

"Roman, I—" The thrust he gave me cut off my words.

Forgetting my protest, I reached for my purse and grabbed my cell phone. When Angela answered, I admitted somewhat of the truth.

"Hey, sis. I'm back."

"Did you enjoy your trip?"

"Immensely."

"Oh shit, *immensely*," she stressed excitedly. "I can't wait to hear about this. The boys are still sleeping, but I can wake them—"

"No, don't. I have a favor to ask. I'm drained from the trip. Do you think you and Kinston can keep them one more day so I can recoup?"

"Now, Lah, you know you didn't have to ask."

"Okay. I'll call you before I get ready to pick them up." Roman nipped at my nipple between the thin fabric of my sundress, causing me to shudder. "Listen, sis, I'll talk to you later."

"Wait. I need to tell you something real quick," Angela protested.

Roman pumped inside of me, causing me to squirm. "Sis, just tell me later when I call. Love you."

"Okay. Love—"

I'd disconnected the call before she could even finish. I knew I'd hear her mouth about hanging up on her prematurely later, but right now, I didn't give a good damn. Right now, I was too busy concentrating on Roman snapping on a fresh condom, putting me on my back, and impaling me again in the back of our RoadRide experience.

Chapter Nineteen

ROMAN

THE SOFTNESS OF the pillow grabbed my attention when I tucked it into me rather than Aquila. My mind was still in a fog from our sex-filled afternoon and late night. The ways in which Aquila and I devoured each other's bodies were indescribable. Her sexual appetite was dope, and her aura was infectious, and I was a happily infected and addicted fiend. On the ship, I was going to ask to be a couple, but after she spazzed out on me, I thought maybe I was moving too fast. Then, she slapped me with a reverse Uno card and apologized without me having to address the issue, and that settled something in me. It was as if all my insecurities about asking her dissipated. But how could I be sure? So, I came up with a game plan to check myself.

Although I wanted the extra time with Aquila because I didn't want our time to end, I also needed to know if it was just the allure of the vacation that had my nose wide open. Before this trip, I was content with finding a companion with benefits, but after bumping into Aquila, I desired more. Yesterday felt like confirmation, but I still hadn't wanted to fully accept what had been browbeating me for the past few days. But as I sat up and stretched, staring around in a slight panic because she wasn't in my bed or my bedroom, I knew that confirmation had been solidified. Aquila had captured something inside of me on board that cruise ship that held a chokehold on me.

I threw the comforter off and hopped out of the bed. I searched my bathroom, but still, there was no sign of her. Stalking down the hallway, I checked the hall bathroom and heard her voice coming from my kitchen, humming a tune. Thankfully, I was able to calm my nerves before she saw me. Taking a beat and a breath, I lazed into the kitchen and saddled behind her.

She jumped and faced me. "You scared the life out of me, Roman. I was looking for your mugs to make coffee for us."

"You don't have to do that." I pecked the side of her neck. "Let's go out and grab some breakfast."

Her body tensed beneath me, and she let out a low groan. "I wish I could, but I have to get to my babies."

On that note, I conceded. I knew she was just as eager to see her sons as they were to see her. I'd preoccupied enough of her time, and being selfish over it wouldn't allow her to take me seriously about wanting to be a couple. Her boys were her world, and I adored those little dudes, so I never wanted to give the impression that I was trying to lock down their mom without realizing they were a part of the package.

"I understand." Leaning in, I pecked her forehead. "I'll take you home to get your car."

With a little shoulder shimmy, she giggled. "Actually, I ordered a RoadRide. It's not the fancy premium package, but I was impressed, so it's RoadRide for me any time I need a car service."

Winking with a smirk, I teased, "You liked that RoadRide, huh?"

"I *loved* every bit of it."

"When does it arrive?"

"I have an hour. I wanted to shower first."

An idea struck me, and I held up my finger. "Humor me." I held her hand and led her to my bathroom. "Can we bathe together? I promise to keep it rated PG," I assured her before her skepticism could kick in.

"As long as you behave."

Tamping down my excitement, I filled the soaker tub as she grabbed her toiletry bag and an outfit from her suitcase. Although I enjoyed seeing her rock my clothing, the sight of her disrobing out of my T-shirt was equally as fulfilling. Her birthday suit was on full display, so when she turned around, I had to force my man below to stay at bay.

Aquila held up a warning finger. "Down, boy."

"I can control my actions, but not his urges." I stroked myself to calm down. "He sees what he wants, so he reacts."

Since we were pressed for time, I stepped into the tub and reached out my hand for hers to join me. When she stepped in, we both settled into the warm water, her back resting on my chest.

"This is just what the doctor ordered. Pun intended." She moaned, her eyes fluttering closed. She stretched out her arms, and her fingers landed on my wrist. "You're still wearing the beaded bracelet. Have you taken it off?"

I shrugged. "At first, I took it off, but it's pretty much a memento."

"You're right." She snapped her fingers. "We have to wear it for the memories since we still don't fully recall our drunken night of fun."

No additional words were spoken as I placed a small kiss on the side of her temple. I lifted her mesh loofa from the small table beside the tub, along with her body wash, and began washing the front of her body and her arms, then easing around to her neck and back. She took care of her essentials below the waist to keep me from getting too handsy. When she finished, I stood to help her out.

Aries Skye

"What about you?"

"I'll take care of myself when you leave. This was for you. I just wanted to pamper you a little bit more before you go."

She muttered a sweet coo and palmed my face. "Thank you."

Quickly, I applied lotion to her body and allowed her to dress while I walked back into my master bedroom, threw on some basketball shorts, and turned on the television. When she entered the bedroom, she announced that her RoadRide would arrive in about fifteen minutes, so she repacked her toiletries. As she sat there, I hyped myself to broach the lingering topic.

Just say it, Patterson. Put it out there before she leaves. I shook out my nerves, and just as she stood, I made my way toward her.

"Before you leave, I wanted to ask you something. Before you shut it down, hear me out, please."

Setting her purse on the bed, she gave me her undivided attention. "I'm listening."

Woo. Okay. Here goes nothing. Clearing my throat, I picked up her hands and held them in mine. "Aquila, I know what we had on the trip was supposed to be a friendly pact, but we surpassed that a few nights ago." I took a beat because my heart was about to pound out of my chest. *Quit stalling, Patterson.* "Qui, I know our time together has been short, but we found something on that ship—something worth exploring beyond the ship."

She waved her hand. "Roman, I don't want a situationship with you—"

"Wait," I interrupted her by clasping her hand again. "I'm not talking about that friends-with-benefits type of stuff. I want to court you." I smiled at her, moving closer as my confidence grew. "Date you." I cradled her chin between my thumb and forefinger. "Exclusively…and see where that takes us."

Aquila's face contorted with contemplation. She withdrew her hands from me and paced back and forth before settling against the dresser. "Roman, let's be honest. Neither one of us went on that trip with any real expectations. We both intended to find someone to hook up with before we bumped into each other. I think we may be letting the fantasy of the trip take over our real life. What we experienced on the boat was special, but that's probably best where we leave it."

My head shook defiantly at her rejection while my insides churned, resisting to accept this crushing defeat. Her lips formed words that I knew for certain her heart and body didn't agree with. There was no way she didn't want to explore what we'd discovered in each other. I knew because she felt for me as I did for her. She wouldn't even be here now if she hadn't. Something deeper was brewing beneath the surface that she didn't want to reveal, and I was determined to uncover it before her RoadRide arrived so we could begin our new journey together.

"I don't believe that, and I know you don't either. Maybe we thought it would start off that way, but you and I know that's not what happened. I felt...*feel*...something, Qui, and I know you do, too. You can't convince me that you don't feel that same thing." I could tell she was about to protest, but I rushed to her and cradled her face. "That's why I suggested that we date. We don't have to label it. We can see where it goes. But we deserve to give this thing brewing between us a fair shot."

Emotions welled up inside me, and I could see her gaze softening as she considered the possibility. So, I revealed my hidden truth to seal the deal. Opening my heart completely, I said, "We deserve the chance that I only ever truly wanted to take with you."

She gasped, covering her mouth as her eyes widened in shock. She was about to say something when her gaze darted behind me, and her brows furrowed. Suddenly, she shouted, "Joel?"

Catching me off guard, I turned and saw that the television was on a local station showcasing the Miami blog news, a local celebrity news and gossip show of sorts. An image of her ex-husband, Joel Oliver, and Jansen Carlyle was on the screen.

"Oh my god," Aquila whisper-screamed, panic consuming her.

That made my ears perk up and tune into the report. The host of the show discussed Jansen Carlyle, a well-known multimillionaire investor, being involved in a sexual scandal with Joel. The issue was that Jansen was married, and apparently, the two were caught by Jansen's wife, Jana.

Hold the hell up. Aquila's ex-husband is gay? Is that why they got divorced?

As embarrassing as I knew this had to be for her, I also had my questions. Did she know? She had to know, based on her reaction. Many emotions ran rampant, but surprise didn't seem to be one of them.

"Aquila, what's going on?"

Her phone pinged, and she peered down at it. Relief flooded her. "I have to go. My ride is here." She grabbed her bags and began scrambling toward the door.

"Aquila, wait."

"I don't have time to talk, Roman. I'm sorry."

Before I could say another word, she opened my front door, and the driver was standing there about to knock. Once she verified it was him, she scanned his photo and company ID information into the app for security measures. Then she directed him to take her bags to the awaiting vehicle. As she stepped out behind him, I clasped her wrist.

"Aquila," I barely croaked out.

"I have to go."

Chapter Twenty

ROMAN

"RO!" KINSTON AND Kannon shouted my name, greeting me as I walked through the gym doors at four in the morning.

I checked the annoyance brewing inside. It's not that I wasn't glad to be back or to see them, but I had hoped to be the first to arrive so I could gather myself and work out in peace.

Since Aquila had left my house, I hadn't been in a good headspace. Our vacation had been nothing short of amazing, and we hadn't been back for a full twenty-four hours before all hell started breaking loose. I left her a voicemail and texted her a couple of times without any response. I knew she had to attend to her children and the drama surrounding her ex, but I wanted to check on her. Don't get me wrong, I wanted answers, but the news about Joel was on constant repeat, and all sorts of allegations were flying around. Joel and Jansen may not have been as popular as our local rappers and entertainers, but they were part of the upper echelon and very well known. Heck, I'd met Jansen at a couple of investor networking events, so I understood the significance of the Carlyle brand and the extent of his influence. While Joel wasn't on Jansen's financial level, he still held a high position due to his family history, legacy, and impact in South Florida.

People often thought that those in front of the cameras were the epitome of power and connection. How wrong they were. The true movers and shakers were the ones behind the cameras. That was where power moves and financial decisions were made, and allegiances were formed. They were the ones who manipulated the front camera people like pawns on a chessboard. The unfortunate thing was that those family members directly affected by the movers and shakers often found themselves on a lonely island, left to deal with the aftermath of their downfall alone, as they were far removed from the world. They suffered in silence while others judged them based on their money, status, and the people in their lives, without understanding or caring that they were human, too. Therefore, I understood how devastating this must have been for Aquila and the boys, which is why I wanted to be there for them. At the same time, I was disappointed that she hadn't reached out to me, even if only out of courtesy.

"'Sup?" I greeted them, snatching my cap off my head.

Kinston reared backward, taken aback by my demeanor. "Damn, Ro. You just came off vacation. I thought you were supposed to come back refreshed with a smile plastered on your face."

"You look like you went and had to fight for your life," Kannon added.

Kinston and he chuckled and slapped fives at the intended joke, but when I didn't join in, they turned serious.

Kinston gave Kannon the side-eye before they both placed their dumbbells down and walked over to me. I knew I couldn't avoid the impending conversation, so I sat on a foam jumping box. Kinston grabbed another jumping box to sit on, and Kannon stood holding on to the rails of the TRX machine.

Kinston tapped my knee with the back of his hand. "Bro, you good? Something happened on the cruise?"

Sitting with my elbows on my thighs and fingers interlaced, my shoulders slouched, I bobbed my head slowly as memories of my time with Aquila scrolled like a quick film through my mind. "My trip was…the best time I've ever had in my life." The tone in my voice contradicted the words I'd spoken.

Kinston and Kannon stared at each other, total confusion consuming their faces.

"So, did you party that hard?" Kannon inquired.

"'Cause you look like shit." Kinston made it plain. "If the trip was that good, something must've happened since you've been home."

My mouth opened to tell them, but then I remembered that doing so meant I'd have to reveal what went down between Aquila and me. Since I wasn't sure about her stance regarding her siblings or in-laws knowing about our tryst, I hesitated to talk to my boys. She had enough on her plate, and the last thing I wanted to do was pile anything else onto it. However, if anyone knew what was happening even on a small scale with Joel, it was these two men—my best friends and Aquila's brothers-in-law. If Aquila had talked to me, I would have known how to handle this situation appropriately. As much as I respected Aquila's need for privacy, I couldn't afford to give that to her wholly. So, I took my chances.

"Don't tell me you met a woman over on one of those islands, and she snatched your soul," Kinston joked, bumping shoulders with Kannon.

"Nah. I met her on the ship."

The sound of light could be heard in the gym; it'd gotten quiet instantly. Both men gawked at me with the same stunned expression. If I had to guess, their shock was less about my admitting to finding a woman but the fact that I'd let her get me down bad. The gym might melt away once they found out who she was.

Exhaling, I explained to them how I'd met the mystery woman. I recounted bumping into her on the first day of the cruise, our long walk and talk, our vowing to be each other's vacation accountability partner, and our taking different excursions together. I recalled with vigor our drunken night together and how this led to intimacy a few times, all the way to her getting off the ship with me and spending the night at my house.

Their eyes furrowed at the last part of my story as they exchanged curious glances. I could see them mentally questioning each other, so I decided to put it out there to uncover the real matter.

"Yes, it was Aquila."

The way Kinston's eyes ballooned made me wonder if they really would pop out of his sockets. "No way! Are you serious? Tell me you're joking."

"We kid about many things, but that is one thing I would never joke about." I stood and started pacing in place. "It was unexpected. I'd planned to hang out as friends, but if you could've seen her on the trip… She was a new person. Carefree. Fun. Sexy. We talked, laughed, and joked for hours. We challenged ourselves to new experiences. We danced like no one was watching. And the sex—"

"And that's where I have to intervene." Kannon put his hand up. "We love Aquila, but we aren't trying to hear about our sister-in-love's sexual appetite."

Kinston acknowledged what he said with an agreed fist bump.

"Well, just know all the BS y'all used to preach to me about those damn Richards sisters, I'm admitting it's true. There's just something about them. Something about…*her*."

Kinston walked over to me and clapped me on the shoulder. "Big dawg, it sounds like you tapped into more than your usual situationships or one-time flings."

Looking up at him and Kannon, I admitted, "I did. That woman sparked something inside me, and my chest has been tender ever since." When they didn't respond, I tackled the next subject they hadn't mentioned. "I heard about the news with Joel and Jansen. Aquila and I heard it together before she left my house."

Kinston exhaled and scratched his forehead. "Yeah, Angela was trying to tell her before she saw the news, but she rushed her off the phone. Now, I know why."

"Listen, don't tell your wives about me and Aquila. I'm not sure if she wants them to know. Hell, I'm not sure I should've told y'all, but this shit with Joel is messing with me, too." I stared them both directly in the eyes. "Is that the reason why they got a divorce? Did Aquila know her ex was gay?" When neither one of them spoke, I pleaded, "Come on. I told y'all about me and Aquila. Y'all are my boys. The least y'all can do is be straight up with me about that."

Neither one of them wanted to give in, but it was ultimately Kinston who broke the silence. "Yeah, man."

I threw my hands up, but Kannon intervened. "It's not something we would've hidden from you if we knew you and Aquila would link up. The family made a collective decision not to speak about her divorce per Aquila's request. Our nephews don't know the real reason. Aquila and Joel blamed it on their inability to get along. They were young, so they didn't ask many questions."

The explanation made sense. I may have been close to the family, but I wasn't part of it. I had no right to think I deserved access to their private information. My issue stemmed from wanting more with Aquila and, honestly, the fact that we had sex. While we lived in a more accepting time, there was still a certain stigma surrounding sex, and I'll admit it bothered me.

Kinston must have sensed the burning question in my mind because he added, "She's been divorced from him for two years, Roman. I can't speak to whether there was any double-dipping between them, but I highly doubt it. I'm sure if there were any reasons for concern, Aquila would have warned you."

"I hear you, and I know y'all are right, but I don't know how to feel that she couldn't talk to me about it at least a little bit while we were getting close."

"I feel that, but can you really blame her? She was on vacation, after all. The last person she wanted on her mind, or even to think about, was that damn Joel. Besides, she wasn't expecting to run into you either, and you weren't just some random guy to her. She deals with the aftermath of her failed marriage every day, and then, to have something so personal exposed for the entire world to judge when she barely wanted her own family to know—can you imagine explaining that to a family friend turned whatever it is you two have? Please give my sis-in-love some grace, bro," Kinston defended, shaking his head as he clarified his point. "I'm not saying you don't deserve answers. The whole situation is sensitive, and honestly, for the most part, it involves Joel's personal business. All I'm saying is to give her some time."

Putting myself in her shoes, I could understand her hesitation and avoidance. I was sure that even sharing that information with her family was difficult, not to mention the thought of having that conversation with me, as Kinston suggested. "I feel what both of you are saying. I respect her need for space, time, and privacy. And she doesn't have to divulge anything she doesn't think is my concern, just as long as she's open about things that affect me."

They nodded, indicating their agreement with my assessment. And it was true. I was caught off guard by the news after I had asked her to date me exclusively, and following our time together, so the reveal surprised me. This conversation helped me understand her perspective and eased my mind. Remembering the straightforward woman I fell for on the cruise, I trusted that once things settled down, she would be in a better headspace to discuss both that and my proposition. For now, all I could do was return to my life and wait for the woman who had suddenly turned my entire world upside down.

"Ready to prep for opening?" I asked Kinston as Kannon finished his private workout and headed to the fire station.

Kinston smiled. "Yeah." He bumped fists with me. "Come on, in-love-ass nicca."

Chapter Twenty-One

AQUILA

NORMALLY, IF I had to be away from my children, I would spend my first few days back with them. With the news of Joel's affair with Jansen made public, having them in day camp was a welcome distraction. They had not heard about it, for which I was grateful, so I made sure to check the parental controls on their devices and prayed that none of the kids in their day camp would bring it up to them. Kids can be inquisitive, and then some are just plain mean. Either way, I didn't want my young children having to answer adult questions about their father.

As for me, I had been fielding phone calls for the past day. Joel and his family tried to contact me, but I refused to speak with them. I didn't have the energy for the spin job they were trying to build with me. I was also angry that Joel could let this happen. Bloggers and reporters had reached out to me as well, but to no avail. I wasn't emailing, texting, or answering anyone whose contact information I didn't already have or didn't recognize. The last thing I wanted was to be dragged into Joel's predicament any more than I already was, which was by default. The only people who could reach me were my immediate family. The only other person I wished to speak with but couldn't out of sheer embarrassment was Roman. Although the shame wasn't mine to carry, I did because it wasn't as if I were blindsided; I knew.

How could I explain that in a way that was understandable? In hindsight, it sounded foolish, even to me. Right now, I just wanted to tuck my tail and hide away from the world until this catastrophe blew over.

The sound of the doorbell made me check my security cameras to see who had dropped by unannounced. If it turned out to be a nosy reporter, I swear I would give them the news story they weren't looking for and call the police while doing it. When I activated the view from my cell phone, it was none other than my sisters. I stood up from my comfortable sofa and answered the front door. Upon seeing them, I fell into their open arms.

"I'm so glad y'all are here," I admitted as we shuffled inside my house.

While I had spoken to my sisters, I hadn't seen them since the day I picked up my sons. Even then, it was more of a quick drive-by pickup. The realization of how much I missed and needed them didn't hit me until they were standing in my living room with me. I wouldn't take this for granted either since it was midday on a Monday, and I knew both of them should have been at work.

Typically, my house was vibrant and full of light, but my blinds and curtains were closed, and the only illumination came from the recessed lights in my kitchen. We collapsed on my sofa in the dimly lit living room, and I leaned my head back as they surrounded me, leaning in with hugs. That alone meant the world to me as one of my greatest nightmares unfolded.

"Have reporters still been calling you?" Nissi asked.

"Calling, texting, and emailing." I palmed my forehead. "You'd think Joel was Diddy or somebody. It's downright ridiculous."

"Next time you get an inquiry, give them my name and email. I'll give them a statement," Angela said, fuming.

"No, sis, I can't put your job at risk. Besides, it'll blow over soon."

"I'm a paralegal. It's what we do. Parsons won't get rid of me. He'd probably help me formulate a professional cuss-out with a nice harassment lawsuit threat." She sat up and leaned her head against mine. "But I know you won't do it. I hate that happened to you, especially after your vacation."

"I guess I should've talked to you and Joel before I got off that ship. At least now I understand why both of you wanted to speak with me."

My mind drifted back to when Joel called me on the ship and when Angela mentioned she had something important to discuss. That reminded me of my next memory—Roman. Just a few short days ago, I was having the time of my life with the most unexpected person. If I could press the rewind button, I'd be right there in his MegaSweeties suite, tangled with him under the sheets, dancing with him at the club, or defying death with some water sport that he'd hyped me to try. He was a breath of fresh air, and now, I was back home suffering from a lack of oxygen. Thoughts of him brought an instant smile to my face.

"*Oop!* Wait a minute. What's that blush about?" Angela gasped, catching me in my private thoughts.

Nissi sat up and peered at me with a smile forming on her face. "*Uh-oh.* Now, you were all sad and blue just a second ago. What brought this mood change on?"

"Or *who?*" Angela interjected and then snapped her fingers. "You didn't have this look until I mentioned that cruise, which you never told us about. I think you met someone. Pray tell. Who has you all in your feels, Lah?"

I wanted to protest because I hated discussing my private affairs, but right now, I needed something to feel good about. Talking about my time on the cruise with Roman seemed like the perfect remedy to soothe my aching heart. Having been out of the dating scene for more than ten years, I also needed their advice on how to handle this situation with Roman. Besides, much of my business was out in the open for public scrutiny; what harm could telling my sisters about my trip do?

"First of all, you all weren't slick with those clothing choices you gave me." I pointed my finger back and forth between them with a scolding glare. "But, I suppose they helped." A sly smile spread across my lips.

They perked up, turning to face me on the sofa with their undivided attention.

"Girl, hurry up and proceed," Angela practically yelled at me. Her enthusiasm was infectious.

"I met someone on the cruise." I could barely get the sentence out without those two hooting and hollering. "Y'all, it was everything I needed and more. We spent every day together—"

"Every day?" Nissi interrupted. "Hold up. You were only gone for seven days. When did you meet this man?"

My shoulders hunched as I admitted, "On the first night. I literally ran into him at full speed. I was trying to break free from being stuck in the Macarena line and ran straight into a wall of muscles. After making sure we weren't hurt, we started a conversation and walked around the ship. We made a pact to be each other's vacation accountability partners, dedicating time together every day—on the ship, on the islands, during excursions, dining, clubbing, talking—"

"Having sex," Angela probed, trying to see if that was where I was headed.

Demurely, I nodded to their cheers.

"Was it good, sis?" Angela asked, bouncing giddily on my sofa.

I glanced between them as Nissi also sat on pins and needles waiting.

"Better than good. Oh my god. The things that man did to my body. It was a whole experience. I've never felt that way, not even with Joel."

"Ha." Angela's eyes rolled upward. "That's not even surprising in the slightest."

I gently tapped her on the arm, but I couldn't hide my amusement at her jab at Joel. He deserved a bit of pettiness for the mess he'd created.

"Aw, man, so you get off the ship only to deal with your ex's craziness. Where is this guy? Can you visit him, or can he come see you? Did you even get his contact info? I hope he doesn't live across the country or in another country," Nissi blurted out, talking faster than a mile a minute.

"Actually, he's here in Miami."

Angela shifted back with her hands on her hips. "Now, I know you're not sitting up here pining over Joel's BS when you could be laid up under your cruise-ship lover."

Nissi gasped, nearly falling out of her seat. "Wait a damn minute! That extra day you needed when you returned… You spent it with him, didn't you?"

"You better get it, Lah." Angela shimmied, slow rolling her body.

This was the part of the conversation I wasn't ready for, so I stood up and started pacing. I hoped it would calm my nerves, but it wasn't working. Oh well, there was nothing I could do except drop the other shoe.

"Yeah, we did, and that's part of the problem. We both saw the gossip story on television together. He knows that my ex-husband is gay."

Nissi gawked in confusion. "And?" She flipped her hands upward. "Who cares? You've been divorced for two years, and I know you've been celibate for longer. Joel is your past, not your present."

Angela tucked her feet, sitting yoga style on the sofa. "I mean, she has a point. Did you explain that to him?"

Stopping my pacing, I faced them. "Besides the fact that Joel is gay, I didn't have to explain anything else to him. He already knew the other important details." Both of my sisters' faces fell into blank stares at that confession. Before they could recover, I dropped the bomb on them. "The man is Roman."

"ROMAN," they both shrieked, jumping up at the same time.

"Let me get this straight." Angela folded her arms across her chest. "You mean Roman Roman. As in Roman *Patterson*. As in Roman, my husband's best friend. As in Roman, the co-owner of KinRo Fitness. As in Roman, the man you've known for at least seven or eight years. *That* Roman?"

Biting my lower lip, I nodded. "Yeah, *that* Roman."

Both of them fell onto the sofa and uttered, *"Wow."*

Now, it was my turn to be confused. "Why don't either of you seem surprised?"

"It's surprising that you connected with him, knowing he doesn't prefer to settle down," Angela admitted, and Nissi agreed. "But it's not surprising that he likes you."

"How? He was with Nia, which is another reason I'm hesitant to continue down this road with him."

Nissi scoffed. "Joel must've truly had your blinders on. The way that man used to defend you when Joel would mistreat you in front of us. It was obvious, sis."

"So, why didn't either of you say anything to me?"

"*Umm*, ma'am, you were married, and he *was* screwing my bestie for a minute," Angela offered as if I were stupid for being clueless.

"But is he still screwing your bestie, though? I don't want things to be weird between Nia and me. I love her, too."

Angela grinned. "Well, it's a little too late for that, but I mean, both of them stated that their situation was purely physical. According to Nia, that has been over for a long time. Remember when we had spa day together before Nissi's wedding, and she told us they were done? That was how many years ago? I think you're just making excuses because you're scared. There's nothing wrong with being scared, but if you both like each other and want to explore where things could go beyond the bedroom, you should go for it."

"I know it's tough to talk about Joel, but you have nothing to be ashamed of. Roman has been our friend for a long time. You should discuss Joel with him. I'm pretty sure he, of all people, would understand. He's been there throughout your marriage and its dissolution. Give him some credit," Nissi added.

"But let me ask, do you all want to try for more?" Angela inquired.

Walking back over to the sofa, I sat between my sisters. I placed my hands on each one of their knees and confirmed, "He asked to date exclusively right before we heard the news." They were about to get excited, but I held my finger up. "But we're forgetting one important fact: Even if Nia isn't a factor, and even if he wants to give us an honest chance, I have children. If I'm going to date exclusively, it must be with intention, not out of sexual tension. Regardless, Roman has never mentioned that he wanted children. In the past, he's even admitted that marriage and family aren't in the cards for him. I don't want to waste our time by diving into something he'll eventually walk away from."

We all settled back onto the sofa, resting in our quiet reverie. Eventually, Angela broke the silence. "There's only one way to resolve these questions, sis. Talk to him."

Chapter Twenty-Two

AQUILA

I T HAD BEEN a whole month, and I still hadn't talked to Roman. Not that we hadn't communicated; we just hadn't had *the* talk. It was entirely my fault, too. Instead of heeding my sisters' advice, I leaned on my excuses as a crutch. The main excuse was dealing with the fallout from Joel's shady affair. Although it didn't affect the boys and me directly, it did impact us indirectly with the nosy public as we navigated through scrutiny and finances. Scrutiny was something we had to manage. Finances, on the other hand, I didn't have to handle, so instead of getting into a tit-for-tat with Joel, I decided that our attorneys would manage all financial communications.

It felt like every day I came up with a new excuse to avoid talking to Roman about Joel or the idea of dating. My first excuse was that I was busy fulfilling the cupcake orders for the day camp. After that, it turned into getting the boys ready for back to school, and then the latest excuse was that since the boys were in school, I had to assist with the PTA and volunteer, or that I was busy kickstarting my catering career. Despite everything, Roman kept reaching out. He tried to call, but either I didn't answer or kept the conversation short. Still, I responded to his text messages, checking in on the boys and me. I even got clever about scheduling my training sessions with Kinston by planning them when Roman wasn't scheduled to be at the gym. Nevertheless, Kinston never missed a chance to advocate for his friend.

Despite my avoidance, I missed him. That's how I knew it was more for me than just some fling on a ship. However, the fact remained that Roman was not one for relationships, marriage, or family. He'd said it himself. While I can't say that I wanted to remarry anytime soon—or ever—I came with a ready-made family. My boys would never be up for negotiation, and being with me meant accepting them. Roman sought to date me exclusively, and that exclusivity required seriousness about me *and* my children. Still, he made it so difficult to move on, especially during moments like these.

"Good afternoon, Ms. Richards. Your weekly special delivery." The deliveryman handed over the beautiful array of flowers.

This week's arrangement featured a beautiful assortment of pink roses and yellow sunflowers—all courtesy of one Dr. Roman Patterson. For the past month, he had sent me a different arrangement of summer flowers each week to brighten my day and remind me that he was thinking of me. They arrived like clockwork every Friday. This time, there was an additional gift in a box. I thanked the deliveryman who had become a familiar face before wishing him a good day. After closing the door, I leaned against it and pulled out the card.

Qui,

I hope these flowers brighten your day the same way you brighten the lives of those around you. Missing your light. Whenever you're ready, I'm here.

Yours,

Dr. Roman Patterson

P.S. Aht. Aht. That box of candy is for the boys. You missed your session at the gym this week.

My heart melted at the sentiment. Clutching the card against my chest, I awed at the sweet note, and then I fished my cell phone out of my back pocket. Placing the vase, along with the box of chocolates, on my foyer table, I snapped a quick picture and texted it to Roman.

> **Me:** These lit up my day. I'll be sure to give the boys their gift, although I'm sneaking at least one of those chocolates out of the box.
>
> **Dr. Patterson:** That's good, but if you sneak one, I'm having Kinston tack on thirty extra seconds to your plank holds.

I couldn't help but laugh at that. He knew plank holds were my nemesis, and I had no doubt he would ask Kinston to do something foolish like that. Knowing my brother-in-love, he absolutely would oblige. Hater. I lifted the vase to place it on my kitchen island as the doorbell rang, startling me. I opened the door without thinking, only to be met by the one and only Joel Oliver.

"What the…Why are you here?"

"Because you've been avoiding my phone calls, and I need to talk to you, and I want to see my boys." He eyed me strangely. "But I see why you're not answering my calls." He pointed at the flowers.

Just that quickly, my day had dimmed. How dare he come over here unannounced and make assumptions? "First of all, our boys have an hour before they are out of school, and secondly, not answering your calls has nothing to do with my flowers."

"Fine. I'll follow you to the school. I want to see my children."

"Oh no you won't."

His forceful words triggered my gut reaction, meeting his arrogant attitude with the same amount of bark. He knew that

I'd told his mother that I was limiting visitation until the chaos died down. And I meant that. The reality was that the noise had started to quiet…and the boys missed him. That thought alone made me waver, and I hated that I was always the one considering everyone's feelings.

I exhaled slowly. Even though the words about to come next tasted like surrender, they would be delivered with a clear warning.

"I'll take them to the neighborhood park after I pick them up. If you really want to see them, meet us there. You can show up—if you're serious. If not, don't you dare bother. And Joel, on everything I love, you better not make me regret this."

"Dad!" Sante screamed as he and Junior ran up to Joel.

"Hey! How are my boys doing?" He picked up Sante and tossed him in the air.

"Mom said you were busy working. That's why we haven't seen you." Sante hugged him around the neck. "I've missed you."

"I've missed you both, too."

"Can we go play now?" Junior asked. That's when I noticed he was less excited than Sante to see his father.

"I want to talk to Dad some more," Sante said as Joel placed him back on his feet.

"Well, you can stay. I want to go play."

Joel and I were concerned as Junior's attitude shifted from sweet to sour. Gently approaching him, Joel placed a comforting hand on his shoulder. "Son, what's the matter?"

Junior huffed. "You said you'd always have time for us even when you and Mom weren't living together. We haven't seen you in a long time. You moved out and forgot about us."

Joel kneeled in front of Junior so that they were face to face. "You're right, son, and I apologize. There is no excuse, but I had some important issues to handle. It wasn't because I didn't want to see you all. I love you guys. I just needed to straighten some things out in my life. I'm sorry for making it seem like I forgot about you."

Junior clicked his tongue, but he didn't utter another word.

Joel's brows furrowed and arms crossed as he assessed his namesake. "Son, I'm telling the truth. What is really going on with you?"

"Whatever." Junior huffed. "This wouldn't happen if you all stayed married and we lived together again."

We may have been outside, but I felt all the air around us evaporate. This was the first time I had heard this from Junior. Neither of them had expressed their sadness over our failed marriage other than when we initially sat down to tell them we were getting a divorce. I kept them occupied to shield them from the pain and tried to overcompensate for Joel's absence. I thought it had worked, but leave it to Joel and his philandering ways to reopen a wound. Perhaps I was also to blame for not allowing them to see their father. However, until Joel was ready to be honest with our children about the real reason we could no longer be married, I had to do what was necessary to protect them from the shock and even greater emotional turmoil they would undoubtedly face. They needed to hear it from Joel, not from me, his parents, a nosy news reporter, a meddling blogger, or an insensitive classmate.

"Son, your mom and I care for each other very deeply. Sometimes, adults need to be separated to get along better. You remember how you and Tim had that huge fight over a ball and decided to stop being friends?" When Junior nodded slowly, he continued. "Well, that's similar to what happens sometimes when two people can no longer stay married. They conclude that they're better off apart than together."

"Do you understand?" I leaned in to address Junior and Sante. "We never want to do anything to hurt either of you. No matter what happens between your father and me, we love you both with all our hearts."

Instead of replying right away, Junior wrapped his arms around my neck and hugged me. "I understand. I love you, Mom."

"I love you most," I whispered in his ear. "How about giving your dad a hug, too?"

He let go of me and then reached over to hug Joel who reached for Sante and wrapped both of them in his arms. They stayed like that for a few seconds before Joel pulled back. "You guys go play while I talk to your mom."

The boys rushed to the playground equipment while Joel and I sat on a bench where we could keep an eye on them and chat. I had to hand it to Joel, that was quite the explanation he gave to Junior. Although I knew this wasn't the right time or place to explain the real reason we couldn't be together, it was clear that an explanation would need to come much sooner rather than later—or possibly never.

"You know you're going to have to tell them. They deserve the truth."

"Well, I was hoping that I didn't have to tell them."

My soul was instantly vexed. Typical Joel. So damn typical. He'd rather hide in the shadows and let them suffer in silence than share the truth so they could heal and move forward.

"How is that going to work, Joel? Are you planning to introduce Jansen or any other guy to them as a long-lost uncle? Be fucking for real."

In a move that shocked me, he slid closer and draped his arm over the back of the bench. "I was hoping that you and I could work on us again."

Speechless. I was stunned speechless. And it wasn't because this was some grand, sweeping gesture. How could this man who put me through the turmoil of his sexual desires, the pain of sleeping with one of our closest friends, and the disappointment of all his broken promises sit here with a straight face and tell me he wanted to work on us after his affair fell apart? What in the *Real House Husbands of Miami* was going on?

"Please tell me you're joking, or have you actually signed a contract with Bravo for a reality TV pilot?"

Joel swiped his hand over his bald head. Nervously, he broached the topic once more. "I…*uh*…Aquila, I'm sorry. I regret breaking my promise to you. I apologize for taking you and our vows for granted. I'm sorry for falling for Jansen. I should've put a stop to it when he first made his move, but I was attracted to him. It started innocently enough—a flirty comment here, a compliment there—then it escalated, and I didn't know how to stop it because feelings started developing."

This was one of those rare occasions when Joel revealed his truths in hopes of winning me over. While I knew that would never happen, I would take this opportunity to find out all the answers I had always wanted to confirm.

"So, you and Jansen did have an affair behind my and Jana's backs?"

A telling sign of Joel's nervousness was when he rubbed his hands together, which he was doing vigorously. "While you and I were married, we never penetrated each other, but we did kiss and fondle." He slid his hands down his face and admitted, "And we did perform oral on each other."

Hearing his confession jarred me because I hadn't expected him to fully acknowledge his wrongdoings. I was so stunned that I had to rephrase my question to ensure I'd heard what I thought I did. "So basically, you cheated emotionally and physically."

He sat quietly, not acknowledging what he had just admitted, then shrugged and finally managed a shaky, "Yeah." Clearing his throat, he continued, "It's the reason I didn't touch you the last year of our marriage."

I blinked rapidly upon hearing him not only confess but also confirm his infidelity. It meant only one thing: He needed me. Unfortunately, none of what he said was news to me. I had long figured this out. The only unclear part was exactly how intimate he and Jansen had been. Other than that, I was aware of everything else. I had been with Joel for over ten years and had known him since I was nineteen. I knew him as well as I knew myself.

"You're admitting all of this to me for what?"

"We're no longer together, and I shouldn't have lost my family by getting involved with Jansen. I had to dig deep to understand what I truly wanted in life. What I want is to have my wife and children back."

Anyone listening would probably fall victim to his pleas. They'd deduce that he'd made a mistake and lapsed in judgment. They might even believe that he was being upfront and sincere and tell me I should fight to reunite my family dynamic.

But I knew Joel.

I allowed him to try to run this game for long enough. It was time for me to call a foul on the play and stop this before he started to annoy me.

"First, thank you for finally telling the truth. However, allow me to paint the true picture: Jana has Jansen by the balls, so he walked away from your relationship. Now you're livid and desperate because you risked everything for him, and he didn't choose you. If I had to guess, you face losing what you've built because your father wants to strip his bisexual-turned-homosexual son of the family restaurant and has more than likely threatened to remove you from his will, too. So, cue trusty Aquila to perform her Black Girl superhero act—throw on the cape and turn from Clarkesha Kent to Superwoman. Does that about sum it up?"

"Come on, Qui—"

"Don't *you* call me that."

He backed up in shock at the venom in my tone. "Okay." He raised his hands. "I apologize. I know I've been a terrible person to you. I don't have the right to ask this, but is what I'm asking unreasonable? Think about our sons. It's obvious that Junior wants us together again. We should prioritize their happiness over our own."

He'd entered executive-level master manipulation status, and I was convinced he held a Ph.D. in gaslighting. I was grateful that I could finally see him for who he truly was. But now, all he'd done was infuriate me.

"I'm going to stop you while you're ahead. I came to hear you out and allow you to see your sons. What you won't do is use Junior's pain to manipulate the situation or use my past kindness for weakness. I am not the same Aquila anymore. There is no way on God's green earth I'd ever reconcile with a man who thinks any of that is acceptable. Not anymore."

"Or maybe you don't want to reconcile with me because another man has your attention, sending you flowers and shit."

The audacity.

"*Wow.* Just *wow.*" With that, I rose from the bench and gathered our sons without offering an argument or rebuttal. I let the boys say their goodbyes to Joel before we left him to stew in his aftermath.

Chapter Twenty-Three

ROMAN

WELCOME TO THE second annual KinRo Fitness Kreme of the Krop athletic training. I am one of your head coaches, Kinston Jordan, and this is your other head coach, Roman Patterson," Kinston introduced us to the group of twenty male high school athletes. "You can call us Coach K and Coach Ro. Every person with a KinRo Fitness t-shirt is one of our staff members who will be assisting us with this special camp. At the end of these next two weeks, we will have equipped you with the skills needed to help improve your strength, agility, and speed. In order to do that, it requires a few things from you. And what are those things, Coach Ro?"

When I didn't readily answer, Kinston turned to me to see me staring out at the young men, but my mind wasn't there. I hadn't heard him when he directed the question toward me. Suddenly, I realized Kinston called my name and became embarrassed by my slip-up.

"My apologies. What was the question?"

Kinston kept his composure, but his stare shot daggers at me. "I was just telling the young men the few things we need from them during this camp, and I asked you what they were."

I dropped my head with my hands on my waist. The first one was a rule that I had already fumbled. "Number one, we need your undivided attention."

"That's right, gang. We need you here with us, paying attention at all times. Or, in other words, the opposite of what Coach Ro just did." Chuckles went up in the air and served as a decent icebreaker for all of us.

After we finished our introductory speeches, we sent them to the table to get assigned their personal gear bag and camp t-shirts. Cami and the staff assisted us, ensuring we stayed healthy and hydrated so everything operated smoothly. Even Kannon and his best friend, Jovan, were there to assist.

"Are you all right, boss man?" Cami asked, approaching me and Kinston while the young men grabbed their t-shirts. "I saw you zoned out for a second over there."

Kinston slapped me on the shoulder. "He's fine, Cami. He's just got his head in the clouds about a certain someone." When Cami looked confused, Kinston covered his mouth with a balled fist. "Oh, she doesn't know."

"Know what?" Cami inquired.

"Know that Kinston needs to go and start the group on the first set of drills." My demeanor clued him in that I didn't want to talk about it.

Kinston pointed at us. "My bad. I'ma just head over there." He exited quickly, realizing he'd placed his foot in his mouth.

I already couldn't stop thinking about Aquila, so the last thing I wanted was to discuss her, especially with Cami. If anyone outside Aquila's family was as close to her as I was, it was Cami. They had formed their bond when Cami served as an alternate trainer for a few of Aquila's sessions. Cami always pressed me about approaching Aquila. She was the only one who noticed my starry-eyed admiration for Aquila at the grand opening yacht party. Ever since Aquila's divorce, Cami had been insistent that I shoot my shot. The moment Cami learned about the cruise, she would be relentless.

"So, are you going to tell me about your lady friend, or will I have to beg Kinston to spill the tea?"

"Now isn't the time, Cami."

She turned on her heels. "Okay. Kinston it is."

Just as she was about to leave—since I wasn't going to stop her—Kannon waltzed up to us with Jovan in tow. Cami knew that I was just as close to Kannon as I was to Kinston, and if Kinston knew, then Kannon did, too. The moment I saw them, I knew my business was about to be laid bare in the parking lot of KinRo.

"Just the man I wanted to see," Cami stressed, staring at Kannon.

Kannon's steps stuttered as he glanced between us and put two and two together about what Cami must be referring to. "It sounds like you're about to snoop for information I'm not authorized to dish out."

As Cami went to protest, I held my hand up. "You know what. It's fine."

"I assume she's trying to find out about you and Aquila," Kannon inserted, leaving Cami and Jovan's mouths gaping.

My head bob was confirmation of the news. Before she could launch a litany of questions, I provided the ChatGPT version. "We linked on the cruise, and she's been avoiding me since we returned—or rather avoiding the conversation about us dating."

It was true. Despite my best efforts to win over Aquila and show her how much I cared for her and her boys, she still hadn't opened up to me. An entire month had passed. After a month of sending flowers, countless text messages, unanswered calls, endless daydreams, and restless nights, I was no closer to her than on the day she walked off my front porch without looking back. I don't know what kind of hex Aquila put on me, but I couldn't get her out of my mind or my system.

When days turned into weeks without us pursuing anything beyond our vacation, I decided to be grateful for our time and come to terms with the idea that the trip would be all that existed between us. How wrong I had been. No matter how hard I tried, I couldn't purge Aquila and move on. The sad part was that I knew she had feelings for me just as I had for her, but she was running scared. That's what made it so frustrating. We could be living life enjoying each other if only she'd take one leap with me. Unfortunately, it seemed that Joel Oliver had wreaked such havoc in her life that she couldn't see past the devastation to appreciate the sunshine we created together. Now, I was left feeling blue from missing her when I'd rather be basking in her rays of light.

Jovan chuckled and slapped his hands with Kannon. "Man, those Richards sisters are hell. So, now Miss Bad and Bougie has Mr. Never Settle Down in a chokehold. I never thought I'd see the day. But y'all tried to warn him. I'm just glad they don't have another sister in the mix, or I'd have to move back to New York to escape whatever is in this Miami water they have y'all drinking."

At that, Kannon slapped his hand away. "Nah. I ain't co-signing that. Besides, Jasmine has you on partial lockdown as it is. You'll be in our shoes soon enough."

Jovan waved off Kannon's comment, but Cami spoke up. "You men irk my nerves. You act like falling in love is so horrible, then you fall and find out it's the best thing that ever happened to you." She turned to face me. "But first, I'm upset with you *and* Aquila for not clueing me in on y'all's hookup, and secondly, what did you do to make her avoid you?"

"Hand to God, I haven't done anything. When we got back, she friend-zoned me. Hell, ice-zoned is more like it. She won't talk to me—at least not about anything other than surface-level bullshit. I've tried several times to meet up, but she has a Ph.D. in dodgeball."

I chose not to mention Joel since I wasn't sure if Jovan or Cami had heard the news, and it wasn't my place to say anything. Even though she had shut me out, I would still protect her and respect her privacy.

Kannon roared in laughter at that. "Sounds very Aquila."

At that, everyone joined in, except for me. It might have seemed comical to them, but I was dead serious. I didn't want to be the one pissing in everyone's cereal, but what seemed minor to them was completely frustrating to me. That was the reason I didn't want to have the "Aquila and me" conversation, and it would be inappropriate to bring my attitude into their space, especially when we were supposed to be training, motivating, and uplifting the youth. As luck would have it, Tyrod approached us, letting us know that the youth had everything squared away with t-shirts and gym bag essentials, so Jovan and Cami went back to divide them into groups so Kinston and I could begin the session.

Kinston made his way back to me after the others had dispersed, and I asked the real question I'd been wanting to pose all morning. "Real talk. How's she doing? After that whole Joel fiasco, I want to make sure she's okay, you know?"

Kinston nodded in understanding. "Actually, she's been doing better considering the circus surrounding Joel and Jansen. She managed to weather it and keep the boys from being exposed, so we were all happy about that. The crazy part is that Joel tried to worm his way back into her life once things calmed down."

An unease settled over me. I understood what he was saying and truly believed she would never reunite with Joel, but he had been her husband for years, and he was the boys' father, so even the most far-fetched idea was possible. "She didn't consider it, did she?"

Kinston sucked his teeth. "Man, hell naw. The whole family would've imploded if she even thought about getting back together with that clown. Besides, I'd prefer to keep my wife out of federal lockup, which is exactly where she would've ended up had Aquila even remotely mentioned rekindling with Joel. Right now, she's focused on pursuing her dreams. Since the summer camp gig, she's secured a couple of jobs for a baby shower and an anniversary celebration. News about her has spread in the community from the affluent people whose kids attend the camp. She is currently looking for more private catering opportunities. It's great to see her embracing and going after her goals, especially since things are a bit shaky with the Oliver restaurant."

A relieved smile graced my face. I was glad to hear she was indeed over Joel and his madness. I was proud to learn that Aquila was pursuing her dreams and not letting Joel and his antics prevent her from doing what was best for her. That's when it dawned on me—if I couldn't get her to come to me, perhaps I could do something that would bring me to her. As we walked over to the group of young men, a plan formed in my mind. I'd make a few phone calls as soon as today's camp was over. A sly grin spread across my face. One way or another, Aquila would see me, and this time, she wouldn't be able to escape my home turf advantage.

Chapter Twenty-Four

AQUILA

$\mathcal{E}$CSTATIC COULD NOT begin to describe the feeling surging through me. There was also a sense of nervousness since I was still in disbelief that my client had taken a chance on my catering for the event I was currently preparing for. Who would have thought a batch of cupcakes could launch me into my dream career? Certainly not me, but I was grateful and intended to keep moving forward. First, one of the mothers asked me to make baked goods for her baby shower, and another inquired whether I could create the cake and cater her sister's anniversary celebration. Even when I didn't prioritize my goals, they made room for me, just as they had for this current event.

The call came in three weeks ago from Daniel, my sons' summer camp director. His fraternity's big brother mentorship program was holding its Black and Gold Guys and Gals Gala for high school youth. The reservation was for one hundred people. I couldn't believe they actually wanted a vegan chef, but Daniel's glowing review must've impressed the planning committee. Well, that and the fact they were in a bind. The previous chef had canceled, and they needed a replacement. I was more than happy to oblige, especially given the size of the paycheck.

Since I didn't have staff, I was able to recruit a couple of culinary arts students from the local university to assist in exchange for course credit and a small payment. Kannon and Angela also stepped up to serve as honorary sous chefs for the evening. I appreciated all my helpers because I knew I couldn't do it alone. The students, Angela, and Kannon helped me set up and would be responsible for replenishing food and drinks throughout the evening. By the time everything was set up in the ballroom and ready in the kitchen, there was thirty minutes left before the event began. Always one to bring class and charm, I changed in the restroom into a cute little black dress and red-bottomed heels. I let my freshly retouched knotless Boho braids hang freely and then slipped on my newly made custom chef's apron that one of my old college friends created at my last-minute request. I hadn't even properly vetted the business name I wanted, so we quickly embroidered Aquila's Creations on it.

"Look at you, number one stunna!" Angela bellowed when I reentered the kitchen. "And I love that apron."

Blushing, I palmed my cheek. "Thanks, sis. I feel awful that you all have to wear those plain black ones, but I didn't want to invest in too many aprons until I finalized my actual business name. I could kick myself for not choosing an official name when Daniel asked me to make the cupcakes. I was so focused on prioritizing everything else over my own needs—"

Angela walked up to me and placed her hands on my shoulders. "Hey, hey. None of that. Not tonight. Tonight, we're celebrating your win. This is your fourth private chef job, and it's a big deal. The food is amazing, the setup is absolutely fabulous, and you're *serving* while serving."

I couldn't help but giggle at that. Angela always came through with uplifting words. I wished I could be more like her at times. She never let anyone see her sweat or took life too seriously. For the life of me, I didn't understand how she managed to maintain that kind of composure, especially after everything she'd been through.

I was so logical and analytical that I operated with a statistical mindset. If it didn't add up, it didn't make sense. But she was right. To hell with all this negativity; tonight was a celebration.

I pulled Angela into an embrace and thanked her for the much-needed words of encouragement. Just then, the kitchen door opened, and I was greeted by the woman officially in charge of hiring me for the event.

"Mrs. Andrews."

"Nonsense. Call me Julia." She stepped into the kitchen, looking stunning in her black-and-gold ball gown. "I just wanted to stop by and check on everything. Also, I wanted to tell you that everything looks and smells amazing. The appetizers are fantastic. Nobody can even tell they're vegan. You're onto something."

Her sentiments had me nearly dancing. "Thank you, Julia. I aim to please."

We shifted our conversation to the side so Angela and my other workers could return to preparing the meal. "I didn't want to settle the tab in front of anyone else." She slipped an envelope into my hand. "This is the remaining balance. Keep an eye out for my call. My fortieth birthday is coming up next month, and I need a caterer."

The heavens were opening up. If I hadn't been stunned into place, I might have keeled over in shock. She wanted to hire me. This was becoming real. My dream. A reality. Somehow, I found my voice. "Sure thing. We'll discuss themes and costs whenever you're ready."

"Perfect!" she exclaimed excitedly. "I'll call you soon. But I'm going to let you get back to your work." She took my hand. "And don't forget to come out and mingle."

When she left, Kannon and Angela came over to me. Angela and I jumped up and down like we did as teenagers when we got our first paycheck from our part-time jobs, while Kannon clapped and bowed in admiration. It was indescribable. Tears welled up in my eyes, but I refused to let them fall, even if they were happy ones. I had to stay professional, and the last thing one of the guests needed to see was a crying chef, misinterpreting it as something being amiss. No, I'd save them for later with a nice glass of Pinot Gris.

The urge to share my good news consumed me. The funny part about irony was that it showed up at the most inopportune times. Ironically, it was Roman I wanted to call and tell all about my good fortune. A wave of sadness threatened to overwhelm me because that line of communication was likely closed, and for that, I had no one to blame but myself. Memories of him cheering on my dreams from the cruise filtered through my mind, along with his text messages and weekly bouquets of flowers. But this week, I hadn't heard from him or received any flowers, and honestly, it stung. At every turn, he'd tried to be there for me, and I'd pushed him away, all because…of what? Secondhand embarrassment? Fear? Hesitation? The exact reason failed to register in my mind. While it may have been a mix of feelings, none of them mattered to me right now. The truth was that I missed Roman and what we'd connected over on that cruise, and no excuse felt good enough anymore, plain and simple.

Tucking the envelope into my apron pocket felt like a reflection of what I needed to do with my feelings: tuck them away so I could be Chef Aquila and provide the guests with the dining experience their one-hundred-dollar-a-head tickets deserved. When I pushed through the doors, the Richards charm I'd been blessed with flowed over me as I waltzed from guest to guest, introducing myself and asking about the food. To my delight, everyone praised the appetizers and eagerly awaited the coursed meal. My helpers were worth their weight in gold as I watched them busily replenish trays, ice, and punch.

"Aquila." Daniel Goldman's voice floated from behind me before I turned to greet him. He grasped my hand in his and lifted it, placing a soft kiss on the curve of my knuckles.

"Daniel." I gulped at the shock of his gesture and subtly removed my hand so that he couldn't linger. "Nice to see you."

"It's always a pleasure." He regarded me. A glint of seduction lingered in his gaze.

Daniel looked debonair in his black tuxedo with a white button-down shirt, complemented by his gold bow tie. He radiated every bit of the historical blackness that he embodied. There was no denying that. As handsome as he was, I didn't share the burning desire he currently displayed for me.

"I had been looking for you to tell you how amazing the appetizers are. Thank you for taking this gala to task." He stepped closer into my space before uttering the last sentiment. "And to tell you how stunning you look."

How he could tell what I wore beneath the apron was puzzling to me. It was a stylish frock, but the true style lay beneath it. Clearing my throat, I stepped back. "Thank you, Daniel. Although I'm unsure how I could possibly look appealing." I gazed down at myself with my hands lifted to the sides. "At any rate, I also wanted to see you to thank you for helping me obtain this opportunity."

His brows knitted together as confusion danced in his eyes. "I'm sorry, Aquila. I wish I could take the credit, but all I did was confirm your recommendation. The person who truly made the recommendation and sealed the deal is…"

Just as Daniel was about to finish his statement, a hand clapped him on the shoulder, prompting both of us to turn and see who it belonged to. My eyes met a familiar pair that caught me completely off guard, but Daniel appeared unfazed.

"Well, actually, this man right here." Daniel acknowledged. "Aquila, this is—"

"Roman." His name slipped from my lips like a rustle in the wind.

He drank a sip from the tumbler in his hand, which had to be tea since it was an alcohol-free event because of the teens present. "Aquila Richards." He tilted his head, his eyes fixed on me. Neither of us ever looked away. "He's right. I made the recommendation."

"Oh, so you two know each other?" Daniel intervened.

However, neither of us paid him any attention. The dryness and roughness in my throat threatened to choke me as I tried to swallow the parched sensation away in search of relief. "Wait. What? How'd you…?" The words came out in broken staccato.

Still holding the glass in his hand, he pointed toward Julia. "Her husband is in the frat, and he's my client. I called him because he invited me to this event, as a couple of young men in their mentor program are also in our athletic training camp," he explained. He then added, "And to answer your earlier question to Daniel, you could wear a brown sackcloth and still look exquisite." Seduction dripped from his compliment, accompanied by a slow wink.

Jesus. Tingles ricocheted all over me, reminding me that Roman still had control over my body and its reactions. I tried to pull away from the telltale signs of my attraction to Roman before anyone noticed, but it didn't matter. Daniel picked up on it and Roman's not-so-subtle hint.

"Well, I guess I should *go*…and mingle." He gave a curt smile, which he tried to cover with a faint laugh.

"You do that," Roman damn near ordered, still not taking his eyes off me.

Daniel cleared his throat. "Right," he bit out, his eyes narrowing in my direction. "Aquila," he said tersely.

My eyes flashed as he broke the trance between Roman and me. Blinking, I focused on Daniel. "It…It was good to see you again, Daniel."

"Likewise, Ms. Richards." The words swooshed out like a rough gust before he walked away.

Roman wasted no time in diminishing the distance between us, but I circumvented whatever he was about to say by raising a hand. My attitude dripped with disdain as I regained my composure. "You didn't have to be rude to Daniel on my behalf."

Roman leaned closer to me, pressing his chest into my outstretched palm, and leveled me with a conqueror's bloodthirsty gaze. "When it comes to you, I'm gonna be a rude man, the caveman, and the fucking boogeyman if necessary to make sure motherfuckers know you're mine, on my mama."

Mercy. I had to clench my thighs together because while my mouth was trained to form a clapback, my puss was meowing, "Yes, daddy." But I ran me, not it and not Roman. While I was not interested in Daniel, he was still a friendly associate, and I valued our relationship. I needed Roman to respect that.

"He's a friend and the director of my sons' summer camp."

"And a man who is clearly attracted to you who needs to understand his role and remain in it."

Although he understood Daniel's intentions, I didn't want him to think he could just waltz into my life and pick and choose who I associated with. "Sir, you can't dictate who my friends can be."

Roman let out a guffaw before taking a sip of his drink and shrugging. "On the contrary, he can be both things you said he was—a friend and the director—but what he can't be is your man."

Well, damn. I couldn't remember the last time I was rendered speechless, but this moment would definitely stay in my memory bank. I had to take a breath to calm my nerves. To be honest, while I felt a bit guilty about how Roman bested Daniel, I wasn't upset because of his rude interruption. Daniel had made me a little uncomfortable with his persistent belief that he had a chance, and I wanted him to stop pursuing me. So, in reality, I was grateful that Roman had initiated the ceasefire.

What troubled me was discovering that Roman was behind my landing this job. While I thought I had earned it through my own merit and the recommendation of my food itself, it turned out to be a "favor" job—pity work. I hated being pitied above anything else. Next to that was the unsettling feeling of being indebted to someone. This once joyous occasion now felt deflated by the one person I had initially wanted to share my good fortune with. That was the true reason for my current attitude.

Roman's shoulders relaxed as his expression softened. He steered me to the side, away from hustling ears and the bustle of the crowd. In the corner, the music masked our voices well enough that we could speak privately.

"Listen, Qui, I didn't come over here to puff up my chest or start an argument."

"No. Maybe you wanted to gloat over securing this job for me as if I'd asked you to." I pointed my finger at his chest. "I'm a grown woman. I don't need you or anyone else to pull strings for me."

He stumbled backward a few steps as if taken aback by my accusation. "Aquila, that's not what this was about, and if I overstepped, I apologize. You know I'm not that kind of man."

"Well, then, what kind of man arc you?"

His head dipped and leveled me with the seriousness of his demeanor. "I'm the kind of man who is trying to show up for you in every way to prove I can be the man you need in your life." He stepped closer and gently tucked one of my braids behind my ear. "And I want to be the man you desire."

Perspiration beaded on my body from the inferno his touch ignited within me. Roman was the man I wanted, but I didn't want another man dictating my life. I had fallen into that trap with Joel. I wouldn't allow myself to be vulnerable to the pitfalls of that mistake again. Joel taught me a valuable lesson about favors—never let anyone think they are doing you one, even if it's the person you should be able to trust the most. The financial support I received from Joel was something I deserved for being the mother of his children and for helping him fulfill his dreams. But *this* was my thing. *Mine.* I wouldn't permit anyone, not even Roman, to believe they had a hand in that success.

Leaning forward, I pointed at him. "The man I *want* will let me be the woman I need to be for myself."

I spun on my heels and was storming away when I heard him say, "And the man you *need* helps his woman realize her dreams." It was enough to stop me in my tracks.

Even over the blare of the music, I heard Roman's footsteps drawing closer to me. I sensed his presence against my back as he inched nearer. The warmth of his broad body radiated against my slim, thick frame. The chemistry between us buzzed uncontrollably, just as it had since we connected on the cruise. It was all-consuming and suffocating. Suddenly, I felt a hand clasp around my arm, and I tensed.

"I'm not here to hinder you from pursuing your dreams or from being the amazing mom and doting sister you are. I only want to add to your life. To multiply. That's what a good man does; he never subtracts or divides." He leaned in so close that his lips brushed my ear. "I know Joel destroyed, but I only want to help restore…if you'll let me."

Before I completely lost my sense of decorum, I bolted out of there and back to the kitchen as if I were on fire. Of course, Angela pulled me aside and insisted that I explain what had happened.

For the rest of the event, I kept myself busy in the kitchen, finding every excuse to let my hired staff go into the venue to help. Angela and Kannon even ventured into the crowd to make sure the plated dinners were served. I only resurfaced at the end for the formal thank-you from the committee and to schmooze with prospective business owners. Throughout it all, Roman and I maintained our distance from each other. Still, I could feel his presence and his lingering gaze on me without needing to acknowledge him. Our souls spoke even if our mouths did not.

When Kannon packed the last of the catering trays into my trunk, he turned to me. "You know, Roman is serious about wanting to give this a shot with you." The look I shot him had him quickly defending his words. "And I'm not just saying that because he's my friend. Real talk. You're my sis-in-love. I would never advocate for someone who wasn't right for you."

I should've known Angela would spill the tea to our brother-in-law. Deflating a bit, I concurred. "I guess you're right because you abhor Joel."

Kannon huffed and flicked the tip of his nose to signal that I was right about that. "Exactly. And you know I'm not one to meddle in other people's business, but I can see you're feeling him just as much as he's feeling you."

"Is it really that obvious?" I buried my face in my hands.

Kannon placed a comforting hand on my shoulder and chuckled. "Just as painfully obvious as it is that you aren't interested in Daniel Goldman."

I playfully punched his arm for that jab.

He lifted his hands. "I'm going to give you advice that I've heard you give to your sisters over these past few years: *Talk to the man.* He may have had his ways, but he's no Joel." We both winced at that thought.

Angela crept out of nowhere and leaned into me. "In other words, he's a good man, Savannah."

We burst into tearful laughter. I knew she had been waiting for that comeback for a long time. It was the same line from the movie *Waiting to Exhale* that Nissi and I had teased her with when she was contemplating reconnecting with Kinston during their rough patch before they got married.

Holding their hands, I nodded. "I hear you." I embraced both of them before they got ready to get into their cars and leave.

Before Angela walked away, she added, "Besides, sis, any man willing to go to such lengths to see you succeed deserves a chance to win your heart." With her arms folded, she bumped my hip with hers. "Take it from someone who also ran scared from a loving relationship, and someone very wise once gave me similar solid advice."

The realization of Angela's turbulent times with Kinston ran through my mind, and I had advised her to hear him out. She left me with that piece of advice, and as I sat in my car, Roman's words filled my mind and seared into the crevices of my heart. For so long, I had been afraid of what we could be, but enough was enough. I refused to be ruled by fear, whether personally or professionally, any longer, so I took a bold leap of faith.

"Aquila?" Roman answered on the third ring; his voice carried the weight of confusion.

Before I could change my mind, I quickly rattled off a heartfelt list of pleas. "Roman, please let me say this before I lose my willpower." His silence encouraged me to continue. "I'm sorry, not just for tonight but for the past couple of months. Tonight, I blamed my attitude on you trying to control me, when in reality, I've been avoiding you for several reasons, but the main one among my excuses is fear. Having a marriage fail after ten years has changed me. It's hard for me to trust men and my decisions about them. Having my boys adds extra weight to that fear because I'm a package deal, and anyone who wants me must want them, too. Still, I don't want to look up one day and see that everyone in my life has moved on except me. I don't want to risk missing out on what could be. I don't want to lose the opportunity with you. So, here I am, scared and all, saying I want to leap off the boat's deck and dive into unknown waters with you."

Roman's weighted exhale felt like he had been waiting for permission to breathe. "*Wow.* I wasn't expecting this. That is a very drawn-out way to say you want your man."

"I know, right?" I giggled at his playful teasing. "I can be a piece of work, but I think you've proven you can handle me."

"Qui." He groaned. "Don't start no shit you can't finish tonight."

"Well, what about tomorrow?" I blurted out, astonished by my own frankness. "You've been catering to me. Let me treat you. I want to take you out on a date."

His rumbling chuckle melted me. The joy in his reaction felt deeply satisfying. His infectious excitement spilled over to me. I needed it because I'd never asked a man out before. I had hidden behind old-school traditions to save face for the Oliver family and brand, but I was ready to run wild and free with Roman.

"Sounds like a date," he answered.

Chapter Twenty-Five

AQUILA

IF I HAD a million bucks, I'd spend it all just to see the sheer adoration on Roman's face again. After he agreed to go on a date with me, I knew I had to make this night as spectacular as possible. Dinner and a movie were nice, but I wanted to show him my appreciation for the months he'd spent attempting to win me over. The weekly flowers and the recommendation for the client warranted an unforgettable evening.

I knew he loved hip-hop and old-school R&B. Since the only concerts in town featured newer hip-hop artists, I chose one that was tolerable to my music palate. So, old-school R&B it was. Thankfully, I found a concert festival that fit the bill. This particular night was a fusion of the nineties and the golden era. Staying true to my promise to pamper him, I picked him up, much to his protest. He only agreed after I promised this wouldn't turn into a regular occurrence. For a West Coaster, he harbored several Deep South values. Though I considered myself a bit of a progressive woman, I had to admit that part of his personality made me swoon because it reminded me of my daddy, Nisante Richards. He may have lived in Miami his entire adult life, but that North Carolina upbringing never left his bloodstream.

Once we arrived at the concert, all our cares were whisked away by the incredible performances of New Edition, SWV,

Xscape, Tamia, and Ginuwine. Their music had us dirty winding in the crowd, while the DJ took us way back between intermissions with tracks by Ron Isley and his brothers, who had us slow grinding on each other, and Frankie Beverly and Maze, who had us two-stepping and electric sliding until the end of the show. By the time we left, we had sweated out every drop of hydration and were completely worn out, but we'd had the time of our lives. My edges were proof of that. Thank goodness I was still rocking the Boho braids for a little longer; otherwise, my usual silk press would've been more like a wool puff. Seeing the childish grin on Roman's face made it all worth it.

Afterward, we decided to stroll along the beach boardwalk to enjoy some of the ocean breeze. Although we had eaten before the concert, our stomachs chimed in with hunger pangs from a night filled with dancing, so we stopped at an ice cream truck and got a few scoops. While he treated himself to two heaping scoops of chocolate with chocolate chunks, I chose an orange sorbet.

"This made foregoing my original cheat day worth every bite." Roman pointed to the cup of ice cream with his spoon as he hummed his satisfaction. "Thank you for this, Qui. I haven't had this much fun since our cruise."

"I'm glad you're enjoying yourself. I wanted to make amends for everything that's occurred since I left your house in a huff."

His stride slowed slightly at the mention of that fateful day.

"Well, you did." He spooned another mouthful of ice cream before continuing, "But I'd still prefer to discuss what led you to flee my house and act as if I were the second coming of the bubonic plague ever since."

My shoulders slumped at his comparison. "I deserved that," I agreed after swallowing a scoop of my sorbet. "Can we sit and talk for a minute?"

Roman extended his arm for me to lead the way. I found a nearby bench that wasn't occupied and sat down. He sat beside me, and I slightly turned sideways to face him. Before I could speak, he interjected.

"Before you begin, I want you to share only what you feel fully comfortable sharing. Please know that I prioritize your privacy and peace above my persistence."

I stretched my hand across his and held it tightly. "You don't know how much that means to me. Truly, I appreciate your patience and understanding." He squeezed my hand in return, nodding his gratitude. "Honestly, I can't hide or sugarcoat what you heard on the news. It's true. My fleeing that day had nothing to do with you. It had everything to do with my embarrassment and frustration with Joel."

Clearing his throat, he dipped his head and asked, "Did you know?"

Heat filled the base of my neck, and I scooped another spoonful of sorbet to cool down and calm my nerves. My eyes closed as I attempted to gather my thoughts when I felt the warmth of Roman's hand gently rubbing and caressing my back. It was soothing to my soul. I swore that with him, it was the little things that made me feel like a schoolgirl eager to check the yes box.

"That's a loaded question. The simple answer is that I didn't know about Jansen until recently. Regarding his sexuality, yes. It was the reason I divorced him. Without going into too much detail, our marriage had been on the brink of destruction for some time before the divorce, as you've occasionally witnessed. That situation culminated when he admitted his propensity for men and his desire to explore more with them. By then, our marriage was severely fractured. That admission confirmed for me that we were far beyond repair. We divorced *amicably*—using that term loosely—for the sake of our children and to avoid public scrutiny."

To ensure I told him everything I wanted to say, I continued, before he could speak. "Although he claimed he never cheated on me, I made sure to get tested every several months as a precaution for my health." Turning to him, I added, "That's another reason I ran from you. I was afraid of your reaction. To protect our children, his sexuality was not something that was supposed to be discussed, but his and Jansen's actions left all of us exposed to public scrutiny. And honestly, that's why it's hard for me to build something new. Joel was my best friend before he became my husband. Therefore, trust is an issue I struggle with, both within myself and with others."

Silence enveloped us as we finished our sweet treats. The night breeze rustled around, offering refreshing coolness after sharing the heaviest parts of my life. Roman discarded our cups into a nearby receptacle before responding to my confession.

"I'll admit, at first, I felt a certain way about you not telling me, but I understand the sensitivity of the subject. Also, regardless of my feelings, that was still your family matter. I appreciate you sharing as much as you have with me. If I can offer any advice, it's to not let his actions dictate your life. We can't predict how other people will evolve. You can only go by what someone presents to you. That's life. Your ex's actions are on him. Don't take that burden on yourself. It wasn't your responsibility to uncover the lies; it was his responsibility to tell the truth."

His last words landed with a thud in my heart, and I melted. I had run from what we could have because of my past with Joel, while Joel was off being happy with Jansen—or had been before they were discovered. I made a definitive decision to choose my happiness because I deserved it, too, and Roman was just the missing piece I needed to add to my newly acquired happy life.

"Can I tell you the truth?" I asked, leaning into him.

He met me halfway. "Always."

My eyes fluttered to meet his as our yearning gazes danced together. "I don't want to be afraid to explore dating you if you still want to give it a try."

His finger glided along my jawline, sending shivers down my spine. "That's what I've been praying for. You unlocked a hidden vault inside of me on that cruise ship, and I need you, and only you, to be the explorer. I can't promise I'm gonna get it right all the time, but I promise to always try for you."

His words were sweet melodies to my ears and heart. Still, I had to address the final elephant looming in the room.

"You have to accept that I'm a package deal. My sons are nonnegotiable."

"Don't you know bundle deals are better?" he joked, making me giggle and playfully punch his arm. "Seriously, those are my guys. They're part of their mama. How could I ever want their mother and not want them?" He lifted my chin. "I want all of you, which includes them."

His sentiments made my heart flutter as a blush crept up my cheeks.

"What do you say? Can we try this thing together?" he probed.

Terrified and all, I was going in. "For you, I will."

Our lips met, and the passion we had discovered on the ship was reignited in that sultry kiss. When we pulled apart, he lingered on my lips. "You do know that means you're mine."

Giggling, I inquired, "And what exactly does that mean, sir?"

"If Daniel or any other man is playing in your face, I reserve the right to play in theirs. When it comes to you, I'm with all the shits."

"So, does that mean you're mine and mine only?"

"Abso-fucking-lutely."

Within the next few minutes, we were back inside my car, tongue-lashing each other down. Something about the seriousness and sincerity with which Roman laid claim to me on the bench at the boardwalk was like an aphrodisiac, and a blaze had swelled inside of me. We were supposed to be en route to his house for a nightcap and conversation, but our hands and mouths spoke their own language. The surrounding trees provided a silhouette around my vehicle, giving us privacy against the dark night sky.

"Baby, if you don't stop," he panted between kisses, "we might not make it back to my house."

I blew a harsh breath and whined, "I don't want to stop."

Roman's mouth twisted into a yearning grimace, his sultry eyes fixed on my pouty lips. He took that skillful tongue I was eager to get reacquainted with in more ways than one and traced the curve of my lips with it. "Say less, baby."

Unbuckling his seatbelt, he climbed out of the passenger seat and into the back-row seat of my SUV, and I followed suit, prepared to satisfy our any-time, any-place urges. We cackled like a couple of teenagers as we continued to kiss and fondle each other in the back of my car, rekindling the raging inferno between us. Roman trailed his tongue along the crease of my neck and sent quivers through my body. His mouth on me was a feeling I didn't believe I'd ever grow tired of. My hands found their way underneath his shirt as I explored the feel of his chest and rock-hard abs. His nips pebbled at my touch and mine at his as he tenderly massaged my nipples between his fingers while deepening his sucks along my clavicle. When he took one breast into his mouth, my back arched, and my head fell backward in ecstasy. I felt his steeliness against my inner thigh. Our bated breaths filled the car in a rhythmic cadence. His body inched downward, and his cool tongue drew a trail down the center of my chest and down to my navel as he lapped at my sensitive skin.

"Help me get these pants down." Roman's voice came out gravelly and strained.

He'd enjoyed the sight of my painted-on jeans that accentuated my assets while we were on our date, but the restrictive material was a nuisance now. Rather than continue to fiddle with my pants, I pushed up to the seated position, causing him to return to an upright position. In a move that shocked him, I kneeled in front of him instead of slithering out of my jeans. Within seconds, I'd unzipped his pants and unleashed the monster straining against his confines.

"Baby, what are you—"

"Tonight is about you."

Before he could object, I nestled his hardness inside my happily awaiting mouth. The feel of his taut and curved caramel dick made my tastebuds water. Aside from it being a masterpiece, it was scrumptious to my palate. My hands gripped his thighs as I inhaled him, traveling deeper on his length. The slow bob of my head helped to moisten him as I greedily slurped, gliding him in and out. His legs tensed as I felt my hair being tugged at my movements' rhythm. His breaths turned from smooth sighs to ragged pants. Sliding up to the tip, I popped his member out to inhale some air and gazed up at him. His hooded lids lowered to me, and his expression begged me not to stop.

"Do you like it sloppy?" My strangled question came out with a moan.

"*Aww* fuck," Roman stretched out in agonized pleasure; his head collapsed against the headrest. "And nasty," he added between groans.

Flipping my braids out of my face, I leaned back down and allowed my saliva to ooze from my lips and slide down his pole before devouring his length again while double fisting him. His entire body strained as his grip tightened around my tresses. As I sloppily bobbed and hummed on him, he began to lift from the seat.

"Qui, I'm about to come, baby. *I'm about to come.*" Roman moaned between gritted teeth. *"Ahhh!"*

I was on a mission. Roman was getting acquainted with a side of me I'm sure he didn't think existed—a side that only Joel had known back in our early days. While I loved the way Roman pleased my body, my secret passion was sucking dick. I craved it. It'd been so long since I indulged, so he fed a dormant frenzy. With the way he felt and tasted in my mouth, I had already become addicted. I knew he was being polite by warning me to give me a chance to pull away from him, but I was a swallower, and I wanted every last drop of his hot load. His deep groans and tightened abs let me know he was near. When his balls drew up, I knew I was about to be blessed with my liquid reward.

"Aquila!" he roared as I jerked the white gold into my throat.

Saving some, I lifted and rubbed his leaking tip around my lips. When our eyes met, I licked his remnants off my lips and then delivered one long swipe to his dick, before showing him the beautiful mess of saliva and lingering sticky remnants on my face.

"So good." The seduction in my voice purred as I gave him a sexy wink.

He fell against the seat, squeezing his eyes closed before refocusing on me with a satiated smile. He brought his hand to my face, palmed my cheek, and glided his thumb over my lips. I parted them and sucked on the tip of his digit. His mouth formed an *O* as he slowly exhaled. Lust and possessiveness filled his lascivious gaze.

"Aquila Richards," he stretched out, "you are full of surprises."

"I'm sure my initial timidness surprised you, but once I'm comfortable…" I let my sentence fade into the knowing gaze we exchanged.

Roman licked his lips, motioning for me to come to him. I climbed his mountainous frame until I was straddling his lap and my arms wrapped around his shoulders. He gripped my ass to him, and I could feel his still semi-hardened erection as it brushed against my swollen sex, which was screaming for attention at this point. He brought his hand to my neck and pulled my face to his, kissing me deeply.

"And you think I'm about to play about you? After this, you'll be lucky if I don't start knocking off heads just for looking in your direction."

I howled in laughter. "Crazy man."

"I'm serious." He turned my chin so that we were squarely faced. "Qui, *I'm serious*," he reiterated to emphasize his words.

I tightened my forearms around his neck, leaning his head toward me. "As long as you know I'm just as serious, Dr. Patterson."

Flashes of all the times Joel broke my heart flooded my mind, making me feel my countenance sink. Roman's hand on my chin pulled me out of those painful memories. When I focused on him, his eyes were filled with concern.

"Where did you go?" he asked, his brows furrowed with worry.

Despite my resistance, my bottom lip started to quiver. "Please don't hurt me." My voice trembled, and I buried my face in the crook of his neck to shield him from witnessing the devastation of my past wounds.

He wrapped his powerful arms around me and held me close. I burrowed into his broad chest, finding respite in his soothing embrace. His hands stroked up and down my back as he muttered reassuring sentiments and planted soft kisses on my temple. When he felt calmness return to me, he lifted me.

"I may not know everything you've experienced, but I have no intention of causing you any more pain. My track record might not look promising, but I'm a man of my word. When I say this is where I want to be, I stand on that." He extended his pinky finger to me. "Trust?"

Recognizing his sincerity and the deepening feelings that were growing by leaps and bounds for this man who was also one of my closest friends, I nodded and linked my pinky finger with his. "Trust." With that, we intertwined our fingers and sealed it with three gentle pecks.

"Now, can we finish this at my place? I owe you for the show you put on tonight, and I need more space than this cramped spot to do everything I want to do to you."

I shrugged. "It's yours, isn't it?"

His manhood pulsed beneath me. "Let's go—now," he growled, his primal urges renewed.

"Yes, Dr. Patterson."

Chapter Twenty-Six

ROMAN

As I LAY in the bed with Aquila in my arms, it was a dream come true. Our date had long since ended, and now we were vibing. After bringing her back to my place and sexing her body down properly, neither one of us had a desire to depart from the other. Her sister Nissi had volunteered to keep her boys while we were on our date, and with one phone call, she agreed to keep them overnight. Apparently, they were a huge help in keeping baby KJ occupied to the point that they had all worn each other out and were asleep, so she and Kannon could spend the night catching a movie and having an adult drink. I loved their family dynamic. Now that we'd turned the page and started dating exclusively, I was excited to learn more about Aquila's family, especially her boys.

Those little dudes were already my little homies, whom I got to hang out with two Saturday mornings out of the month. Now, I had the pleasure of incorporating them into my daily life, and I couldn't wait. Knowing that the dynamic between Aquila and me had changed, I was happy I'd already built a rapport with them. I hoped it made for an easier transition from solely being friends with their mom to now dating her.

"What's on your mind?" Aquila's voice broke the silence surrounding us.

I looked down to find her full attention on me as I stroked up and down her arm. Our naked bodies were intertwined underneath my satin sheets. Her soft fingertips stroking from my pecs to my abs felt like home. *She* felt like home. I'd lived in this house for five years; it was the first time I felt settled.

"Just thinking about your boys—how our relationship is going to develop and transform."

She turned and propped on her elbow. "Are you worried?"

"Maybe a bit nervous about how they'll take the news, but honestly, I'm excited."

"Well, that's good." She lay back down against me.

Her lackluster response to my enthusiasm was somewhat disappointing, but I attributed it to her being tired. We had worn each other out tonight, but if I had anything to do with it, we'd be completely exhausted before the night was over.

"So, can you help a brother out? Tell me more about them. Give me a little home-team advantage."

I could feel her slowly exhale as if she were contemplating what to divulge. After a few short seconds that felt like minutes, she finally spoke, "*Umm.* There isn't much to say. They're your typical little boys. Both of them are into video games, Junior more than Sante, but of course, he'll follow his big brother to the ends of the Earth. Sante still loves to play with action figures, but he gets upset when Junior refuses to play with them unless I make him. They love sports and action movies. Mostly, they're rambunctious as can be. Sante is my little comedian and truly a little mama's baby. Junior is at that age where he wants to be mama's baby, but not in public because it's embarrassing. Almost everything I say or do is embarrassing to him these days, but he and Sante are my world. I love them immensely."

I hugged her closely. "It's a phase. Trust me, your boys will always be mama's babies. Every man loves his mother."

She shot me a glance. "Please don't tell me I have to compete with your mother," she joked.

"Nah, never that. I love my mama. That's my sweetheart. Like your sons, I'm a mama's *baby*, not a mama's *boy*. There is a difference. She doesn't run me, nor does she desire to. My mother was adamant that she raise independent children. As soon as she finds out about you, she will be on my neck for marriage and grandkids." I kissed her forehead and added, "Besides, there are some things you can do for me that my mama can't do."

We burst into laughter as she playfully tapped me. "Well, I certainly hope not."

"Hell nah. Ain't no funny family business going down with the Pattersons."

She moved to lean against the headboard. "Speaking of the Pattersons, tell me more about your family."

I brushed my hand down the waves of my hair. As much as I loved my family, talking about them was hard for me. Like Aquila, I struggled with trust issues when it came to sharing about them. I was a staunch protector of them. It already took a lot for me to open up, but sharing openly about the ones I cherished most felt like trying to crack the Da Vinci Code—damn near impossible. For Aquila, I would take baby steps. It was only fair. If I wanted to know her intimately, she deserved the same courtesy.

"There's really not much to share about them. You know my mom works in the medical field, and my dad is in tech. I have a younger sister, Gracyn. We're a close-knit family, but they're pretty busy with work, so I rarely see them. My mom dislikes that I chose to stay on the East Coast instead of returning home so she can see me more, but she's adjusted to the distance. At least, she pretends to handle it well. They're your traditional Black family. Not overly religious, but we pray together. I'm the spitting image of my dad, and he's my hero. My sister is the perfect blend of both of them. She's beautiful. She's also my biggest supporter and friend, and my greatest headache. I'll protect her as if my life depended on it."

Peering at her smile and approving look, I wondered, "Why are you staring at me like that?"

"It's just astonishing to see this side of you. I know I keep harping on the distorted image of you as a playboy, but you genuinely seem to be all about family. It's just a different perspective for me."

"I'm all about my family and…" I paused before pulling her into my lap. "I'm all about you, too. You and your boys. I don't want you to think I'd enter your lives unless I was serious about it. I am."

She toyed with my fingers before admitting, "That's what has me baffled. How are you so sure so soon? It's not that I don't believe you when you say you're ready; it just seems a bit fast, as if you've gone from one extreme to the other. I don't want to feel like I'm rushing you into a lifestyle you're not prepared for."

I leaned my head against the headboard and closed my eyes. For the most part, I was a private person, which is why my family ideology and my deep love for them caught Aquila off guard. None of my friends truly understood how much family meant to me. They all knew I was loyal as a friend, but somehow equated the fact that I had dated a few women—okay, quite a few women—with not being family-oriented. In a sense, I understood it. Although I never expressed that I wasn't into family, I never gave the impression that I *was* either.

"I'm sure because I've always wanted you since your last name was Oliver."

My eyes popped open just in time to see her mouth fall agape at my revelation. She attempted to say something, but everything came out in a jumbled mess of awkward sounds and noises. Sitting up, I lifted her hands and softly caressed them in mine.

"I know this sounds far-fetched to you, but the truth is that from the moment you walked into KinRo and signed up with our old receptionist, Lauren, I've been attracted to you. By the time you joined, we had a strict no-fraternization rule, so I could never approach you. Then, when I found out you were married, it sealed the deal for any hopes I had. So, I settled for you being a client and then, eventually, friends. When the entire Kannon and Nissi and then Kinston and Angela situations unfolded, it gave me more opportunities to be around you outside of just the gym, and the more I was around you, the more those old emotions resurfaced. Still, it was hopeless because of Joel, whom I've long wanted to boot from your life myself, given how he treated you. Unless an opportunity ever arose, all I could do was admire you from afar, so I lived my life while you lived yours. Then, a very attractive, very timid, and very *single* woman named Aquila Richards—formerly Oliver—literally ran into me on a cruise ship."

Aquila's eyes danced around. It was clear she was trying to connect the dots to make my confession make sense. "It's not that I don't believe what you're saying, but I'm confused why you dated or slept with Nia or whatever if that's how you felt. I understand that you two are done and have been for a while, but if that's the case, why didn't you approach me once I was first divorced?"

Nia. I knew this conversation was going to come back around. I had to tread lightly. Even though I didn't mean any harm, I understood I needed to deliver this news with a modicum of respect and humility. Nia was Angela's best friend and also a friend of Aquila's. I didn't want to offend either of them. But the cold, hard truth was that Nia was the greatest mistake of my life.

"I only pursued Nia because of that dinner at Kannon's house when the entire dinner table insisted we hook up so we could all be on some couple and friends shit. My boys were the ringleaders in that crusade."

"So was Joel," she faintly uttered.

And there it was. I was glad I didn't have to say it. The last thing I wanted was to sound like I was using her ex-husband as a scapegoat to date Nia. "Yes. So was Joel," I reiterated. "I sensed that he felt my emotions for you that night, so he joined in to undermine me. But I don't pursue married women, no matter how I feel." I dragged my hand down my face. "That's why I was never truly interested in Nia; you were married, so I thought, why not? That's the reason I never approached you after you and Joel ended things. I knew you'd never give me a chance because of Nia. If I had a crystal ball to foresee the future, I never would've gotten involved with her."

The shock of my words must have been too much for Aquila, as she stood wrapped in the sheet and began to pace the floor. As if a light bulb had switched on, she turned to me. "That's why you defended me at the dinner against Joel," she stated more than asked.

Slowly, I bobbed my head in agreement as I reflected on the friends' dinner that started with me defending Aquila and ended with my friends coaxing me to hook up with Nia.

"And on the party bus for Kinston's birthday, when Kinston and Joel got into it and Joel got right in my face, you defended my honor. You were the one who laid hands on him," she said as realization crossed her face. "You weren't standing up for me because you disliked Joel, but because you liked me. My sister was right."

I held up a finger. "Oh, I definitely dislike Joel, but yes, my intervention had more to do with the fact that he was treating the woman I secretly longed for like crap, and all I could think was that you'd never have to worry about that if you were mine."

And there it was; my hidden truths laid bare. Then, what she said struck me. "Wait. What did your sister say?"

"When I told them that you and I connected on the cruise, they were shocked but deduced that it made sense that you liked me because of how you'd defended me in the past. I didn't feed into what they said until just now."

A solemnity fell over Aquila before she turned away from me, directing her attention to the floor. I didn't know whether to approach her, so I remained patient until she gave me a sign. She walked to the opposite side of the bed and sat down with her back toward me. I climbed to my knees and placed my hands on her shoulders. She looked over at the nightstand and gently traced my beaded bracelet, which matched hers—the ones we got in Turks and Caicos. I placed my hand over hers, and we interlocked fingers. Her head fell back against my chest lazily, and we sat there, basking in our shared silence. When she turned to face me, I captured her lips in a kiss, hoping she'd accept it. When she deepened the kiss, I eased around her body and leaned her back against the bed as I hovered over her.

"Can I have you again?" My lust-filled voice exposed my intimate musings.

"Sure. I think you've waited long enough, Dr. Patterson."

Chapter Twenty-Seven

AQUILA

THE SOUND OF the doorbell startled me. It couldn't be noon already. I tapped my phone to verify, and sure enough, it was, which meant I was behind schedule. I needed to leave the house in an hour to set up for my client's party, and the last batch of cookies still had another fifteen minutes. I'd have to skip the extra shower I'd planned and hurry to get out the door on time. I dusted off my hands on my apron and ran to the door.

"Joel." I swung the door open quickly and ushered him inside. "Thanks for being on time. Looks like I'm the one running behind."

He closed the door and followed me through the house. He sat at the kitchen island while I scrambled to gather everything I needed to pack. "No problem. Is there anything I can help with?"

Record scratch. I stopped in my tracks and turned, my eyes widening in surprise. Even though we'd found common ground for the sake of our kids, I wouldn't expect him to help with anything beyond our children. Just the offer itself left me bewildered. Who was this new Joel, and where did he come from?

It had been a little over a month since that wild day at the park. Ever since I stormed out on him, he had been cordial, which was all I wanted. He called me the next day to apologize for what he'd said and told me he wouldn't pressure me to rekindle our marriage. I couldn't help but pry for more details about Jansen.

Surprisingly, he was forthcoming that Jansen chose his wife, stipulating that they would no longer talk or see each other in any capacity, nor would the Carlyles assist the Olivers financially. It was as if they had never known each other. Joel maintained that while it hurt, he knew that would be the outcome because Jana was ruthless, unlike me. When he reflected on how I handled the situation compared to Jana, he realized how much he had taken me for granted, which prompted him to broach the subject of getting remarried. He admitted he allowed his ego to lash out at me, but accepted my answer. However, he still wanted to leave the rekindling discussion on the table for when or *if* I was ready. I would never be ready for that, but I took my wins where I could. Since then, we have been able to speak amicably over the phone about the kids and finances. He halted the petition to lower alimony to give me time to get my business off the ground, for which I was grateful. Even though I knew he was still struggling to get the restaurant out of arrears without alerting his father, he expressed that he understood the difficulties of starting a business and that the first year was the most crucial. He agreed he wanted me to be successful because I deserved it, but also for the boys. To assist, he stepped up with caring for our sons and spending more time with them. As much as I didn't want to admit it to him, I needed the extra help and was thankful beyond measure that this was something I didn't have to battle him about.

But with Joel, one could never tell. I wasn't sure if he was trying to turn over a new leaf or if he was banking on wooing me back with changed behavior, but either way, that was never going to happen. It wasn't because I had Roman in my life; it was simply because I was no longer in love with Joel Oliver, and I wouldn't force myself into a relationship that didn't serve me just to please others. Not anymore. Being with Roman only reinforced my decision. I still hadn't confirmed that I was dating anyone, let alone Roman, to Joel or my sons. It was still new, and I didn't want to open that discussion too soon. I needed to be sure that what we were building was solid and secure first, because once that information was out, I had no idea how any of them would react. Admittedly, that scared me. For now, Joel's belief that I didn't want to be with him without the additional knowledge of my dating life would have to suffice.

Joel shrugged. "What? You're in a rush. You need an extra pair of hands. I kinda know my way around a kitchen, and I'm here, so use me." He lifted his hands.

"Dad!" Sante yelled, entering the kitchen and running up to him.

Joel lifted him into his arms. "Hey, buddy. Where's your brother?"

"Upstairs packing. I'll go get him." Sante was out of his arms and headed upstairs faster than the speed of lightning.

Once Sante ran off, I took Joel up on his offer. "Can you take the cookies out of the oven once they finish, put the rest of these brownies and cookies in the containers, and load this in my car?"

"You've got it." He stood and washed his hands at the sink.

I took off my apron to take a quick shower and throw my clothes on. On my way up the stairs, I saw Junior moseying down with both his and Sante's backpacks.

"Hurry up and put those in your dad's car." Junior nodded, but I caught the eye roll and stopped him. "What's that look for?"

He hunched his shoulders and shook his head as if he were uninterested in talking to me. I stood in front of him with my arms folded, making it clear that wasn't going to fly with me.

Huffing, he said, "I'd rather go with Auntie Nissi or Auntie Angela. Dad doesn't keep his promises, and I don't want to go with him."

I pulled him into an embrace. Joel had made his fair share of mistakes regarding the boys since the divorce, but he'd been on point ever since the park. Junior had seemed to come around, so I was unsure where this new attitude came from.

"What promise did he break?" Junior's wide eyes sparkled with panic. I rested my hands on his shoulders to comfort him. "You can tell me."

Although reluctant, he let out a swoosh of air and confessed, "I overheard him tell Grandma that he was trying to move back into our house, but he's not, Mom. When I asked him on the phone last night if he was moving back, he said no. So that means he told a fib to Grandma."

That damn Joel. Apparently, he hadn't told his parents I had rejected his proposition, and instead of being honest, he was stringing them along with lies. Now, his lies were affecting our child, putting me in the position of having to defend his reckless antics once again.

"Listen, I don't want you to stress over that. At the end of the day, your dad has always been there for you whenever you or I call him, right?"

Junior grudgingly nodded. "Right."

"Then that's all that matters." I patted his shoulder. "Give your dad some grace. This adjustment is tough on all of us. He's doing the best he can. We all are. Okay?"

Junior offered me a half-hearted smile. "Yes, ma'am."

With that, he headed downstairs, and when I heard him and Joel greet each other, everything seemed restored. I rushed up the stairs to take a prostitute bath—since a shower was impossible—so I could be ready in time. As for Joel, I would bide my time to confront him about his lies because the real truth of the matter was not about us getting back together, but rather that he was still hiding his sexuality, and the sooner he faced that, the better it would be for all of us.

Chapter Twenty-Eight

ROMAN

*E*VEN THOUGH IT was a chilly December morning, the pep in my step couldn't be denied. It felt as if I was walking on cloud nine every day, and that sensation could only be attributed to one person: Aquila. With each passing day, we discovered more about each other, forging a bond that felt solidified by our monogamous commitment. While I agreed to 'date' Aquila—albeit exclusively—to allow us both time to decide whether we wanted to put an official label on our relationship, I was confident that she was the woman I wanted in my life for the long haul. It felt awkward to admit it, considering how much trash I'd talked about my boys, but now, I was part of the "when you know, you know" club with them, because with Aquila Richards, I *knew*.

Somehow, deep down, I'd always known. Always hoped. Even when hope felt distant. Even when the possibility seemed non-existent. There had been a soul-stirring pull on my heart that I could never shake or comprehend. Now, three official months into our courtship, here I was, completely smitten with the one woman I never thought in a million years could be mine.

Yet, despite all these giddy feelings and a seemingly promising future, a sense of dread plagued me. It had nothing to do with Aquila or our current status. It was entirely about the world around us. As long as we remained in our bubble, that was all that mattered and all that existed. However, there was a world outside our bubble. Although some of those outside knew about us, for the most part, it was just our original inner circle. My parents and sister knew of Aquila, but I doubted her parents knew about me. We hadn't discussed them apart from general conversation, nor had I been invited to meet them. I didn't dwell too much on not meeting her family because I was sure she wanted to ensure our relationship carried more significance than simply dating. However, my greatest concern was telling her boys that we were dating. I was certain they weren't aware, and just like her parents, I hadn't been invited to meet them, other than seeing them at the gym. Since I had an established bond with them, I felt uncomfortable being around them, as if we were hiding in plain sight. Besides, the sooner they knew their mother was dating, the quicker they could adjust to my presence in their lives. The issue was that I didn't quite know how to broach that subject with Aquila. On the one hand, I felt my feelings were valid enough to have a discussion. On the other hand, I worried I'd be overstepping because those were her children, and ultimately, it was her decision when to introduce someone new into their lives. So, I remained in limbo, but sooner or later, we'd have to tell them. I preferred sooner, while it seemed she was a proponent of later. My hope was that delaying the revelation of our relationship to her boys wouldn't hurt us in the end. Without their approval, any desire to advance further could easily fizzle out. Aquila was all about her children, and I couldn't see her wanting to continue if it meant sacrificing their feelings. For now, all I could do was hold on to hope that my worries were unfounded.

The ringing of my cell phone snapped my attention. I took a moment to stretch, then leaned back in my chair and lifted my cell from my desk. The name scrolling across my screen was unexpected.

"Hey, stranger," the voice purred through my speakerphone. Exhaling, I greeted, "Nia."

"Well, don't break out the fanfare."

"What's up?"

Scoffing, she *tsk*ed. "*Hello, Nia. How are you? I'm busy, so can I call you back?* That's how normal people greet each other…with pleasantries, Roman. I don't know who pissed on your side of the bed this morning, but save the rudeness for them."

Pinching the bridge of my nose, I realized she was right. She had nothing to do with what I was dealing with. Hell, she didn't even know. She'd been away for months on a travel nurse assignment. Acknowledging this, I let go of my attitude.

"My bad. You're right. Let's start over. Hey, Nia. How are you?"

"Better now that you've calmed your feisty ass down."

I patted my chest as though she could see me. "I deserved that. My apologies. I shouldn't have taken my stress out on you."

"That brings me to the reason for my call. I'm back in town, and it sounds like you could use a stress reliever just as much as I could."

This time, her soft voice had returned, infused with sugary undertones that suggested exactly what kind of time she was on.

"Nah. I'm good."

"Oh, come on. It's chilly outside, and it's been a while since we've kept each other warm. I can do that thing you like. I know you're not going to turn *that* down."

The "thing" she did paled in comparison to the "*things*" Aquila did to me, but I would never expose my baby's sexual prowess to anyone, nor would I embarrass Nia. Irritation crept in because I loathed when a woman couldn't take no for an answer—a residual effect of my previous client-slash-bedroom-buddy-turned-stalker's behavior. People loved to nail men to the cross for relentlessly pursuing women who didn't want them, but women could be just as ruthless, if not more. Still, Nia was only responding to what we used to share. Obviously, she didn't know what had happened since she'd been away. I had no problem informing her, but I did want to gauge Aquila's opinion on the subject first. Until then, I'd let her down easy and hope she'd catch the hint.

"Nia, what we had was cool, but—"

"Oh shit. You met somebody," she bellowed, interrupting my rejection.

I couldn't help but smile as it spread like wildfire, thinking about who that somebody was that I was now dating exclusively. "Yeah, I did. We're solid, and I'm not interested in betraying what we're building."

There was a pregnant pause, and finally, Nia uttered, "Damn."

"Are you all right?"

She inhaled sharply. "Yeah, I…*umm*…I guess I'm just shocked, is all. I knew you were looking for a constant, but this seems more like a permanent situation."

I leaned forward, propping my elbows on the desk. "That's the goal."

"Wow. She must be an amazing woman."

"She is." It was all I was willing to offer for now.

Nia cleared her throat. "Well, that's good for both of you. I wish you the best and hope everything works out." I could hear the pang of hurt in her words, and while I felt bad for her, it was what it was.

"Thanks. I wish you the best, too."

We ended the call, and I sat back with my arms behind my head, hoping and praying that Nia wouldn't become a problem for me and Aquila.

Chapter Twenty-Nine

AQUILA

THE AMOUNT OF exuberance I felt when I heard Angela's car horn made me think I should be low-key ashamed. Angela, Nissi, Nia, Ciara, and I were all set for some girls' time. Back in the day, I rarely hung out with my sisters and their friends during their famous girls' night out, mainly because Joel was always missing in action, and I hated to burden my parents with babysitting. Often, it would result in a million questions about my absentee husband, and I didn't want to face the ridicule. So, instead, I stayed home and played super mommy. Now, I'd learned to fully embrace the "fuck them kids" mantra. In fact, I was the one who rallied the children tribe and dropped KJ, Sante, Junior, and even Fawn off at our parents' house.

Fawn was staying with Kinston and Angela this weekend and decided to help out the grandparents by watching the boys tonight. She was such a sweetheart, and we all loved her immensely. Kinston tried his best to hold on to as many years with her as he had left. She'd be sixteen in just a few months and was currently a sophomore in high school. So far, she had wavered between wanting to return to California to attend UCLA or attend her parents' alma mater, the University of Miami. Her mother was rooting for California, while the rest of us were cheering for The U, especially Kinston.

At any rate, with all the kiddos now under the care of their grandparental babysitters, my sisters had come to pick me up because I planned on getting margarita-wasted. My body demanded it. Business had picked up tremendously, and leading into the holidays, I'd been booked and busy. There were no complaints from me, but I understood the importance of maintaining a work-life balance. Tonight, I planned on lifeing the hell out of the balance. Roman provided balance, too, but we also needed some time apart. We'd been enjoying our new-couple bliss for three months, so a little downtime with the girls was necessary. While we were having girl time, the guys were having their bro time. Roman, Kinston, Kannon, Jovan, and Zach—Ciara's husband—were heading to one of their favorite sports pubs to enjoy some beers and watch football. It was a win-win for everyone.

My sisters hooted at me when I stepped out of the house, strutting toward Angela's Beemer. Climbing inside, we cackled and high-fived each other—a clear signal that the silliness and foolery were about to ensue.

"Look at you looking all hot and stuff." Angela beamed at my ensemble.

"*Mmm-hmm.* Get a man, and she wants to show off all the assets," Nissi jeered with a finger snap.

A catchy tune grabbed Angela's attention as she bumped the music, and she and Nissi started yelling and pointing at me. "Get it, sexy!"

Joining in on the fun, I pursed my lips and twerked in my seat to the rhythm of the song. Since dating Roman, we'd been exploring each other's musical tastes more and more, and oddly, I had developed a new infatuation with what I called Gen Z street bangers. There's nothing like a little young school ratchet bop to get the blood pumping. I wouldn't attend any concerts or buy albums, but I'd enjoy them during some adult fun or workout sessions. Although that wasn't exactly the vibe Roman aimed for when introducing me to his music style, he conceded that a little hood hip-hop was better than none.

"OMG! Who is this woman, and what have you done with our Lah?" Nissi screamed as Angela turned down the volume and backed out of my driveway.

I lifted my hands. "I'm just a new-and-improved Lah."

Angela teased, "She's been Romanfied."

"And Roman has been Aquilafied," I tossed back as my sisters erupted in deafening hollers.

"Okay, sis," Angela sang. "It sounds like your relationship has progressed."

"We're still dating and taking it slow, but what we have is strong and solid."

On that note, I received enthusiastic cheers of approval as each of my sisters offered me their hands in a low high-five. The rest of the way, we shared stories about our children, work, and, of course, the challenges of keeping tabs on our hard-to-raise parents. If we thought raising kids was a tough job, it didn't compare to trying to raise our senior citizen–aged parents who were too grown for their own good. By the time we reached our favorite spot, we were all caught up on each other's lives and ready to gossip and sip with our girls.

Per usual, Ciara was punctual and had secured a high-top table for us. We met her at the table and started our round of hugs. Before we could all sit down, however, Nia strolled over to us, and we greeted her with the most enthusiasm since she'd been away on a work assignment for months, making this our first time seeing her since early July. No sooner had we taken our seats than our waitress came to gather our drink and appetizer orders.

"I've missed this so much," Nia squealed. "Y'all have to catch me up on everything."

"And we will, sis, but tell us about your time away. I think this is the longest work travel you've had in a while," Angela said, as we agreed.

"It is," Nia confirmed as the waitress brought our margaritas and appetizers. She bit into the pita bread with dip and took a sip of the mango margarita. "I've been craving one of these."

"You didn't hang out with the other nurses while you were away?" Nissi asked.

"I did, but it just wasn't the same. It felt like having drinks with a co-worker, and no one makes my mango margarita quite like this place."

After that, she launched into a story about her time in Seattle, the people she had met, her wildest cases, and her one-time hook-up with a local male nurse. Without a doubt, she had us in hysterics with that failed experiment, as she referred to it.

"He tried his best not to be placed on schedule when I was around, and when he couldn't avoid it, he just ignored me, which I was fine with me, with his two-pump, nut-head ass." Nia finished her story, and we laughed until we were in tears.

Once we gathered ourselves after her hilarious story time, Ciara jumped into discussing the renovations she and Zach were making to their home. The conversation flowed around the table, with Nissi doting on baby KJ and telling us about Kannon expressing a desire for another child. Then Angela shared all the school activities Fawn was involved in. We all admired her accomplishments and felt so proud of her. By then, we had a couple of margaritas in us, and the conversation turned salacious as they began talking about new bedroom toys they wanted to try and positions they were perfecting with their spouses.

"All I'm saying is stick with your husbands because the dating pool is filled with swamp water," Nia said, her mouth dropping open as her eyes met mine. "My bad, Aquila."

"No worries." I snickered, tipsy from the liquor. The last thing I cared about was my failed marriage when I had Roman by my side.

She snapped her fingers. "Wait a minute. You've been quiet over there. The last time I saw you, you were getting ready to leave for that singles cruise. How was it? Over there, keeping the tea to yourself."

The entire table fell awkwardly silent because we hadn't considered this aspect of our reunion during the planning. I could tell that my sisters and Ciara were waiting to see how I would address the situation without overstepping my boundaries. My current status with Roman was not up for public discussion, but it was also something I didn't want to conceal, not from Nia or anyone else, for that matter. However, I would be cautious about how I approached the topic to ensure everyone remained copacetic.

I took a long sip of my Coronarita before I answered her question. "The trip was fantastic. I rested and relaxed. It was the break I never knew I needed. Thank you for suggesting it."

She stared at me as if waiting for me to finish until she realized that was all I was going to say and scoffed. "That's it?" she inquired. "What happened? What did you do, and where did you go? Better yet, did you find someone to do?" she joked between bites of our shared chicken wing appetizers.

I'm sure my face looked dreamy as I reminisced about the excursions, the food, and the amenities aboard the cruise ship, all filled with memories of Roman, too.

"I did meet someone."

Ciara coughed and pounded her chest to clear it while sipping her peach margarita. "I'm sorry. Something must have gone down the wrong pipe." She eyed me as if to ask if I was sure.

I settled back and nodded, resolute in my decision to tell Nia the truth. Under the table, Angela squeezed my hand as a gesture of encouragement. That provided me with all the motivation I needed to continue.

"It's kind of funny, actually. The person I met is from Miami, and he's a man I've known for years," I said, trying to deliver the news gently.

"That's wild," Nia said, her eyes shining with anticipation. "You went all the way out of the country to meet a man in your own backyard."

"Literally," Nissi uttered before sipping on her drink. "*Ow,*" she shrieked lowly. "Sorry, I bumped my knee."

But I knew Angela had kicked her.

"So, are you and Mister Man seeing each other now that you're off the cruise?" Nia continued her inquisition.

"Yes, we are. We're dating exclusively and seeing where it will go from here."

Nia was elated as she reached across the table to high-five me. "All right, girl. So basically, the best water must be at sea because you're doing that. When do I get to meet him? I'm sure you all have since I've been away."

Unease settled among the women, and I knew I had to rip the bandage off and say it. "You've already met him." When her expression turned puzzled, I added, "It's Roman. Roman and I are dating."

It was Nia's turn to have a full-blown coughing fit. Her eyes bulged as she shook violently. It got to the point where Nissi and Ciara had to pat and rub her back while Angela signaled to the waitress for water. Hurriedly, the young lady rushed to the bar and returned with a glass, handing it to Nia, who drank and leaned back as she fanned her face and settled down.

"I'm sorry. Did you say *Roman*? As in Roman Patterson?" Nia asked, her face completely stoic and unreadable.

Leaning forward, I gestured. "Yes. That would be the one." I tried to keep my voice steady and gentle so it wouldn't come across as a gloat. "Listen, Nia, I honestly didn't know how to tell you, and Roman assured me there was nothing between you two."

Right on time, Angela chimed in. "Exactly. And you told us a few years ago that it was just sex and that you all were no longer involved with each other."

Nia shot a glare at Angela. "And I also said I'd let him spin the block. We weren't dating or had anything official, but it's not like we weren't keeping the door open for our sexual trysts."

Now, I understood that the news might have caught her off guard, but she had no claim to the man. *My* man. At least he was mine when it came to any other woman wanting him to be available for them to...spin a fucking block. Maybe I was misinterpreting her words. This was Nia. She was Angela's bestie and my friend. I'd calm down and give her the benefit of the doubt.

"Girl, I know it may feel awkward for you. Believe me, it is for me, too—"

Nia tossed aside the napkin she had used to wipe her mouth and hands. "*Girl?* Oh, so *now* we're girls. Were you thinking about us being *girls* when you went and screwed Roman and decided to start dating him without even asking if I was okay with passing the collection plate?"

Blinking, I tossed myself back into my seat, trying to wrap my mind around what she had just said. The Holy Spirit had better activate before the Lah spirit in me did, because our girl or not, Nia was testing the wrong waters with me, especially regarding my Roman.

Before I could respond, Angela jumped in. "Come on, Nia. It's not that serious. You and Roman were nothing. You said it was just a test drive for you. Roman and Aquila have found each other and are exploring something real and meaningful for them. It may have caught you off guard, but don't pretend it's that deep. Don't act like that."

"That's rich coming from someone who claims to be my bestie. We've been best friends since we were kids, and you didn't have the decency to tell me?"

Angela's mouth fell agape. "It wasn't my business to share."

"Bullshit." She snorted with a scoff. "You could tell me everything else that wasn't your business to share except this? We talked often. Not once did you think you should mention, 'By the way, my sister is fucking your fuck buddy.'" She then turned her vitriol back to me. "Matter of fact, *you* have my number, Aquila. I could've heard it directly from the violator's mouth."

Nissi scooted her chair away from Nia. "Now, hold on. You may feel a certain way, but you can't sit here and disrespect my sisters. We're extending grace because you're our friend, but please don't ever think you can get it twisted."

Nia cocked her head to the side. "You're really going to come at me like that when your sisters are dead-ass wrong?"

Ciara comfortingly patted Nia's hand. "Let's just take a beat. It all came at you at once, so you're having a knee-jerk reaction. You don't want to say something you might regret later."

"Screw you, Ciara," she said, snatching her hand away. "What I'm experiencing is an epiphany about some women I thought were my friends who wouldn't lie or betray me. Instead, you all want to support Aquila in her wrongness instead of acknowledging that. Now, I understand why she landed a man so quickly. She's cut from the same murky waters as these men."

That last bit was the last straw. Completely taken aback by her obtuse comments, I lashed out. "Now, wait a minute." I raised a finger in the air and leaned forward as if I were schooling her. "We are all fair and straightforward individuals. You may be upset because your little side piece of dick was taken away, but I won't let you denigrate me or anyone else, especially my sisters. Angela didn't speak on it because she was asked not to and because it wasn't her place. As for me, I wanted to wait until you got back so I could tell you in person, like the real woman and friend that I am. But what I will not do is apologize for what Roman and I have and what we are building together. According to both of you, sex was all there was, and he was done with that from you long before I came along. So, enough with the nonsense, and accept the loss on the guy you were never going to get another taste of anyway."

Nia let out a sadistic chortle before she downed the last of her margarita. Lifting her purse from underneath the table, she reached inside, placed a hundred-dollar bill on the table, and stood.

"You got it, *sis*," she hissed, then leaned over her chair. "Just know this: Since you're capping for your man, you'll always be just another notch on his checklist of women because he's still hung up on some chick named Tamia." Noticing my confused expression before I could hide it, she seized the moment. "Oh, didn't know about her, did you? Ask about her."

She stood erect before pulling out her car keys. "And as for the taste, you're new to these dating streets, so let me put you up on game: I got that sampler platter two weeks before he went on that little cruise. Have fun with your friendly neighborhood street-dick slinger." She tossed a heated gaze at Angela. "And since you love to play about canceling friendship contracts, you can go ahead and permanently cancel mine for real. All of you."

Nia stormed out of the restaurant, leaving us reeling from the devastation she had caused. None of us could find the words to say. As if on cue, her confession collided in my mind and heart. She'd slept with Roman right before the cruise. Hot tears puddled in the corners of my lids as I felt three sets of eyes fixed on me with empathy and concern.

"Excuse me," I said meekly as I shot up from my chair and dashed to the restroom to collect myself.

Chapter Thirty

ROMAN

LAST NIGHT OUT with the fellas was one for the history books. We hadn't drunk and had that much fun in a long time, and my thirty-six-year-old bones felt it this morning. I was grateful that Cami was here at the gym because she would have to take the lead coach role today. Kinston was at home, probably sleeping off his liquor-induced haze, but I had the misfortune of leading this morning's family fitness on this beautiful Saturday, even though the beer and brown liquor sloshing in my belly begged to differ. I thought I could handle it, but my body was proving that my rolling thirties were nothing like my roaring twenties.

I hadn't heard from Aquila since yesterday afternoon, even though I tried calling last night when I got home and again this morning before heading to the gym. I wasn't worried. She deserved the beauty rest if her time with her girls was anything like mine. Plus, there was still a chance she might show up this morning with the boys for the weekly family fit day. I didn't have to wait long to find out because Aquila burst into my office just as Cami sat with me at my desk, finalizing the playlist.

Cami and I both peered up at the sudden intrusion.

A smile spread across Cami's face. "Oh, hey, Aquila."

The look on Aquila's face quickly stopped Cami and me from speaking any further. Her eyes nearly appeared murderous. I was concerned she'd start frothing at the mouth soon.

"I guess I should be worried about Cami, too, along with Nia and some mystery bitch named Tamia?" Aquila spouted, folding her arms across her chest.

Cami's expression shifted as she looked at me. Sympathy radiated from her gaze. "It's best if I give you both space."

"Yeah, thank you." I stood, never breaking my focus on Aquila. "Sorry about this."

"It's no problem, boss man. Just talk to her," Cami advised, easing past Aquila and offering her a sympathetic smile despite the venom Aquila had directed at her.

No sooner had Cami left than Aquila started in on me. "I asked you. I damn near begged you not to hurt me, and what did you do? Exactly that."

As I moved to lock the door, I turned to face her, my eyes wide, wondering where these unfounded accusations were coming from. "Baby, slow down. I have no idea what you're even talking about right now. I was out with the guys last night. When I left the sports bar, I went straight home…alone."

She dismissed what I'd said. "Yeah, last night, but what happened right before the cruise?"

No lie. I was still lost as to what she was even going on about. "Qui—"

"Don't you dare *Qui* me right now."

Stepping back, I put my hands in my pockets to indicate de-escalation. "All right, Aquila. I have no idea what the hell is happening. You barged into my office at my place of business, making a scene and talking nonsense about something I don't understand, claiming it happened months ago. You're gonna need to help me make sense of this."

The searing flames nearly scorched my face from the intense glare she gave me. Her hands spread to brace her hips as she spat, "Nia," through gritted teeth. "Does that make it plain enough for you?"

My shoulders slumped at the reminder that Nia was back in town. I'd forgotten our conversation the other day so quickly. That's how much of a nonfactor she was in my life. My mind raced with thoughts about what might have happened between her and Nia that led to Aquila being upset with me. Then I recalled their girls' night out. Of course, Nia was part of their plans. Had Nia and she argued about us? Before I could dive deeper into the situation, Aquila filled in the missing pieces.

"She was upset that you and I were together. *That* I can handle. If she needed time and space away from me to cope with the fact that we were dating, then so be it. I'd give her that. It's the lying that bothers me. You screwed her right before the trip?"

My mind drifted back to that time. Like an old movie reel, the memories flashed back to me. A day after the date from hell with that one girl who claimed to be an RN, but in reality, was a CNA, Nia and I ran into each other at the gas station. We flirted a bit, and she followed me back to my place. We had a few drinks, and then one thing led to another. Before long, we found ourselves tangled in a quickie on my sofa. It was a brief sexual release that we both seemed to need at the moment, and I honestly hadn't seen or talked to her since until she called me the other day wanting to meet up again.

"Ah, damn." I sighed, dropping my head into the palm of my hand. Immediately, I explained what had happened between Nia and me. "But I swear, baby," I said, easing up and cradling her arms. "That's all there was. I didn't even remember it until you brought it up."

She shrugged out of my grasp. "Maybe you don't remember now, but back when we were on the cruise, I'm positive you recalled it. I kept asking about Nia, and you made it seem like it was a long time ago between you."

Now, that was facts. I couldn't deny it. Back then, I clearly remembered. "I admit it. Back then, I did remember. But to be real, it was a meaningless moment. I was already afraid you wouldn't give me a chance because Nia and I had history. I was even more scared to tell you about our recent encounter because I was sure you wouldn't believe me when I said we were over, and we wouldn't have what we have now."

"So you stood in my face and lied to me."

"No. I stood right in your face and told you the truth. There is nothing between Nia and me. There wasn't anything then, and there isn't anything now." I exhaled to calm my nerves so she could see reason. "How can you hold me accountable for something that happened before you and hasn't happened since? She called me a few days ago wanting to hook up, and I told her I was dating someone. While she was trying to sully my character, did she tell you that? I bet not because her only goal was to hurt you, just because she was butt hurt. Neither you nor I should be blamed for how she feels when she knew exactly what our situation was."

It seemed I had finally gotten through to her for the first time since she bulldozed into my office. The steam rising from her chest seemed to deflate a bit as she mulled over my explanation.

"She seemed pretty upset for someone who believed that it was sex only."

"Did she say we were something more? Because if she did, I could resolve it right now and call her up with you present. I have nothing to hide when it comes to Nia." I tossed my hands in the air. "I'll accept responsibility for not telling you that like two or three weeks before the cruise we screwed, but I'm telling you that a nut is all I ever got from her or asked of her."

Aquila fell quiet as she contemplated and then plopped into the chair beside my desk. "She called you a fuck buddy."

"That's all she could call me. That's all we were. *Were*. Past tense."

Aquila toyed with her fingers before giving me the saddest puppy eyes. "Are you sure there's nothing more to this between you two? I went all in for you...*for us*...and she blindsided me with this. I felt foolish and betrayed."

Kneeling in front of her, I clasped her hands in mine and kissed them. "I'm so sorry she made you feel that way and that my omission contributed to it. I'd never do anything to hurt you— ever. That's my word. I never expected Nia to act like this, and now she's a part of my past that I regret because she had no right to make you feel bad about your decision or about what we have. But I promise you—swear to you—and guarantee you that there is nothing between Nia and me. I feel nothing. I don't desire her. The only woman I desperately want in my life is you, baby. Only you."

Her head bobbed slowly, and I leaned in to hug her, but she thwarted my attempt. "I believe you about Nia, but we never even scratched the surface on the other issue."

My brows furrowed because I didn't remember anything besides the Nia subject.

"Who is Tarnia?"

The blood damn near drained from my body. However, I was saved by Cami.

"Sorry to interrupt," she stated as she entered my office. "I need you in the session. Warmups are done."

When Aquila left the gym yesterday, it was with the understanding that we would finish our conversation later. I was grateful for the reprieve because it gave me time to figure out how to handle her question. I swear, if I didn't feel that Nia would turn an ice cube into an iceberg, I would call her and curse her out for revealing things to Aquila that I needed to say in my own time. It baffled me how she could spill information to Aquila—someone she called a friend, to hurt her as if she had the inside track on my life. The only reason she knew anything remotely personal about me was by happenstance. It had nothing to do with any firsthand information because I didn't talk to her about my personal affairs. Aquila knew more about me than everyone in my inner circle, aside from my immediate family. Yet, Nia had successfully made Aquila feel different, and for what? Over some sex?

If I really wanted to put her business out there and keep it a bean, Nia had reached out plenty of times to hook up since I'd stopped communicating with her years ago. The only reason I even entertained her that one time before the cruise was that my ego was bruised from the nursing girl, and I was looking for something guaranteed to slip into. I wouldn't have even called Nia for that. Seeing her at the gas station just saved me from scrolling down my contact list because there were a few baddies that I could've called and would've considered before Nia crossed my mind. And that's on God. The big one. Not the little one. Out of respect for her and Aquila, I'd never reveal that to them. But Nia was making it really hard for me to maintain my gentlemanly demeanor. I'd let her get away with it this time because I understood that the thought of Aquila and me was fresh to her, but if she kept it up, the kid gloves would come off, and I'd have no choice but to hurt her feelings. I wanted to respect her as a woman and as their friend, if she'd let me. However, if it came down to protecting her feelings or losing Aquila, I'd choose Aquila every time.

"Oh, my goodness, Roman. What are you doing here?" Aquila answered the door frantically, retying her silk robe with a bonnet still in place over her hair. "It's seven o'clock in the morning."

"I'm here to finish our conversation. I didn't want to give you a chance to get inside your head, so I pulled up. When it comes to you, I'm pressing up every time."

She stepped outside and pulled the door closed.

"It smells like you're cooking."

"Yes, I was. It's almost time for me to wake up my sons."

"Great! Then we can head inside, chat, and you can wake them up so they can have breakfast."

Her body tensed as her forehead creased with worry. An uneasy feeling hung in the air as she stood, shifting from foot to foot. The mere fact that I'd arrived unexpectedly was solely due to what I'd mentioned, but now, I was glad I did for another reason. Yes, we'd address Nia's mention of Tamia, but I also had a grievance to air.

"Are we going to stand out here in this chilly air, or will you let me into your home?"

Shivering from the cold, she rubbed her arms before turning to open the door. "Please don't wake up my children."

She guided us into her insulated sunroom, adjacent to her living room. She switched on the electric firepit, and the room quickly filled with warmth.

"Stay here. I'll turn off the food and change into some clothes."

I nodded, and she shuffled out of the sunroom and returned to the house. I sat on the cushioned wicker furniture and relaxed, absorbing the warmth as I patiently waited. After about five minutes, Aquila re-entered the room, donning a pair of leggings and an oversized sweater that exposed one of her shoulders. It turned me on. Yes, I loved her in sexy outfits, swimsuits, and dressed up, but the at-home Aquila with a messy bun and fuzzy socks was the best. This form of her was the one that showed that she was mine all the time, not just on special occasions. But I kept my mind and my man below at bay so we could tackle the subjects at hand. She sat down on the wicker sofa and faced me, and I initiated the conversation.

"What did Nia tell you about Tamia?"

Aquila propped herself up on her elbow and curled her feet beneath her. "She said that I would just be a notch on your checklist since you still had feelings for Tamia or something to that effect."

I grimaced, rolling my eyes. "Just as I suspected. She was out there talking nonsense. She knows nothing about Tamia or my history with her. She overheard a conversation with my sister one night. My sister called while Nia was in the bathroom and commented about Tamia. It triggered me, and we went back and forth a little before I remembered Nia was still there. So, we ended the phone call."

"Clearly, this woman is significant in triggering your emotions, especially for Nia to sense that you still have feelings for her. What are you not sharing with me? Because I'm beginning to think you have a habit of concealing information."

Exhaling, I moved closer to Aquila. "Qui, we all have things we'd rather not discuss and can't talk about until the time is right." I ran my hand down my waves and clarified, "I'm not hiding anything. I'm just a private person. There's a difference. I want you to understand that."

She shrugged as if she were frustrated. "I guess, Roman."

"Don't do that, Qui. Don't shrug it off or act like it doesn't bother you, especially since I can see that it does. I'm going to tell you about Tamia, but I want you to understand that my not mentioning her wasn't due to any lingering feelings or some loyalty I have to my past. Just as you needed to come to me about Joel in your way and in your own time, I needed to approach you about Tamia. But Nia took that away from me."

The mention of Joel must have earned me newfound favor, as I heard Aquila release a slight gasp before observing her visibly soften once more. She didn't say it aloud, but I sensed the shift in her spirit, recognizing that I deserved some grace, too.

"So, Tamia is my ex. We dated in my mid-twenties." Interlocking my fingers, my gaze fell to the floor. "What's wild is that she wasn't even supposed to be an ex. We were just kicking it, having fun, having sex, just being young and reckless. Then, suddenly, we went from that to almost walking down the aisle."

A flurry of unfinished questions erupted from Aquila before she focused on one. "What happened?"

There it was, the million-dollar question. It was the truth I hadn't dared to voice for years, for many reasons—shame, anger, defeat—but most of all, hurt. Peeling back the scar tissue of that wound would leave me vulnerable to such deep pain that I feared I couldn't recover. That's why only my family and, by chance, Cami were the only ones who knew. My hands trembled as I fidgeted with a nonexistent spot on my palm, emotions I'd tried to keep buried beginning to overwhelm me.

A gentle touch caught me off guard. Aquila's hands covered mine, and the trembling stopped. It was as if her touch were the cure for my past pains. Healing energy swept through me, calming my nerves and soothing me like a bathed and burped newborn. When I felt her hand on my cheek, I leaned into her soft caress. Her orbs bore into me and broke down every barrier Tamia had caused me to build. Her next words only reaffirmed what I now knew.

Aries Skye

"You don't have to hide from me. I've got you the same way you have had me. Trust me to be for you what you've been for me so many times."

Her thumb brushed away the tears streaming down my face as I swallowed my apprehension and revealed my secret. "I've faced this almost entirely alone because I'm private and haven't shared it with anyone except my family. She was pregnant, Qui. I never loved her, but I didn't want any baby mama situations. I was raised in a two-parent household, so there was no way I was going to let my kid grow up without me being part of their life. I thought marrying her and making her an honest woman was the best way to handle it. I believed she wasn't a bad woman, but rather someone whom I could learn to love in time."

More tears fell, and Aquila continued to wipe them away, giving me space to express myself. "She...*umm*...she aborted my baby without telling me. She said it was her body and her choice, that she wasn't ready for kids and didn't know if she ever would be. I get everything she said about her body, but didn't I deserve a say, too? That baby was just as much mine as it was hers. I would've taken care of the baby by my damn self if I had to. No question. Why kill my bloodline?"

Sympathy shone in Aquila's eyes as I sniffed and wiped away the last remnants of my tears. I cleared my throat. "At any rate, I ended things with her without her ever knowing I was going to propose, and I cut off all communication with her. But real talk, that shit gutted me."

Aquila crawled to me, straddled my lap, and cradled my face in her hands. "*Aww,* Roman. I'm so sorry. You shouldn't have had to go through that alone."

"There was one person who helped me sort through things."

Her eyes lit up as the light bulb went off. "Cami."

"Yeah." I exhaled. "She saw me at a bar, drowning my sorrows in a glass of Tennessee whiskey. Despite my protests, she stayed with me all night, refusing to let me drive home alone. I let my drunken tears flow onto her that night, and ever since, she's been like a protective guardian angel. She has kept that night and the conversation between us a secret for years. I admire her for that, which is why we share a close brother-sister bond."

"And now I feel terrible for coming at my girl like that. I treated her the same way Nia treated me, all because I was so frustrated and angry. I need to apologize to her."

"I'm sure she'll understand." I brushed my fingers gently along her cheek. "In a nutshell, that's what Nia was referring to. I don't have any unresolved feelings for Tamia, but that relationship caused me to move differently for a long time. Nia overheard my sister asking me to stop letting my past with Tamia hold me back from being the man I was raised to be. Nia lashed out at you and tried to use me to provoke you because she knew she wasn't the one I chose."

Inquiry spread across Aquila's features as she lifted my face to hers. "That's why people have you misconstrued. It's not that you don't want a family. You were hiding behind the pain of losing your own," she surmised.

When I agreed, Aquila embraced me tightly for the longest time as we basked in my heart's truth. "Roman, I don't know what to say to all of this. I'm sorry I allowed Nia to get in my head and toy with my emotions, but mostly, I'm sorry you had to endure that type of betrayal."

"Thank you, but my past pain is entirely on Tamia. Discovering it the way you did is something I must share the blame for, along with Nia. I should've told you. I have to learn to open up more for you because you deserve it. Regarding allowing Nia to influence your thoughts, we learn and grow. As long as we're growing together, that's what matters most to me. I want you to feel secure in what we're building."

She pressed her forehead against mine and extended her pinky finger. "I am. Promise that we'll both rely on what we know about us and not let anyone or anything come between that."

I stared at her pinky for a second. "Even you? We may have resolved your hang-ups about me and Nia, but my hang-ups about you not discussing us with your sons still remain."

She shifted out of my lap and sat back on her haunches. Gliding her nails along the creased lines on her forehead, she argued, "That's complicated."

"Uncomplicate it."

"How do you suppose I do that, Roman?" she asked, her tone sharp with the question. "Junior has already shown that he's struggling with the divorce between his dad and me. He blames the dissolution of our marriage for his father's absenteeism, and Joel adds fuel to the fire by refusing to tell the truth."

"You, Joel, and I know that isn't the truth, though. So maybe instead of hiding behind his lies, you stand in your truth, Qui."

"What do you mean?"

"Tell your sons about us. Give us the chance we need to incorporate them into our budding relationship."

"I don't know if they're ready."

"If not now, when?" I pressed, rising to my feet. "We've been dating for three months. I don't think there will ever be a right time. All we have is right now. We'll never know what they can and can't handle if we never try. Joel has been hiding who he is from them, and you don't agree with that, yet we're imitating him. And to keep it a bean, quite frankly, if you want honesty and transparency, you have to be willing to offer that to others in return. That starts with us and extends to the people who need it most from us—your sons."

Aquila leaned forward, resting her face in her hands. At last, she rose from the sofa, and I could see the determined expression on her face as she approached me and embraced me.

"You're right," she said, withdrawing and holding my hands. "I'm sorry for what I've done to you and them. I've been hiding us from them out of fear of their rejection, and that's not fair to any of us. Now, I'm coming to you about Nia and Tamia. I must sound like such a hypocrite to you."

This time, it was my turn to cradle her face. "No. You sound like a woman trying to navigate life and relationships the best way you know how. Just as you had to bring certain things to my attention, you deserve the same courtesy. The great part is that neither of us has to face things alone anymore. We can tackle them together as a team."

Her beam was infectious. "How'd I get so blessed to have a man like you in my life?"

Wrapping my arms around her waist, I pulled her close to me. "Careful now. You almost sound like I'm official and not just dating material."

She clasped my biceps, boring deeply into my soul. "Maybe that's because you are."

"Baby, don't play with me like that," I boomed, cheesing from ear to ear. "You want to make it official official. I mean, that's what I want. It's what I've been wanting. But are you sure that's what *you* want?"

"Dr. Roman Patterson, do you want the official title of my man?"

Biting my lip, I dipped my head so that we were eye-to-eye. "So long as you accept the official title of my woman first."

She squeezed her index finger in the come-hither motion, and I leaned down so our lips were barely apart. "I accept," she whispered.

My heart swelled, and I became so overwhelmed with emotions that I planted a kiss on her that was so electrifying she swooned. "I accept, too."

Turning, she interlocked her fingers with mine as she held my hand. "Come on. It's time I woke the boys up for breakfast and introduced them to my man."

I sat at the breakfast table, sweating bullets, while Aquila went to wake the boys. I had practiced what I would say a million times, but none of that practice came to mind. I would have to wing it and pray it worked. When I heard footsteps, I thought it would be best to stand. I didn't want to appear domineering by sitting at the head of their table.

"I told you guys that we have company this morning—"

Aquila's words were cut short when Junior saw me and yelled, "Mr. Roman!"

Excitedly, Junior and Sante ran up to me and initiated our individual greetings, which we typically did at the gym.

Junior slapped hands with me. "What are you doing here, Mr. Roman?"

Aquila walked over to where we stood and interrupted, "Why don't we all have a seat? We have something to discuss with you both."

The boys took their seats, and Aquila and I sat across from them at the table. Taking a deep breath, Aquila started the conversation. "So, I wanted to talk to you guys about how you would feel if I started dating."

"Like having a boyfriend?" Sante giggled and covered his mouth.

Making a face at his silliness, Aquila gestured. "Yes, Sante. Exactly like that. How would you all feel if I had a boyfriend?"

A few seconds went by before Sante spoke up. "I guess it would be cool. I mean, as long as your boyfriend is cool."

As if a light bulb went off, Junior moved his head back and forth between Aquila and me, staring at us with contemplative eyes. "Wait. Is that why Mr. Roman is here? Is he your boyfriend?"

I leaned forward, staring directly at Junior with a softened expression. "How would you feel about that, little man?"

Before he could answer, Sante squealed, "That would be so cool. You're so much fun, Mr. Roman, and I love hanging around you. Would that mean you get to hang around us all the time?"

His enthusiasm brought a smile to both my face and Aquila's. "I'd definitely get to spend more time with you, my man."

"Awesome!" Sante flexed a muscle. "I get to work on my guns."

We burst into laughter. "Oh, Lord." Aquila shook her head in amusement.

Sante hopped up and ran around the table. "I like you, Mr. Roman, so if you want to be my mommy's boyfriend, that's fine." He pointed a finger at me. "But you better not be mean to her, or I'll have to give you a knuckle sandwich." He balled his fist and shook it at me.

"Nisante Oliver!" Aquila gasped.

I patted her hand. "It's cool, Qui. He's one of your protectors; that's what little man is supposed to do." I slapped fives with Sante. "You don't have to worry about me being mean or mistreating you or your mommy. I promise. In return, I ask that you respect us. Deal?"

Sante rubbed his chin as if he were genuinely contemplating it, then extended his hand for a handshake. "Deal."

I shifted my attention to Junior. "And what about you, my dude?"

When he didn't respond, Aquila turned to Sante. "Baby boy, why don't you head upstairs and play with your action figures for a while? I'll call you down when it's time to eat."

"Cool! Don't eat up all the food, Mr. Roman," he shouted as he dashed out.

"I promise I won't."

Aquila stretched her hand across the table, and Junior took it. "What about you?"

My stomach pitted because Junior wouldn't look at either of us. His gaze was fixed on the dining table as if the answer would somehow rise from the wood. Finally, he shrugged, withdrew his hand, and said, "Whatever" before standing up.

"Junior," Aquila said, her tone conveying a stern warning.

I patted her hand. "Please. Let me." She nodded in approval, and I stood, walking around the table to Junior. "Do you mind if we talk privately?"

"We can talk," Junior said, walking toward the sunroom as I followed him.

Once we entered, Junior turned to face me. "You wanted to talk, so talk."

Other people might have seen his bluntness as disrespect, but I understood. He was a young boy growing into a young man. Puberty was beginning to kick in, so his actions and words were changing. He was learning how to process his own emotions, on top of dealing with the aftermath of his parents' divorce and watching a man he admired date his mother. It was a lot for his young mind and heart to receive.

I sat down on the wicker sofa and invited him to join me. He settled into the chair beside me and stared. "When I was about your age, my dad's career took off. He was making a lot of money, and he wanted to move my sister, my mom, and me to this wealthy neighborhood. I was upset." When I glanced at him, I could see he was intrigued because this story wasn't what he had expected. I was pleased because it meant I had his attention, and we could have a real conversation.

His curiosity got the better of him, and he asked, "Why were you upset? I love living in a wealthy neighborhood."

"I bet you do because you were born and raised into it." I chuckled. "For me, it was new. Moving meant I was away from my school and my friends, but you know what made me more upset?"

He leaned forward. "What?"

"Nobody ever asked me how I felt about it. Not my sister. Not my mom. But especially not my dad. And that hurt. I felt like nobody cared how I felt."

"Tell me about it." Junior's voice sounded as if I had tapped into his exact feelings.

"Yeah. Well, eventually, I got over it. I liked the new school and made new friends. But you know what helped me get over it?"

"What?"

"Every other weekend, my dad would take me back to the old neighborhood to play hoops with my old friends. I still visited them and spent time together. I was invited to their birthday parties and to hang out. I realized as I grew older that even though he didn't ask, he understood that those people and that old neighborhood were important to me. At the same time, he had to improve life for his family. To this day, I still have those friends. Some of them are successful, while others, not so much. As for me, I have benefited from both worlds. I learned some tough lessons in that neighborhood, but in my new one, I gained opportunities with school, work, and experiences that I never would've had in the old place. Both experiences have shaped me into the man I am today."

"Well, that means your dad made the right decision, right?"

I nodded. "Right. He did. Even if it didn't feel like it to me then." I focused on him as his mental wheels began to turn with my words. "That's kind of the same thing here. Your parents may have made some decisions that you don't like, but they believed it was best, and all you can do is make the best of it. But what I love is that, unlike my parents, your mom cares enough about how you and your brother feel and asks, no matter how difficult it is. For that, try to appreciate that she considers your feelings. I'm not saying it will change her mind, but I know your mom will make sure you all get through it together. And if it's cool with you, I'd like to be a part of your lives and do the same."

Minutes passed before Junior finally stood up and walked over to me. "Will it still be cool to talk with you and work out together?"

"Of course." I tapped his chest. "We could even have a no-girls-allowed session just for the fellas."

He smiled and dapped me. "I'd like that."

"So, what do you say?"

He seemed uneasy as he asked, "So, you really like my mom?"

"Yeah, I do. Your mom is nice, and she's pretty cute, too."

"*Eww.* That's enough." His outburst caused my chuckle to erupt into a bellow. "Okay, fine. I think you're cool, and if you want to date my mom, I'm okay with it."

I eyed him skeptically to ensure this sat well with him. "And you're sure?"

"Kinda. Let's see how it goes. Is that okay?"

We slapped palms. "I respect it. Always have your mom's back. Your dad's, too. Your parents will always be your parents, and they love you. And I'm here for you guys, too."

His face beamed for the first time. "Cool."

When I stood, he hugged me. Just then, Aquila tapped on the door and walked in to see us embracing. "Everything good in here?"

Junior playfully hit my arm. "Yeah, we're cool. Mr. Roman can be your boyfriend."

She crossed her arms, watching him with a playful expression. "Oh, well, thanks for the permission."

He ran over and hugged her. "Can we eat now? I'm starving, and Mr. Roman's stomach is talking, too."

"Aye, man! Don't do me like that," I shouted as he ran out, laughing at his joke.

Aquila waltzed over to me and kissed my lips. "*Aww.* It's okay. Let me feed all three of my babies so we can start our day."

"I like the sound of that." I pecked her lips softly.

"So does your stomach because that bad boy is screaming."

Laughing, I chased her out of the sunroom to have my first official breakfast with my girlfriend and her sons.

Chapter Thirty-One

AQUILA

$\mathcal{D}$ECEMBER CAME AND went so quickly that it felt like a fleeting moment in the year. I attributed this to the whirlwind of activity. So much had happened in the past month that it seemed we'd experienced an entire year within those brief days.

While the boys were happy to have Mr. Roman in their lives, Junior still sometimes wavered in his attitude about him being my partner. He didn't openly resist, but there were moments when he subtly withdrew from his usual banter with Roman. It made me anxious, but Roman's composure during this time calmed my spirit. No matter what, Roman kept engaging with Junior while giving him the space to process. That seemed to help because Junior had gradually opened up to Roman over the past couple of weeks. Their relationship wasn't exactly the same as it once was, but Junior was making an effort, which was more than I could ask for.

On the other hand, Sante was thrilled that one of his favorite men in his life was playing a bigger role. Their mainstays were their grandpas, uncles, and Joel. However, Sante also admired the workout guy, Mr. Roman, as he called him. In his eyes, he was as cool as his Uncle Kinston. That elevated Roman's status in Sante's life as Mommy's boyfriend.

Overall, our relationship reveal wasn't the disaster I had imagined. It made Sunday dinners at the house and planning family time together, including Roman, much easier. What I loved about my man was that he didn't dominate our time together. There were times when he would bow out gracefully so the kids and I could have our time. I think that was Junior's turning point. He realized that Roman wasn't there to take his mom away from him; he simply wanted to be accepted as part of our family.

Roman had even met my parents over the holidays as my official boyfriend, rather than Kinston and Kannon's friend and one of my trainers. I also had the chance to speak with his parents over the phone—a wonderful step in our journey together. Naturally, our friends were completely supportive of us progressing in our relationship, except for Nia, who hadn't communicated with any of us since that disastrous girls' night. She also hadn't reached out to Roman again. At least she respected our decision, even if she loathed us. I had apologized profusely to Angela countless times for ruining her lifelong friendship. Angela never blamed Roman or me; she explained that Nia's feelings were her own, and if she ever came around, she'd be mature enough to listen and forgive. But she'd still cuss her out about it once they were cool again, which was so typical of Angela. Although I wished the situation with Nia were different, there was nothing I could do to fix it, and I had accepted that it wasn't my place to try.

Today marked the start of a brand-new year, so I was putting all things of the past behind me and forging forward to a new, bright future with my man, my man, my man.

"After the partying we did last night, I don't see how you and Roman have the energy to attend a networking event tonight," Nissi said over FaceCall while I dressed.

"I'm tired, but for this, I'll make time. I have a household to maintain and a career to build. I can rest when I retire."

"*Yasss,* boss babe," Nissi cheered, snapping her fingers. "Have I told you how much I admire that you are pursuing all your dreams, sis? It's good to see you *living.*"

"*Aww.*" My hand flew to my heart as my cheeks reddened with pride. "No lie. What a time to be alive and thriving and not just surviving."

"Come on with a Word," Nissi belted with a praise dance. "You need to put that on a t-shirt, baby."

Laughter emitted from the pit of my belly. I swear I loved my sisters for life. We had our differences, but nobody stood by and for me like they did. And I felt the same way.

"Girl, you're so crazy. Let me get off this phone. Roman will be here any minute."

"Where are the boys going to be?"

As I sat down to put on my pumps, I shared, "Believe it or not, Joel is going to come over and take care of them. He has to work in the morning, and since it'll be late when I get in, he volunteered to keep them at the house since he didn't get to ring in the new year with them."

Nissi's face morphed into a surprised smile. "Look at Joel, being a daddy for real."

"Bye, girl." I cackled. "Love you."

"Love you roundtrip."

We disconnected, and I walked to my vanity to slip on my diamond teardrop necklace and matching earrings. A reflection caught my eye in the mirror, and I looked up to see Junior standing in the doorway of my bedroom.

"You look pretty, Mommy."

"Thank you, my Pooh."

His face lit up at the nickname. He could pretend all he wanted around others, but he loved it when I called him that. I'd learned that he enjoyed it in private these days. Before we could continue our conversation, the doorbell rang.

"Let me grab the door. Check on your brother for me, please."

"Yes, ma'am."

We headed in opposite directions. When I answered the door, it was Joel—right on time. I had to admit that he had improved over the past few months. He kept his promises to the boys, paid alimony and support on time and in full, and showed up when needed. I had no idea what sparked the change, but I was grateful nonetheless. I didn't even bother to ask why, nor did I confront him about what Junior confided to me, fearing he might revert to his old habits. As my mother often says, sometimes you have to leave well enough alone.

"Hey, Joel. Come in." I ushered him inside and shut the door. "Thanks for watching them and keeping them here so I don't have to travel late tonight to pick them up."

"It's no problem at all," he said, easing his jacket off and placing it on the back of the sofa before he sat down. "You look gorgeous."

"Thank you."

The boys barreled into the living room and tackled their father with hugs. I couldn't hide my gleam. This moment right here was what I had always longed for since our divorce. Peace. Happiness. *Unity*. All the pieces were falling into place, and internally, I sent up praises to the Heavenly Father.

"All right, boys. Don't act brand new with your father. You know your bedtimes, no junk food after eight, and no soda. Only water and juice."

Immediately, grumbles permeated the air.

"Aye. None of that. Listen to your mama," Joel intervened.

Before I could relish the fact that this was the first time in all of eternity that I could remember Joel ever having my parental back, the doorbell rang again. Joel turned to me, his brows furrowed. Sante jumped up as I walked to answer it.

"Hey, baby," Roman said, waltzing through the door. He paused for a beat and scanned my body from head to toe. "*Wow. You look amazing.*" He leaned in for a hug, nuzzling his face against my cheek and inhaling my scent.

"As do you, baby."

"Mr. Roman," Sante yelped as he bounced in front of us.

"My man," Roman shouted, slapping fives with Sante as they did their ritual greeting dance. "You good?"

"Yep!" Sante grinned.

"Hey, Mr. Roman," Junior spoke from the sofa beside Joel.

"'Sup, man," he greeted, then directed his attention to his father. "Joel."

Joel raised an eyebrow. "Roman," he acknowledged, but his name sounded more like a question than a greeting.

Roman faced me. "Are you ready? We really have to get going."

"Sure. Let me grab my purse in the back."

As I walked toward the hallway, I heard Joel trailing behind me. "Aquila, a moment, please."

Joel stopped me in the hallway, and I paused briefly to see what he needed. "Make it quick, please. You know how bad the traffic is in downtown Miami."

"So Roman is taking you to this event?"

I rolled my eyes. "Really, Joel? Isn't that obvious?"

"I thought this was an event for you—for your little bakery thing."

The offense hit me so hard that I was stunned and speechless. Just when we were doing so well, old Joel reared his atrocious head. Taking a moment to breathe, I chose to respond calmly.

"First of all, Roman invited me to this event, but it's meant to benefit my *catering business*, Joel. Is there anything important you need from me so we won't be late?"

He relented and stepped back. "No. Just wanted to clarify the details."

"Good. Consider them clarified."

I turned on my heels and marched into my bedroom, grabbed my purse, then locked and closed the door. Taking a moment to breathe, I shook off the irritation that Joel had ignited before rejoining Roman and the boys in the living room.

"All right, boys. Behave. I'll see you tonight," I said as they approached. Each of them hugged me, and then they both fist-bumped Roman.

Joel remained silent as Roman and I left the house, and I locked the door behind us. After getting into Roman's Maserati and heading to the venue, Roman addressed the situation at the house.

"What was Joel's issue before we left?"

"He asked me about you attending the event," I replied, shaking my head. "I guess since I didn't give him all the details about tonight, he felt out of the loop."

Roman scoffed and rubbed his fingers down his beard. "Nah. He just feels some type of way about me."

"Well, I don't know why. He knows we're a couple."

"Doesn't matter. Hearing that we're a couple isn't the same as witnessing it. This is the first time we've come face-to-face since we've been in a relationship. It seems he didn't think it was that serious between us for me to get involved in helping your business."

"I don't give a damn about what he believes or doesn't believe regarding my personal life. I am no longer his concern. He's focused on the only concerns we share."

Roman stopped at the red light and turned to look at me. "I know you don't. But he gives all the damns. Can't say I blame him, though."

"*Huh?*" My nose scrunched at his assessment.

"I'd feel like an idiot, too, to see you on your boss shit with the next man. Those L's are a hard pill for us men to swallow."

We settled into a quiet reflection of what he'd said before I leaned over and eased my hand between his thighs before whispering in his ear. "Funny, but I don't want to talk about my ex. My only focus is on this business and my man."

"*Qui,*" he stretched out. His voice was strained as I felt his manhood jump under the palm of my hand. "Don't make me drive this car to my house. The only networking you'll be doing is making those cheeks meet when I clap 'em together. Keep playing with me."

"You better not," I howled, falling into my seat.

"Keep your little ass over there for the remainder of this drive."

"Yes, Dr. Patterson," I teased.

"A'ight. Keep on."

Although we arrived about fifteen minutes late to the function, we didn't miss much. I met several movers and shakers in the entertainment, travel, hotel, hospitality, restaurant, and retail industries. I exchanged digital business information and even landed three callbacks for upcoming events. I also learned about a grant program and decided to apply for funding for a location outside my kitchen. The night was wonderful, filled with excellence among Black entrepreneurs, CEOs, and investors, accompanied by delicious food, endless bubbly, pulsating music, and great company. I thoroughly enjoyed myself and was truly grateful that Roman had invited me.

Speaking of Roman, the atmosphere was truly his environment. He could navigate and work a crowd unlike anyone I'd ever known. His charismatic charm and business acumen were to be studied and admired. This was his element, and I understood wholeheartedly why Kinston chose him to be his business partner. Besides the fact that he was wise with money management, the man was a magnetic and charismatic genius wrapped in one sexy bow—my sexy beau.

As we cruised the Miami streets, I placed my hand atop his. "Thank you for tonight."

I saw the profile of the smile that graced his face. He lifted my hand and kissed it. "You're welcome. Anything for you, baby. I'm so proud of you."

"For what?"

"For going out there and showing off your boss skills. Your confidence has grown by leaps and bounds, and it looks so sexy on you. Seeing you taking charge and making your dreams come true makes my heart swell. That's all I want for you."

His words melted my heart and my kitty. "*Aww*, babe," I purred. "But if you don't stop, my good sis down below is going to ride stick shift down this highway."

"Shit. Twin, where have you been?"

I doubled over. "I can't with you. You are so damn crazy."

"Nah. I'm like Day-Day. *I ain't never had no shit like that ever happen to me. I'm trying to see what that be like*," he said, mimicking the famous line from the movie *Friday After Next*.

"If Joel weren't at my house, I'd show both of us what it be like."

"Don't remind me." He groaned.

We grew silent as we shared the same sentiment. I was grateful for Joel's help, but in some ways, he was cockblocking, even if unintentionally. He was involved with his sons, so I had to embrace the victories I had. We continued the ride, letting the tunes of Black country music serenade us. Roman had become a fan, too, and I loved that we could vibe together. Everything with him felt so effortless. Life with him was just…better.

As we pulled into my driveway, the carefree mood I was in faded at the sight of a black Maybach next to Joel's Audi. "What the hell?" The words slipped out as I unbuckled my seatbelt before Roman could turn off the ignition.

"What's going on? Whose car is that?" he asked as I rushed out of the vehicle, not giving him a chance to come and open my door.

My feet flew in my stilettos with Roman right on my heels as I struggled to open my front door. When it finally unlatched, I threw it open and shouted, "Joel!"

"What's wrong, Aquila?" Roman repeated as he attempted to calm me down.

As soon as we turned the corner from the small foyer into the living room, my eyes met Joel and the boys. I hurried over to my sons and hugged them.

"Is everything all right? Why aren't you boys in bed?" The words rushed out as I frantically scanned up and down to make sure no hair was out of place.

"We're fine, Mom," they said together, gazing at me with wide-eyed confusion written on their faces. "Dad, let us stay up to see Grandpa."

That's when my focus gradually shifted and rose to the owner of the Maybach, marked unmistakably with the license plate OLIVER1 on the rear bumper. A pair of deep-set hazel eyes looked down at me, mirroring those of my ex-husband. Thurgood Oliver loomed over us with his husky six-foot-three frame. The same bald head and beard closely resembled his son's, the only difference being that his silky beard was flecked with salt and pepper. His hands rested in the pockets of his designer slacks, his button-down shirt had rolled-up sleeves, and his shiny dress shoes reflected off my hardwood floors. His outfit suggested he had come straight from somewhere without having gone home to change into something more casual.

"Thurgood, what are you doing here? I was worried something had happened to the boys. Is Ivy okay?" I referred to Joel's mother and his wife.

"She's fine." He dismissed my question with a wave. "I'm here because my son asked me to come over."

That brought me back to my feet. He didn't come off as abrasive, but that was never Thurgood's style. He had a silver tongue that he used to win over his opponents, not realizing they were dealing with a snake in the grass.

My eyes darted to Joel. "Why would you call your father over here?"

Thurgood cleared his throat. I followed his gaze, which was directed straight at Roman. "This is a *family* matter."

Roman stepped forward and stood next to me, adjusting his suit jacket. He extended his hand toward Thurgood, his diamond cufflinks shining against his crisp white button-down. "We haven't met. My name is Roman Patterson." Thurgood stared blankly at Roman's hand, never bothering to take his hands out of his pockets. Roman lowered his hand, fiddled with his cufflinks, then sniffed, and squared his shoulders. "As Aquila's man, any matter concerning her is my concern." He pointed to himself with both hands. "Unless she tells me to leave, I'm staying."

Thurgood flicked the tip of his nose while Joel stood beside his father. Their identical gazes turned to me, as though expecting me to intervene. However, I wouldn't. I had no idea what they had contrived, but until they let me in on it, Roman was staying put.

Folding my arms, I reiterated, "What's going on?"

Thurgood shrugged nonchalantly. "My son has informed me that he approached you about reuniting his family."

The moment those words came from his mouth, I went into defensive mommy mode. "Boys, go to your rooms, *now.*" My voice was stern and authoritative. It was so stern that they both turned on a dime and scurried up the stairs to their rooms without question.

My eyes narrowed to slits. "How dare you say that in front of my kids."

"*Our* kids," Joel seethed. "Besides, we tried to warn you that this was a private conversation."

I refused to acknowledge his last statement because the only person they wanted to leave was Roman. Having the boys awake and present for this ambush was wholly intentional. Ignoring Joel, I directed my next words to Thurgood. "You've got exactly one minute to state the nature of your bringing up claims that happened months ago."

"My *nature* is that we have always been remarkably generous to you, Aquila. Our family has consistently held your best interests at heart. You are aware of my plans for Joel to expand the family restaurant and brand. You were part of the Oliver family for years. Any opportunity you have to repair and mend that relationship, you should seize it. This concerns your children's legacy. Why would you risk that by choosing some gym owner over the inheritance promised to you and my grandsons?"

Pompous and audacious. I didn't have to worry about Joel not inheriting that from his father. "What *exactly* are you saying?"

Thurgood shrugged casually. "I'm proposing you accept my son's offer. You won't have to worry about stipends anymore, and you'll have full access to everything related to Oliver to expand your own brand. I'm sure all that sounds much more appealing than continuing whatever *this* is." He gestured between Roman and me.

Immediately, I saw red. Memories of the night before my wedding flooded my mind as I recalled being coaxed into a lackluster marriage arrangement, my heart aching because I was in love with a man who had only asked for my hand in holy matrimony to gain his father's restaurant and the inheritance from his will. I accepted my role as a provisional wife and made my bed without fulfilling my dreams, silencing my voice, masking my hurt, and never finding true and everlasting love—for Joel. All I received in return were my beautiful children and a lavish lifestyle that served me financially, yet starved me mentally and emotionally.

"Whatever *this* is." The repeated words fell from my lips. "Whatever *this* is, it's none of your business or your son's. But I'll tell you what it *isn't*. It *isn't* me accepting a loveless union to maintain pretenses for a family that has never cared about what I need or deserve. It *isn't* me shouldering the family's bullshit secrets and lies to protect a brand name. It *isn't* me shrinking myself so he can shine. It *isn't* me neglecting myself to cater to a man who hasn't once bothered in that miserable sham of a marriage to protect or uplift me." I stepped into Thurgood and Joel's space. "So, respectfully, I don't give a damn about you or your son's proposition, and *disrespectfully,* fuck both of you."

The sensation of a warm hand wrapping around my waist drew my attention to Roman, who gently pulled me away from Thurgood and Joel and shifted me slightly behind him.

"I think—"Thurgood attempted, but was interrupted.

"*I* think you heard what Aquila said, so you and your son need to leave because, unlike my lady, I'm all about that action first."

"Who are you to threaten me or my father?" Joel seethed, turning to me as he pointed at Roman. "Is this what you want, Aquila? A thug who only knows how to resort to violence instead of using his words?" He hissed in disgust. "You've always wanted my wife, and the only reason she's entertaining you now is because she's hurt. But I'm here to help her heal. You're beneath us. You always have been and always will be."

I gripped Roman's bicep, praying he wouldn't get loose. Roman pinched the bridge of his nose before lowering his hands and crossing them in front of him. His stance was protective, as if he were my bodyguard.

"See, that's where you've got me mistaken. I respect *my* woman, her home, and her children, so in here, I'll handle this like a gentleman." He stepped closer to Joel until they were eye to eye. "*In here,*" he stressed. "But you are right about one thing. I've always wanted *my* woman. I got her, too, and I take *real* good care of her heart, which *I* helped heal." Roman pretended to brush lint off Joel's shoulder and winked at him. "I also take real good care of other things, too."

"You both need to leave, now," I demanded of Joel and Thurgood before this mostly civil conversation took a turn for the worse.

They headed to the exit with Roman and me right behind them. Roman opened the door. Joel walked out first, shaking his head and muttering to himself. Thurgood stepped out and turned to us.

"Aquila, I urge you to reconsider. Even in the divorce, my son has made it quite comfortable for you. You can't possibly live on a minimal catering budget, and I'd hate to see your alimony payments reduced or terminated altogether because you refuse to see reason."

Did this bastard threaten me? Anger shook my core. My body began to convulse with tremors, and my fists clenched at my sides. Just before I unleashed my pent-up fury, Roman slammed the door in Thurgood's face and locked it. He looked down at me, and the wave of emotions coursing through my veins transformed into a wail as my tears burst forth. He pulled me into a tight embrace, and I collapsed into his warmth. His cocoon was the soothing shield I desperately needed. He kept me from letting the Olivers witness my breakdown and possibly use it against me. I'd never felt so grateful to be wrapped in his comfort.

"Why does he keep doing this to me?" I cried, burying myself in his chest.

"*Shh*, baby," he whispered. "Everything is going to be fine. I promise."

Chapter Thirty-Two

AQUILA

FOR THE PAST two months, I'd been battling with Joel over his proposal to reunite. It was nearly driving me insane. It's easy for people to say not to talk to him, but I had to see him because we shared children. He used every meeting as an inopportune time to bring it up. I would've asked the courts to let me drop our children off at his parents' house and arrange visits through them, but I'd be subjected to the nonsense from Thurgood and Ivy.

My parents refused to be the go-between because my father preferred to stay out of prison. At his tender senior age, he couldn't care less about spending the rest of his days behind bars, but that wouldn't be fair to my mother, who might end up with her own sentence out of retaliation for her husband being locked up. Saying they disliked the Olivers would be an understatement. Their disdain bordered on hatred. To be honest, mine did, too, but unfortunately, I bore children into their lineage. I'd never regret my babies, but I sure as hell regretted who their father and grandparents were.

With spring bringing a blossoming season of new beginnings, I decided to let their idle threats and annoyances roll off me like water from a shower. Dwelling in their insanity was only counterproductive for me. I couldn't function properly as the mother, caterer, big sister, daughter, and girlfriend if I were always weighed down, letting their actions hinder mine. So, I added a new mantra to the mix: Fuck them Olivers.

"Hey, babe." My beam couldn't be contained as Roman's face appeared on FaceCall. "How's your day?"

"Cool. I'm about to go on lunch break, and I was wondering if you could join me."

I glanced at the time, which showed 12:32 p.m., and then back to the oven. "I just put the last batch of those muffins in for my client, who has a conference tomorrow morning. If you have time, feel free to stop by. I'll whip up some veggie tacos for us."

"Can't. I have another training session in the next hour."

I pouted. "*Aww.* I'm sorry, babe. But you're still coming over for dinner tonight, right?"

His pearly whites showed first; then, he bit his lip. "Heck yeah. You know I'm not missing any meals from my baby."

"Just when I thought you would say you wouldn't miss a chance to see me." I pouted and picked up my latte to take a sip.

"Oh, I ain't missing no dessert either."

I coughed, nearly spewing the rest of the latte out of my mouth. I grabbed napkins to wipe the droplets that ran down my chin and on the counter. "Oh my gawd. I can't with you."

"But dessert is coming with dinner, isn't it?"

This time, I licked my lips while eyeing him sexily. "Oh, absolutely."

Roman started to tell me something, but I was distracted as I opened the mail I had picked up just before his call. My heart raced when I noticed it was from the courthouse. My tunnel vision kicked in as I quickly scanned the paperwork, and my jaw dropped.

"Aquila? What's wrong, baby?" Roman's voice reminded me that he was on the line.

My throat went dry as salty tears filled my eyes. "That bastard," I croaked.

"Who?"

Dropping the paperwork on the countertop, I wiped the wetness spilling down my cheeks. "Joel! He filed for custody of the boys, claiming it's in the best interest of our children, along with moving forward with the petition to reduce my alimony based on my new income. I must appear in court if I want to contest this petition since the judge has put a hold on the reduction. If I don't show up, the petition will be granted, and the reduction will take effect. But I don't even care about that. I can't believe he'd try to take away my sons. I'm so sick of him and his family." Hot tears streamed down my face, and I could do nothing to stop the wails. "Roman, they have so many people in their corner at their disposal. What am I going to do? What if he wins? What if he takes my boys?"

"Don't do that. Don't imagine the worst. We're going to get through this. I promise you."

"How? I'm not sure what information they provided to get this set in motion, but I'm pretty certain that no matter what I present, the so-called judge will side with Joel." I sniffled as the endless stream continued to flow. "And we both know why he did this. I'm so tired and frustrated, baby. They won't let me be happy and live in peace."

"Listen to me. I've got you. For now, set that aside and stay focused on your business. When I come over tonight, you can vent to me as much as you want, but you're not going to let him stress you out. This is exactly what he wants to achieve, so don't give in to his demands."

Roman's words carried a confidence that I did not. Too exhausted to argue or debate the issue, I wiped my eyes and nodded. The scent of the muffins reminded me that they were baking and reinforced exactly what Roman had told me. Regardless of this letter, life still moved on. I had no choice but to keep moving with it.

Dinner had been relatively quiet—at least on my end. I swirled most of my food around the plate while my man and boys devoured their meal. Watching Roman and the boys, especially Sante, engage in jokes and small talk made my heart smile. Since that confrontation with Joel and Thurgood a couple of months ago, Junior had been somewhat hot and cold with Roman and me. We'd both tried to get to the bottom of his iceberg, to no avail. He hadn't been disrespectful, yet he wouldn't fully open up to us either. Tonight, my energy mirrored his on several occasions, making me realize we all needed counseling before the powder keg exploded. I was sure his attitude stemmed from the mixed emotions surrounding his father. Mine were, too, and I was a grown adult still struggling to process the aftermath of my divorce. Therefore, I somewhat understood how he felt. All of us should've already been in therapy, but like so many, I misjudged that sometimes our happiness was mere bandages masking our underlying suffering. Once this custody and alimony petition was resolved, I'd focus on my sons and my mental health because God knows Joel didn't care at all.

After dinner, the boys rinsed the dishes and loaded them into the dishwasher before saying good night to Roman and me. They bounded upstairs to bathe and go to bed. Once they were done, we'd go up and tuck them in. While they bathed, I sat in the living room with Roman, venting about the petition and anything else I needed to release from my pent-up emotions. Roman sat quietly, offering comforting back rubs as he allowed me to pour out all the contents of my bleeding heart. I was in the midst of another tirade about Joel and his asinine family when we heard footfalls approaching speedily in the living room. Junior rushed in, donning his favorite football pajamas.

"Stop it. Just stop it," he yelled.

"Junior," Roman and I boomed, our tones blended in a unified cadence.

Tears poured down his little face. "All you do is fuss about my dad. All he does is fuss about you. I'm sick of it. I'm tired. None of this would be happening if you two just stayed together. You were happy together."

"Pooh—"

"No!" He halted me, his tone harsh and definitive. "Dad wants us to be a family again, but you won't let him. You won't let him because of Mr. Roman. He told me."

"Junior—" Roman attempted.

"Why can't you just leave my mom alone, huh? Just be the exercise guy again. My mom and dad wouldn't fight anymore."

My heart shattered into a million pieces as I sprinted from the sofa and wrapped my arms around him. It was all I knew to do. It was all I could do. How could I explain that he was wrong? No matter what I had to say, now wasn't the right time. All that mattered was that my son, my firstborn, was hurting, and I needed to tend to him. I knew Roman was panicking, but I couldn't worry about that now. As much as I wanted Roman and what we had, my child needed me more than ever. Yes, Joel was to blame for our impossible situation, but none of that mattered. I would deal with him when I could. Right now, my allegiance had to be to my son and comforting him.

Junior collapsed in a heap of tears into my arms, and I rocked him for a long while until I called Roman's name. Slowly, he appeared in front of us, and when our eyes locked, he knew. He understood without me saying a word.

"Baby," he pleaded, the emotion in his voice causing it to crack.

"Please go," I cried, my voice so overwrought with emotion that it sounded hoarse and barely audible.

He took a step toward me, but I lifted my hand, stopping him mid-motion. His eyes went wide, filled with emotion, and they searched mine before his gaze drifted to Junior. His lips pressed together as a single tear broke free and careened down his cheek. My insides instantly hollowed. The pain in him reached deep inside of me, and it gutted me—gutted *us*. I mouthed, "I'm sorry," even though I knew those words weren't enough to heal us or save us.

His eyes shut tight, like he was trying to hold something in— or hold something back. I could see the war playing out behind his closed lids; the ache of the desires of our hearts clashing with my verbal request. When he opened them again, acceptance flickered through the disappointment. He squared his shoulders, swallowed the pain, and placed a gentle hand on Junior's back.

"All right, buddy. I'm gonna go, but I just want you to know I love you, and I love your mama, too. One day, I hope you can accept that."

Without another word, he turned and bounded out of the house. My mouth fell agape because it was the first time he'd uttered the words. He *loved* me. It was in that very moment that I admitted to myself I might have lost the man I also loved. The man I was *in love* with, and it hurt. It hurt like hell.

Chapter Thirty-Three

ROMAN

THE PAST TWO weeks felt like I'd been walking around as a soulless creature. Nothing in life felt the same. Of course, I went through my normal routine, but I knew I was going through the motions. I hadn't spoken to Aquila since I'd left her house that night after Junior's meltdown. I didn't reach out to her; similarly, she didn't reach out to me. We were in a state of limbo, and I hated it. Oddly, I understood that neither of us was being selfish. It was vital for her to tend to her children, particularly Junior. As much as I wanted to help her and be there for him, I wasn't his father, and due to his father's jealous interference, I was now the enemy in his mind. While repairing Junior's perception of me was important, it was a thousand times more crucial for Aquila to ensure that she cared for his mental and emotional well-being. So, we existed, caught between our hearts' desires and our current dilemmas.

Still, no matter what, I was determined to get my woman back. I'd fight until the day I released my final breath. No lie, I wanted to knock Joel's head between the window and the wall, but I knew that wouldn't resolve anything. True, it would've made me feel so much better, but it would've caused more harm than good. Besides, if I did lay my hands on him and his punk father, I might not have ever turned them loose, then I'd be facing an entirely different set of charges. Instead, I'd operated in a manner that none of them expected of me; the way I typically handled people who stood in my way. I'd contemplated this since our initial confrontation, but I opted not to take action, thinking the situation would be resolved. Now, the gloves were off.

I peered at my Cartier watch to see that it was time to get going. I stood, slipped on my navy blue suit jacket, and straightened my diamond cufflinks. After I buttoned my jacket, I swiped my keys and the manila folder off my desk.

"Hey, bro."

Kinston and Kannon stood at my door. Their expressions were priceless as Kinston paused mid-sentence, stopping whatever he was about to say to me.

"'Sup, y'all."

"Well, we were coming to treat you out to lunch to cheer you up, but it looks like you're doing just fine," Kinston informed me.

"Did you and Aquila work things out? For the past two weeks, you've looked like the *Walking Dead*, but today, you look like new money," Kannon added.

"Nah. We still haven't talked or seen each other. That doesn't mean work stops." I walked over to them and patted each on the shoulder. "I appreciate you fellas for trying to cheer me up, but I'll have to take a rain check on that lunch. I have a business meeting."

"No problem," Kinston said. "But remember, you can always talk to us if you need to. I know this has been a tough time for you."

Slowly, I exhaled. "It has. I'm just maintaining and doing the best I can with each new set of twenty-four hours that the Lord blesses me with."

"Shit. I feel that," Kannon said, slapping hands with me.

"Before I get out of here, how is she?"

Kinston and Kannon glanced at each other and answered simultaneously, "Maintaining."

Kinston bumped fists with me. "She misses you, man. Real talk."

Hearing that both hurt and healed me. I swallowed deeply to bite back the emotions threatening to well up inside. "Tell her I miss her, too."

"We got you, big dawg." Kannon bobbed his head.

I pulled each of them into a one-armed embrace before we headed out of my office to part ways.

"Good afternoon, Mr. Patterson. How are you?"

"I'm well, Macie, and yourself?"

"I'm fabulous."

"That's wonderful. Is our guest here?"

"Yes, sir, in Conference Room A, as you requested, with a bottle of bubbly chilling. If you're ready, I'll take you back."

I gestured for her to lead the way as she guided me through the building to the conference room area. During our walk, I greeted everyone we encountered. When we reached the door, Macie opened it and stepped inside.

"Hello, Mr. Oliver. Mr. Romero is here," Macie stated, stepping aside for me to walk in.

Once I was inside, Macie eased out, closing the door behind her. Joel sat at the conference table with a flute of champagne and coughed, causing some of the bubbly to spill from his mouth. He grabbed napkins to dab his chin. As I sat across from him, his eyes widened in shock and confusion.

"What are you doing here? And who is Romero? I thought your name was Roman?"

I raised my hand. "Let's begin as gentlemen. Hello, Joel. Thank you for accommodating this meeting on such short notice."

"Cut the shit, Roman. What kind of games are you playing?"

*Tsk*ing, I inhaled. "See, that's the difference between you and me. I don't play games. I make moves, especially when it comes to my *wife*."

The gasp Joel released echoed around the room as his eyes widened like saucers. I leaned back, reveling in the news as my thoughts drifted to the moment Aquila and I had exchanged our wedding vows.

July 19—Turks and Caicos

After the club, we left the boat, too full of energy and drinks to settle down. We headed out to have some fun before we set sail. The nightlife was an eclectic island atmosphere, allowing us to soak in the culture. We felt wild and free, and it was different yet naturally perfect. Aquila twirled around as we traipsed the streets during the street festival with some of the new islander friends we'd made.

"I love it here," she slurred.

Pulling her into my chest, I moaned. "That's all I wanted."

She encased me in her arms and stared into the depths of my soul. "Roman, you make me so happy."

Just as our lips were about to meet, a woman interrupted us with a smile. "We're ready for you."

Aquila and I grinned at each other as we interlocked hands and followed the woman, jogging and laughing like teenage lovers. Once we reached a grassy fire pit by the shore, dancers took part in a cultural dance to Junkanoo. They grabbed Aquila's and my hands, encouraging us to join in. We danced in a circle as if no one were watching. After the music faded, an older man stepped forward and greeted us.

"It's time. Come," he said as he led the way to the beautiful altar.

He offered us words of encouragement. Then, the lady who guided us there pulled out two beaded cord bracelets. She placed one in each of our hands, and we put them on each other's wrists while the man recited the marital vows, which we each repeated.

"May these symbolic bracelets keep you forever connected in the circle of life. Each cord represents your commitment to hold tightly to each other, and each bead symbolizes the contributions you make to each other's lives. You may now salute your bride," the officiant said.

Aquila and I kissed passionately, sealing our union.

The next day, we woke up in my suite on the boat, unaware of what we'd done. After Aquila left to prepare for our next day in Bimini, I discovered the ceremonial certificate and a prayer note in an envelope containing a picture of us at the altar. That's when some of the previous night's memories suddenly flooded my mind. Though much of it was still fuzzy and incoherent, what stood out was that Aquila and I had decided to commit to each other. No, it wasn't legally binding, but it was symbolic. That was the information I had wanted to share with Aquila during the month she'd ignored me. I finally told her when we returned to my house the night we rekindled, when she took me on the date.

This mutual understanding and getting to know each other period was essential for both of us as we considered whether we could continue to build our relationship. Although we might not be legally married on paper, something significant happened that night that bound our hearts, and it wasn't just the liquor. Regardless, she was mine, and hopefully, one day, I could officially call her Mrs. Patterson. But Joel didn't need to know the details; he just needed to understand that she was not now nor would she ever be Mrs. Oliver again.

"*Wife?*" Joel repeated.

"That's what I said. As her *ex*-husband, none of that is your concern, but I'll tell you what is."

I slid the paperwork over to him. He opened the manila folder and nearly keeled over when he saw what it said.

"Wait. How…How'd you get this?"

"You know me as Roman Patterson, the gym owner, but allow me to introduce myself to you as the founder and CEO of Romero Investments." Raising my hands, I pointed to the area around us. "This is my company."

"You're lying."

I wagged my finger at him. "Oh, quite the contrary. As my father says, I may tell you a joke, but I'll never tell you a lie." I pointed to the folder. "As you know, since you accepted the offer and the funds, that paperwork shows that Romero Investments is the primary investor with majority holdings in the Oliver Brand restaurant. Now, I don't need to explain what that means, but to clarify so that we're both on the same page…" I leaned forward, pressing both hands on the table. "That means I own your ass."

"You motherfu—"

Shaking my head, I interrupted him. "Please don't write a check—or should I say, *another* check—your ass can't cash." I stood, walked to his side of the table, and leaned against it. "I have a proposition for you if you're willing to be a trouper and listen."

Joel rolled his defeated eyes. "What's your proposition?"

"I propose that the Oliver Brand continue to operate under your management. All I want in return is my initial investment. Once that's repaid, I'll gladly return the majority ownership to you while retaining a minority share. The funds for the minority share will go into an account for Aquila because, without her, you wouldn't have a stake in your family business. It seems only fair that she benefits from this little arrangement. What she does with the money is her decision. She can spend it, save it, give it to the boys, or toss it over the Brickell Avenue Bridge for all I care."

Joel leaned back in the leather chair, completely stunned. "What's the catch?"

Smirking, I patted his shoulder. "I'm glad you asked. Sign this addendum to confirm that you will remove your custody and alimony petition and, of course, allow it to continue under the initially agreed-upon terms. You must also cease any attempts to reconcile with Aquila. Whenever she mentions your name or your family, she had better not have a single negative comment regarding her emotional and mental well-being. Additionally, I expect you to resolve this reconciliation issue with Junior and Sante so they can come to terms with the fact that you and their mother have moved on with your lives."

He slid the paper over to review and sneered, "Any-fucking-thing else?"

"Ah, yes, there's one more thing." I raised my finger. "This stays between you and me. There's zero leniency for broken NDAs. Of course, my attorney phrased the addendum in better terms than this good ol' gym owner could, but that's the gist." I stood and faced him. "So, what do you say? Keep your family's hard work and legacy, or let me take it over?"

Joel jumped to his feet. "What happens if I don't sign this?"

My jaw clenched, and my nostrils flared, emphasizing my menacing scowl. "Then, I will tear down the Oliver Brand and rebuild it so that your family's legacy will barely be a memory. Trust me, my bite is a helluva lot worse than my bark. As I said, I'm about that action, chief."

When Joel's eyes squinted in recognition, I chuckled. "As pleasant as it would be to lay hands on you, fighting with my deep pockets always gets the job done. Speaking of which…" I reached into my inside jacket pocket, retrieved a pen, and extended it to him. "Whenever you're ready."

Chapter Thirty-Four

AQUILA

"MOM, I FINISHED the dishes," Junior said as he entered the sunroom where I was sitting with a glass of wine, reading the novel, *Soldiers of Love: Beautiful Scars.*

Setting the goblet on the coffee table, I marked my place in the book and beckoned him to come over. He approached and plopped down on the sofa next to me. To my surprise, he wrapped his arms around my waist and squeezed tightly. I returned the gesture, finding comfort in his affection.

"You're voluntarily doing dishes *and* giving me hugs." I peeked down at him. "Don't get me wrong, I appreciate it, but what gives?"

We shared another hug before he pulled away and glanced up at me. He shrugged. "I don't know. Just wanted to do it, I guess."

In return, I shot him a glance that reeked with skepticism. "What did Dr. Soto say?"

"Speak my truth, not hide it."

"Exactly." I pointed at him. "So, let's try that again."

After the fallout from Junior's breakdown, I signed us all into therapy. Junior enjoyed it much more than I expected, and even though it had only been three weeks, the transformation felt miraculous. I felt like I was finally getting my son back, and our bond was not only restored but had improved.

"I just wanted to do something to make you happy again." He sighed. "You don't think I see it, but I know you're sad, Mom." He hung his head low. "You've been sad since you sent Mr. Roman away."

His intuition was spot-on there. While I felt overjoyed that my boys were on track for healthier mental and emotional states, mine was in shambles. I missed Roman terribly. My soul felt depleted. I floated through my days, poured my sorrows into wine at night, and put on a waterworks show every bedtime, only to rinse and repeat the process. All that drama, and I hadn't even seen any of the Olivers, nor had my alimony been reduced. In my mind, it meant that if Joel couldn't have the man he truly longed for, he would be hellbent on making sure I didn't have the man I wanted, either. And it had worked.

I embraced him. "I'm sorry you've witnessed that, but I can't sugarcoat my feelings, Junior. I do miss Roman a lot."

Junior gave me a sheepish expression. "Yeah, I…*umm*…I miss him, too."

Surprise couldn't begin to describe what I felt. Just as I was about to ask a ton of questions, Junior added, "Mr. Roman is cool, and when he was around, we had a lot of fun and did family things together. We don't do that with Dad."

"I thought you didn't like him and wanted your dad and me to get back together." I'd said it before I could prepare how to phrase that statement, but I couldn't reel it back in now.

"I know." He sighed. "Dad said that Mr. Roman was the reason we couldn't be a family, but now that Mr. Roman isn't around, Dad still isn't here. And when he is around, all you two do is fight, even though Mr. Roman isn't here. I don't want you and Dad back together. You guys fuss more than me and Sante."

His admission astonished me. Although I was upset that he had to witness the unbearable relationship between his father and me, I couldn't help but feel vindicated as he gained firsthand insight and formed his own conclusions. If Joel hadn't been such a troublesome liar, we would have never reached this point.

"Pooh, I'm so sorry you've had to bear all this. What I really need for you to accept is that no matter if I'm with Roman or not, your father and I are not reconciling."

"Do you guys love each other—I mean, you and Dad?"

Rubbing my hand down his back, I explained as best I could, "I'll always have love for your father because, without him, I wouldn't have you and your brother. We can be cordial and maybe even friends again one day, but I won't ever love him like a wife loves her husband. Honestly, your dad doesn't love me like a husband loves his wife, either."

He didn't readily respond, but instead grew quiet—clearly turning over everything I'd just said. I watched him with bated breath, hoping my truth hadn't created a setback. Then, I saw something shift—a quiet surrender. It was as if he were beginning to accept that life as he knew it had changed. When he turned an inquisitive look at me, I wasn't sure what to brace for next, but I said nothing, giving him the time and space to say whatever was on his heart.

"Do you love Mr. Roman?"

Tears welled at the mere mention of my love for Roman. Oh, how I longed to be with that man. My heart physically ached without him. Wiping the droplets away, I nodded. "Yes. Very much so. I'm in love with him."

At my confession, sympathy shrouded Junior's expression. Slowly, he stood and wrapped his small arms around my neck. "I'm sorry, Mom. If you want Mr. Roman to be your boyfriend again, you can."

His words and his resolve left me shocked, to say the least. "What made you say that?"

"Because I love you, and if someone told me I couldn't be around you anymore, I would freak out."

I burst into laughter, sniffling back my tears. "True, but also language, son."

"My bad." He covered his mouth, pulled a tissue from the box on the side table, and gently dabbed my face. "I love you, Mom."

Taking his hands into mine, I declared, "I love you most."

We chatted a little longer before I sent him upstairs to finish his homework ahead of bedtime. Even though my relationship with Roman was uncertain, I felt as if a weight had been lifted from my shoulders after my conversation with Junior. I might have to pay Dr. Soto triple for her efforts because this turnaround was nothing short of a miracle.

Just as I downed the last of my wine, the doorbell rang. No one had informed me they were coming, so I activated the security camera on my phone and saw Joel standing at my front door. Irritation coursed through me. Every time I had a breakthrough with Junior, it was like he had radar that detected it was time to disrupt my life. Not this time. Not tonight. He would face all the smoke for whatever flames he came to stoke because I wasn't going to tolerate it.

"What are you doing here?" I didn't waste a second before asking him as soon as I opened the door.

He held his arms up in surrender. "I come in peace."

"That's rich coming from the master of chaos."

He cleared his throat. "I deserved that."

Folding my arms across my chest, I couldn't stop the heated venom from spilling out. "I don't need you to validate what I said.

I know you deserved that, just as there is a CVS receipt list of things you *don't* deserve."

He had lit the fuse, and now that I was ignited, I was about to let my venomous sparks fly, but Joel usurped my tirade before I could continue.

"I didn't deserve you as a wife or my amazing kids. I made many mistakes and poor choices, all of which have severely impacted my decisions." His confession deflated all my comebacks, and my mouth clamped shut. When he noticed I had no rebuttal, he added, "As I said, I come in peace."

I let him inside and closed the door behind him. However, I stopped him short, ensuring he didn't go farther than the foyer. "Whatever you have to say, say it right here."

Adhering to my demand, he turned to face me and put his hands in his pockets. Rising onto his toes, he exhaled and paused for a moment. "I just came here to let you know that you no longer have to worry about me interfering in your life. I've come to realize that our time has come and gone. I want to co-parent our sons amicably and put an end to the bickering between us. And before you say anything, I know the arguments were my fault. I take full responsibility for everything I did, and I'm sorry."

I wasn't sure if I believed him because I'd heard this same song and danced this same dance before; quite frankly, it was time to change the tune and exit stage left from the dance floor. Apparently, my body language reflected my internal thoughts.

"I know you may not believe me, but if you don't, at least believe this: The restaurant brand is financially secure. We had a large investor come through. I handed the reins over to my father because, truthfully, I'm tired of living under his thumb. The way you're living in your truth is the same freedom I desire, so I'm claiming it. He'll return to operations until he finds a suitable replacement when he officially retires."

Floored. I was floored at the bombshell he'd dropped. "How is your dad handling it, and what will you do about a job?"

Joel rubbed his fingertips across his forehead. "He's not thrilled, but he's not going to give up the investment money. As for him and me, we're only on speaking terms when it comes to settling the restaurant affairs. It breaks my mother's heart, but until he changes or accepts that I can only be who I am, we have nothing to communicate about. I love him, but he has lived his life. I'm not turning mine over to him. As far as work goes, I will continue with the celebrity catering events. Those worked better for me, which is the one aspect I created with my family name that belongs solely to me. Besides, my dinners are much more lucrative due to lower overhead expenses, which brings me to my next point: I dropped the custody and alimony petition. The original agreement will remain intact under the previous terms."

My insides were kung fu fighting me to do a cartwheel at this news, but I tried to keep my excitement in check because I wasn't sure if this was another one of Joel's schemes or truly the end of the foolishness.

"Thank you. I appreciate that."

Joel chuckled. "*Geesh*. Don't sound so enthused."

"I'm reserving my reaction for when I receive the official notice from my attorney."

"That's fair." He smiled before he faded back into seriousness.

"I'm also prepared to tell the boys the true reason we divorced. If I'm going to live my life and embrace who I am, I need to explain my sexuality. Jansen and I may be finished, but that doesn't mean I'm not open to companionship with someone new."

Someone could have blown a breath and pushed me over. His willingness to admit that to our children proved that this was a new page in Joel's chapter, one that I admired. It was about time.

I was sure this would also help the boys as they went through therapy.

"Absolutely. We'll pick a day and time to prepare them for the conversation. I also want to let Dr. Soto know. Perhaps she can be of assistance or even have us come into the office to have the discussion."

"I'd love that." Joel nodded. "Whatever you think is best, I'll do it." Glancing at the time on his watch, he looked back at me. "I have to head out, but it was nice talking to you."

I opened the door, and Joel stepped over the threshold. He was about to keep walking when I grabbed his hand. "Wait. Who was the investor that bailed you guys out?"

"It's on my dad, so I'm not at liberty to discuss."

"Fair enough." A weighted pause fell between us. "Joel, if you're serious about telling the boys and embracing your sexuality, I'm proud of you, and I'm willing to help you in any way I can. Our boys need us to be friends, at least."

Tears welled in his eyes, and he embraced me, taking me off guard. I embraced him back, and it felt as if the weight of the world drained from his body. "Thank you. I really need that." He pulled back from the embrace, and the gratitude on his face was evident. "You're a good woman, Aquila. Always have been. You deserve true happiness."

There he was. The Joel I first met in college, my old best friend. I prayed this version of him was here to stay, and somehow, I had faith that it would.

I offered him a bright smile and nodded. "Be good to yourself, Joel."

"You, too, Lah. You, too."

When I shut the door, I did a celebration dance, then ran to grab my cell phone. I had a man to reunite with, and I wouldn't wait one extra second to get him back.

Chapter Thirty-Five

AQUILA

"QUIET DOWN, EVERYONE. It's time for the prayer," my mother announced at the dinner table.

It was another famous Sunday dinner at my parents' house. This time, however, we were complete with Roman by my side. As I glanced around at everyone, the feeling of family enveloped me, seeing Nissi with Kannon and KJ, and Angela with Kinston and Fawn. Having Roman there completed our family circle with my boys and me. Everyone held hands and bowed their heads as my father, who sat at the head of the table, cleared his throat.

"Actually, since it's Roman's first official Sunday meal with all of us, how about you do the honors and say grace?" my father said.

"Nisante, don't put him on the spot," my mother fussed.

Roman held up a hand. "It's perfectly fine, Mrs. Abigail. I don't mind. Besides, I have so much to be thankful for." He squeezed and kissed my hand to the sound of everyone's coos.

"All right then. Go ahead, Roman."

"If all minds are clear." He paused and began. "Most gracious and heavenly Father, we thank You for this time with family and friends and the gift of life that You've given us to share. It serves as a constant reminder that our fortunes in life should never outweigh the people we cherish. We thank You for this meal we're about to enjoy. Bless the hands that prepared it and the mouths that will partake, and may it provide nourishment to our minds, bodies, and souls. We ask this blessing in Your Son Jesus' name. Amen."

A hearty "amen" went up from everyone at the table.

"You might have to say grace all the time, Roman. Powerful and short. You sure you don't have any southern roots in your family?" my father teased.

Chortles went up around the room. "I do, but we rarely saw them."

My father waved off his comment. "Don't need to. It's in your bones."

We all began passing bowls of food around the table as everyone filled their plates. Once mine and Roman's were done, I turned to him. "That was a great prayer, babe."

"Thank you. I've been practicing. Ain't no way I would tank prayer in front of your dad."

We all dove into the delectable meal that my mother and I had prepared, which included both vegan and non-vegan options to satisfy everyone's palate. Small talk flowed between us as we devoured the savory dishes. Watching Roman interact with my family so effortlessly made my heart sing. Butterflies filled my belly just seeing how we had all come full circle over the past few years. Love and happiness filled the room. I was so full that I started speaking before I realized what I was sharing.

"Roman and I have been holding something from you guys that I feel it's time you knew."

Angela gasped. "You're pregnant!"

Shaking my head, I *tsk*ed. "What? No."

"Darn it. My money was on pregnancy, too, sis," Nissi added, slapping hands with Angela.

Ignoring them, I clasped Roman's hand as we lifted our arms to show our matching bracelets. "When we were on the cruise, we got married in Turks and Caicos."

A resounding "what" rose as everyone dropped their silverware. The room went silent before a gamut of questions spilled from one person to the next.

"Before you all lose your minds—"

"Too late for that," my dad chimed in.

Roman clasped my hand and cleared his throat. "Allow me, baby." To which I handed him the floor. "Aquila is trying to explain that we had a symbolic wedding. It's not legally binding in the States, but it's one we're choosing to honor now that we're in a committed relationship with each other."

"Exactly. Considering everything I've experienced in marriage before, I'm not sure I want to make it legal just yet. However, emotionally, mentally, physically, and spiritually, I see myself as Roman's wife, even if my last name is Richards."

"Likewise, I consider myself her husband. Perhaps one day, we'll both be ready to take that next step, so I can exchange these bracelets for rings. If that's all right with you, Mr. and Mrs. Richards."

"I'm at a stage in life where I'm just happy my daughters have men in their lives who love them unconditionally. If you ever decide to take that leap, you both have my blessing," my dad said.

"And mine, too," my mother added.

We hugged them before taking our seats.

"That means Mr. Roman is our stepdad," Junior announced to the table while everyone congratulated us.

"Wait. So the boys knew?" Angela said as they giggled and nodded. "And you didn't tell your favorite auntie?"

Sante held up a finger to his lips. "We were sworn to shushcrecy."

Bellows of laughter rang out over his mispronunciation of *secrecy*. Honestly, it tracked, so no one argued with him.

"I just know there's an adult story behind this that we need to discuss at our next girls' night out." Nissi jogged her eyebrows at me.

Of course, I'd be willing to share my memories of that night with them, but my thoughts immediately drifted to Nia. Other than spending time with my sisters now and then, we hadn't had an official girls' night out since everything happened. Nia still wasn't talking to us—or at least to me—and I felt terrible.

"Speaking of that, have you spoken to Nia?" I asked Angela.

She flicked her hand back and forth. "Sparingly." She took a sip of water and added, "She's still upset, so our conversations have been surface-level. I miss her friendship, but I can't rock with her unless she accepts what you two have. I love her wholeheartedly, but if she asks me to choose between my friendship with her and my relationship with my sister, my family will always win out. That includes you, too, Roman."

I held my hand to my heart, and Roman patted his chest. "We appreciate that, sis," he said.

"We'll pray that God works on her heart," my mother said.

"Get Roman to pray for it. Seems like his prayers go straight to heaven's gate," my dad joked, making the adults at the table erupt.

As the table settled and laughter mellowed into clinks of silverware and conversation, Angela's thoughts about Nia hit me like a gut punch. The way things unraveled between us still sat heavy on my heart. I never meant to break any bonds of friendship—but somehow, I did. Or maybe she did. Maybe we both did. For all of our sakes, I wished I could turn back time, undo the silence, and the sharp words. But Nia had drawn a line—one I wasn't sure if she'd already crossed to the point of no return.

In a perfect world, we could talk it out, work on repairing what we felt had been broken, and maybe even find our way back to friendship. But if Nia thought she could make Angela choose sides or scare me into letting go of Roman after everything we'd overcome, she'd need more than thoughts and prayers.

So, I smiled, nodded, passed the bread, and let the warmth of incorporating Roman into my family mask the chill in my chest. Hope for restoration was what I longed for. But I was already bracing myself for the fallout.

Chapter Thirty-Six

AQUILA

$\mathcal{E}$VERYTHING IN MY life was like the sweet scent of cherry blossoms in June. Although I was skeptical, Joel had kept his promise. He removed the custody and reduction petition, made his payments in full and on time, and maintained cordial communication. We even met with Dr. Soto, who helped us inform our sons about their father's bisexuality. Sante understood as much as his young brain would allow. Junior grasped it and did not judge his father. His understanding stemmed from the reality that we lived in an ever-changing world, and he had classmates who were gay and some who identified as non-binary. They were discussing topics we never imagined addressing during our own formative years. At any rate, it helped make the announcement smoother and allowed us to have a long, deep, and heartfelt conversation as a family.

My catering business was thriving, thanks to the clients I had met through word-of-mouth advertising and networking events.

Roman's life was thriving as well. He and Kinston were looking to expand their gyms to a third location and were in talks to add spa services based on Roman's experience with the spa on the cruise ship. They were now offering a wide variety of supplements and merchandise. I was his biggest cheerleader and even became the spokesperson for their gym brand, as he'd asked. Overall, my relationship with Roman was flourishing. We supported each other completely. We took care of each other's hearts, and he was a wonderful and positive influence on my sons. In short, life was good.

I couldn't wait to discuss everything with my sisters. Since it had been a minute since we had spent time together, we decided to organize another girls' night for the three of us. We had nothing against our other friends, but given the previous incident, we just wanted to spend some time by ourselves.

"Okay, I low-key have PTSD from the last time we were here." I was referring to the visit that ended with Nia and me clashing.

"Let's not focus on the negativity of the past and try to have fun," Nissi coaxed, stroking my back comfortingly.

Taking a page from her book, I agreed and strode excitedly to the table Angela had reserved for us on the restaurant's back patio. When we got there, Nissi and I were deep into a roasting session when my laughter came to a hard stop.

"See, I knew this didn't feel right," I fumed, tossing darts at Angela, who was sitting at the table with none other than Nia.

Angela stood up. "Sis, just hear me out." She walked over to me, and I shrugged Nissi's hand off my shoulder because I was upset about being ambushed like this. "Nia wants to talk. No fussing or arguing. Let's have a mature conversation."

I took a beat to gather myself. Although the way this little reunion was set up was foul, it needed to happen so we could all move on with our lives, whether that be as friends or not. Cautiously, I swallowed the sting of this coup and agreed. "Listen, I'm all for all of us working on the friendship. But if she starts in on my relationship with Roman, I won't be responsible for my reaction."

"Fair game," Angela yielded.

We all sat at the round table, with Nia and me directly across from each other. Nissi placed her purse on the hook underneath the table, but I left mine on top. I didn't need any hiccups if I needed to make a speedy exit. I sat back and crossed my legs, showing off my toned muscles in my fitted jeans and sky-high pumps.

"Well, hello, Nissi and Aquila," Nia addressed us.

Nissi greeted her in return.

After a brief pause, I waved my fingers. "Nia."

Angela inhaled deeply. "I told my sister you were here to work things out, so let's keep it cute but also a buck. That's the only way this will have any chance of working."

My gaze shifted to Angela, then back to Nia. She was about to speak, but I interrupted her before she could say anything. "Since you had the last word the last time we talked, I guess it's only fair for me to make the first point. Nia, you may have been Angela's best friend, but you were our girl, too—Nissi and me. Your overreaction was out of line and outright disrespectful. I let it slide because I understood how everything unfolded, but this time, it's on me. I advise you to tread light about what you say to me about me and Roman."

Just then, the waitress came to our table. "Are you ladies ready to order drinks?"

"Not yet," all the other women said.

"No. I haven't decided if I'm staying yet," I answered.

The waitress' mouth formed an "O" shape. She quickly made her exit and left us to our private meeting.

Nia fanned her wrist in the air. "I deserved that."

Those words triggered an audible sigh of relief between Angela and Nissi. Still, I had my guard up.

"Listen, I won't pretend that hearing about Roman and you didn't hurt. It did. Still, that gave me no right to react the way I did and say the mean things I said. I can admit I was on one. Hell, I hadn't had good sex in months. Blame it on being deprived."

At that, soft chuckles went around the table. Even I had to let out one.

I shrugged. "Well, I can't blame you for missing that, especially from Roman."

"Okay, bish, you got the man. You ain't gotta remind me," she tittered jokingly. We sat silently for a brief moment before Nia's shoulders slumped and sadness settled in her eyes. "Aquila, I'm sorry. Roman and I weren't even serious. You and he deserve happiness. If you've found that in each other, then who am I to hate on that?"

Although I appreciated her apology, I had to ask the burning question. "I hear you, but why the sudden change of heart?"

"Girl, I haven't been mad about it for a long time. I didn't reach out because I felt more embarrassed than anything. I thought all of you hated me. What you all didn't know was that I had called Roman earlier that day to hook up. He turned me down because of his current relationship, and admittedly, it stung. I mean, the man was my go-to fuck buddy. So, then to go out with my girls and find out in that way that you were the one in a relationship with Roman mixed with the margaritas and my horniness, it was like adding propane to an open fire. My mind started wandering with crazy thoughts in the moment, and I lashed out in the worst way." Placing her hand to her chest, she bowed her head in humbleness. "I say this wholeheartedly, I am sorry, Aquila, and I wish you and Roman the very best." She reached across the table and motioned for my hands, and I gave them to her. "So, can I please come back into the friend circle? I miss my bestie, and I miss you guys."

Pursing my lips, I scanned her up and down. "I don't know." She looked as if she'd burst into tears. The grin I'd been withholding broke out across my face, and I let out a chortle. "Girl, I'm just kidding. I had to serve you your own medicine."

"You nearly made me pass out. You know I don't like nobody but y'all asses. Who else am I going to talk trash with, confide in, and have bougie girl drinks with?" She dramatically clutched her chest.

Angela intervened. "Nobody but us. Besides, you could never replace me. I may be imitated, but I can never be duplicated."

That was our Angela, right on time with the quick-witted comebacks. They hugged each other tightly for a long time as Nia repeatedly apologized to her. Tears flowed freely between them, and Nissi and I allowed them to have their moment. Nia was like our fourth sister, so having her back felt like a piece of us being restored. We were battle-tested, but at least not battle-scarred, proving in the end, friendship wins.

"Let me get some, too." Nissi hopped up, and Nia embraced her tightly, too.

"So, can we order those drinks now?" Nia asked as she and Nissi returned to their seats. "This calls for a round of shots for all of us."

Nissi and I cheered our agreement.

Angela held up her hand. "That will be a round of shots for you three."

"Girl, what are you talking—" Nia started and then gasped, covering her mouth.

Nissi and I looked at each other, our eyes ballooning. "Oh my gawd," we shrieked in unison.

Angela smiled. "As of today, I am entering my fourth month of pregnancy. Before you all get upset, Kinston and I decided to keep it a secret to ensure I made it through the first trimester.

This is why I've stayed away from you all as much as I could these past few months. I knew you would notice if I saw y'all too often, or my big mouth would spill the tea."

We all jumped up and ran around the table hugging her and rubbing her belly, sharing our excitement over our new little bundle of joy. This day was filled with surprises and happiness. Life was truly in full bloom for all of us.

Chapter Thirty-Seven

ROMAN

REFLECTING ON THESE past months, I couldn't believe how my life had changed. This time last year, I was simply searching for a steady companion after years of casual encounters. Not only did I find a companion, but I also discovered the only woman I'm proud to call my very best friend, my confidant, my breath of fresh air, my lover, and the absolute love of my life. I wouldn't change or trade this for anything in the world. Yeah, I was proudly simpin' over one Aquila Richards, and Kinston and Kannon would never let me hear the end of it. For Aquila, I'd take every joke they could throw my way. That woman meant everything to me, and I'd spend the rest of my life giving her just that.

"Babe, what's the name of the restaurant? I want to check out the menu for vegan options," Aquila said, tapping on the Google app on her phone.

"Actually, we're already here," I said, pulling into the parking lot and parking my car.

Aquila panned the area and then gave me a puzzled look. "*Umm*, babe, this must be ultra-exclusive because it seems pretty empty around here."

"Woman, sit tight until I come and open your door. Your man has got this handled."

I unbuckled and exited the car, opened the passenger-side door, and took Aquila's hand as she stepped out of my ride. Together, we walked to the front door and opened it. Once inside, I pressed a switch, and the entire place illuminated. The vibe was both chic with an upscale feel, featuring dark mahogany chairs and tables draped with white tablecloths and red table runners. Dozens of boxed red roses brightened the area, with golden luminaries illuminating each table. The brick back wall was decorated with green leaf accents and a neon sign that read, "The Happy Place," clearly for photo opportunities.

Aquila was mesmerized. "This is so fabulous, Roman. Is this a private dinner?"

"For now," I answered, slowly turning her to the left. "But I was thinking in the near future, it could be a place for you."

Straight ahead was an empty bakery showcase, and behind it stood a bustling kitchen filled with state-of-the-art stainless-steel commercial-grade appliances. The red neon sign mounted on the back wall read, *Lah's Lavish Creations*. Aquila's hands flew to her mouth, and pools of tears crested in her lids.

"Ro...Roman," she stuttered. "Is this? What is this?"

"This is what you said you needed to elevate your business. I want to help you achieve every goal you've set for yourself. It begins with you having a space where you can cook, but that can also serve as a small eatery. Customers can place custom orders, grab and go, or dine in."

She spun around, shock still evident on her beautiful features. "Babe! Oh my goodness, what have you done? I can't let you do this. You have your own ventures to pursue. I'm so thrilled, but I can't accept this."

Without a word, I took her hand and led her to the back of the building, behind the kitchen, to a room marked *Aquila's Office*. I opened the door to find a desk, a leather chair, shelf space for books, and a leather sofa. I encouraged her to sit on the sofa while I took a seat at the desk.

"You can, and you will allow me to do this for you because I can afford it."

"But how? I don't want you spending your business funds on me. That's for you."

Crossing my arms, I exhaled as I prepared to deliver the news. "So, I have a final confession to make." With pursed lips, she shot me a sidelong glance, and in response, I gave her a sheepish look. "Please don't think I don't trust you, but there's a reason I keep my life extremely private, and so do those closest to me. It's not just about me; it involves my family."

Concern was etched across Aquila's face. "What is it, babe?"

"The reason I can afford this is because I own an investment firm. My father isn't just into tech; he *owns* a tech development company, and I'm a silent partner. In fact, I own several companies. Besides KinRo Fitness, which you know about, I also own RoadRide. All of these have helped me branch out and create Romero Investments."

She shrieked. "Your middle name. OMG! KinRO, ROadRide, ROmero Investments all pay homage to you, Roman."

With a chuckle at her quick wit, I nodded in agreement. "Yes, my investment firm carries my middle name, providing an extra layer of anonymity, and including *RO* serves as my personal mark of alignment between companies. Alongside my father, my mother is also a respected neurosurgeon. My parents are multimillionaires, and I am one, too. I prefer a low-key lifestyle. This also benefits me in dating because I need to be sure that a woman is interested in me, not just for material gains and success."

I witnessed the instant realization strike her. "That's the true reason Tamia was with you."

Thick emotion welled in my throat, causing me to pause. Unshed tears that I had kept hidden for the child I lost at the hands of a woman I thought I could trust began to seep out. Aquila stood and rocked me in her arms as I finally let go of the last of my hurt tied to that tucked-away pain.

"Everything about you makes sense now," Aquila murmured.

Once my tears had subsided, I dried my face. "My bad, baby. I didn't mean for this to become an impromptu counseling session."

She cupped my cheeks in her hands. "Hey, we're here for each other, no matter when, where, or how, remember?"

She leaned forward and kissed my forehead, and in return, I offered a soft peck to her lips. We basked there for a while before I broke our connected silence.

"So, are you accepting this place, or do I need to place it on the market—"

"You better not." She bounced up and down in my arms. "Baby, I can't believe you did this. It's accented in my favorite colors. It's exactly what I dreamed of. How did you know?"

"Because I listen to you, and I love you."

Stepping out of my arms, seduction crept into Aquila's gaze as she slowly slipped out of her dress, leaving only her bra, panties, and heels. "Let me show you how much I love and appreciate you, Dr. Patterson."

Before she could pounce on me, I stood and lifted her. She wrapped her legs around me, and we kissed fervently. Our tongues tasted and teased as we nipped at each other's lips, earlobes, and neck. It wasn't long before we'd both discarded our clothing and were naked on the leather sofa. As I sat with her straddling me, we kissed and uttered our sentiments of gratitude and affection to each other while her slick wetness rubbed back and forth on my rising member. When I couldn't take anymore, I smacked her ass so she could mount on this ride and jockey me like the stallion she was.

Sliding down my shaft, inch by inch, her moans turned to wails at how stiff I was beneath her. When she finally completed the journey of securing me deep inside her walls, we both groaned at the feel. The warm feeling of her insides coated me like a fitted glove. She was just perfect for me.

"*Qui.*" The grunt dragged out of my mouth. "Ride me, baby."

"It's so hard and deep," she said, groaning.

"Let me guide you through it."

I placed my hands on her hips and helped her roll them back and forth until she caught a good rhythm. The sight of her taking all of me as she rode was amplified by the sexy heels she wore. My sweet vixen was giving me everything she had tonight. She could've asked me for the sun, and I would've risked limb and life to snatch the motherfucker out of the sky to give it to her. I'd gladly perish from incineration for her. I smacked her cheeks as she shifted to bounce up and down my shaft. Her juices slid down, making a gooey mess of my dick, and I loved it. I loved seeing her essence rain down over me, knowing I was responsible for the pleasure she experienced.

"Roman," she whined. "Right there, baby. It's so good."

"*Mmm-hmm.* I feel it, baby. Damn."

I met her thrust for thrust as we kept digging for depths that we hadn't touched with each other. Sweat beaded down our bodies as the gushing sounds rose louder and louder. When she gripped my neck and tossed her head back, I knew her crescendo was near.

"*Mmm-hmm.* Drench me. I want it all."

"Shit. I'm coming," She released, bucking on me as she lost complete control, showering me with her love.

"That's it, baby. Good girl. Good fucking girl."

I stood, still locked inside of her as her walls spasmed all around me. I slammed her back against the wall and continued my quest to find her lost treasure. Her moans turned to full-on wails as I plummeted inside of her to a sweet and steady beat. She sniffled as droplets ran down her face. Her stomach muscles clenched as she tried to run from the feeling, except she had nowhere to go. All she could do was take every ounce of the pleasure I was unleashing onto her. Her feet locked around my waist as she took flight and squirted all over me.

"Fuck me, Dr. Patterson!" My name came out in a broken cadence.

Hearing my name and feeling her downpour sent me over the edge as I prepared for my ascent.

"Qui!" I pelted with a hard grunt as my body tensed, and I spurted never-ending loads inside of her sweet spot to the point my entire body convulsed. "Fuck, I love you."

"I love you for infinity."

Once our breathing normalized, I gently slid out of her and set her on the sofa. When I turned to grab my clothes, she giggled.

"Well, it's definitely mine since we christened the place."

I grinned. This woman. "Hopefully, we can create another first in this place, too." I walked back and knelt in front of her, holding a velvet box. She began to heave as soon as she saw it. "Breathe, baby."

Fanning her face, she tried to gather her bearings.

"Baby, never in a million years did I think I'd find love on board a cruise ship, but even crazier was that I never thought I'd get to experience it with the crush of my life. Now that you are the love of my life, I want to have you as my wife for the rest of my life. I'm ready, and if you will have me, it would be my greatest honor to have you as Mrs. Dr. Roman Patterson. Will you make this official and marry—"

"Dude, yes. Hurry up and give me my ring."

I slid the custom princess-cut diamond ring onto her finger, and we locked pinky fingers, then kissed like delicate lovers, whispering sweet sentiments of love.

"Just one question," Aquila inquired.

"What's that?"

"Can we christen this place once more? I want to show my fiancé how grateful I am that he'll be my future husband."

When she climbed off the sofa and kneeled, I already knew what time it was. "Say less, Future Mrs. Dr. Patterson. Say less."

Epilogue

AQUILA

TWO MONTHS LATER

$\mathcal{J}$ ULY, THE MONTH Roman's and my journey to forever began. At first, we planned to go on a couple's cruise to celebrate the occasion, but I thought of an even better idea. His family wanted us to spend Thanksgiving with them, but instead of waiting months to meet the boys and me in person, I figured our summer vacation could be dedicated to showing California some love. We could hit the beaches and meet Roman's family. Everyone loved the idea, especially the boys, who were convinced they would meet every Hollywood celebrity and Kendrick Lamar. The schedules even aligned for Roman's sister to be there, so we'd finally get the chance to meet everyone.

When we first arrived, I was blown away. Roman's parents' home resembled a compound. The mansion spanned over fifteen thousand square feet. Naturally, I fell in love with the designer gourmet kitchen. It was a chef and baker's dream, featuring quartz countertops and an oversized island; the custom wood beams, inset cabinetry, and wine chiller were perfect for entertaining, while the commercial-grade gas double oven and refrigerator represented the ultimate culinary fantasy, complete with a butler's pantry. I felt like I was in Food Channel heaven. Meanwhile, the boys were more excited about the indoor gym, outdoor basketball court, and an outdoor pool, complete with two slides. As Roman mentioned, they'd made additions and renovations over the years, so even he was thrilled by some of the features, especially his mother's foresight regarding grandkids, which led her to add a theater room and a billiards room.

After seeing how truly affluent his parents were, I became a bit nervous about their acceptance of me. Yes, we'd often talked over the phone, but that was before I witnessed their status. My level of financial freedom would be deemed middle class compared to theirs, but they were the humblest people I'd ever met. They were grateful for their lot in life, but they didn't allow that to determine who they were on the inside—the total opposite of the Olivers.

I completely understood how Mr. Robert and Dr. Genesis Patterson could raise a son like Roman Romero Patterson. Most importantly, they adored me and my children. If this estate wasn't surprising enough, I nearly went home to glory when Roman's sister walked in. No wonder this man was so private. His sister was Gracyn Patterson, better known as the ultra-famous supermodel CYN. She was so gorgeous that looking at her felt like being in the presence of an angel. She was that captivating. We had to remind Sante that she was his aunt because I swore he fell in love the moment he laid eyes on her. After that wore off, Gracyn and Sante became best buddies. She and I fell into an easy vibe with each other, and I knew we'd become close friends. Just like her big brother, she was an amazing soul and a joy to be around.

We had a great cookout, and Mr. Patterson let me join him at the grill to prepare vegan options, which Gracyn was elated about. After a day of dancing, trash talk, and pool time, we decided to wind down by watching a movie in the theater, so everyone headed to their rooms to shower and change into pajamas.

"I am so grateful we chose to come here. Your family is wonderful."

Roman came up behind me after I slipped on a sleep tank that read, *Future Mrs. Patterson,* and wrapped his arms around my waist. "And they are your family, too."

He kissed my temple when I leaned into him. "And I'm proud to be a member. But I do have one question because you're not slick."

He furrowed his brow. "What's that?"

"While on the grill, I heard your dad ask you about a restaurant investment." I turned to face him, wrapping my arms around his neck. "Were you the one who purchased the Oliver restaurant?"

"Woman, you heard a little bit and ran with it." He kissed my forehead. "The last thing I want to do is worry about the Olivers. As long as Joel can co-parent peacefully with you without all that bickering and stress, that's all that matters."

Roman bit his lip and smiled at me, and I knew. He didn't have to confirm. Rather than press for him for a verbal admission, I chose to let it go. He'd gotten the Olivers off my neck, and Joel and I were co-existing as great parents and good friends, so for that alone, I was thankful. Just thinking about it turned me on in the worst way. He was such a badass businessman, but even more important, he was such a good-ass man. My man. My future husband.

"Keep looking at me like that, and I'm going to make sure my mother has all the grandbabies she wants filling the rooms in the house."

I grew silent as I smirked, heading toward the bedroom door.

"Wait. Baby, what was that smirk about?" Roman asked, walking quickly behind me.

I shrugged giddily. "I don't know what you're talking about, Dr. Patterson." With that, I scurried out of the bedroom with Roman pleading playfully for an answer.

THE END

BONUS INFORMATION

BONUS #1

Congratulations to Mr. Kinston and Angela Jordan, who welcomed a twin boy and girl into the world:

Kinston O'Mari Jordan II and Royalty Marie Jordan

BONUS #2

Congratulations to Mr. Roman and Aquila Patterson, who welcomed a baby girl into the world:

Miracle Joi Patterson
6 lbs. 4 oz.
19 inches
Born to the parents of
Roman Patterson and Aquila Richards-Patterson
On February 3

DEDICATION

This is dedicated to the power of
second chances in life and love.

ACKNOWLEDGMENTS

My Forever Thank-Yous

To my God, the creator and blesser of this precious gift of writing. Without you, there is no Aries Skye, but with you, I can touch the skies.

To my backbone, greatest supporter, and number one fan, my husband. You inspire me to write these whimsical fairytales because you ensure I live them every day. I love you.

To my precious womb fruits, you are my reasons, and I pray I inspire you also to have a reason.

To Black Odyssey Media, I may have given these characters a voice, but you gave them a home.

To Black Queens Who Write, you ladies propel me to give my best. Your sisterhood is everything to me. Shannon and Crystal—thank you for the writing sessions and advice.

To Pretty Girls Do Read: thank you to my dynamic PR team for helping to propel the Aries Skye brand with sass and class.

To my Skye's Sweeties: Crystal, Tameka, Jaleesa, Robyn, and Rese Alisa, you ladies are my MVPs. I cannot say thank you enough for all that you selflessly do.

To my Sweethearts: the readers, bloggers, friends, and family who tirelessly support all things Aries Skye, I am grateful to you all. You opened your readers' space for my words, and that is more than I could've ever dreamed of.

To the unexpected light of Aquila and Roman's story. You all grabbed hold of me and never let me go, proving that even in the smallest of nuggets, extraordinary stories exist.

OTHER BOOKS BY ARIES SKYE

Love on the Ninth Floor—Available Now
Love on the Rebound—Available Now
Supreme—Available Now
Savior—Available Now
Love on the Edge—Coming Soon
Love Me Down to Christmas—Coming Soon

A NOTE FROM ARIES SKYE

Oh my goodness! Can you believe we have reached the end of the sisters' stories? I can't. This has been a ride. Again, I appreciate everyone who has picked up these books and enjoyed learning more about my writing and the Richards sisters. I ask that if you haven't, please go and leave a review, whether you loved it or didn't. If you're in love with this Black romance journey that I'm on, please visit my website and subscribe. I promise not to drown you with emails or sell you an extended warranty for your car, but I'd love to keep you abreast of upcoming titles, events, and freebies.

www.authorariesskye.carrd.co

I'm also available on social media:

Instagram and Threads @ariesskye_

Facebook, TikTok, YouTube & Lemon 8: @authorariesskye